De... ...e art of storytelling. ... ...amut, and sh... ...es to pen entertaining books that embody matters of the heart. She's an RWA m... a BA in English from the University of Illinois. When Denise isn't writing, she enjoys watching true crime TV and chatting with readers. Follow her on social media on Instagram: @Denise_Wheatley_Writer, Twitter: @DeniseWheatley, BookBub: @DeniseNWheatley and Goodreads: Denise N.Wheatley

USA TODAY bestselling and *RITA*® Award-winning author **Marie Ferrarella** has written over 300 books for Mills & Boon, some under the name Marie Nicole. Her romances are beloved by fans worldwide. Visit her website, marieferrarella.com

Discover more at millsandboon.co.uk

THE HEART-SHAPED MURDERS

DENISE N. WHEATLEY

This book is dedicated to all of my fellow
true crime junkies.

Keep sleuthing, friends!

Chapter One

Lena Love kicked a rock out from underneath her foot, then bent down and tightened the twill shoelaces on her brown leather hiking boots.

The crime scene investigator, who doubled as a forensic science technician, stood back up and eyed Los Angeles' Cucamonga Wilderness trail. Sharp-edged stones and ragged shards of bark covered the rugged, winding terrain.

"Watch your step," she uttered to herself before continuing along the path of her latest crime scene.

Lena's eyes squinted as she focused on the trail. Heavy foliage loomed overhead, blocking out the sun's brilliant rays. She pulled out her flashlight, hoping its bright beam would help uncover potential evidence.

An ominous wave of vulnerability swept through her chest at the sight of the vast San Gabriel Mountains. She spun around slowly, feeling small while eyeing the infinite views of the forest, desert and snowy mountainous peaks.

The wild surroundings left her with a lingering sense of defenselessness. Lena tightened the belt on her tan suede blazer. She hoped it would give her some semblance of security.

It didn't.

Lena wondered if her latest victim felt that same vulnerability on the night she'd been brutally murdered.

"Come on, Grace Mitchell," Lena said aloud, as if the dead woman could hear her. "Talk to me. Tell me what happened to you. *Show* me what happened to you."

A gust of wind whipped Lena's bone-straight bob across her slender face. She tucked her hair behind her ears and stooped down, aiming the flashlight toward the majestic oak tree where Grace's body had been found.

Lena envisioned spotting droplets of blood, a cigarette butt, the tip of a latex glove…*anything* that would help identify the killer.

This was her second visit to the crime scene. The thought of showing up to the station without any viable evidence yet again caused an agonizing pang of dread to shoot up her spine.

Grace was the fifth victim of a criminal who Lena had labeled an organized serial killer. He appeared to have a type. Young, slender, brunette women. Their bodies had all been found in heavily wooded areas. Each victim's hands were meticulously tied behind their backs with a three-strand twisted rope. They'd been strangled to death. And the amount of evidence left at each scene was practically nonexistent.

But the killer's signature mark was always there. And it was a sinister one.

After murdering his victims, the predator would carve a heart into the chests of his victims with what looked to be a sharp blade.

"Ugh," Lena groaned, shivering at the gruesome thought of his actions.

The entire state of California, along with the victims' families and the media, had put an immense amount of pressure on the LAPD to catch the killer. As a result, Lena was recently assigned to the case.

The sound of a crackling tree branch stopped Lena dead in her tracks. She almost stumbled forward when the tips of her boots dipped into the dusty earth.

She quickly gathered herself and aimed her flashlight toward the noise. Bears and mountain lions were known to frequent the trail. So were hikers.

Unfortunately, so were serial killers.

Lena swallowed hard, questioning whether she should turn around and leave. But her resolve was stronger than both her fear and common sense combined.

"Maybe you just shouldn't have come out here alone…"

She did an abrupt 360-degree turn and waved her flashlight in the air. The stream of yellow light landed on several tree limbs that were swaying in the wind. Her shoulders relaxed a bit at the sight.

"See?" she said to herself. "It's nothing. You're good."

Lena chalked her panic up to paranoia and continued along the path.

"Come on, Grace," she whispered once again while shining her light along the edge of the trail. "Speak to me. Give me something to work with here."

Lena paused. She noticed what appeared to be two oddly shaped black lumps sticking out from underneath a tall shrub.

She stepped off the path and walked farther into the wooded area, then pressed the button on the back of her flashlight, increasing its brightness.

Are those lumps of coal? she asked herself while slowly moving in. *Remnants from a barbecue grill, maybe?*

But as Lena got closer, she realized that the lumps looked more like leather than sedimentary rocks.

"What the…?"

Lena dug around inside her pocket and pulled out a pair of latex gloves. She slipped them on, then bent down.

She pressed her fingertips against the black matter. It wasn't hard enough to be stone. But the smooth surface was firm.

She leaned farther into the brush. Shined her light down directly onto the objects. After a few moments, Lena realized that she was staring at a pair of black leather work boots.

"Bingo!" she exclaimed, thrilled to finally get her hands on a possible piece of evidence.

She reached down and grabbed the boots. But when she tried to pick them up off the ground, they didn't budge.

"Come on," Lena grunted, wondering if the hot sun had caused the rubber soles to disintegrate into the dirt.

She pulled harder. The boots still did not move.

"*What* has these stuck?" Lena asked aloud.

The investigator gave the boots a firmer tug. Suddenly, one of them lifted off the ground. It kicked up so swiftly that it knocked her square in the forehead.

"*Ow!*" Lena yelled, falling backward onto the ground.

She closed her eyes and gripped her head. A bump was already beginning to form.

Lena slid her hands underneath her. The rocky soil scraped against her palms. She ignored the pain and brought her knees in close.

Just as she began to stand up, Lena was knocked back down again.

"*Dammit!*"

She was completely discombobulated. Strangely, the work boots she'd been trying to grab were now positioned directly in front of her.

Lena recoiled when they moved in closer. A shadowy figure hovered over her. Within a matter of seconds, she knew she was in danger.

Just as she opened her mouth to scream, a man pounced on Lena. She tried to kick him off, but his weight pinned her legs to the ground.

She tore at his arms. He overpowered her, his hands moving past her flailing limbs and going straight for her neck.

"No! Stop!" Lena attempted to yell. *"Help!"*

Her muffled screams were silenced by the howling wind. The attacker's hands were now wrapped firmly around her throat. Lena's voice was a mere whisper. Her vocal cords had been immobilized. And she was too deep into the woods to be seen from the trail.

This is it, she thought, tears falling from her eyes as the pressure behind them increased. *I cannot believe my life is going to end this way...*

Just when Lena felt herself losing consciousness, the predator loosened his grasp on her neck.

She gasped, choking on the huge puff of air that swept through her lungs. But before she could truly catch her breath, the attacker ripped open her blazer and tore at her blouse.

Pearlized buttons flew through the air. She emitted a guttural scream, punching her assailant in the chest.

He continued to overpower her. Lena's blows did nothing to deter his assault.

Your pepper spray, she thought. *Get to your pepper spray!*

She struggled to reach down inside the pocket of her black cargo pants. Just as she wrapped her fingers around the canister, Lena felt a cold, sharp blade slice into her skin.

Her mouth fell open. But nothing came out. She was too stunned to make a sound.

This can't be happening. This can't be happening!

The blade continued to carve into her chest. That's when it struck Lena. She was being attacked by the serial killer she'd been pursuing.

You will not be his sixth victim, Lena told herself. *Fight back. Fight!*

Burning pain tore through her chest. She bit down on her bottom lip and snatched the pepper spray from her pocket. Lena held the canister directly in front of his masked face, closed her eyes and hit the red button.

"Aah!" he grunted.

As the man howled in pain, Lena opened her eyes slightly.

He was up on his knees, still hovering over her while covering his face with his gloved hands.

She quickly jumped up and kneed him in the groin. His screams caught in his throat. A hissing wheeze oozed through his mask.

When he rolled over and curled up into the fetal position, Lena took advantage of the moment. She jumped up and hurried back toward the trail, tearing down the pathway toward the canyon's entrance.

Lena wanted to turn around to see if her attacker was following her. But she was too afraid of losing her footing. So she kept moving forward.

She could feel the blood pouring from her chest. The chilled mountain air stung the open wound. But the gash was the least of her concerns. All Lena cared about was reaching her car and getting the hell out of there.

As the trail began to open up, she heard faint footsteps pounding behind her.

Just keep going, she told herself. *Keep going!*

After what seemed like forever, Lena finally reached the parking lot. It was practically empty.

Her wide eyes darted anxiously. A surge of relief eased the terror running through her limbs when her silver Jeep came into view.

Lena charged toward the vehicle. But as it got closer, sharp cramps began to shoot up her legs.

Don't you dare stop now, her inner voice screamed as the sound of looming footsteps persisted. *Keep going!*

She fought through the pain and forced herself to run faster. Lena grabbed her keys from her back pocket, pounding the fob until the button unlocked the doors.

She reached the car door, then turned around. A shadowy figure appeared at the parking lot's entrance.

It was her attacker.

He quickly limped toward her, holding his groin with one hand while swiping his eyes with the other.

Lena emitted a short, panicked scream.

"Get back here, you *bitch*!" he yelled.

She inhaled sharply. Her fingers trembled as she grabbed the handle and threw open the door.

His heavy footsteps were drawing nearer. Her assailant was getting closer.

"Aw, is she *scared*?" he taunted. "Did you actually think you were gonna catch me? It'll never happen, sweetheart. But I caught *you*. And after I finish what I started on that delicate little chest of yours, I'm gonna kill you!"

"Stay away from me!" Lena tried to shout. But her voice sounded more like a whimper than a command.

The cramps in her legs intensified as she struggled to climb inside the Jeep. She grabbed the side of the driver's seat and pulled herself up.

Finally, she was in.

Lena's chest heaved with panic. She pressed down on the brake and frantically pushed the start button. The door hadn't closed all the way before she threw the gearshift into Drive.

Her attacker was only a few feet away. He ran toward the front of her Jeep, still holding his groin. She looked into his pale gray eyes. There was something oddly familiar behind their cold, menacing glare.

One thing was for certain. He appeared determined to take her out. And judging by the blood that continued to seep from her chest, he'd almost completed his mission.

Lena rammed her right foot down onto the accelerator. She slammed her door shut, then tore through the parking lot.

She craned her neck, blinking back tears while glancing in the rearview mirror. Lena watched in horror as her attacker jumped inside a black sports car. Its huge spiked chrome wheels screeched loudly as he sped after her.

Lena's chest tightened. Thin streams of air barely filled her lungs. She whipped her Jeep around the mountain's sharp turns, all while struggling to catch a glimpse of her assailant's license plate. It was obscured by a black shield.

Stay calm. Just get to the hospital. Stay calm. Just get to the hospital, Lena kept telling herself.

When she reached the bottom of the mountain, Lena made a quick right turn onto a desolate road. She pulled behind a large dumpster, making sure her Jeep was hidden from the main street.

The sound of her attacker's roaring engine filled the air. Lena's eyes were glued to the side-view mirror.

Please keep going. Please keep going, she repeated over and over again.

Her prayers were answered when the car flew past the side road.

Lena's chest heaved with relief. She waited several minutes before spinning around and creeping toward the main street. It was clear. She sped off toward the hospital.

When she pulled into the emergency room's lot, Lena opened the console and pulled out a stack of napkins. She pressed them against her wound. Blood quickly soaked into the stark white paper, turning it into a bright shade of crimson. The sight, along with the intense pain, caused her to cry out in agony.

She pulled down the sun visor and slid open the mirror.

Lena stared at the wound on her chest. She studied the curved, half-cordate symbol.

After I finish what I started on that delicate little chest of yours, I'm gonna kill you!

The attacker's words echoed through her mind. The half-shaped heart he'd carved into her skin would be a permanent reminder that she was almost murdered by her most elusive suspect to date.

And now, it was a race against time to catch him before he really did finish what he'd started.

Chapter Two

"Ouch," Detective David Hudson hissed after a splash of hot coffee spilled from his cup and singed his hand.

"Gotta wait for it to cool off, hon," Milly called out from the police station's front desk. "I just brewed that pot about ten seconds ago."

The receptionist, who doubled as the 9-1-1 operator, didn't miss much that went on around the station. Or their entire town of Clemmington, California, for that matter.

"Yes, ma'am," David uttered through clenched teeth. He waved his hand in the air, hoping that would help ease the sting.

"Why don't you grab a few ice cubes out of the freezer?" Milly suggested, staring at the handsome detective from the corner of her eye while fluffing her tightly curled silver bouffant hairdo. "Apply them to your burn so you won't get a blister. I can help you if you want…"

"Stop flirting, Milly!" Detective Russ Campbell yelled out from his office. "Hudson's young enough to be your grandson!"

"I'd say that's pushin' it, Campbell!" Milly growled. "Oh, and by the way, mind your business! Nobody out here is talking to you."

"If it's within earshot, then it *is* my business!" Russ barked back.

David chuckled at the bickering twosome. They seemed to get entangled in some sort of altercation at least three times a day.

"Thanks for the advice, Milly," David said, extending his muscular arm and giving her an affectionate fist bump.

Milly pulled her fist away from his and emitted an explosion sound effect through her puckered ruby-red lips. She then wiggled her stubby fingers, which were adorned with vintage gold rings and long acrylic French tips.

"You're welcome, sweetheart," she murmured. "It's good to know _somebody_ appreciates me around here."

"We all appreciate you," he assured her.

David then turned around and headed back to his office.

On the way there, he could feel Milly's piercing green eyes watching him as he walked away. David was used to that sort of attention by now and didn't give it much thought.

For years, the detective's fellow townspeople tried to talk him into leaving small-town Clemmington behind and heading to Hollywood. They were convinced that his dark, deep-set eyes, smooth cocoa-brown complexion, lush lips and athletic build would garner a lucrative career in the entertainment business.

But David, who downplayed his rugged good looks, found nothing appealing about being in the limelight. He was fully dedicated to life in his hometown and work in criminal justice.

David entered his small, modest office and closed the door. He walked past an old silver filing cabinet and slammed his fist against the top drawer. Per usual, it popped right back open thanks to all the dog-eared files stuffed inside.

David pulled his well-worn black mesh ergonomic chair out from under the rustic cherrywood desk. He sat down slowly, clenching his jaws as pain shot up his thighs. Yesterday was leg day at the gym and his quads had yet to recover.

Just as he took a sip of coffee, which had finally cooled down, David heard a knock at the door. Before he could say anything, it slowly opened.

He looked up and saw Miles Love, one of Clemmington's most well-respected police officers, standing in the doorway.

"Hey, Dave, you got a sec?"

"Yeah, of course, man. Come on in."

David's eyelids lowered as he watched the officer saunter inside the office. Miles was usually cheerful, but today his face appeared twisted with worry.

"What's with the long face?" David asked him. "You having woman problems again?"

"I wish that was the problem…"

Miles slid his hands inside the pockets of his black uniform pants, blinking rapidly while staring down at the floor.

David pointed at the chair across from his desk. "Do you wanna have a seat and talk about whatever it is that's bothering you?"

Miles shook his head from side to side without looking up.

David's concern grew. A feeling of dread overcame him as he watched the color in Miles's reddish-brown complexion drain from his face.

"Nah," Miles mumbled. "I'd rather keep standing. I, uh—I guess you haven't checked the breaking news alerts on your cell phone lately."

"No, not recently." David grabbed his phone and punched in the security code. "Why? Did I miss something?"

Miles looked up at the ceiling, his chest now heaving as though he were having a panic attack. "It's Lena. She, um…" He paused, his gravelly voice cracking underneath the weight of his words. "She's been attacked."

David froze. His cell phone slipped out of his hand, thumping loudly when it slammed against the desk. "She's been *what*?"

"She's been attacked," Miles repeated.

"When did this happen?" David asked, struggling to remain calm for the sake of Miles, considering Lena was his sister. "*How* did this happen? And do they know who did it?"

"It happened yesterday. Lena was alone, investigating a crime scene when she was assaulted. The LAPD thinks it was done by the serial killer they've been pursuing. So does she." Miles paused. He dropped his head in his hands and pressed his fingertips against the corners of his damp eyes. "That—that *animal*…"

"I'm so sorry, man," David whispered.

The detective swallowed hard in an attempt to keep down the mix of pain and guilt creeping up his throat. He ran his hand down his goatee, his mind racing in a million different directions.

"Wait," David said, looking back up at Miles. "If the attack happened yesterday, why are you just now finding out about it?"

Miles shrugged before emitting a deep sigh. "Lena said she didn't want to worry the family before getting herself checked out at the hospital. Honestly, I think it's a pride thing. You know how she is. My baby sis can't stand the thought of failing at something or making a misstep."

"Humph, don't I know it. So you had to find out about this through the media?"

"Yep. Unfortunately."

"That woman…" David writhed his hands together, hoping that the pressure would somehow purge the frustration stirring inside his body. Hearing Miles speak of Lena's stubbornness triggered thoughts from their past.

David and Lena had been high school sweethearts. They were deeply in love. But that love wasn't strong enough to keep her in Clemmington.

They'd always planned on attending the local college and building a life together in their hometown. But during their senior year, Lena decided that she wanted to attend southern California's Pacific Western University and enroll in the school's prestigious forensic science program.

David was disappointed but confident they could maintain a long-distance relationship during those four years. However, when Lena informed him that she planned on moving to LA after graduation and working for the LAPD, that confidence faded.

He was shocked by the news that Lena didn't want to return to Clemmington. Aside from their relationship, David assumed she would want to work for their hometown's police department since her father served as the chief of police, and both of her brothers were police officers. But he'd been wrong.

Lena craved the excitement of working in a big city and welcomed the challenges of LA's multifaceted criminal investigations. When David expressed his desire to remain loyal to Clemmington, the pair acrimoniously parted ways.

After Lena moved away for good, David was left feeling abandoned. And now, he was regretful. Because had she stayed by his side, she never would've been attacked.

Miles cleared his throat and slowly backed out of the doorway. "I'd better get to my parents' house and check on my mother. Can you hold things down until I get back? My father and brother already left for LA to pick Lena up and bring her back here."

David shot straight up in his chair. "Wait, Lena's coming here? To Clemmington?"

"Yes. She's too traumatized to stay in LA. So she's gonna take a leave of absence and come home for a while and recuperate. But I don't know..."

David looked on curiously as Miles ran his hand down his beard, his voice trailing off. "You don't know what?"

"I'm just wondering how things are gonna go when Lena gets to town. She wasn't on the best of terms with my family when she left Clemmington. We all felt betrayed after she chose to work for the LAPD instead of our police department."

David felt a pull inside his chest after hearing those words spoken aloud. Apparently, he wasn't the only one still affected by Lena's departure.

"You know," David began, "nobody was more disappointed when she moved away than me. But at this point, that's all irrelevant. We've got to put our differences aside and make sure she's okay."

"Oh, I agree with you one hundred percent. But are *you* gonna be able to do that after everything you two have been through?"

The lawmen stared one another down. David was surprised that Miles had brought up the couple's tumultuous past. But Miles was well aware of their unresolved issues that they never addressed before Lena left town.

"Of course I'll be able to do that," David insisted. "I can't bring our personal issues into this situation. Right now, my only concern is Lena's well-being."

"Yeah, okay. We'll see…" Miles replied, his low tone dripping with skepticism. "I'd better get to my parents' house. I'll be back later this afternoon."

"Please send Mrs. Love my regards. Tell her I'm thinking of her and the family."

"It would be nice if you stopped by and told her that yourself. I'm sure she's expecting to see you once Lena gets home."

David stared blankly at Miles. A pang of uncertainty thumped inside his gut. As concerned as he was about Lena, he wasn't ready to see her just yet.

"I'll give you an update on things when I get back," Miles continued without waiting for a response, as if sensing the pressure in David's hesitation. "Call or text me if anything goes down. Not that things ever do in this town."

"Will do. Thanks for keeping me in the loop."

"No problem."

The minute Miles left his office, David turned to his computer. Despite his coffee now being lukewarm, he took a long sip, then pulled up the *Los Angeles Times*' website.

There it was. The top story, flashing across the screen.

*Famed Crime Scene Investigator Lena Love
Attacked by California Serial Killer!*

David's stomach flipped as he gazed at the beautiful photo of Lena that accompanied the story.

Do not start with that, he told himself before turning his attention to the article.

As he studied the details surrounding Lena's attack, any ill feelings David held toward her slowly dissipated. They were replaced by the sudden desire to protect her.

Chapter Three

Lena sat at her parents' dining room table, her hands clenched together tightly. She couldn't seem to control her jittery knees as they bounced against the sharp oak edge.

"Here you go, honey," Lena's mother, Betty, said. She set a cup of chamomile tea in front of her. "Be careful. It's hot."

"Thanks, Mom."

The sting of guilt singed Lena's skin when she looked up at her. The skin underneath Betty's swollen eyes was a pale shade of burgundy. Lines of worry ran down her quivering chin. Her wavy, salt-and-pepper hair was pulled back into a disheveled ponytail.

Betty placed her hand on Lena's back and began massaging it, just like she used to do when Lena couldn't sleep as a child.

Lena closed her eyes and exhaled. After several moments, her mother stopped abruptly. When she opened her eyes, Betty was hurrying over to the curio cabinet.

She threw open the doors and began pulling out glasses, then vigorously wiping them down. Lena wanted to ask if she was okay, especially considering the glasses were already gleaming. But she didn't. She realized that her mother was trying to keep busy in hopes of calming her frazzled nerves.

Lena picked up her white porcelain teacup and blew on the steaming liquid, then focused on the wall in front of her.

A portrait of the family hung in the middle. It had been taken right after Lena's college graduation, before she'd broke the news that she planned on moving to Los Angeles and working for the LAPD.

Everyone looked so happy in the picture. But shortly after the photo shoot, nothing was the same. Things had been strained between them to say the least, which was why Lena hadn't been back to Clemmington to visit in several years.

She turned away from the picture and glanced around her parents' spacious, ranch-style house. The sight brought tears to Lena's eyes. Her mother, who was a retired elementary school teacher, had maintained the home beautifully. It's where Lena and her brothers grew up, and not much had changed since she'd moved away.

The family room's neutral color scheme and rustic decor brought back memories of game nights and get-togethers among their classmates. The pang of nostalgia caused Lena to realize just how much she missed those nights, along with her parents and siblings. It also made her wonder whether leaving had been a mistake.

Just as her mind drifted toward thoughts of the attack, Lena's father, Kennedy, and brother Jake sauntered into the dining room.

The Love men looked as though they could've been triplets. They were each slightly over six feet tall, with muscular builds and strong, refined features. The only traits that set them apart were Kennedy's bald head and thick mustache.

"Dad and I threw together some turkey sandwiches,"

Jake said to Lena, placing a platter filled with mini hoagies in the middle of the table. "We, uh, we figured you may be hungry."

"Thanks, Jay. I appreciate that," Lena told him, even though she had no appetite. Eating was the last thing on her mind.

Her father remained silent while pulling a cream-colored chair away from the table. He sighed deeply, sitting down slowly while running his fingertips across his forehead's frown lines.

Lena felt herself growing sick at the thought of stressing her family to this extent. It was the reason she didn't initially tell them about the attack. Between their tense exchanges and the trauma of being assaulted, she was tempted to pack up and go back to LA.

Her rigid muscles relaxed a bit when Miles came strolling into the room. He was the only one in the family who'd stayed in regular contact with her after she moved away.

"I'd better go check on the pot roast," Betty muttered before rushing toward the kitchen.

Lena shifted in her seat and looked up at Miles. When he walked over to her chair, she noticed a silver flask discreetly tucked in his hand.

"What is that you have?" she whispered.

"Whiskey. Have some. It'll help calm your nerves."

Lena glanced over at her father and Jake, who were both busy digging into the sandwich platter. Sitting in her parents' home made her feel as though she shouldn't be drinking alcohol, despite being way past the legal age.

"A shot of whiskey is exactly what I need right now," she told Miles. "Hit me."

As he poured the brown liquor into her cup, the doorbell rang.

Lena jumped in her chair, still on edge after being attacked.

"Relax," Miles said. He gently placed his hand on her shoulder. "You're good. That's probably David."

"David!" Lena exclaimed, her eyes widening. "What is he doing here?"

"He wanted to come by and check on you. Make sure you're okay. Why don't you go get the door while I go into the kitchen and check on Mom?"

"Wait, no. I don't want to. Why can't you—"

Before Lena could finish, Miles gave her a sly grin, then turned around and left the room.

She turned to her father and Jake, who were staring down at their plates. Lena couldn't help but think they were focusing on their food in an effort to avoid talking to her.

Aside from asking if she was okay a few times on the drive from LA to Clemmington, the ride had pretty much been silent. She knew they felt badly about the attack and didn't want to drill her. But Lena also realized that hurt feelings still lingered within the family over her move.

The doorbell rang again.

"You've gotta face him at some point," Lena's father said quietly. "Regardless of what went on in your past, David does still care about you. So go on. Answer the door."

Lena wanted to roll her eyes. But instead she nodded her head and slowly slid her chair away from the table. Before standing up, she took a long sip of her spiked tea.

"Is somebody going to get the door?" Betty called out from the kitchen.

"I'm getting it now!" Lena replied.

"Don't be scared," Jake snorted.

"Oh, stop it," she shot back, swiping his shoulder. When he gave her a smirk and a wink, Lena couldn't help but appreciate the snarky gesture.

Maybe the icy atmosphere is starting to melt... she thought.

"Stop teasing your sister," Kennedy said.

"Thank you, Daddy."

Lena took her time heading to the door. On the way there, she stopped in front of the mirror hanging on the living room wall and ran her fingers through her hair.

What are you doing? she asked herself, waving her hand at her reflection.

The doorbell rang a third time.

"I got it!" she called out before any of her family members could say a word.

Lena took a deep breath. She tucked her fitted white blouse into her dark blue jeans, then finally opened the door.

The sight of David almost knocked her down. She hadn't seen him since she'd left Clemmington. He certainly hadn't looked this clean-cut, fit and handsome before her departure.

"Hello, Lena," he said, his smooth voice flowing like Dennis Haysbert's in an Allstate commercial. "It's, uh, it's good to see you."

"Hi. It's—it's good to see you, too."

David handed her a bouquet of yellow roses. "I hope these'll help lift your spirits a bit."

"You remembered," she murmured, holding the bouquet to her nose and inhaling its sweet, fruity aroma. "Thank you."

"Of course I remembered. How could I ever forget your favorite flower?"

The pair gazed quietly at one another for several moments. A slight tingling began to flow through Lena's body.

What in the hell is going on? she asked herself. The last thing she'd expected was to feel this way upon seeing David.

The spell was broken when her mother entered the living room.

"David," Betty said, "thank you so much for coming over. Come on inside. Can I get you something to drink?"

"Oh no, Mrs. Love," he said, stepping across the threshold. "I'm fine. I just wanted stop by and check on everyone. And of course see how Lena is doing."

As he entered the house, David's muscular forearm brushed up against Lena's arm. She took a deep breath and stepped back.

When he paused and glanced over at her, the scent of his woodsy, aquatic cologne filled her nostrils. That tingling she'd been feeling transformed into full-blown pulsations.

"Are you okay?" he asked.

Lena could've sworn she heard a tinge of amusement in his voice. "Yep. I'm fine."

Betty approached David and gave him a warm hug. "Well, we really appreciate you stopping by to check on us. I'll leave you two alone so you can talk. Plus I need to get back to my pot roast. David, why don't you stay for dinner?"

He hesitated, then turned to Lena.

When David raised his eyebrows, she realized that he was silently asking for her permission. She nodded her head.

"Thank you, Mrs. Love," David replied. "I'd love to stay for dinner. As long as it's all right with Lena."

"Of course it is," she responded a bit quicker than she'd intended. "I—I mean, yeah, that's fine."

"Good," Betty said. "I'd better go and get those sandwiches off the dining room table before your father and brothers ruin their appetites. And here," she continued, taking the bouquet of flowers from Lena, "I'll put these beautiful roses in water for you."

"Thanks, Mom."

Betty paused, her eyes darting back and forth between Lena and David. The huge grin on her face said more than words ever could.

"Thanks, Mom," Lena repeated, through clenched teeth this time.

Betty caught the hint and hurried out of the room.

Lena turned to David and chuckled lightly, embarrassed by her mother's behavior.

"Sorry about that," she said before pointing over at the couch. "Why don't we have a seat. Are you sure you don't want anything to drink? Soda? Tea? Water?"

"No, I'm good. I think I drank about three pots of coffee today. But thank you."

Lena led the way as she and David sat down on the beige sectional sofa. She kept a safe distance, considering she was still waiting for the body tingles to stop. When she noticed David staring at her intently, Lena glanced around the room in search of something to say. The last thing she wanted to discuss was her attack.

"I have to tell you something," she blurted out.

"What's that?"

"I was drinking chamomile tea spiked with whiskey before you got here."

"Oh no. Not you. I can't even see Miss Top Shelf Wine and Champagne drinking whiskey."

"Yeah, but I was. After everything I've been through? I needed it. Blame Miles. He's the one that gave it to me."

"Ugh," David groaned, throwing his head back. "Here you go. Blaming one of your brothers for your wild behavior, per usual. I see not much has changed around the Love residence."

"And as long as I can keep getting away with it, things never will."

Lena was surprised by how relaxed she felt with David. Despite their complicated past, it was as if no time had passed between them.

She looked up at him. There was a pained look behind his eyes. She was suddenly hit with a bout of remorse.

Lena knew David was still hurt over the way she'd left Clemmington. But it wasn't just that. She could sense that he was upset by her assault.

"So, on a serious note," he said, "how are you doing?"

Lena's eyes fell to her lap. The high energy in the room shifted. It was replaced by a heavy gloom. She was quickly reminded of why she was back in Clemmington.

The moment when Lena's attacker knocked her to the ground flashed through her mind.

Stop it, she told herself, shaking her head in an attempt to erase the memory.

"I'm hanging in there. I mean, of course I'm still shaken up." She paused, curling her trembling hands into tight fists. "I just can't believe what happened at that crime scene. How did *I* end up getting assaulted by the killer that I'm pursuing, and almost killed, and…"

When Lena's voice trailed off, David slid in closer toward her.

"Are you sure it's the same suspect you've been after?" he asked. "Or could it have been a random attack?"

Lena cleared her throat, swallowing a lump of nausea. She held her hand to her chest. Her fingers pressed against the thick bandage covering the scar underneath her blouse. That half-heart-shaped wound was a clear indication that her attacker was their serial killer.

The LAPD hadn't revealed the particulars of her assault to the media, specifically the details surrounding her scar. And in that moment, Lena wasn't ready to share them with David, either.

"It definitely wasn't a random attack," she told him. "City officials are feeling an intense amount of pressure to solve this case now that a fifth victim has been found. The mayor held a press conference a few weeks ago and introduced me as the newest member of the investigative team. After mentioning a couple of high-profile cases that I helped solve, I vowed to find the killer. *That's* why he's after me."

"So you think he trailed you to this latest crime scene you've been investigating?"

"I do. He was probably staking out the forensics lab. That's where I was before heading to the Cucamonga Wilderness trail."

David shook his head. "I don't like the way LA's city officials are handling this situation. At all."

"What do you mean?"

"That press conference put you in a very precarious position. We do things differently in Clemmington. We protect our own. Our police department never would've shined a public spotlight on you like that."

"Yeah, that probably wasn't the smartest thing to do," Lena muttered, wincing as she rubbed the back of her neck.

"Are you okay?"

"I'm fine," she replied, once again leaving out the details of the half-shaped heart that had been carved into her chest.

"Good. I'm glad you're back in Clemmington, Lena. I hope you'll stay for a while. Lay low and allow yourself some time to heal. What you experienced was extremely traumatizing. Maybe you should even consider letting another forensic investigator take over the case while you focus on your recovery."

Lena leaned into the back of the couch. "Humph. I don't know about all that. It sounds like the right thing to do. But honestly, I don't know how long I can just sit still. And I definitely can't see myself letting the case go. I've been investigating this killer for a few weeks, and I'm too close to cracking it to turn back now."

David stared at her, his steely eyes defiant.

"Your ambition always did override any advice I could ever give you," he said.

"I just like to finish what I start. That's all."

"Except when it comes to us," David shot back just as Betty walked back into the room.

"You two ready for dinner?" she asked cheerily.

"I am," Lena replied, quickly hopping up from the couch and heading to the dining room. It was bad enough that David had popped up at the house unexpectedly. The last thing she was prepared to do was hash out their unresolved issues.

He stood up and followed closely behind her. She could feel his intense gaze on her back.

"This conversation isn't over," he murmured.

What have I gotten myself into with this trip back to Clemmington...?

Chapter Four

David strolled into the police station and headed straight to the breakroom to grab a cup of coffee.

"Good morning, Detective Hudson," Milly sang out. "Looks like you've got a little extra pep in your step today."

"Do I?" he asked curiously.

But David knew exactly what Milly was referring to. Ever since Lena had come home, there was a rousing energy flowing through him that he couldn't seem to contain.

"Yes," Milly replied, propping her elbows on the edge of her cluttered desk and clicking her nails together. "You do. I wonder if it has anything to do with what's going on inside Chief Love's office."

David's eyebrows furrowed with confusion. He almost asked her to elaborate before realizing he didn't have time. He needed to check in with the chief on an act of vandalism that occurred earlier that morning across town.

"We're going to have to reconvene on whatever it is you're referring to," he told her. "I've got a few things I need to take care of."

"Suit yourself," Milly told him. She flipped through a stack of reports and began sliding them inside manila folders. "In the meantime, I hope you guys catch whoever defaced the front of Mr. Young's beautiful art gallery."

"I'm sure we will."

David entered the breakroom and acknowledged the few police officers who were gathered around one of several white folding tables. They nodded their heads to him, then turned their attention back to a video they were watching on Officer Lee Underwood's cell phone.

After pouring himself a cup of coffee, David glanced down at his watch. It was already after nine o'clock.

Put a move on, he told himself, holding his cup steady while rushing to his office.

He tossed his briefcase down onto the desk and grabbed a notebook, then headed to Chief Love's office.

"Come on in, Detective," the chief said. "Have a seat. I hope it's okay that Lena is here. She was getting antsy sitting in the house all day. So she came down to the station to keep her dear old dad company."

"And once again get grilled on why I left Clemmington," Lena interjected. "Don't forget to add *that* little detail."

"Hey, if you wanna hang out with the boss, then you have to deal with the trash talk. It comes with the territory."

David chuckled at their friendly father-daughter banter. He was pleasantly surprised to see the pair getting along so well considering they were discussing such a touchy subject.

Lena turned to David and threw her hands in the air. "I cannot believe that after all this time, my father and brothers are *still* salty that I moved to LA."

"Your family just misses you, that's all. Take it as a compliment."

"I bet we're not the only ones who've missed her…" Chief Love said.

David's eyes lowered as he noticed a smirk on the chief's face.

Just let it go and sit down, David told himself before taking a seat next to Lena.

"*Anyway*," David said, "should we go ahead and get this meeting started?"

"Yes, we should," Chief Love replied.

While the chief flipped through his planner, David glanced over at Lena. That rousing energy he'd been feeling intensified as he discreetly studied her.

She was dressed casually in a fitted denim jumpsuit and white sneakers. Her hair had been pulled up into a messy bun, and her glowing skin appeared makeup free. Only a sheer coat of gloss covered her full lips. She looked relaxed, and absolutely beautiful.

"But before we get started," Chief Love said, "I've gotta get in one last word."

"Uh-oh," Lena mumbled, slumping down in her chair. "Here we go…"

"Lena," he continued, "you come from a family of law enforcement officers. We run Clemmington, California. Why would you have ever wanted to ruin the family legacy?"

She leaned forward, gripping the arms on her chair. "I cannot believe you want to talk about this right now. Seriously, can I just recuperate in peace?"

Lena turned to David as if waiting on him to chime in.

He stared down at his notebook, not wanting to get in between the father and daughter. Not only that, but he needed to focus on something other than her stunning face.

"I plead the Fifth," David told her. "My arms are too short to box with the Love family."

"Oh, come on, Dave!" Chief Love insisted. "You may have dated my daughter back in the day, but you're *my* guy. You should be on my side."

"I'm on Sweden's side," he joked before flipping to a blank page in his notebook. "Now, what's going on with this act of vandalism? Milly mentioned that someone defaced Mr. Young's art gallery?"

"Yes, that's what it looks like." The chief slid several pieces of paper across the desk. "I had Jake and Miles drive by there earlier, assess the scene and take these photos."

David leaned forward, studying the pictures. The words *One Two I Am Coming For You* had been spray-painted in black across the gallery's storefront glass.

"Hmm, that's strange," David said. "What time did this happen?"

"According to Mr. Young's security cameras, around three o'clock this morning."

"Were the cameras able to capture a decent image of the perp?"

The chief leaned back in his chair and propped his hands on top of his head.

"Not really. All Mr. Young could gather was that the offender appeared to be male. He was dressed in what looked to be dark green camouflage hunting gear and a full tactical face mask. I'm surprised he went to such great lengths just to vandalize a storefront."

"Why don't I go by the gallery and take a look around?" David suggested as he jotted down notes. "I'll see what I can find and hopefully take a look at those surveillance tapes."

"That sounds good," Chief Love said. "Hopefully you

can question Mr. Young and find out who he thinks may have done this. When Jake and Miles went by there earlier, he was too upset to speak with them."

Lena picked up one of the photos and studied it intently. "Poor Mr. Young. He's so sweet and doesn't bother anybody. And his art gallery means everything to him. He takes so much pride in it. I can't imagine who'd want to do something like this."

David picked up the other photos and eyed each of them again. "'One two I am coming for you…'" he read aloud before looking up at the chief, "Maybe this message wasn't aimed at Mr. Young."

"What do you mean?" Chief Love asked.

"Well, for starters, I agree with Lena. Mr. Young is a beloved member of this community. And even though he was upset when Jake and Miles stopped by, if he had a clue as to who would have done something like this, he would've reported it."

"I'd like to think so," the chief replied. "But where are you going with this?"

"The art gallery is located in one of the most visible areas in town. Maybe the perpetrator just wanted to leave this message somewhere he knew it would be seen in hopes that his target would receive it."

As soon as the words were out of David's mouth, his stomach dropped.

This message may have been left for Lena…

He glanced over at her, hoping she wasn't thinking what he was thinking. She was still staring down at one of the photos, seemingly oblivious.

David then looked up at the chief. He too was studying one of the pictures, rubbing his chin curiously. David couldn't tell whether he and his boss were on the same page or not. If they were, Chief Love wasn't letting on.

"I'm gonna head over to the gallery now," David said, slamming his notebook shut and hopping up. He was irritated with himself for almost saying too much. Lena had already been through enough. The last thing he wanted to do was cause any alarm, especially if his suspicions didn't hold much merit.

"Hey," Lena said, grabbing his arm, "is it okay if I ride with you? I'd love to take a look at the scene, too."

David stared down at her. There was a hunger in her intent gaze. The look was a reminder of how much she loved her work.

David turned to his boss. Chief Love shrugged his shoulders and scooted away from the desk.

"Well," the chief began, "Lena is a crime scene expert. You never know what she may find. And she had a great relationship with Mr. Young back when she still lived in Clemmington. She and her brothers actually used to volunteer at the gallery whenever he had openings. So it may not be a bad idea for her to ride along."

Lena pointed at her father. "Exactly. Plus, if I don't get back to some semblance of my normal life, I just may lose my mind."

David looked on apprehensively as she stood up and grabbed her purse.

"Are you sure you're ready for this?" he asked her. "You know…after what you've been through?"

"Listen, Detective Hudson," Lena said, brushing past him and pausing in the doorway, "I am a pro. This is what I do. And it's just an act of vandalism. It would be different if you were investigating a murder scene. Trust me. I can handle this. Now, let's hurry up and get to the gallery before Mr. Young calls a cleaning service to have the graffiti removed."

David paused, giving the chief one last time to talk his daughter down.

"You heard the lady," Chief Love quipped. "You'd better put a move on before Mr. Young compromises the crime scene."

"Thanks, boss," Lena said to her father.

She spun around and strutted out of the office. David followed behind her, fighting off a mix of frustration and excitement.

Milly perked up when the pair walked past her desk. "Where are you two off to?"

David's eyes shifted at the suggestive tone in her high-pitched voice.

"We're going to check out the crime scene at Mr. Young's art gallery," he told her.

"*Ohhh*. And Miss Lena Love is joining you?"

"Yes, I am," Lena replied. "It's time for me to get back into the swing of things. Even if it is with the Clemmington PD as opposed to the LAPD."

"*Please,*" Milly snorted, the red beads on her bracelets jingling loudly as she waved Lena off. "The LAPD ain't got nothing on us."

"If you say so," Lena retorted.

"But seriously, hon, I'm glad to see you're doing okay," Milly said before giving her a sympathetic smile. "You had this entire town worried for a minute there."

"Thanks, Mills. I know a lot of the townspeople were pretty disappointed when I moved away. So hearing that means a lot."

David gently placed his hand on Lena's shoulder.

"We'd better get going. Milly, we'll be back in a bit. Call my cell phone if anyone needs me."

"I most certainly will, Detective. *Byyye* you two."

He threw her a look as she grinned and wiggled her fingers at the pair.

The people of Clemmington may have held a grudge toward Lena when she'd left town. But they certainly seemed to have softened up quickly now that she had returned.

Including you... David told himself.

As soon as the thought crossed his mind, he pushed it aside. He'd already gotten hurt once when she moved away. And he knew she'd be returning to LA eventually.

So don't fall for her again...

Chapter Five

A burst of adrenaline flowed through Lena's veins when David pulled up in front of Mr. Young's art gallery.

The building stood prominently on the corner of Clemmington's busiest downtown strip. Its contemporary glass exterior was a stark contradiction to the surrounding brick storefronts.

Today, however, the gallery appeared bleak. Yellow crime scene tape had been wrapped around the perimeter. Large, sloppy black lettering was scribbled across the high-end pane of glass.

"How obnoxious," Lena mumbled as she eyed the damage. "I can only imagine how sick Mr. Young must've felt when he saw this."

"I'm sure he was devastated. And even though the gallery is located in a small town, it is a prominent California exhibition room. Mr. Young has featured premiere artists from all over the world. So to see it being treated like a piece of trash is really disheartening."

"It really is." Lena reached down inside her beige leather hobo bag and grabbed her cell phone. She climbed out of the car and began taking photos of the windows.

"Hey!" she heard someone yell from the doorway. "Is that who I think it is?"

"Mr. Young!" Lena exclaimed, rushing toward the front of the building. "It is so good to see you!"

She embraced the popular curator, surprised by how frail he'd become since the last time she had seen him.

His pale skin was wrinkled with worry. His eyes were sunken in, and the light that once radiated from them had dimmed. The thick blond braid that used to swing down his back had whittled down to a short silver ponytail.

But it wasn't just age that had affected Mr. Young's appearance. Judging by the fearful scowl on his face, he'd clearly been shaken up by the act of vandalism.

"I am so sorry about what happened here," Lena told him. "I hope you don't mind my tagging along with Detective Hudson to analyze the scene."

"Of course not. I don't mind at all. I'm actually glad that an expert such as yourself is here to help."

David approached Mr. Young and shook his hand. "Hello, sir. Lena and I are going to take a look around and try to figure out who did this to your establishment."

"Thank you, Detective. I appreciate that. And hey, you never know. Lena just may end up cracking this case all on her own. She's got that LA expertise under her belt." He reached out and patted her arm. "Speaking of LA, we were all so devastated after hearing that you'd been attacked. I just—the whole town was just…"

"Thanks, Mr. Young," Lena said after his voice broke. "I'm working on putting all that behind me and moving forward. Hopefully being back home with family and friends will help me to do that."

"I'm sure it will," he assured her.

An awkward silence fell over the group. Lena hated how the subject of her attack triggered an uncomfortable energy every time it was brought up. She fiddled with a metal button on her jumpsuit, hoping David would step in and say something.

David cleared his throat and turned to Mr. Young. "So, if it's okay with you, I'd like to take a look at the surveillance tapes. I want to get a good look at the perpetrator and gather whatever evidence can be pulled from the video."

"Of course, Detective. Follow me. I'll take you to the back room where the security system is set up."

Just as the threesome headed inside the gallery, a red pickup truck pulled in front of the building.

Two men jumped out. Lena watched as they pulled buckets and mops from the cargo bed.

"Oh good," Mr. Young said. "My maintenance crew is here. I asked them to come and get rid of this…this *filth*."

"Do you think you could have them hold off on cleaning for now?" Lena asked. "Just until I'm done surveying the scene?"

"Absolutely. Hey, guys?" Mr. Young called out. "Clemmington PD needs to investigate the property before you begin washing down the windows. Would you mind giving them a few minutes? Maybe go next door and grab a coffee while you wait?"

"Sure, no problem, sir," one of the men replied, giving Mr. Young a thumbs-up, then walking over toward Martha's Sip & Savor.

"Okay," Mr. Young continued. "Let's go check out that CCTV footage."

"Listen," Lena said. "Why don't you two go in and start reviewing the footage? I'll stay out here and take a look around before the cleaners come back."

David hesitated, looking up and down the street. "Are you sure? You're okay being out here by yourself?"

Lena tilted her head to the side and emitted a soft

chuckle. "Of course I am. And technically, I'm not by myself. I'm standing out on a busy street. Not to mention we're in Clemmington. What's going to happen to me here?"

When David didn't budge, Lena reached out and nudged his shoulder.

"Come on," she teased. "I'm a big girl. Trust me, I'll be fine. I'm just going to search the area for any evidence, then take a few more photos of the graffiti. I'll come inside as soon as I'm done. Okay?"

David craned his neck, staring down the street again as if he was searching for something. Several moments passed before he finally replied.

"Fine. But don't take too long. If you're not inside this gallery in the next fifteen minutes or so, I'm coming back out here."

"Yes, sir," she said, already holding up her cell phone and taking pictures of the window. "See you inside."

Once David was gone, Lena immediately went into investigator mode. She slid her phone inside her back pocket and pulled a pair of latex gloves out of her purse. She slipped them on, then grabbed a plastic baggie and small flashlight.

Lena walked over to the left corner of the building and shined the flashlight down onto the pavement. As she searched the area, a serene feeling floated through her body. Even though she wasn't investigating a high-profile crime scene back in LA, being on a job felt good.

"Come on," she whispered, moving in closer to the building. "Show me something…"

She willed a piece of evidence to appear; a spray-paint bottle or cap that could reveal a fingerprint. Or a piece of clothing accidentally left behind that might match up with the perp's gear in the surveillance footage.

Just as she bent down and studied the gap in between the art gallery and coffee shop next door, a loud car engine roared in the distance.

Lena shot straight up. She peered down the street. A black vehicle slowly turned the corner. She watched as it crept down the road toward the gallery.

Despite memories being triggered by the engine's piercing rumble, Lena turned her attention back to the investigation. But when the noise grew louder, she stood back up and focused on the approaching car.

As Lena got a better look at the vehicle, her limbs went numb. She immediately recognized its obnoxious twenty-four-inch spiked chrome rims. They were attached to the black sports car that chased her from the Cucamonga Wilderness.

"No, no, no, no," Lena whispered. "It can't be him. It *can't* be him!"

The car pulled over toward the curb and stopped abruptly in front of her. She cringed at the sound of its revving engine. A cloud of exhaust billowed from underneath, smoking out the street.

Lena wanted to scream out for David. But she could barely breathe, let alone yell.

Her eyes were glued to the vehicle. She struggled to see inside. But she couldn't make out the person behind the dark tinted windows.

Lena held her breath, waiting for him to jump out and attack.

Don't let him get the best of you this time. Defend yourself. Fight back!

She tried to position her body into a defensive stance. But terror had locked up her arms and legs.

Flashbacks of the assailant slicing his knife into her skin flooded Lena's mind.

I cannot go through that again…

The roar of the engine suddenly ceased. The driver cracked opened the door.

Lena's chest tightened. She recoiled at the sight of a large silver blade.

Just as a black combat boot slipped out of the car and hit the pavement, David came bursting out of the gallery.

"Lena!" he called out while jogging toward her.

She gasped, taking in a huge breath of air. As David approached her, she pointed at the car.

"David! I think that's the—"

But before Lena could finish, the driver slammed the door and sped off.

"Listen," David continued, oblivious to her frightened state, "I've got great news. Miles just texted me. They apprehended the suspect that vandalized the gallery."

Lena stared up at him, blinking rapidly. "Wait…" she uttered, still pointing at what she thought was the suspect's car as it flew around the corner. "They what?"

"They arrested the alleged perp! Officer Underwood was over by the high school and caught some teenager scribbling graffiti across the back of the gymnasium. With black spray paint no less."

"Really?" Lena asked, now wondering if her mind was playing tricks on her. Had she really seen that exact same sports car the night of her attack? Was it an actual knife blade that appeared through the crack of the car door?

Maybe not… Lena thought before turning to David.

"What about the surveillance video?" she asked. "Were you able to get a good look at the perp?"

"I haven't watched it yet. Miles sent the text message letting me know they'd apprehended the suspect right after we sat down. But Mr. Young is going to turn the footage over to me."

"Okay. Good."

Lena felt the tense muscles in her shoulders relax a bit. She knew her attack had left her traumatized. But she didn't realize it'd left her paranoid, as well.

"Let's head back to the station so I can talk to the suspect," David said. "We'll review the surveillance tape once I receive it and see if the young man in the footage resembles the kid they've arrested. Were you able to find any evidence out here?"

"No, I didn't see anything."

Lena contemplated telling David about the man in the black sports car. But she decided against it for fear of sounding neurotic, which would make her appear unstable and land her right back at her parents' house 24/7.

Just stay calm, she told herself. *That man was not your attacker. You're just on edge...*

But as Lena followed David back to the car, she wondered whether she was simply trying to fool herself.

Chapter Six

"A toast," Kennedy said, raising his glass of champagne in the air. "To my oldest son, Jake, formally known as Officer Love, who I am now proud to call *Detective* Love. Congratulations on your promotion, kid."

"Thanks, Dad," Jake said, grinning from ear to ear as he clinked his glass against his father's.

The Love family was standing in the middle of the living room, celebrating Jake's advancement within the department. A few members of the Clemmington PD had joined them, including David.

"Congrats, big bro," Lena said, nudging Jake playfully with her hip.

"Thanks, lil sis. I appreciate it. And hey, I'm glad that you're here to share this moment with me."

David looked on as the two siblings tapped their glasses against one another's, then took a sip of champagne. He smiled, glad to see them healing their rift.

"Yeah, man, congratulations," David chimed in.

"Excuse me, everyone," Betty said. "I hope you didn't get too full of Kennedy's grilled steak, chicken kabobs and corn on the cob, because I'm serving up red velvet cheesecake for dessert."

"Aw, big brother's favorite," Miles teased.

"Shut up, dude," Jake shot back.

Lena leaned into David. "One thing about these two. No matter how old they get, they will never outgrow their sibling rivalry," she whispered.

David chuckled and wrapped his arm around her. "You think this is something? You should see them down at the station. The joke-telling never stops."

"I can only imagine," Lena murmured before looking over at him curiously.

David quickly dropped his arm to his side.

"Oh…sorry," he uttered. "I didn't mean to, um…"

"Relax. It's okay. We didn't just meet yesterday. And I'd like to think that we're friends. Friends can put their arms around one another, can't they?"

"Yeah," he said, his nonchalant shrug a total contradiction of the thrill he felt as her body pressed against his. "Friends should definitely be able to put their arms around one another."

David looked at Lena. Their eyes locked. Just as his gaze drifted down toward her lips, Betty's voice boomed in the background.

"So, if anyone would like a slice of cheesecake, meet me out in the backyard on the deck."

Jake and Miles brushed past Lena so quickly that they almost knocked the glass out of her hand.

"What gentlemen!" she called out, grabbing a napkin and wiping away the champagne that had spilled onto the front of her silk magenta tank dress.

"Sorry!" they yelled in unison.

David picked up a few more napkins off the coffee table and handed them to her. "That won't leave a stain, will it?"

"No, it should be fine once it dries. I just wish my brothers weren't so overzealous over dessert."

Detective Campbell approached the pair. "So maybe that move to LA was good for you after all," he interjected.

Lena paused and turned to him. When she didn't respond, he pressed on.

"You know, because it got you away from your brothers and whatnot."

David watched as Lena's darting eyes filled with apprehension. He could sense that her mind had drifted toward thoughts of the attack.

"I—I don't know, Russ..." she stammered.

"Should we go out onto the deck and grab a slice of cheesecake?" David asked, detecting her discomfort.

"Yes," she responded before the words were barely out of his mouth. "We should."

As David led her outside, Detective Campbell continued to hound her.

"So how's it been, being back in Clemmington?" he queried, probing.

"It's been nice, actually. I've enjoyed reconnecting with my family. And as you know, I've been spending time down at the police station, helping out with some of the investigations."

"Getting back to work so soon hasn't been tough on you after your attack—"

"Hey, Russ," David interrupted, "why don't we lay off of the heavy talk for now. This is a celebration. Let's sip champagne and eat cheesecake and focus on Jake's promotion."

Russ threw his hands in the air as the threesome stepped out onto the deck. "My bad. Sorry, Lena. I was just wondering how you're doing, that's all. I certainly didn't mean to offend you."

"You didn't," she assured him before gently placing

her hand on David's arm. "You know how this guy is, though. He's just looking out for me."

"Yeah, well, I wouldn't mind looking out for you, too. Maybe we can get together sometime next week for drinks. Or dinner even. Whatever you're comfortable with."

David clenched his teeth together, resisting the urge to punch Russ in the jaw. The detective was a known ladies' man throughout the town of Clemmington as well as several surrounding areas. Between meeting women online and hanging out at all the hot spots, Russ's contacts list was endless. And he didn't mind bragging about it. The last thing David wanted was for Lena to get caught up with a player like him.

He turned to Lena, anxiously awaiting her response.

"Honestly, Russ," she began, "I'm just focusing on my recovery right now. But I do appreciate the offer. Thank you."

"So I take that as a no, then?"

"Did she stutter?" David shot back, unable to conceal the smirk on his face.

"All right then, Lena," Russ said, slowly backing away while ignoring David. "Maybe some other time."

The cringey exchange was interrupted when Betty walked over and handed David and Lena two slices of cheesecake.

"Here you go," she said. "I wanted to make sure you both got a piece before it's all gone. Kennedy and those sons of mine are already on their second helpings."

"Of course they are," Lena said, then snickered. "Thanks, Mom."

"You're welcome, honey." Betty leaned in and kissed Lena on her cheek. "I know it may not be under the best circumstances, but it certainly is nice having you home. I think I'm getting spoiled."

"Yeah, me, too," David said. When Lena and her mother both turned to him with surprised looks on their faces, he cleared his throat. "I mean, I agree that it's been nice having Lena around. You know, down at the station helping out…"

"Nice save, sweetheart," Betty muttered, patting his arm before walking off.

"Thanks for the cheesecake!" he told her before glancing over at Lena. "That mother of yours is something else."

"Oh, you don't have to tell me. She doesn't miss much. I think it comes from all those years of teaching young, mischievous students."

"I couldn't agree more."

David bit into a mouthful of cheesecake and looked around the Love family's spacious backyard. The lush green lawn was surrounded by colorful philodendron plants and butterfly bushes. The cedarwood fence was lined with bright green horsetail reed bamboo. A Western Redbud tree stood in the middle of the yard, its magenta-colored blossoms blowing gently in the breeze. It was a beautiful setting for the joyous occasion.

"So," he said to Lena, "no interest in Russ, huh."

"Russ *Campbell*? Please. None whatsoever. That man is a known playboy. He's even dated a few of the female LAPD officers. And when they found out about one another? Whew! That drama lasted for a good couple of months around the station."

"Typical Campbell behavior," David said. He took a deep breath, stabbing his fork into his cheesecake before continuing. "So, uh, speaking of dating, are you seeing anyone?"

"Me?" Lena practically choked. "No. Not even close. I've been so wrapped up in my work that I haven't had time to even think about dating." She paused, her eyes squinting as she stared at David. "What about you? Are you seeing anyone?"

"Nah. I'm single as a one-dollar bill."

"Oh, so you're *single* single," she replied before they simultaneously burst out laughing.

"Yep," he replied. "I sure am. Like you, I've been totally focused on work."

"Hmm, interesting…"

David watched as Lena slid a piece of cheesecake into her mouth. He stiffened up at the sight of her glossy lips, puckering as she chewed.

Chill out. You're at your boss's house…

David felt something stirring deep within him. He shifted his feet, anxious to shake it off. He couldn't.

You have got to get out of here…

"Hey, listen," he said. "I, uh, I'd better get going."

"So soon? But what about the fireworks show? You know my dad and Miles are going to surprise Jake with what they're calling *the most epic pyrotechnics display of all time.*"

"Yeah, sorry I'm going to have to miss it. But I, um, I need to get over to my sister's house. I promised her I'd help move some things out of the basement and into the garage."

David didn't feel too bad considering he wasn't lying. Technically. He *had* promised his sister he'd help with the clean out. He just wasn't due to be at her place for another couple of hours.

"Okay." Lena sighed. "Well, thanks for coming by and celebrating with us."

"Of course. Thank you for having me."

"Can I walk you out?"

"No, no," David replied brusquely. "I mean, I'll be fine. You just stay here and enjoy the party."

He hoped she hadn't sensed the abrasiveness in his voice. But David felt an urgent need to leave before he made a fool of himself.

"I guess I'll see you at the station tomorrow, then?" Lena asked.

"Yep, see you tomorrow."

And with that, David charged out of the backyard without saying goodbye to anyone else.

Chapter Seven

Lena gripped the car door handle as David peeled around the corner and flew down Robinson Avenue. He pulled in front of Nancy's Country Mart and slammed on the brakes, double-parking next to a squad car.

The pair jumped out and ran toward the entrance, ducking underneath the yellow crime scene tape on the way inside.

"Was anyone hurt?" David asked Russ, who was standing in the doorway.

"Not that I'm aware of. But double-check with Jake and Miles. They're both inside near the cash register, talking to Nancy."

As the two detectives continued to talk, Lena took a few steps back and eyed the store.

It had been burglarized sometime during the middle of the night. Nancy hadn't discovered the break-in until she arrived to open up earlier that morning.

The mart, which had been a Clemmington staple for years, was one of Lena's favorite stores. Its charming red wooden structure resembled that of an old country barn. Bales of hay were stacked on either side of the white-framed doorway, and miniature pumpkins lined the ramp leading up to the entrance.

The inside of the store looked more like a high-end

marketplace. Shiny white oak floors, chrome shelving units and sleek recessed ceiling lights created a sophisticated atmosphere. One side of the mart contained a variety of gourmet meats and cheeses, specialty breads, and international wines. The other side housed unique toys and gifts, luxury beauty products, and a mini floral department.

Today, however, the normally pristine store had been ransacked. The front picture window was shattered. Graffiti had been spray-painted along the walls. A slew of items were strewn across the floor. Silver art display panels had been pulled from the walls, along with the paintings hanging from them.

"Lena, did you remember to bring your forensics kit?" David asked her.

"Of course," she told him, pulling the black plastic case from her tote bag. "I seldom leave home without it."

"Good. Just making sure since we ran out of the station so quickly. I'm gonna head to the back and talk to Nancy and the other officers. Why don't you start processing the scene?"

"I'm on it," Lena replied, pulling a pair of latex gloves out of the pocket of her gray skinny jeans. When David threw her a look, she pulled an extra pair from the pocket of her black leather moto jacket and handed them to him.

"Thanks for looking out for me," he said.

"No worries." She reached inside her forensics kit and grabbed a couple pairs of disposable white shoe coverings. "You'd better put these on, too. Don't want to contaminate the scene."

When he reached for the booties, Lena felt David's fingers glide over her hand. She ignored the shivers that shot up her arm and bent down, slipping the covers over her black combat boots.

"You ready, Hudson?" Russ asked him.

Lena glanced back up and saw that David was still standing there, staring down at her.

"Yeah," he told the detective without taking his eyes off her. "Right behind you."

She slipped past the men. "I'd better get started. David, I'll circle back with you once I survey the store and see what I can find."

"Sounds good. Thanks again for helping us out, Lena. I know you keep hearing this, but we're lucky to have you back home, lending us your expertise."

She turned to him and nodded her head. "Thank you for that. Being back in Clemmington is beginning to feel more and more therapeutic."

"I'm glad to hear it."

The pair stood there, neither breaking their gaze.

Russ cleared his throat and stepped in between them. "We'd better get moving," he told David.

Judging by the scowl on Russ's face, Lena knew that the suggestion was driven by jealousy rather than business. She backed away, not wanting to take the focus off the investigation.

"I'll catch up with you in a bit," she told David.

Time to get into forensic investigator mode...

Lena slipped on a pair of eye goggles, then pulled a bottle of black granular powder from her kit. She sprinkled the substance along the frames of the broken windows, the kicked-in door and the doorknob. She then used a soft brush to dust off the excess powder. When fingerprints appeared, Lena took photos, then lifted them with clear adhesive tape.

From the corner of her eye, she noticed David talking to a couple of policemen. But his focus was on her. After a few minutes, he walked over.

"How's everything going?" he asked. "You good? Need my help with anything?"

"No, I'm okay. But thank you."

Lena knew that David was worried about her mental state after the attack. She appreciated his concern but wanted to prove that she was fit for the job.

"I was actually able to lift several fingerprints from the store's entryways," she continued while placing the tape on a latent lift card to help preserve the prints. "So we'll run the data through the FBI's Integrated Automated Fingerprint Identification System in hopes of coming up with a match."

"Sounds good." David paused, his soft expression filled with concern. "So, um, are you sure you're—"

"Detective," Lena interrupted. "I thought you were going to speak to Nancy and the other officers about the break-in."

David threw his hands up and took a step back. "I am, I am. I just—I wanted to make sure you feel comfortable being here. This crime scene isn't just graffiti on a window. This one has escalated."

"I'm fine. I promise. Trust me, I've seen much worse. Being here isn't triggering feelings of fear or anxiety. So go on. Do your thing. I'll catch up with you shortly."

"Yes, ma'am."

Once David walked off, Lena turned her attention back to the scene. She walked over to the store's wine display, which had been completely destroyed. Glass bottles were shattered everywhere. The wood crate shelves were crushed. Pools of red and yellow wine covered the floor.

Lena bent down and noticed a stained shard of glass. The deep shade of burgundy didn't appear to be wine. She picked it up and took a closer look.

It was blood.

Excellent, Lena thought, hoping that the evidence would lead them to a suspect.

She pulled a piece of butcher paper out of her bag and carefully wrapped the glass, then slid it inside a brown paper bag and secured it with red evidence tape.

Lena then stood up and continued studying the perimeter. Her eyes landed on a piece of metal sticking out from underneath a rack of T-shirts that had been knocked over.

She stepped carefully through the debris. The rod appeared to be an arm that had broken off the clothing rack. But when Lena grabbed hold of it, she realized that the fixture was actually a steel pipe.

"What have you got there?" she heard Miles call out.

Lena looked up and saw him standing near the floral department, watching her intently. The look of concern in his eyes told her that he too was worried about her well-being.

"I'm thinking it may be a weapon that our perp used to do some of this damage," she told him, her strong tone filled with confidence. It was her way of discreetly letting him know that she was fine. "We'll process it and see what comes up."

Miles gave her a thumbs-up. She nodded her head, then turned her attention back to the scene.

Just as Lena slipped the pipe inside a brown paper bag and sealed it with evidence tape, she heard a loud whimper. Nancy was leaning against the checkout counter, doubled over in tears while her daughter Sarah rubbed her back.

Poor woman, Lena thought. The store owner took so much pride in her establishment.

Lena walked over to the register.

"Nancy, I am so sorry about this burglary."

Her head popped up. Nancy's round, doll-like face

was streaked with tears. Her signature brunette beehive, which was normally perfectly coiffed, was completely disheveled.

"Oh, Lena," she wailed, "I'm so glad you're here. Please help me find the *animals* who did this to my beautiful store!"

"I promise you that I will do everything in my power to find them. Have you contacted your insurance company yet?"

"No, not yet," her daughter Sarah replied. "I'm going to call our agent as soon as I can calm my mom down."

"Okay, good. Once we're done processing the scene, your insurer will send out an adjuster who'll assess the damage. That'll get you on the road to repairing and rebuilding this place. Your beloved market will be back up and running before you know it. I'd also recommend filing a business income and extra expense claim. That way you'll receive a settlement that will cover lost profits while the store is closed for repairs."

"Thank you so much, Lena," Nancy said, wiping her nose with a tissue. "I appreciate that." She backed away from the counter and eyed the store wearily. "Have you found any evidence yet that might identify a suspect?"

"I have, actually. I've got a few items here in these bags that could help us track down the culprit or culprits. I'll know more once we send them off to the crime lab and have them processed."

"Humph. Good luck with that," Russ muttered underneath his breath.

Lena turned around and glanced at the detective, who was standing behind her taking photos of a smashed jewelry display case. He paused, shrugging his shoulders.

"Just being honest," he whispered to her.

Lena subtly shook her head from side to side in hopes

of quieting him. They both knew that many of California's crime labs were notoriously backed up. The wait on getting forensic results back could take months. But she didn't want Nancy to hear that, considering how upset she was.

Lena cleared her throat and turned her attention back to the store owner. "I know that you've already been questioned by law enforcement. But I have to ask, do you have any idea who may have done this?"

Nancy stared off into space. Her quivering lips tightened. "No, I don't. Unless it was some punk high school kid. Like the one who vandalized Mr. Young's art gallery. But all he did over there was spray-paint graffiti on the window. Not break in and destroy everything."

When her voice broke, Sarah wrapped her arm around her mother. "It's okay, Mom. We'll rebuild the store. It'll be even better than it was before. And in the meantime, law enforcement will figure out who did this."

"Yes, we will," Lena confirmed.

"I hope so," Nancy sobbed. "I'm just glad we weren't here during the break-in. Can you imagine what would've happened to us if we had been?"

"No," Sarah replied. "But luckily we weren't. So let's not even think about that." She tightened her grip on her mother's shoulder before turning to Lena. "Do you know if anyone has checked around the outside of the store yet?"

"Detective Hudson and a few other officers are examining the front now."

"What about the back? Have you seen it?"

"No, not yet."

Nancy's eyes filled with a fresh batch of tears. "Please, go look. Paint's been splattered all over the back exterior. My sunset mural is completely ruined!"

"And there's a strange message spray-painted across the top of it," Sarah added.

"Really?" Lena asked. "What does it say?"

Sarah tapped her fingernails against the counter and stared up at the ceiling. "You know, I don't remember. But it reads like some kind of weird nursery rhyme. You'll see it when you go out there."

"Okay. I'll go check it out now."

"Thank you," Nancy mumbled before leaning over and propping her head against her daughter's arm.

Seeing the store owner so distraught caused a hot streak of anger to shoot straight through Lena. She set her evidence bags down behind the counter, then marched toward the back of the store, bursting through the exit.

She stepped out into the alleyway. Aside from a few nearby dumpsters, the vicinity was empty.

Lena stared up at the store's red wooden wall. Obnoxious splatters of paint covered the mural's green palm trees and orange setting sun. Graffitied words were scrawled above it.

She moved farther into the alley, shielding her eyes from the sun while studying the phrase.

Three Four Kicking Down Your Door, it read.

"Yeah, you kicked down the door all right," Lena muttered. "And did a whole lot worse."

She pulled out her camera. As she began taking photos of the wall, Lena paused.

"'Three four kicking down your door,'" she said out loud.

Her mind flashed back to the message left on Mr. Young's gallery window.

One Two I Am Coming For You...

Just as Lena began to make the connection, she heard the roar of a thunderous car engine.

Lena froze. A burst of panic imploded inside her chest. She dropped her camera down by her side and stumbled toward the doorway.

Her head swiveled from right to left. She peered down each end of the alleyway. There were no cars in sight.

It's nothing, she told herself. *Maybe it's just—*

Before she could finish convincing herself, the engine roared once again.

"Okay," she whispered. "This is happening. This is really happening. *Again.*"

Lena tried to spin around and run back inside the store. But just like a nightmare, her body suddenly became immobilized. That numbing fear returned, seeping through her limbs like venomous snake poison.

Get back inside the store. Get back inside the store!

The words reverberated through her mind. But her legs refused to cooperate. The only thing she could move was her head.

Once again, there was no sign of a car. Yet there was the sound of approaching footsteps.

Oh good. Law enforcement is finally making their way back here...

Lena leaned her stiff body against the wall. She inhaled slowly as the footsteps drew nearer.

But then she realized that they weren't coming from inside the store. They were coming down the alleyway.

Heart palpitations thumped against Lena's rib cage. The sound of the pounding shoe soles reminded her of the moment she was being chased down the Cucamonga Wilderness hiking trail. She closed her eyes and held her breath, desperate for someone to show up and rescue her.

The footsteps quickened. Lena forced her eyes open. She scanned the alley.

A man dressed in green camo army fatigues was

charging toward her. His face was covered in a full mask. Tactical gloves and military boots covered his hands and feet.

Lena winced as his eyes penetrated hers. He balled his hands into tight fists, swinging his arms in rhythm with his legs. When he seemed to notice her watching him, his speed increased.

This is it. I am going to die. With all of Clemmington's law enforcement officers right inside this store, I'm gonna die.

Just when the man stopped a few feet away from Lena, David came flying through the back door.

"Hey!" he said. "Guess what?"

Lena was unable to speak. She could only lean over and crumble into David's arms.

"What's going on?" he asked her just as the man in the fatigues approached them.

"Hey, what's up, Lena?" the man said.

Her head swiveled. She looked over at him. He removed the mask, revealing a handsome bearded face that was smiling from ear to ear.

"Ryan!" Lena practically screamed before swatting his chest. "You just scared me half to death! Why were you charging at me like that?"

"Sorry. I was in the middle of a run when I heard that my mom's store had been burglarized. So I got down here as fast as I could."

"And what's up with the outfit?" David asked him. "Getting ready for basic training early?"

"Yes, sir. I'm due to arrive at Fort Benning in Columbus, Georgia, next month. When I get there, I want to be as prepared as possible."

"Fort Benning, huh," David replied. "So you're going out for the infantry. That's gonna be pretty tough, you know."

"I do know. Both physically and psychologically. But I'll be ready."

"I bet you will. Why don't you go around to the front of the store and have your mom step outside? I've still got my team inside processing the crime scene. I don't want anything to contaminate the potential evidence."

"Will do, Detective Hudson. Do you all have any idea who may have done this?"

"Not yet," Lena told him after finally pulling herself together. "But we're working on it."

"Good. I hope you catch the bastard soon."

"That's our hope," David assured him.

Once Ryan headed to the front of the store, Lena turned to David. She contemplated telling him how terrified she'd been while watching Ryan charge down the alleyway.

Nope, she told herself. *Keep your mouth shut. He already questioned whether or not you were mentally ready to be here in the first place...*

"I've got good news," David said.

"I could use some good news right now. What's up?"

"Nancy pulled me to the side after overhearing Russ discussing how long the crime lab may take to process the evidence."

"Oh no," Lena moaned. "I tried to shut him up about that. Nancy's already so distraught. I didn't want him adding to that."

"Well, her anger prompted me to call down to the lab and ask if we could bring the evidence there and process it ourselves."

Lena reached out and gripped David's arm. "*Really?* And? What'd they say?"

"They said yes."

"David, that is awesome! I can't believe they're giving us personal access to the lab."

"Trust me, the facility director was very hesitant until I told her that the famed, highly skilled Lena Love would be the one processing the evidence. I couldn't get your name out of my mouth before she told me that we're more than welcome to utilize the lab."

"Aw, how nice of her. I'm flattered. By her *and* you. So, thank you."

"Just stating the facts. She did say we'd better get down there soon because they're extremely busy. Were you able to find any viable evidence other than the fingerprints?"

"I was. I'll show you everything once we get to the lab."

As the pair headed back inside the store, David paused, staring up at the vandalized mural.

"Wow," he breathed. "Whoever broke into this place was out for blood. What a vicious attack."

"Did you see the graffiti they scribbled at the top?"

David took a step back. "'Three four kicking down your door,'" he read. He crossed his arms in front of him, his eyes blinking rapidly. "That phrase is a continuation of the message that was spray-painted on Mr. Young's window. Remember? 'One two I am coming for you'?"

"I do remember. I was actually putting that together just as Ryan came charging toward me. What do you think it means? That our perp has a personal vendetta against Mr. Young *and* Nancy?"

David didn't immediately respond. His jaws clenched, as if he were holding something in.

"I don't know," he finally said. "But we'll figure it out. In the meantime, let's get back inside the store and finish processing the scene so that we can head to the lab."

"Right behind you."

Chapter Eight

"You know," Lena said, "I have to admit, I was pretty disappointed after I failed to collect any evidence from Mr. Young's art gallery."

"Well, now's your big chance to help us figure out who broke into Nancy's store," David told her. "So have at it."

She and David were standing at a corner station inside the Definitive Solutions Crime Lab. Lena was busy processing the evidence while he looked on.

She slipped on a pair of latex gloves, opened one of the brown paper bags and pulled out the metal pipe.

David leaned in and inspected it. "My guess is that our suspect used the pipe to shatter the windows and damage items inside the store."

"I think you're right."

Lena placed the pipe inside a cyanoacrylate fuming chamber and closed its clear glass door.

"Now, what is this thing?" David asked, pointing at the large square machine. "It looks like an oversize kitchen cabinet."

"This machine develops latent fingerprints on evidentiary objects. Hopefully it'll capture any prints that were left on the pipe."

"And how do you make that happen?"

"Well, I'm going to start by adding cyanoacrylate,

which is a strong, fast-acting adhesive, to the chamber's heating element. Then I'll set the fuming cycle time. After that, I'll hit the start button and begin the process."

David peered inside the machine. "And what happens once it starts...*fuming*?"

"Right. Fuming." Lena glanced over at David, enticed by the inquisitive expression on his handsome face.

Focus, she told herself before turning back to the machine.

"Once the fuming process begins, vapors from the adhesive will blend with the machine's humidity. Those fumes stick to the fingerprint residue on the pipe, which will reveal the print's ridges. Once that's done, the pipe will be ready for forensic analysis. If the fingerprints match someone's in your system, then, voilà. We'll be able to identify our suspect."

"That is absolutely fascinating," David said, his wide eyes revealing his awe.

When he gave her a round of applause, she curtsied. "Thank you very much."

Once Lena got the fuming process going, she took a deep breath and glanced around the bustling laboratory.

The stark white floors and walls were spotless. Staffers dressed in lab coats and protective eye goggles shuffled past long steel tables. The workstations were packed with techs injecting chemicals into test tubes, studying samples through microscopes and importing information into computer software systems.

"Hey," Lena said, "any word on whether Nancy turned over the store's surveillance footage yet?"

"I don't know. Let me check." David pulled out his cell phone and tapped the notifications. "Oh, Miles just texted me a few minutes ago. They've got the footage. They're reviewing it now."

"Good." Lena picked up another brown paper bag and opened it. "I just wish there were eyewitnesses who would've come forward with some sort of information."

"There may be. You never know. We posted news of the break-in on Clemmington PD's website as well as our social media accounts, and included the tip hotline. So we could still receive information anonymously. Especially now that Nancy has put up a reward."

"That's true. Rewards do oftentimes attract credible tips."

Lena changed gloves and pulled out the shard of glass. David stared down at the fragment.

"Wow," he breathed. "Judging by the amount of blood on that thing, our suspect must have a really nasty cut somewhere on his or her body."

"I'd say so. And once they're identified, that wound could link them to the crime scene."

Lena placed the piece of glass on a clean board, then picked up a handheld X-ray fluorescence spectrometer.

"Okay, now what is that thing?" David asked. "It looks like a grocery store scanner."

"Okay, so we've gone from a kitchen cabinet to a grocery store scanner, huh," Lena said. "This is actually an XRF analyzer. It's a device used to test the chemical composition of materials. So in other words, it collects potential biological evidence."

"Gotcha. You know, I've never actually watched any of these forensic testing procedures. It's pretty amazing. You have no idea how impressed I am with you right now."

"Why thank you. But I'm just doing my job."

"Quite well, might I add…"

Lena glanced over at David. His crooked grin was

filled with flirtation. She cleared her throat and quickly turned her attention back to the analysis.

"You know," she said, "we had to drive forty miles outside Clemmington to get to this lab. The facility services several counties. *And* they're short-staffed. The wait time on processing evidence is ridiculous. You should talk to my father about ordering a few pieces of forensic equipment and setting up a small lab inside Clemmington's police station."

David dropped his head as he side-eyed Lena. "And who's gonna pay for all that?"

"I'm sure there's enough money in the town's budget to cover it. Plus my dad is good friends with the mayor. I imagine he'd make an exception for something so important."

David waved his arm around the lab. "Lena, Clemmington could never afford all of this—"

"David," she interrupted, "you don't need all this. Just the basics. A fuming chamber similar to the one I'm using, a tamper resistant drying cabinet to safely store evidence, a high power microscope, extraction software for digital evidence and the XRF analyzer."

He sighed dramatically and leaned against the table. "Okay, so say we do get the green light to install a lab. Who's gonna run it? No one on our staff knows how to operate all that fancy equipment."

Lena turned away from David and stared inside the chamber. Her skin tingled under his intense gaze as he awaited her response.

"You'll just have to hire a forensic scientist," she told him. "I'm sure there's someone out there who would love to work for the Clemmington PD."

"*Someone?* What about you? I mean, you do seem pretty happy being back here. And let's not forget, your father does run the police department. I think it'd be cool for you to work with him and your brothers, especially now that you all seem to have healed that rift. Not to mention…"

David hesitated. Lena watched as he broke eye contact, focusing on the shard of glass lying on the table rather than her.

"Not to mention what?" she asked.

"I—well, I hope I'm not speaking out of turn here. But I just think that you're over LA. Especially after the…"

"The attack?" she queried after his voice trailed off.

Her chest tightened at the sound of those words. She inhaled deeply, struggling to ease the pressure.

Breathe. Calm down… she told herself.

"Yes," David murmured. "After the attack. All I'm saying is that you may feel more comfortable being back here in Clemmington."

"Is there any other reason why you think I should move back?"

"Well, I mean, I'm here, too—"

The loud buzzing of the fuming chamber's timer cut David off.

Lena jumped, startled by the noise. She was also disappointed that it had interrupted the moment.

She waited to see if David would finish his statement. He didn't.

Lena glanced down at her watch. "We'd better get the rest of this evidence processed before the lab director kicks us out. The facility will be closing soon."

"With the famous Lena Love working inside it? I highly doubt that. I'm sure the director will make an exception and stay open late for us."

"Let's not push it. Plus I'm starving. I haven't eaten all day."

"Neither have I," David said. "Why don't we go to The Dearborn Grill for dinner after we're done here? Misty is serving up her spicy glazed salmon tonight."

"Mmm, that sounds delicious. I'd love to."

"Cool. I'll step out and make a reservation while you finish up. Be right back."

Lena watched as he jogged toward the exit. Just as she became fixated on his flexing biceps, the fuming chamber's buzzer went off once again.

Stay focused, she told herself. *You're here to recuperate, not reignite an old flame...*

"Thanks to you," Lena said, "I am now dying to try that spicy glazed salmon. But I'm gonna need a nice glass of Riesling to go along with it."

"I second that," David said. He steered the car around a corner and headed toward the restaurant. "And I'm off the clock, too. So you can't report me to your father and tell him I was drinking on the job."

"Ha ha, very funny."

Lena's cell phone buzzed. She pulled it from her handbag and opened it using the face ID feature. An email message from an unfamiliar address popped up on the screen.

Unknown@Unknown.com

The subject read, *Five Six Up To My Old Tricks...*

Lena's phone almost fell from her hand. She stared straight ahead, focusing on nothing in particular as a sickening chill seeped through her pores.

She thought about Mr. Young's vandalized window.

One Two I Am Coming For You...

And Nancy's mural.

Three Four Kicking Down Your Door...

Her breath caught in her throat.

These attacks have been aimed at me, she thought before sliding down in her seat.

She peered back down at the phone. The body of the email was blank. But there was an attachment.

Lena's index finger trembled as she double-clicked on it. She held her breath while waiting for the attachment to load.

A sketch of a bloody, half-shaped heart appeared on the screen. It matched the scar that her attacker had carved into her chest.

She slowly turned to David.

"He's coming after me," she whispered.

"What?"

"He's coming after me," she repeated, a little louder this time. *"Again."*

"Who's coming after you again?"

"The serial killer."

David stopped at a red light and looked over at her. "Why would you say that?"

"He just emailed this to me."

She held up her phone and showed him the sketch. David leaned toward her, squinting his eyes as he studied the image.

"What is that?" he asked.

Lena forgot that David didn't know about the killer's knife attack on her. She took a deep breath, wiping away tears while summoning the courage to tell that part of the story.

"You know how the killer leaves his signature mark on his victims by carving a heart into their chests with a blade?" she asked.

"I do."

"Well, when I was attacked, the killer began carving a heart into mine. But I was able to get away before he could finish. So he left me with a scar in the form of a half-shaped heart."

"Oh, Lena," David whispered.

When the light turned green, he hit the accelerator, then reached over and clutched her hand. "I am so sorry. I had no idea the assault was that vicious."

She reached up and pressed her other hand against her chest. "No one knew. I asked the LAPD to keep that information confidential. I wasn't ready to talk about it. That part…that was just too much."

"I completely understand."

"And the subject of the email says, 'Five six up to my old tricks.' The killer is the one who vandalized the art gallery, and Nancy's store."

Lena felt as though her chest was caving in. She tried to take a breath as panic sucked the air out of her lungs.

"That's what it's looking like," David agreed quietly. "That high school kid we suspected of vandalizing Mr. Young's store never admitted to it. He only confessed to spray-painting the school's gymnasium. And since we couldn't get a clear visual of the suspect in the gallery's surveillance video, we couldn't charge him for both crimes."

Lena locked her phone, unable to look at the bloody half-shaped heart any longer.

"I think those two vandalisms happening on the same day was a complete coincidence," she said. "It's clear that the killer is doing all of this to alert me that he's here in Clemmington and coming after me. We've got to figure out a plan of action."

David's temples pulsated as he ground his teeth in frustration. "For starters, you're going to have to keep a low profile around town from here on out. Be careful with the apps you use on your cell phone so that he can't track your location. You never know what type of software that maniac has in his possession. And if you post on social media, make sure your location tracker is turned off."

"I will," Lena said, opening the settings app on her phone and confirming that the GPS locator was turned off. "What else?"

"Forward that email to me. I'll have our digital forensic investigator take a look at it and see if he can trace the sender's IP address back to a specific individual. And as a precaution, we're going to have eyes on you twenty-four seven. Do you feel safe staying at your parents' house? If not, you're more than welcome to stay with me."

Lena was surprised by his offer. Before she could respond, David continued. "Wait, I hope that wasn't too forward. I mean, it's not like you don't have your dad there with you, and two law enforcement brothers stopping by regularly. I just—I figure that I should at least offer."

"And I appreciate it. But I should be fine at my parents' place. However, whenever my father's not home and my brothers aren't around, it would be nice if I could have a squad car out front watching over the house."

"Of course. We can definitely make that happen. And it goes without saying that I'll be keeping an eye on you, as well."

"I'd appreciate that, David."

He slowed down as they approached the restaurant. "Are you sure you're still up for dinner?"

"Definitely. After this new development, I'm really in need of that glass of wine. Or two."

"Same here," he agreed.

David pulled into the parking lot and maneuvered the

car into a space near the entrance. He then turned to Lena, reaching out and once again clutching her hand.

"Listen. I want you to know that I've got your back. And I promise not to let anything happen to you again."

"Thank you," she whispered.

Despite the terror surrounding the situation, Lena was overcome by a comforting sense of security. And in that moment, she knew there was no one else she'd rather have protecting her than David.

Chapter Nine

David rocked back in his chair. He propped his hands on top of his head and stared up at the ceiling.

"I cannot believe this is happening," he muttered. "What a nightmare."

Miles, who was sitting on the other side of David's desk, nodded his head in agreement. "Yeah, we've gotta figure something out here. I cannot see my sister go through another attack. Or worse…"

There was a knock at the door.

"Come in!" David called out.

Jake opened the door and shuffled inside. "Sorry I'm late, guys. I was in the chief's office, giving him a run-down on what's going on with Lena."

"How's he doing?" David asked. "Is he all right?"

"He's hanging in there. You know he's a tough guy. But underneath it all he's worried. And pissed off. And ready to hunt down this psychopath who's coming after his baby girl."

"You did tell him not to share the news with Mom yet, didn't you?" Miles asked.

"Of course. He said he'll hold off for now. But eventually, she needs to know."

"Well, I'm planning on making sure we've got eyes on the house twenty-four seven," David said.

"And my dad has law enforcement patrolling the streets," Jake added. "They're on the lookout for anyone or anything that appears suspicious."

"Good." David sat up straight in his chair and pointed over at Miles. "Did you stop by your parents' house on the way to the station this morning?"

"I did. I checked in on Lena. And I dropped off coffee and muffins from her favorite bakery to try and lift her spirits."

"How's she doing?"

"She appears to be hanging in there." Miles sighed. "But you know how she is. She'll never let us see her sweat."

"True," Jake said. "But underneath that tough exterior, I'm sure she's terrified."

"Yeah, well, she wasn't afraid to express her disdain in having to sit around the house all day," Miles said. "Believe it or not, she wanted to come down to the station and check up on the evidence that was collected at Nancy's."

David shook his head. "That woman. I'll give her a call and let her know that Russ is taking over the forensic aspect of the investigation—"

David was interrupted by another knock at the door. "Come in!"

He looked up, shocked to see Lena burst inside his office.

"Lena!" he exclaimed. "What are you doing here? How did you even get here? I thought I told you not to leave the house without letting me know in advance—"

"Look, we can talk about that later," she interrupted, marching right past Jake and Miles. She approached the side of David's desk and slid her tablet computer in front of him. "Take a look at this."

David leaned down and focused on the bright screen. It was set to the front page of the *Los Angeles Times*.

"What am I looking at here?" he asked her.

"Check out the main headline at the top of the page."

David pressed his fingertips against the screen and enlarged the page. "'LA's heart-carving serial killer strikes again,'" he read aloud. "Another murder victim found."

"Wait, when did this happen?" Miles asked.

"According to the article, yesterday," Lena told him. "The same day that Nancy's Country Mart was burglarized."

"So what do you think?" Jake asked. "Is the killer going back and forth between LA and Clemmington to commit these crimes?"

"Or do we have a copycat killer on our hands?" Miles questioned.

Lena groaned loudly, throwing her arms out at her sides. "Who knows? Either of you could be right."

"This is truly baffling," David said while scrolling through the article. "The thing that worries me is that we seem to be dealing with a spree killer. The man is murdering his victims pretty closely together, without taking much of a cooling-off period in between attacks."

"What are the details of this latest killing?" Jake asked.

"It says here that the victim's body was found by hikers, deep inside the Angeles National Forest's Cooper Canyon. They haven't revealed the identity because some of the family members have yet to be notified. But she was in her early thirties, petite and brunette. She was found strangled with her hands tied behind her back. And a wound had been sliced into her chest in the shape of a heart."

David glanced up at Lena. His eyes inadvertently traveled down to her chest. He quickly looked away, hoping he hadn't made it obvious that he was thinking of her scar.

"Yep, that's the killer's modus operandi," Lena said, not seeming to notice. "He's followed that same ritual with each of his victims. And who knows. It could be that the killer isn't working alone."

"Which would make this case that much more complicated," David told her. "Have you spoken to LAPD's chief about this?"

"No, not yet. As soon as the article alert pinged on my phone, I skimmed it and drove straight here."

"Which you should not have done," Jake retorted. "Like David said, we want eyes on you at all times. Until we catch this killer, we don't want you roaming around town alone."

"Yeah, well, I figured if the killer is busy committing crimes in LA, he can't be in Clemmington right now—"

"Lena," David interrupted, "we don't know what this psycho is up to. So we need to take all the precautions that we can. As the saying goes, better safe than sorry."

"I know, I know. So what's our new course of action?"

David handed her the tablet. "Why don't you start by calling LAPD's chief? Find out if they have any updates on the case. Was there any evidence at the scene? Are they any closer to catching the killer? While we're busy trying to come up with a course of action, I'd like to know theirs. And—"

David was interrupted by a knock on his door frame.

The foursome turned around. Chief Love was standing in the doorway, a stern expression on his face.

"Lena, what are you doing here?" he asked. "You're supposed to be at home, laying low."

She stormed over to her father and handed him the tablet. "This is why I'm here."

Chief Love scanned the article. The further in he read, the deeper his eyebrows furrowed.

"Humph, another murder," he said, sighing. The chief scrolled down to the end of the article. "But wait, if he committed this murder in LA yesterday, are we sure he's the one who burglarized Nancy's store?"

"That's what we're trying to figure out," Lena told him.

"Well, keep me posted. I'm glad to know I've got four great minds inside this office working on the case."

"Five, counting yours," Jake chimed in.

"Thanks, son." Chief Love paused, wrapping his arm around Lena. "I'm hopeful that together with the LAPD, we'll catch this psycho soon. In the meantime, I need to get back to my office and return Nancy's five phone calls. According to Milly, she's anxious to find out whether we've identified a suspect. Speaking of which," he continued, turning to David, "what's the latest on those forensic lab results?"

David grabbed his notebook and flipped it open. "I spoke with the lab director this morning. She's put a rush order on the results. So it's just a matter of time before I get them back. And Russ is running the fingerprints that Lena lifted through the FBI's ID system."

"Let me know as soon as you've got something. And as for you," Chief Love said, giving Lena's shoulder a gentle squeeze, "let this be the last time you leave the house alone. Especially without telling one of us first. We can't afford to take any chances at this point."

"Yes, sir," she mumbled.

David watched as Lena picked imaginary lint off her emerald green tunic. He felt for her, knowing how anxious she was to help with the investigation but having to stand down because she was a target.

"All right, then," the chief said. "I'll let you four get back to it while I call Nancy."

As soon as he left the office, Lena grabbed a chair from the corner and pulled it up to the desk. She sat down, then removed her notebook and a pen from her handbag.

David looked over at Jake and Miles. The three of them stared at one another, their expressions weary. It was clear that they were all worried about her.

David cleared his throat. "So, uh, Lena? How are you feeling after finding out that the killer has struck again? Are you okay?"

She snapped the top off her pen and began scribbling in her notebook.

"Yes," she replied without looking up. "I'm fine. Just ready to get to work and start planning our course of action. So, what are we thinking? Where do we go from here?"

The determination behind her stoic expression was chilling. David was in awe of her fearlessness.

"Well, for starters," he began, "I'm thinking we should probably order lunch. Looks like it's gonna be a long day inside the station."

"I agree," Miles said. "We've got a lot to unpack here."

Jake stood up and walked over to the whiteboard. He grabbed a black marker and wrote the words *Next Steps: BOLO.*

"Okay," he said. "While you all think about what you want to order, let's talk about the suspect. What do we know about him? How does he look? What does he usually wear? What kind of car may he be driving?"

All eyes turned to Lena since she was the killer's only surviving victim.

"Well," she said, shifting in her seat, "I didn't get a good look at his face because he was wearing a mask. But I do know that he's got cold, pale gray eyes. He looked to be about five feet eleven inches or so. Slightly stocky build. And he was dressed in tactical camouflage gear."

David could see a change in Lena's disposition. Seeing her in distress caused his chest muscles to tighten.

"And he drives a black sports car with a really loud engine and huge, spiked chrome wheels."

"How do you know what kind of car he drives?" David asked.

"I, um… I saw a car here in Clemmington that looked similar to a vehicle that chased after me the night I was attacked."

"What?" both Jake and Miles yelled in unison. David was too stunned to even speak. He held his hand up in an attempt to calm her brothers, who were now gathering around her.

"Lena," David said in a calm voice, "why didn't you report that to us? Don't you think it's something we should've been made aware of, so that we could—"

"No!" she insisted, jumping up from her chair and pacing the floor. Jake and Miles immediately backed off. "I shouldn't have made you all aware of it. You know why? Because everybody would've thought I was being paranoid. And suffering from PTSD. And you would've forced me to sit inside the house nonstop even sooner than you already have."

Her voice broke. David stood up and walked around the desk. When he put his arm around her, she quieted down and leaned her head against his chest.

"Guys," he said to Jake and Miles, "could you please give us a minute?"

They both nodded their heads. Miles gently squeezed

Lena's arm on the way out the door. "Sorry if it seems like we're ganging up on you—"

"Seems," she interrupted sarcastically.

"You know what I mean. We're just worried about you."

When Lena remained silent, David spoke up.

"Thanks, Miles. Hey, would you mind asking Milly to order us a couple of pizzas and cartons of iced tea from Ronaldo's?" He quickly looked down at Lena. "Wait, are you good with pizza?"

"I don't have much of an appetite. But sure. Get whatever you all want."

"Will do," Miles said before following Jake out of the office.

Once the door was closed, David led Lena over to a chair.

"Why don't you have a seat. Let's talk."

She sat down slowly, staring down at her hands.

"David?" she whispered. "If you all don't allow me to stay involved in this investigation, I'm afraid the killer will never be caught."

David paused. He sat down next to her and held her hand.

"I can understand why you feel that way. You're highly skilled at what you do. But we've got to keep you safe, Lena. Which means you can't keep anything from us. If you see something, you have to say something. Don't let your passion for your work get you killed. Deal?"

"Deal."

"And with that being said, I really think you should consider stepping away from the investigation. Take a break. Let the police handle the—"

"No," Lena interrupted. "I will not back down from this case, David."

He fell silent for several moments before responding. "Understood."

David instinctively leaned down and kissed her softly on the forehead. She raised her head. Their lips were inches apart. Just as the pair moved in closer, there was a knock at the door.

They both jumped back.

"Come in!" David called out, much louder than necessary.

Jake and Miles shuffled inside the office.

"Your boss sent us back in here," Jake told them. "He said that if we don't get to work immediately and start putting a plan in place, he's gonna fire us all."

"That man…" Lena said, slowly shaking her head.

David quickly walked back around his desk and took a seat, hoping the brothers hadn't noticed him and Lena getting close to one another.

"All right then," he said. "Let's get to it."

Chapter Ten

Lena rolled over onto her back and stared up at the clouds painted across her bedroom ceiling. She pressed her fingertips into her temples and rubbed them rigorously. Being cooped up in her parents' house had left her head spinning.

Or maybe it's the fact that you keep your eyes glued to that tablet...

Even though Lena suspected she may have been suffering from a bout of cybersickness, she grabbed her iPad and pull up the *Los Angeles Times*' website.

Do not read that article again. Do not read that article again...

But Lena ignored the voice in her head and began scanning the latest report on the serial killer for the hundredth time.

It is believed that the unidentified victim is their killer's seventh attack, the article read. The sixth was Lena Love, LAPD's own forensic investigator. She was assaulted while processing the fifth victim's crime scene on the Cucamonga Wilderness hiking trail. Unlike the killer's other victims, Love survived the attack.

According to Herschel Scott, LAPD's chief of

police, Love was on the cusp of catching their elusive killer.

"Trust me, Lena was on his heels, and he knew it," Chief Scott told reporters. "I believe that's what drove his attack. Had Lena not been assaulted, the killer would be in police custody right now."

Love has since taken a leave of absence from the force. We here at the *Los Angeles Times* wish her a speedy recovery.

Lena slammed the tablet down onto the bed. She tossed off her frilly white comforter and jumped up, frantically pacing the floor.

"I should not be stuck in this house," she said to herself. "I should be on the scene, helping to catch the killer!"

"Lena?" her mother called out. "Are you talking to me?"

"No! I—I was leaving someone a voice mail," she lied, so that her mother wouldn't think she was losing her mind.

Even though it feels like I am.

"All right," her mother said. "I made coffee if you want a cup. And Miles dropped off your favorite muffins again this morning on the way to work. They're in the kitchen."

"Thanks! I'll be out in a minute."

Lena skulked over to the window. She parted the embroidered cream curtains and glanced up and down the bustling street. Neighbors were out and about, tending to the lawns surrounding their bungalows and ranch-style homes, jogging along the winding road's sidewalk and carrying groceries into their homes.

She stared up at the swaying palm trees. The sight made her long to be back in LA, working on the case that had grown so personal.

If only you could turn back the hands of time, she thought, wishing she hadn't gone out to that hiking trail alone.

Right before Lena stepped away from the window, she noticed the ever-present squad car parked a couple of houses down. It was a constant reminder that she was being hunted by a crazed maniac.

"Ugh," she moaned. "Time to go out and relive the same day over again."

Lena took a quick shower, then slipped into a lavender sweatshirt, black leggings and a pair of sneakers.

She left her bedroom and headed to the kitchen. On the way there, she heard her mother whispering hysterically.

"Where was the body found?" Betty hissed. "On the *Juniper hiking trail*? Oh no, Kennedy. Lucinda and I used to walk that trail all the time. That is terrifying! What do you think happened to her?"

Lena hovered closer to the kitchen door. Her mother was leaning against the sink, gripping the phone to her ear.

"I cannot believe something like this has happened here. In *Clemmington*. And you said the victim was strangled?"

"Oh my God," Lena whispered into her palm.

"Well, if there was a heart carved into her chest," Betty uttered, "that means it must be the same killer who attacked our—"

Her voice broke as she emitted a long sob. "I'm sorry. I'm trying to be strong, Kennedy. But I just… I hope this isn't a warning that he's coming after our daughter next!"

Lena fell against the wall. The nerves in her legs weakened underneath the weight of her mother's words. A bout of nausea hit her stomach. She tried to swallow the lump of panic climbing up her throat. But her mouth was so dry that she almost choked instead.

"I know," Betty continued. "I promise that I'll hold it together for the sake of Lena... No, of course not. I won't mention a thing. I'll act as if nothing has happened. You just better make sure this doesn't leak to the press... All right. Call me as soon as you've got an update. Be careful... I love you, too."

Lena quickly stepped away from the kitchen doorway just as her mother disconnected the call. She walked over to the living room's Victorian bay windows, running her sweaty hands down her leggings while staring outside.

"Lena?"

"Yes!" she practically screamed after being startled by her mother's loud tone.

"Are you coming for your coffee and muffin?"

Lena hurried through the living room and entered the kitchen. When she noticed the lingering tears still glistening in her mother's eyes, her gaze fell to the beige stone tiles.

"Yep," she said, struggling to sound upbeat despite what she'd just heard.

Betty spun around and busied herself at the counter. "I'll get you a cup and saucer."

Lena wanted to rush up to her mother and hug her. But she didn't want to appear as though she'd overheard the conversation. So instead, she walked over to the sliding glass doors and looked out into the backyard.

Her Jeep, which was parked in front of the garage door, came into view. And then, she was overcome by that all too familiar urge.

Lena's arms fell down by her sides. She balled her hands into tight fists, then released them, then balled them up again. Her feet shuffled from right to left, as if she were at the starting line of a race and preparing to take off. Her mind began to shift. Everything around her shut down. Nothing else mattered, except getting to that crime scene.

"Lena, are you okay?" Betty asked.

She swiveled around. Her mother was standing at the breakfast nook placing a cup of coffee and platter of muffins on the table. Her eyes appeared as though they'd finally stopped weeping. But her lips were now twisted with concern.

"Yeah, Mom. I'm fine."

Lena glanced down at the nook's padded blue bench. Her purse was sitting on the edge.

"You know what?" she continued. "I think I'm gonna have my coffee and muffin out on the deck. Get some sun, meditate, maybe even do some yoga."

"I think that would be good for you, sweetheart."

Betty walked over and wrapped her arms around Lena, squeezing tightly. Then she planted a series of kisses all over her face, just like she used to do when Lena was a child.

"Mom!" Lena squealed. "That tickles!"

"I know. And I don't care. You're never too old to be showered with love and affection by your mama."

"Yes, ma'am," Lena said, giving her a firm hug.

"Okay." Betty sighed. She stepped away from her daughter while dabbing her eyes. "I'd better go take these rollers out of my hair and put on a little makeup. I've got a video conference call with a couple of my mentees from the women's group. They're new to teaching this year, and I promised I'd help them enhance their curriculums."

"Aw, that's sweet. Well, while you're doing that, I'll be out on the deck."

"Sounds good. Enjoy yourself, baby."

Lena watched as Betty walked out of the kitchen. Once she was gone, Lena tiptoed toward the entryway, sticking her ear toward the living room. As soon as she heard her mother's bathroom door close, Lena darted back into the kitchen and snatched her purse.

She slipped out of the sliding glass door. After glancing around to make sure that the coast was clear, she jumped inside her car and sped off toward the Juniper hiking trail.

LENA SLOWLY DROVE past the street where the hiking trail's entrance was located. The block had been cordoned off with yellow tape. The entire road was swarming with squad cars, their red-and-blue lights flashing.

Several law enforcement officers were pacing the road. They waved their arms at a few of the residents who lived on the upscale block, motioning for them to go back inside their homes.

"How in the hell are you going to get to this crime scene?" Lena asked herself.

She was very familiar with the trail. She and her friends had hiked it for years. There were several ways of accessing the area that didn't involve entering through the designated entrance.

Lena pulled her phone out of her purse and checked the home screen. There were no new notifications. She was surprised that David hadn't reached out to tell her what was going on. While she was slightly irritated, Lena knew that he was only looking out for her mental well-being.

She contemplated calling and telling him that she was there, then asking if he'd let her through to help examine the crime scene.

Don't be ridiculous, she thought, knowing he would never agree to it.

Lena drove a block over. She parked on a street near the back of the mountain trail and looked around. Aside from a few children playing in their front yards, no one was in the area.

She slowly climbed out of the car. A silver chain-link fence stood at the base of the mountain trail. The climb appeared a bit steep, but doable.

Okay, here goes nothing...

Lena jumped the fence. She steadied herself, digging her feet into the dirt while scaling the trail. Rogue tree roots and wild foliage grew from the dry, red earth. Lena grabbed hold of the shrubbery as she pulled her body up toward the hiking path.

When she neared the top of the foothill, Lena heard a commotion in the near distance. She paused. The voices were to her right. She jogged up to the path and dusted herself off, then set out in the direction of what she assumed was the crime scene.

Five minutes into the trail, Lena noticed red biohazard tape up ahead. It had been wrapped around several massive sequoia trees.

Law enforcement officers were swarming around the outer perimeter while only a few surveyed the area within the tape.

She stepped off the trail and crept closer to the scene, walking discreetly in between the tree trunks. As she searched the inner perimeter for David, Lena noticed the coroner kneeling down near the victim's body.

Tears flooded Lena's eyes as she watched him slip paper bags over the victim's hands and wrap them in tape. Her entire body trembled as the sight brought back haunting memories of the crime scenes back in LA.

"Did you get all of her clothing secured in the evidence bags?" she heard the coroner ask one of the officers.

Russ walked over toward him, carrying several brown paper bags. "I did, along with a few other items we're hoping will contain viable clues."

Lena craned her neck. She noticed Miles and Jake, walking along the outskirts of the crime scene tape with their flashlights focused on the ground.

I wanna get in there, she thought to herself.

Despite her brief moment of PTSD, she couldn't fight her desire to jump in and help. Lena felt as though this was her case to solve. Yet here she was, forced to take a back seat while her entire family worked the investigation without her.

Just as Lena noticed the coroner unfolding a linen sheet, David and her father approached him.

"Are you preparing to take the victim down to the morgue?" David asked him.

"I am. I've processed the body thoroughly, allocated an identifying number and had plenty of photos taken."

Lena watched as her father crossed his arms tightly over his chest. "All right then," he said just as two transporters walked over. One of them unzipped a body bag and placed it next to the victim.

Lena took a few steps closer, watching as the men carefully wrapped the victim in the sheet, then placed her inside of the bag.

"Chief!" Miles called out. "Can you and David come and take a look at this?"

"Be right over," Kennedy told him before turning back to the coroner. "We'll finish processing the scene while you begin the autopsy procedures. I'll be in touch soon."

"Sounds good, Chief Love."

Lena felt herself growing anxious. She stepped back

and forth, contemplating her next move. When she did, dried leaves crackled underneath her sneakers. The noise caused the group to turn toward the trunk that Lena was hiding behind.

She ducked quickly, almost slamming her head against a thick branch in the process. She held her breath, waiting to see if someone would come over and investigate the noise. When they continued talking among themselves, Lena held her hand to her chest and slowly exhaled.

In that moment, she knew she had only two choices. Either approach the scene and ask if she could participate or go back home.

But then Lena thought back on the phone conversation she overheard her mother having with her father. He'd made it clear that he didn't want her to even know about the murder. There was no way he'd want her to get involved in the investigation.

Lena slowly turned around, her shoulders slumped in defeat. Then, as she crept back down the side of the trail toward her car, a thought crossed her mind.

She glanced back at the crime scene. David and her father were standing next to Miles and Jake, who were busy placing something inside an evidence bag.

You may not be able to get in there now. But you will...

LENA STARED UP at the sky. Lush layers of lavender, yellow and orange blended together, creating a beautiful backdrop. It was a complete contradiction of the bleak crime scene up ahead.

She gripped the handle on her forensic kit, then straightened her shoulders. As darkness began to fall over Clemmington, law enforcement had cleared the area where the victim had been murdered. Lena was there at the Juniper hiking trail alone.

She once again managed to elude the police officers who were standing guard at the trail's entryway by climbing up the back of the mountain. Now that she was standing on the outskirts of the red biohazard tape, adrenaline pulsated through her veins. The urge to dig into the scene and see what she could find began to overtake her.

Lena set her field kit down on the ground and pulled out a pair of booties. She slid them over her combat boots, then slipped on a pair of latex gloves and eye goggles.

She slowly approached the tape and stooped down, careful not to disturb it as she crept underneath and entered the killing ground. Lena pulled her flashlight from her pocket and shined it down on the dry, reddish-brown dirt. Her eyes were focused on the forest floor. She studied every rock, leaf and pine needle in search of the tiniest bit of evidence.

A few steps in, Lena noticed a small pool of dried blood that had soaked into the dirt. She quickly whipped open her kit and pulled out a metal scalpel. Lena dug the tool into the dirt, careful to pick up the scoop without disturbing the bloodstain. She then slipped it inside a paper evidence bag and stored it inside her case.

Lena stood up and continued on, moving carefully through every inch of the scene. When a gust of chilly wind blew open her suede navy jacket, she realized that the temperature was dropping. Lena quickly zipped the blazer and kept going.

The eerie sound of dried twigs crackling underneath her feet filled the air. Lena could feel her heart rate increasing. She was suddenly hit with flashbacks of being on that trail back in LA, surveying the scene alone before being attacked.

That was then, this is now, she told herself. *Press on toward the goal...*

Any remnants of overhead light were fading fast. But Lena intended on scouring the scene until there was nothing left to uncover.

Something flapping in the wind up ahead caught Lena's attention. It was outside the crime scene tape, stuck underneath a pile of leaves. She hurried over to the small heap, ducking underneath the tape and aiming the flashlight at the foliage.

A crackling tree limb snapped. Lena jumped up just as the large branch crashed to the ground.

She shrieked at the sight. Suddenly, Lena felt as though she was not alone.

Her entire body stiffened up. She held her breath, pushing thoughts of the killer lurking there out of her mind.

Calm down, she told herself, convinced that he wouldn't be bold enough to return to the crime scene, especially knowing it was under police surveillance. Nevertheless, she kept her eyes glued to the tree, waiting for the killer to jump out at her.

The area remained motionless. No one appeared. Lena sighed with relief, realizing that she'd merely witnessed an innocent act of nature.

She turned her attention back to whatever was tucked underneath the leaves. Lena bent down again and began sifting through the pile. She grabbed hold of the material stuck at the bottom. When a black leather glove appeared, Lena almost fainted.

She tightened her lips before releasing a squeal of elation, then slipped the glove inside an evidence bag.

"What else can I find?" she whispered into the wind, forgetting all about the fallen tree branch that had terrified her moments ago.

Suddenly, the sky lit up. Flashes of lightning flickered

within dark gray clouds. The roaring sound of thunder rippled through the air.

"You have *got* to be kidding me," Lena groaned.

Rain was not in the forecast. So she'd neglected to pack an umbrella.

"Let me hurry up so I can get out of here," she mumbled to herself.

Lena slid back underneath the crime scene tape and continued scouring the area.

She took a deep breath. The musky scent of an incoming storm filled the air. But as long as the rain remained at bay, she would stick to her mission.

The sky flashed with bright lightning. It lit up the area around her. From the corner of her eye, Lena could've sworn she saw a shadowy figure, looming near the fallen tree branch.

She quickly swiveled her head. Darkness filled the air as the lightning subsided. When it flashed again, no one was there.

Your mind is playing tricks on you...

But then Lena heard footsteps creeping over the dried earth. She pivoted in a circle, shining her flashlight into the distance. Nothing but trees appeared. And then, silence.

Raindrops began to slide down her eye goggles, obscuring her vision.

You need to get the hell out of here. Now!

The thick, humid air fogged her lenses. She pulled the goggles off and shoved them inside her pocket. Her feet sank into the muddy ground as the rain went from a drizzle to a downpour.

Heavy droplets splashed against Lena's eyelids, further impairing her vision. She rushed away from the crime scene area and slipped off her booties.

Just as she reached the hiking trail, lightning illuminated the sky. A shadowy figure appeared before her.

Lena recoiled when he placed his hand on her shoulder. Before she could let out a scream, the man called out her name.

"What are you doing out here?" he yelled.

Lena moved in closer. She almost fell to her knees after realizing it was Officer Underwood.

"I—I wanted to search the area for clues," she stammered. "How did you know I was here?"

"Your mother called in to the police station and reported you missing. She figured we might find you at the crime scene."

The officer wrapped his arm around Lena and led her toward the hiking trail's entrance.

"Come on. Let's get you home."

Chapter Eleven

David parked his car in front of the Love family's house. He slowly stepped out and waved at the officer in the squad car across the street, then made his way toward the front door.

"Do not go off," he whispered to himself. "Stay calm. Keep your cool. Do not jump down this woman's throat. She's already been through enough."

But as the words came out of his mouth, David could feel streaks of anger churning inside his stomach. When he'd received the news late last night that Lena had been found investigating the Juniper hiking trail, he thought it was a joke. He just knew that she wouldn't step foot onto that crime scene.

Unfortunately, he'd been wrong.

You should have known better, David thought.

Lena had never been the type of woman who could be contained. When she wanted something, she went after it. Especially when it came to her career. And because she had such personal ties to this case, her passion to solve it ran deep.

"Deep enough for you to risk your own life," he muttered, shaking his head in disappointment.

David climbed the porch stairs and reached up to ring

the doorbell. Just as his fingertip hovered over the button, Chief Love's loud voice boomed from inside the house.

"Lena, this is it!" Kennedy yelled. "I have *had* it with your erratic behavior! You going behind our backs and trying to solve this case on your own is not gonna cut it. Why would you go out and risk your life, *yet again*, like you're some damn superhero?"

"You're gonna mess around and give Mama a heart attack," David heard Jake chime in.

"Can everybody just please calm down for a minute?" Miles interjected.

David went ahead and rang the doorbell, figuring now was a good time to interrupt the heated exchange. Even though he was in full agreement with Kennedy and Jake, he didn't want to see everyone gang up on Lena.

"Coming!" David heard Mrs. Love call out. When she opened the door, he noticed her eyes were red and puffy, and her face was creased with worry.

"David, please, come in. I am so glad that you're here."

"Sounds like I'm walking into the middle of World War Three."

"You may as well be."

David stepped inside the living room where the Love family was holding court. Jake and Miles were sitting on the sectional, Lena was seated across them on the love seat and Kennedy was pacing the floor.

"Can I get you something to drink?" Betty asked David right before Kennedy threw his hands in the air.

"No, Miles!" he ranted. "I will not calm down. None of this would even be happening had your sister listened to her father, stayed in Clemmington and worked for our police force. But *no*. Rather than remain loyal to her family and her hometown, she chose to run to the big city and—"

"*Excuse* me," Betty interrupted. "We have company

now. It would be nice if you all could show some civility toward one another."

The family turned toward David. From the looks on their surprised faces, they hadn't even noticed him enter the room.

"Hello, everyone," he said, nodding his head awkwardly.

The group fell silent. The tension in the air was apparent. David wondered if he should turn around and leave. It felt as though he was intruding on a private family matter.

Lena looked over at him. When he saw the pained expression on her tear-streaked face, his anger toward her immediately subsided.

She glanced around the room, then pointed at David. "Why did you all call him here? So you'd have yet another person on your team to jump down my throat?"

"No, Lena," Kennedy replied. "I've actually assigned David as the lead detective on this case. And Officer Campbell will be handling forensics."

She glared at David, clearly displeased with the news. The look in her eyes appeared as though she felt betrayed by him.

David watched as she sank down farther into the couch. Her slumped posture reeked of defeat. She stared down at her lap, fidgeting with the stray threads hanging from a beige throw pillow.

"Lena," Kennedy said, "why don't you tell David about the evidence you found out on the—"

Before he could finish, she jumped up from the couch.

"I can't do this," Lena insisted before storming out of the room.

Miles hopped up and went after her.

"Hold on," Kennedy called out to him. "Let her go. She probably needs a break from us. I think we all need to take a minute and cool down." He turned to David. "Would you mind going to check on her?"

"Of course not."

"Thank you," Betty whispered, giving his shoulder an appreciative pat.

David walked through the dining room and entered the kitchen, expecting to see Lena sitting at the table. But the room was empty. He walked over to the sliding glass doors and noticed her out on the deck, leaning against the wrought-iron table with her head in her hands.

He knocked on the glass to get her attention. She looked up, her watery eyes blinking rapidly as she stared at him. After a few moments she waved her hand, motioning for him to come outside.

David stepped out onto the deck and slowly approached her.

"You okay?" he asked.

"Not really."

"You wanna talk about it?"

"Not at all."

"Understood."

He walked around the table and sat down, stretching his legs out in front of him.

"You know," he began, "you've been through so much, Lena. Do you think you should talk to someone? A professional?"

"What, a *shrink*?" Lena snorted. "Absolutely not. With a job like mine, danger comes with the territory."

David felt that streak of anger return. He sat straight up in his chair and turned to her.

"Actually, it doesn't," he shot back. "Your job as a forensic investigator does not entail you roaming around taped off crime scenes, alone at night, leaving yourself vulnerable to being—"

"Um, *excuse* me, Detective Hudson," she interrupted, crossing her arms in front of her. "I don't need you telling me what my job entails. I am fully aware of the criteria and have quite a successful track record to prove it."

"No doubt. But clearly your judgment is questionable considering you were willing to put your life on the line to investigate a crime scene that we'd thoroughly processed."

David watched as Lena's lips curled into a smug smirk.

"Thoroughly processed, you say?" she asked.

His eyes lowered. He could sense that she was about to hit him with some surprising news.

"Judging by your silence," she continued, "you must not have heard about the evidence that I collected at the crime scene."

"No," he replied, shifting in his chair. "I didn't. Your family was so upset that you went out there by yourself that they didn't mention it."

"Well, thanks to *me*, there's a scoop of blood-soaked dirt and a leather glove down at the crime lab waiting to be processed. I'd like to examine the evidence myself, but my father insists on holding me captive here at the house."

"I'm not surprised that you found evidence everyone else overlooked. You're exceptional at what you do. And I'm sure the lab's facility director will prioritize processing it."

"My father already spoke to her. She said she would. But you know me. I'd rather process it myself."

"Of course you would. Your need to control is unwavering."

Lena turned away from David and stared out at the lawn. "So is my passion for my work. And my determination to solve this case."

Her steely expression silenced him. He knew from experience that once she shifted into go mode, there was no pulling her out of it.

Lena threw her head back and leaned against the railing. "I just wanna get out of here. I'm actually thinking about calling Chief Scott and talking to him about going back to LA. I'm ready to get back to work."

"That's it," David said. He jumped up from his chair and joined her over at the railing. When she ignored him, he leaned in and forced her to make eye contact.

"Lena, you do not, I repeat, *do not*, need to go back to work. The suspect is obviously following you. If he trails you back to LA, you already know the LAPD won't look after you the way your family would. The way *I* would. I think you need to stay put and let us protect you while we handle the investigation."

"But that's exactly what the killer would expect me to do," she replied. "Hide out here in my hometown, under the watch of my family. He'd never think that I would be bold enough to go back to LA. So while he's busy trying to catch up to me in Clemmington, I'll be back in the city, investigating the crime scenes in hopes of gathering more evidence."

"You have *got* to be kidding me," David grunted.

"Listen. I'm suffocating in this town. My father and brothers are smothering me to death. Every day I'm being reminded of why I didn't stay here and work for the Clemmington PD in the first place. I can't stand being treated like the baby of the family. I just want to do my job, catch this killer and get back to my life in Los Angeles."

David felt a piercing burn sear through his chest. He was quickly reminded of the moment all those years ago, when Lena graduated college and told him she wasn't moving back to Clemmington.

"This place has never been enough for you," he said,

thinking more of the people in it rather than the town itself. "And it obviously never will."

He stood there, waiting for Lena to tell him he was wrong. When she didn't, he turned around and headed back toward the house.

"I hope you'll reconsider going back to LA. Trust me, it's a bad idea."

"Wait, you're leaving?"

"Yes. I'm leaving. I've said my piece. You seem to have your mind made up on what you want to do. But like I said, I hope you'll reconsider."

Lena turned so quickly that her sneakers squeaked against the deck's slippery wood surface.

"I will," she said.

"You will what?"

"I'll reconsider. But on one condition."

David paused. His hand fell from the sliding door's handle.

"And what's that?" he asked.

"You'll talk to my father about letting me process that evidence I collected from the Juniper hiking trail myself."

David's head rolled in exasperation. "Why is that so important to you? Don't you trust that our lab can get the job done?"

"Of course I do," Lena insisted, walking over to him.

She stood so close that he could smell her vanilla-scented perfume floating through the air. Her soft expression dismantled his defensive stance. In that moment, he would've agreed to anything she wanted.

"Can I be honest with you?" she asked.

"Of course."

"Being stuck here inside my parents' house has made me feel…*useless*. To the point where I'm starting to question my own self-worth. Like, what's my purpose? I've worked so hard to get to where I am in my career, and the minute I start focusing on the investigation of a life-time, *bam!* I'm forced off the case and relegated to the sidelines. That's pretty demoralizing, David."

David gently placed his hand on her shoulder. "But think about *why* you were taken off the case, Lena. No one is trying to strip you of your purpose. We all know how talented you are. We're just doing this to keep you safe."

"I know." She sighed. "And even though all that sounds perfectly reasonable, it still doesn't feel good. I can't stand the thought of being completely removed from this investigation. After all I've been through, *I* want to be the one to track down that son of a bitch."

David winced at the menacing anger in her low tone. As a member of law enforcement, he understood Lena's desire to finish what she'd started. Yet as a close friend, he wanted nothing more than to protect her.

"I'll tell you what," he said, slowly removing his hand from her shoulder. "I will see what I can do about getting you into the lab to process the evidence. Meanwhile, why don't we switch gears and drop the topic of the investigation for now? Maybe go inside and check on your family? They seemed pretty wound up when I first got here."

"To put it mildly."

When David threw her a look, Lena rolled her eyes.

"Fine," she groaned. "But only if a glass of wine is included in me walking back inside that house."

"I'm sure that can be arranged," he said. "And hey, you've gotta promise me that you won't go investigating another crime scene. Unless you've gotten the green light from law enforcement and are with the team, of course."

Lena turned to face him, her eyebrows furrowing in response to David's request.

"Let me hurry up and put in that call to my real boss back in LA," she quipped. "Because it sounds to me like somebody who I *don't* report to is trying to make demands."

The smirk on her face told David that she was just joking. But the fact that she didn't agree to his request left him feeling slightly worried.

Just let it go, he told himself. *For now...*

Chapter Twelve

The next morning, Lena stood at her bedroom window. She parted the curtains and stared out onto the street. The squad car that had become a permanent fixture on the block was parked in front of the house.

"Lena!" her mother called out. "I just brewed a fresh pot of coffee. Should I pour you a cup? Maybe make you an omelet—"

"No, thanks, Mom," Lena interrupted, her strained tone filled with frustration. "I'm working on something. I'll be out in a bit."

"Okay. I'm going out to run a few errands. Do you need anything?"

"Nope, I'm good. I'll see you when you get back."

Lena grabbed her cell phone. There were no new notifications. She pulled up the last text message that David had sent.

He'd received word from the forensics lab that the results were in on the evidence they'd collected at Nancy's Country Mart. The perpetrator's fingerprints and biological evidence did not match up with any of the offenders stored in the national DNA database. The disappointing news left Lena feeling even more determined to catch the killer before he struck again.

Lena pulled up Chief Scott's phone number and called her boss back in LA. He picked up after the first ring.

"Chief Scott," he barked.

"Chief, it's your favorite forensic investigator."

"Lena! How are you doing?"

"Ah, I've been better. Let's just say that."

"Well, that's perfectly understandable," he replied quietly. "Things have been pretty brutal for you. You're a tough one, though. I will say that."

"Thanks, Chief. I'm trying to stay strong. This is what I signed up for when I decided to go into the criminal justice field, right?"

"Not necessarily. Your job is to collect and process evidence while law enforcement is on the scene. You shouldn't be subjected to safety issues. However, with that being said…"

Uh-oh, here we go, Lena thought, feeling as though she was talking to David all over again.

"Your safety never would've been jeopardized had you followed the rules and not visited that crime scene alone," Chief Scott continued.

"With all due respect, Chief, I didn't call you for a lecture."

"Then you shouldn't have called me at all. Because you know how I am. I will always be the one to put you in check over your rogue behavior."

Lena closed her eyes and pressed her fingertips against her forehead. "Trust me, you're not the only one. But listen. I'm growing more and more frustrated by the suspect. The way he's taunting me, all while he keeps getting away with murder. I'm beginning to feel as though his crime spree has turned into a personal vendetta against me."

"Rule number one when it comes to investigations is

that you cannot take these cases personal. You have got to keep your head on straight and make good choices. Don't let the killer outsmart you. You're too skilled for that."

"The fact that the perp is trying to outsmart me is actually why I'm calling you," Lena said while sitting down on the side of the bed. "Now that we know he's on the hunt for me here in Clemmington, I think this would be the perfect time for me to come back to LA. I could reexamine the crime scenes there, try and collect more evidence and compare it to the DNA we recovered here in—"

"Whoa whoa whoa," Chief Scott interrupted. "You can stop right there. There's no way in hell I'd put you back on the job right now. Not after everything you've been through. I think you need to take more time to recuperate. I'd also advise you to talk to someone. We can connect you with a licensed trauma and PTSD therapist who would help…"

As the chief rambled on, Lena felt her jaws tighten. She resisted the urge to hang up on him. Nothing coming out of his mouth resonated with the way she was feeling, let alone how she wanted to proceed with the investigation.

"And when I spoke with your father last night," Chief Scott continued, "he made it clear that he did not want you returning to LA and getting back to work."

Lena jumped up and began pacing the floor. "Wait, you talked to my father?"

"Yes, I did. After he heard from one of his detectives that you mentioned coming back to LA to continue working on the case, he called me just to make sure we're all on the same page. Luckily, we are. The consensus is that you need to stay put."

"And let me guess. The detective who shared that information with my father was David Hudson?"

"Yeah, I believe that was his name."

Lena rushed over to her closet and pulled down a pair of jeans and a fitted yellow tunic.

"So will you consider talking to a therapist?" Chief Scott asked.

"I'll think about it," she huffed while throwing off her robe and stepping into her pants. "In the meantime, I'd better go. My mom made breakfast and she's waiting on me."

"All right. Well, thanks for calling. It's always good to hear from you. And, Lena? Please, do me a favor. Make good choices. And stay out of trouble."

"I'll do my best, Chief. Talk to you soon."

Lena disconnected the call and rushed into the bathroom. She quickly applied a light layer of makeup and ran a flat iron through her hair. After slipping on a pair of tan leather wedges, she grabbed her purse and sneaked out the back door.

LENA BURST INSIDE the police station and stormed up to Milly's desk.

"Where's Detective Hudson?" she snapped.

"Well, good morning to you, too," Milly replied, her eyes wide as she leaned back in her chair. "What in the world has gotten into you?"

"I'm sorry. I'm just pissed off. I need to speak with Detective Hudson. *Immediately.*"

Milly pointed the long, purple acrylic nail of her index finger toward the back of the station.

"Check his office. Last time I saw him, he was headed that way with a pile of folders in one hand and a cup of coffee in the other."

"Thanks," Lena muttered.

She shot past the breakroom, noticing Russ and Officer Underwood standing near the vending machine. When she reached her father's office, she slowed down. Just as she inched toward the window and peeked inside, Milly yelled out her name.

"You're fine!" she told Lena. "Your father and brothers are back at the Juniper hiking trail where that poor woman was found murdered. They're giving it another look, just to make sure all of the evidence was collected."

I bet they are, after I recovered that glove, Lena thought to herself.

"Thanks, Milly!" she said before setting off toward David's office.

The door was closed. Lena wanted to kick it in after finding out he'd snitched on her. But instead she took a deep breath and knocked, albeit more aggressively than necessary.

"Come in!"

She grabbed the knob and swung the door open so forcefully that it slammed against the wall. David jumped back in his chair. His mouth fell open, and he stared at her as if he'd seen a ghost.

"Lena! What are you doing here? And how did you get here? Did the officer watching over the house escort you?"

"No, he did not. And before you get to lecturing me, let me ask you this. Why in the hell did you tell my father that I was thinking about going back to LA?"

David moaned loudly and stood up.

"Please. Have a seat," he told her while closing the door. "Can I get you anything? Coffee? Water?"

"Cut the niceties and answer my question. Why would

you sell me out like that? I thought we were friends. You couldn't have kept that information to yourself?"

David walked back around the desk and sat down. He took a long sip of coffee, watching Lena closely as she took a seat across from him.

"Look," he said. "You don't listen to me. And you going back to LA right now is a terrible idea. So I did what I had to do to stop it from happening."

"You are aware that you nor my father have that much power and control over me, aren't you? I can come and go as I please."

"Lena, this is not about power or control. Again, this is about your safety. It's just a shame that we're all more concerned about that than you." David paused and shook his head. "I really believed that getting you back inside the crime lab would've been enough to pacify you. At least for the time being. I guess I was wrong."

"Wait, what are you talking about?"

"Didn't you get my text message?" he asked.

"No," she mumbled while scrambling around inside her purse. "I was so angry after talking to Chief Scott that I hadn't checked my phone."

David sat up straighter in his chair. "Well, I talked to your father this morning and asked if he'd be willing to let you process the evidence you retrieved from the Juniper hiking trail."

"You—you did?" she asked, blinking rapidly as if she hadn't quite comprehended what he'd just said.

"I did."

"But why?"

"Because I know how much it means to you. And I understand how you feel. About everything. I don't want to see you be completely removed from the investigation.

So, after wearing your father down for almost thirty minutes, I finally got him to agree to let you inside the lab."

A slight smile spread across Lena's lips.

"Thank you for doing that, David. It means a lot knowing that *someone* gets how I feel."

"You're welcome," he said, grabbing his keys and wallet. "So, now that we've gotten all that straightened out, should we head to the lab?"

"Yes!" Lena exclaimed.

She hopped up from her chair and ran around the desk, throwing her arms around David. When he returned the hug, she turned her head and kissed him square on the lips.

"Oops!" Lena squealed, jumping back and covering her mouth. "I am so sorry. I—I don't know what got into me. I just—I guess I was just…"

"Too excited to contain yourself?" he asked, chuckling as he headed toward the door. "No worries. I'll chalk it up as your way of giving thanks. Now come on. Let's get out of here."

Lena dropped her head, mortified by her actions but grateful that he'd made light of the situation.

But when she glanced over at David, Lena noticed an intensity in his gaze that appeared far from nonchalant.

Chapter Thirteen

David held the door open for Lena as they exited the crime lab.

"Whew!" She sighed, bouncing down the stairs. "That felt good. Really good. I can't thank you enough for talking my father into letting me process the evidence, David."

"Don't mention it. That's the least I could do, especially considering you were the one who retrieved it from the crime scene. I still don't understand how all of Clemmington PD managed to overlook it."

Lena gave him a wink and dusted off her shoulders. "Hey, what can I say. I'm just that good."

"Oh *really*. Is that what it is?"

"That's exactly what it is."

David couldn't help but smile at her upbeat demeanor. Despite her most recent attack, he was glad to see she was in better spirits. It reassured him that he'd done the right thing by talking her father into letting her analyze the evidence.

Lena turned to him as they headed toward his car. "Hey, I've been meaning to ask you something. Was the woman who was murdered on the Juniper hiking trail ever identified?"

"Yes, she was. Her name was Ashley Duncan. What's

strange is that she wasn't a Clemmington resident. She actually lived a couple of towns over, in Valley Oak."

David noticed Lena's pace slow down a bit. When they reached his car, she fell against the passenger door.

"Are you okay?" he asked.

"I'm—I'm fine," she breathed while holding her hand to her chest. "I just… I wonder if the suspect kidnapped her in Valley Oak, then assaulted her here in Clemmington, just to torment me."

David had already taken that theory into consideration. But he didn't mention it to Lena for fear of stressing her out even further.

"Well, the good news is the lab director promised to have the DNA results back on the evidence you just processed within the next week or so," he said in an attempt to steer the conversation in a positive direction. "Hopefully that'll bring us even closer to arresting the perp."

"Hopefully…" Lena mumbled, her wavering tone less than confident.

"Come on. Be optimistic. We're getting closer and closer every day, and—"

David was suddenly interrupted by a woman's voice.

"Lena? Lena Love?" she called out.

He turned around and noticed a thin, dark-haired woman walking toward them.

"Katie?" Lena called out. "Hey, girl!"

David looked on as the woman ran over, embracing Lena tightly.

"How are you?" Lena asked her. "What are you doing here in this neck of the woods?"

"I'm doing well. I actually just started working here at the lab as a forensic scientist."

"*Really?* Oh, wow, congratulations!"

Lena clutched the woman's arm and turned to David.

"David, this is Katie Winters. She and I attended Pacific Western University together. Katie, meet David Hudson. He's a detective with the Clemmington PD."

"It's nice to meet you, Katie," he said, reaching out and shaking her hand. "Congratulations on the new job."

"Thank you so much. It's nice to meet you, as well."

Katie turned back to Lena and gently placed her hands on her shoulders.

"How are you doing?" she asked softly. "I was so sorry to hear about what happened to you back in LA."

"I'm hanging in there. David and I were actually here processing evidence that I collected from the most recent crime scene in Clemmington."

Katie's hands fell down by her sides as she shook her head. "I can't believe that bastard committed another murder, right in your hometown. It's as if he's following you. I pray you all get him behind bars before he strikes again."

"That's exactly what we're working to do," David told her.

"Good," Katie responded. "Well, I'd better get back to work. My lunch break ended fifteen minutes ago. I'd hate to get fired during my first week on the job. David, it was great meeting you, and, Lena, it was wonderful seeing you. We have got to keep in touch. Is your contact information the same?"

"It is. I'd love to get together and catch up."

"Same here. I'll be in touch soon."

Lena waved goodbye, then turned to David.

"That was so nice, running into her," she said as they climbed inside the car. "It'll be good to reconnect with someone from college who's in the same line of work as me."

"I'm sure it will be," David replied while driving out

of the parking lot. "But you best believe that if you two decide to get together, you'll be chaperoned."

"Oh *God*," Lena groaned. "Are you serious? I feel like a kid all over again."

"Remember, safety first. So listen. I'll take you back to the police station to pick up your car, then follow you back to your parents' house. You know, just in case…"

"I know. Just in case the killer is following me."

David noticed a mist in Lena's eyes as she stared straight ahead. He reached over and nudged her thigh.

"I tell you what," he began. "After I get off work tonight, why don't we go out to dinner? And I don't mean a quick, casual meal. I'm talking suit and tie, fancy dress and high heels type of dinner. How does that sound?"

Lena nodded her head and forced a smile. "That sounds amazing, actually. And much needed. Thank you."

"You're welcome. I figured you'd enjoy doing something nice that would break up the monotony of dealing with this investigation."

"I definitely would. Looking forward to it."

"So am I."

"Mmm, THIS IS really good," David said. He slid his plate of dark chocolate ganache tart across the table toward Lena. "Here, try it. You'll love it."

"I can't," she moaned. "I am stuffed. I ate way too much of my blueberry lavender cheesecake."

"So what are you saying?" David asked as he emptied a bottle of Riesling into their glasses. "You didn't leave room to finish off this delicious wine?"

"I didn't say all that now," Lena protested before they broke out into laughter.

David took a sip of his wine while staring across the

table at her. Lena looked beautiful dressed in a black slip minidress and silver kitten heel pumps. She'd pulled her hair into a sophisticated chignon, which highlighted her sparkling dangle earrings and matte red lipstick perfectly.

David had reached into the back of his closet and pulled out one of his better dark gray suits, which he'd paired with a crisp white shirt and pink silk tie. But all eyes were inevitably on his stunning companion.

"I've had such a great time tonight," Lena told him. "I haven't had this good of a time in…"

When her voice trailed off, he gave her a flirtatious wink.

"In a long time?" he asked.

"A *really* long time. I don't want the night to end."

"It doesn't have to."

Lena tilted her head. "Meaning?"

"Meaning we could take this back to my place. Listen to some music. Crack open the bottle of Cabernet Sauvignon reserve wine that I've been saving for a special occasion."

David's mind inadvertently drifted to the moment in his office earlier that day when Lena kissed him. He wondered if they would pick up where they'd left off later.

"So you consider tonight a special occasion?" she asked.

"I most certainly do."

Lena dabbed the corners of her mouth with her napkin and picked up her clutch. "Okay then. Let's go."

David paid the check, then led her out of the restaurant. When she intertwined her arm with his, he was hit with a bout of nostalgia. David felt as though they were back in high school, and he was once again dating the most popular girl in class.

The pair climbed inside the car. Just as he started the engine, his cell phone buzzed loudly against the dashboard.

"No, don't answer it," Lena said. "I do not want our wonderful evening being interrupted by any nonsense."

"Neither do I. But unfortunately, I've got to check it. Could be an emergency."

David tapped his phone's home screen and opened the new notification.

"This is your father texting me," he said.

"What does that nosy man want?" Lena asked. "He knows we're out at dinner."

"Maybe he just wants to check in and make sure I'm behaving myself," David joked as he began reading the message.

Get down to Roble Park immediately! We've got another murder on our hands. Female victim, strangled to death with a heart carved into her chest. She was new to town. Worked at the forensics lab. She's been identified as Katie Winters.

A freezing chill swept over David. His mouth fell open and immediately went dry.

Lena turned to him and grabbed his arm.

"Hey, what's wrong? Are you okay?"

"Uh—I…"

He was too stunned to speak. So he handed Lena his phone so that she could read the message for herself.

After a few seconds, she let out a guttural scream.

"I am so sorry, Lena," David said before slamming his foot against the accelerator and speeding off toward Roble Park.

Chapter Fourteen

Lena's entire body trembled with shock as she stepped
carefully over the park's dried dirt trail. She and David
hadn't had time to stop and change before rushing to the
crime scene. Thankfully, he had a silver windbreaker and
shoe covers stored in his car that she was able to slip over
her dress and heels.

When Lena laid eyes on the wooded area up ahead, her
muscles tensed. The sight of yellow caution tape wrapped
around massive sycamore tree trunks brought back memories of her most recent attack.

Do not break down, she told herself, knowing this
moment could lead to her being put back on the investigative team.

Despite being traumatized by her own experience, she
was devastated that her friend had been killed and more
determined than ever to catch the killer.

"Are you sure you're okay being here?" David asked,
as if he'd read her mind.

"Honestly? I'm a bit shaken up. I can't believe Katie was
killed. I mean, what's the likelihood that a personal friend
of mine who just got to town, who I just so happened to
see earlier today, is now dead? That's no coincidence."

"Yeah, I don't think so, either. I just hope your father
doesn't reprimand me for bringing you out here."

"I'm sure he won't. He knew we were out together. You had no choice but to bring me considering you needed to get down here ASAP."

"That's true. And if he does say anything, that'll be my argument."

Lena glanced over at David. He was staring straight ahead, the corners of his mouth curled into a slight frown. When he began cracking his knuckles and quickening his pace, she broke out into a slow jog in an effort to keep up with him.

"Hey," she said, reaching over and gently placing her hand on his arm. "Are *you* okay?"

"I'm good," he barked. "Just ready to get to work."

Lena winced at the sound of his gruff tone. It was apparent that he was feeling the pressure to solve the case, especially now that he'd been named lead detective.

"We're going to get through this, David," she said, despite her own feelings of fear and doubt. "Together."

"Thanks," he replied quietly, covering her hand with his. "I needed to hear that. Now, let's see what we've got here."

The pair approached the crime scene tape. The area had been lit up with portable telescoping pole lights. Law enforcement officers were covered in hazmat suits, latex gloves and eye goggles. Lena could barely make out who was who.

David, who had already removed his suit jacket and tie, rolled up his sleeves.

"Hey!" he called out. "Where's Detective Campbell?"

"Right here!" Russ responded, waving his hand before walking over. He was carrying a black case in one hand and brown paper evidence bags in the other.

"You got a couple of extra hazmat suits?" David asked him.

"I do. They're in my other bag. I'll go and grab them." Russ paused, eyeing David and Lena from head to toe. "You two look awfully dressed up. Where are you coming from?"

"Not now, Campbell," David grunted. "Can you please just bring us those hazmat suits?"

"Sure, man," he replied while slowly backing away. "No need to get all huffy. It was just a question."

"Leave it to Russ to be worried about what we're doing while he's in the middle of a murder scene," Lena muttered under her breath.

"I know, right?" David said. "He's a good detective and all, but he is messy as hell. Gossips more than kids in high school."

Lena crossed her arms in front of her and stood on her tippy-toes. She craned her neck, struggling to see over the heads of the officers who were hovering near Katie's body. When she caught a glimpse of her friend's bare leg, Lena cringed and turned away.

She took several deep breaths and fanned her face.

Do not start panicking out here in front of all these officers.

"Are you all right?" David asked her.

"I'm fine." She sniffed, quickly wiping away a few tears that had managed to escape from her eyes.

"Hey, you two asked for a couple of hazmat suits?"

Lena looked up and saw Miles approaching them with the protective gear in hand.

"We did," David said. "Russ couldn't bring them over to us himself? He had to recruit you to do it instead?"

"You know how he is. He claimed the chief asked him to finish processing the scene."

"Yeah, right," David muttered. He took the suits from Miles and handed one to Lena. "That dude is a trip."

Miles pointed over at her.

"Hey, does Dad know you're here?"

"I don't know," she said while quickly slipping on the coverall. "But he knew David and I were out at dinner, and told him to get down here immediately. So, he had no choice but to bring me."

"Well, are you okay with being here?" Miles asked. "Because, I mean… I know that Katie was your former classmate and friend. And I was thinking that the killer may have…"

"Murdered her to send me a message?" Lena asked after his voice faded. "The thought of that chills me to the core, Miles. Knowing he probably followed us to the lab and saw me talking to Katie, then hunted her down and killed her, is devastating. But it also makes me want to go even harder. So let's get to it."

"Let's get to what?" Lena heard someone ask behind her.

She turned around and saw her father approaching them.

"Get to *what*?" Chief Love repeated.

"I thought I could step in and help out with the investigation," Lena finally replied.

"The hell you can. I'm sorry, but I am not about to let you subject yourself to this case. Not after what you've been through. I've got Detective Campbell handling the forensics. Now, you can stick close by until I'm able to free someone up who'll take you back home. Until then, no investigative work for you."

"But, Dad, I—"

"Chief Love," Russ interrupted, "I could actually use some help processing the scene. I'm done collecting evidence from the body, and the medical examiner is on his way for the removal."

When Russ glanced over at Lena, she mouthed the words *thank you*, then turned to her father.

"See, Dad? Detective Campbell needs my assistance. Now that Katie's body has been processed and she'll be taken to the morgue, the hard part is over. Please, let me help handle the rest."

Chief Love glared at his daughter, his forehead creased with doubt.

"I don't like this," he stated. "I don't like it at all."

The chief paused, watching Lena closely. She stood firm, like a soldier at attention in front of her drill sergeant. When she didn't break, he turned to Russ.

"You'd better keep a close eye on her," Chief Love said. "If you see any signs of distress, you pull her off the scene immediately. Am I clear?"

"Absolutely, sir."

Chief Love gave Lena one last look before turning to David.

"Detective Hudson, you come with me. I want to talk to you and Jake about a strategy on how we should be canvassing the town in search of this psychopath."

"Yes, sir," David responded.

When he walked past Lena, he threw her a look of caution, then turned his attention to Russ. The scowl on David's face said it all. He did not want her working one-on-one with Detective Campbell.

"Is there a problem?" Russ asked David before handing Lena a pair of gloves. He didn't wait for David to reply. Instead, Russ wrapped his arm around Lena's shoulders and led her toward the middle of the crime scene.

She could feel David's intense stare burning into her back as they walked away. But at this point, Lena wasn't concerned with either of the detectives' petty schoolboy antics. She'd shifted into forensic investigator mode and was ready to dig into the crime scene.

"What do we know so far?" she asked Russ. "Other than the fact that the victim was strangled to death and had a heart carved into her chest?"

"Her hands were tied behind her back."

"With what sort of ligature?"

"A three-strand twisted rope."

"That's my killer's modus operandi," Lena said. "Have you collected the rope?"

"I have. Along with blood evidence and photographs of a shoe print I found in the dirt near the body."

Russ handed Lena a flashlight. As they approached the body bag, she squeezed the light's handle and stared down at it, fumbling with the switch as if she were having trouble turning it on.

"You need help with that?" Russ asked.

"Nope," Lena insisted, a slight quaver in her voice. She tapped her chest with her fist and cleared her throat. "I've got it."

"The body bag has been zipped up and secured," he said gently. "So you don't have to worry about seeing your friend. And by the way, I'm so sorry that this happened to her. I'm sorry that *all* of this is happening, to you and the rest of the victims."

"Thanks, Russ. I appreciate you saying that."

"Of course. Look, I know I've got a…a *reputation* when it comes to the ladies. But I do have a heart."

"I know you do."

As the pair fell silent, Lena heard a commotion behind her. She turned around and saw the medical examiner and his team approaching the scene.

"Oh, good." Lena sighed, relieved that Katie's body was being removed.

Russ waved them over. After they greeted one another and the coroner took over, the detective grabbed Lena's hand and pulled her away.

"You doing okay?" he asked.

"Yes. I'm fine."

"Good. And you're still up for searching the area for more evidence?"

"Of course. Let's do it."

Russ tightened his grip on her hand. "All right then. Let's check out this spot over here," he suggested, leading her toward a taped-off corner. "I haven't examined it yet."

On the way there, Lena felt eyes on her. She looked up and saw David glaring at them.

She quickly snatched her hand out of Russ's grip. But it was too late. David had already seen them.

"OKAY, TEAM, I think we've got everything we need," Chief Love announced. "Let's wrap it up and get out of here."

Lena closed her eyes and pressed the back of her hand against her damp forehead.

"I am exhausted," she said, sighing. "What do you think? Do we have enough viable evidence here to formulate a solid DNA profile?"

"I think so," Russ confirmed. He secured the latch on his forensic case, then let out a huge yawn. "*Whew!* I guess I'm tired, too. But after this long, insane day, I could go for a drink. How about you? Wanna stop by Lacey's for a cocktail? Or two?"

"And fall asleep on you at the bar? I don't think so."

"Aw, come on. It's just a drink among friends. Plus we haven't had a chance to catch up since you've been back in town."

"Well, considering the fact that I'm pretty much in

the witness protection program at the Love residence, I haven't been doing much socializing."

"It certainly looked like you were out getting your mingle on with David before you two got here. I peeped the little black dress and silver shoes underneath the windbreaker and shoe covers."

"Wow, aren't you the observant one," Lena quipped.

"It's hard not to notice a woman as beautiful as you. But anyway, let me stop before I say too much. If I can't take you out for a drink, at least let me give you a ride home."

"I, um… I think that I should probably—"

Before Lena could finish, David came storming over.

"Are you ready to go?" he asked her gruffly.

"Yes. I am. Hey, are you oka—"

"I'm fine," he grunted before she could finish. "Just tired and anxious to get the hell out of here."

Lena stood awkwardly between the two men as they stared one another down. She writhed her hands before turning to Russ.

"I'm going to head out with David. Thanks for letting me join in on the investigation."

"Anytime. I'll be in touch regarding the evidence we collected. Maybe we can take it down to the crime lab together. Then finally grab that drink."

Lena peeked over at David. If looks could kill, Russ would be a dead man.

"Okay then, talk to you soon," she told Russ without addressing the crime lab or the invitation for drinks.

"Are you coming, or do you wanna meet me at the car?" David snapped.

"I'm coming."

He spun around and stormed away from the crime scene. Lena hurried after him.

They walked to the car in silence. David popped open the trunk and pulled out a plastic garbage bag. He and Lena removed their protective gear and stuffed it all inside. He tossed the bag into the trunk, slammed the lid shut, then threw open the passenger door.

"Why are you so angry?" she asked him.

"I'm not angry. I already told you, I'm tired."

"Do you still want to go back to your place and have that glass of wine?"

David shook his head. "It's been a long night, Lena. I think I'd better take you home."

The rejection caused her heart to pound so hard that it bounced up into her throat. She swallowed hard and slid inside the car.

David slammed the door and climbed into the driver's seat. Without saying a word, he started the engine and sped off.

Lena felt her body heating up as she seethed with anger.

"I cannot believe you're taking Russ's actions out on me. Especially after my friend was just killed and I helped to investigate the crime scene."

David remained silent for several moments before finally speaking up.

"I'm sorry. I just—I can't stand to see you fraternizing with him. He is such a womanizer. And I know exactly what he's trying to do."

"First of all, I wasn't fraternizing with Russ. I was taking care of business tonight. Secondly, I know exactly what he's trying to do, too. And I'm not giving in to it. So don't worry. I have no interest in socializing with your apparent enemy."

"He's not my enemy. He just isn't someone I want you associating with."

The tense exchange was interrupted when Lena's cell phone buzzed. She pulled it from her clutch.

A text message notification appeared on the screen. It was sent from an anonymous number.

She was immediately overcome by a sick feeling. Her hand shook as she opened the text.

Nine Ten I Struck Again...

The phone fell from her hand. She turned to David. "We've got bigger things to worry about than Russ."

Chapter Fifteen

David sat across from Lena at her parents' dining room table. She shuffled through the lab reports, comparing the results from all of the crime scene evidence.

"So the DNA profiles on every sample that we've processed match up," Lena said.

"Yes, they do."

"Which means that we're dealing with one killer. Not a copycat killer."

"Exactly."

"But the killer's profile didn't match anyone's DNA record in the CODIS criminal justice database?"

David sat back and folded his hands behind his head. "Unfortunately, no. It didn't. But at least it's been confirmed that a copycat killer doesn't exist. There's only one person who's been committing these murders."

"Right," Lena said before slamming the reports down onto the table. "But where do we go from here? This is so frustrating."

"I know it is. And I've been thinking about the next steps. This killer that we're dealing with has continuously stayed two steps ahead of us. We've gotta take a risk here. Do something unexpected. Set up a trap that'll catch him off guard in hopes that he'll make a mistake."

"That sounds good. Do you have a plan in mind?"

"No." David sighed. "Not yet. But we need to figure something out. Fast."

Lena grabbed her laptop and opened the lid. "Okay, let's just start brainstorming. Anything that comes to mind, I'll write it down. Then we'll go through everything, keep the good stuff and throw out whatever doesn't work."

"All right. Let's do it."

Betty walked into the room carrying a charcuterie board in one hand and a pitcher of iced tea in the other.

"How's it going in here?" she asked. "Anything insightful coming from those reports?"

"It would be if the suspect's profile matched up with someone's in the criminal database," Lena said. "But it doesn't."

"Oh, that's a bummer." Betty placed the board and pitcher down onto the table, then paused. "Wait, wouldn't that mean the killer has never been convicted of a crime?"

"It would," David confirmed. "Which is crazy. How could someone go from never being arrested to committing all of these brutal attacks?"

"Exactly," Betty replied, slowly shaking her head.

Lena turned to her mother. "But David and I are going to shift gears. We're working on a plan that'll hopefully beat him at his own game."

"Oh, really? Well, good. I'm looking forward to hearing all about it. And on that note, I'll leave you two alone so you can get back to work. Enjoy the snacks and tea."

"Mmm, we will," David said. "Thank you."

As soon as Betty was out of earshot, David grabbed Lena's hand.

"I just thought of something."

"Okay," she said while filling their glasses with tea. "What've you got?"

"Don't faint when you hear this, but what if you go back to LA?"

The pitcher almost fell from Lena's hand. David jumped up and grabbed it, setting it back down onto the table.

"I'm sorry," she said. "But weren't you the same guy who threw a fit when I mentioned going back to LA?"

"Hold on," David replied. "Just hear me out. This is different. We'd technically be using you as a pawn. *No offense,*" he quickly added when she threw him a look. "Listen, the bottom line is, if you go back to LA, the killer will follow you there. We could have you revisit the crime scene out on the Cucamonga Wilderness hiking trail. The suspect will think you're alone, combing the area for additional evidence. But we'll have law enforcement in place, ready to apprehend him the minute he appears."

David waited for Lena to respond. She remained silent, her eyes focused on the charcuterie board rather than him. He leaned in, noticing her fallen expression.

"I'm sorry," he uttered. "That was too much to ask. And insensitive to suggest. I shouldn't have even—"

"I'll do it," Lena interrupted.

"You will?" David asked, watching as her eyes flickered with determination. "Are you sure?"

"Yes. I'm positive. I can't stand the thought of the killer murdering another innocent victim. So if we have to use me as bait in order to track him down, then so be it."

David paused. Lena was now focusing on the pepperoni slices she was placing on their saucers. Her calm demeanor was almost frightening.

"I see you watching me from the corners of your eyes," she said. "Trust me. I'm down with your idea. I know that between the Clemmington PD and the LAPD, I'll be fully protected."

"Of course you will be—".

Before David could finish, Betty came storming into the room.

"Excuse me, but you two will do no such thing!" she insisted, throwing a stack of napkins down onto the table. "Have you both completely lost your minds?"

"Mom, please," Lena said. "You didn't hear the whole conversation. Plus David and I haven't even put a solid plan in place yet. We're just throwing around ideas."

"First of all, I stood my nosy self right outside that doorway and heard every bit of your conversation. Second of all, no matter what type of plan you two put in place, the whole idea is utterly senseless. *Period*. Third of all—"

Betty was interrupted when Kennedy, Jake and Miles came bursting through the front door and into the dining room.

"Dude!" Jake yelled, shoving Miles's shoulder. "Do you know how ridiculous you sound right now? Smoky Pit does not have the best ribs in town. That would be Leon's Barbecue."

"Man, get outta here," Miles replied, shoving him back before approaching the table and rubbing his hands together. "Mmm, what do we have here? A little Brie and Parmesan, with a side of prosciutto and salami, along with a variety of other meats and cheeses?"

When he reached for the board, Betty slapped his hand away.

"Go wash your hands first," she commanded. "But before you do that, I need for all three of you to talk some sense into Lena and David."

"Uh-oh," David muttered as he slid down in his chair.

Kennedy walked over to Betty and planted a kiss on her forehead.

"Is it just me," he began, "or does this moment remind you of the good ole days, back when we still had a house full of kids and their friends?"

"I wish this moment reminded me of the good ole days," Betty muttered. "Go on, you two," she continued, pointing over at Lena and David. "Tell Chief Love about your brilliant little plan to catch the killer."

David noticed Jake walk over to his parents and stand next to Kennedy. He crossed his arms over his chest while looking down his nose at him and Lena. Miles on the other hand stood near his sister, propping his hand against the back of her chair protectively. The lines of allegiance were clear.

David glanced over at Lena. Judging by the look of her downturned lips, she wanted no part of sharing their plan with her family. So he cleared his throat and began explaining the situation.

"Lena and I were going over the killer's DNA results, and discussing how frustrated we are that they didn't match anyone's in CODIS. Without any new and viable leads, we're convinced that the suspect will continue to get away with murder."

Kennedy glanced down at his watch, then back up at David. His right eyebrow shot up toward his forehead. "Um, Detective? Would you mind getting to the punch line? I've had a long day, and I can smell my wife's short ribs simmering in the Crock-Pot. I'm ready to *eat*."

Lena emitted a loud sigh and threw up her hands. "Long story short, David and I were thinking that we could set up some sort of sting operation. I would bait the killer to a certain location, and law enforcement would be there lying in wait."

Betty turned to Kennedy and nudged his arm.

"Can you believe what you're hearing right now?" she asked him. "They want to go back to LA so that the suspect will follow Lena, then lead him to the crime scene where Lena was first attacked."

Jake groaned loudly, slapping his palm against his forehead. "*Really?* Are you two being serious right now? That has got to be the dumbest idea I've ever heard. Lena, why would you want to subject yourself to being attacked yet again? You're not a cat. You don't have nine lives. Keep this up and the third time just might be the charm for the killer—"

"Come on, Jake," Miles interjected. "That's enough. I actually don't think it's a bad idea. Could it be dangerous? Yes. But if the plan is executed properly, we could very well capture the suspect."

"Well, like I said," Betty began, turning to Kennedy, "I think it's utterly senseless. Between the Clemmington PD and the LAPD, we've got two of the best law enforcement agencies on the case. Why put my child in the middle of the investigation and jeopardize her life?"

"Because nothing else we've tried has worked so far," Kennedy replied.

Everyone in the room turned to the chief, their mouths falling open in simultaneous shock.

"So what are you saying?" Betty asked. "That you're okay with this…this awful, dangerous idea?"

"I'm not saying that I'm okay with it. But I am saying that it's worth considering."

Betty turned away from her husband and stared down at the floor. She pressed her fingertips against her temples and massaged them vigorously.

"Okay," she whispered, "I see you've completely lost

the script, as well. I'd better go check on my short ribs before I say something I might regret."

"Yeah," Jake said, his arms falling down by his sides, "I'd better go with you."

Once he and Betty were out of earshot, Kennedy approached the table.

"Listen," he said, "I think you two may be onto something. But let's drop it for now and reconvene tomorrow down at the station. Betty doesn't fully understand the pressure that we're under to get this case solved. So we shouldn't continue the conversation here at the house."

"Understood, sir," David replied. "Thank you for hearing us out."

"Yes, Dad," Lena added, "I really appreciate that."

"You're welcome. See? I'm not always the stern, strict tyrant that you make me out to be."

Lena laughed and nudged Miles's arm. "Maybe not today…"

Miles nodded his head in agreement, then turned to their father.

"But what about Jake?" he asked. "We need for him to get on board with this, too."

"Let me talk to him," the chief replied. "He'll come around. In the meantime, why don't you three start quietly brainstorming some specific ideas and taking notes? The better the plan, the faster he'll agree. Once we have a solid strategy, I'll put in a call to the LAPD's Chief Scott and run it by him."

"That sounds good," Lena said. "I'm so glad we're in the state of California. Since the suspect committed all of these crimes within state lines—"

"Clemmington PD is allowed to make an arrest anywhere in California, by law," Miles chimed in.

Kennedy walked over and shook his son's shoulder.

"Hey, look who's been brushing up on the criminal justice system's laws and procedures. Is that a promotion I see in your future?"

"*Very near* future," Miles responded with a huge grin.

"Keep this up and we just might bring that to fruition. But as for the *immediate* future, let's go check on your mother and brother and make sure they haven't disowned us. David, are you staying for dinner?"

"From the smell of those short ribs, I would love to. But I don't know. Mrs. Love may not want me here after that exchange we just had."

"Aw, don't worry about her. You're like family. She'll get over it just like she does whenever one of her own kids upsets her."

"Thank you, sir."

Once Kennedy and Miles left the room, David turned to Lena.

"Wow," he breathed. "That was intense. I'm actually sweating."

"*You're* sweating. I'm pretty sure my blood pressure is at stroke level. But the good news is, we accomplished our mission. I think this is it, David. If we come up with the right plan, we'll finally capture that son of a bitch."

David took a long sip of tea, then rolled up his sleeves.

"I agree. Now that the room has cleared out, let's dig into this cheese board and start thinking of a master plan."

Chapter Sixteen

NEWS RELEASE
Tuesday, August 10, 2021
Los Angeles Law Enforcement Media Relations

FORENSIC INVESTIGATOR LENA LOVE RE-TURNING TO WORK

Los Angeles: We are pleased to announce that our lead forensic investigator, Lena Love, will be re-joining the Los Angeles Police Department, effective immediately. Love had fallen victim to an attack that we believe was committed by a California serial killer. After returning to her hometown to recuperate with family, she feels ready to get back to work and continue lending her expertise to the department.

Love will be working part-time, primarily inside the forensics laboratory, as she eases back into her routine. Love's crime scene investigations will re-commence at her discretion.

The LAPD continues to pursue the suspect, who is still at large. Anyone with information regarding this case is urged to contact the LAPD's Homicide Division. Anyone wishing to remain anonymous should call Crime Stoppers, or submit tips online.

Lena read through the press release one last time, then looked over at David.

"I think this sounds great," she said, spinning her laptop toward him. "What do you think?"

"I agree," he replied. "For the *fourth* time. Trust me. The LAPD's media relations department did an excellent job on the fake release. I definitely think it'll throw the killer off and convince him that you're back at work in LA."

"Awesome. I'm taking your word for it."

Lena composed an email to the public relations director, giving her the thumbs-up on the release. After cc'ing Chief Scott, she sent the message, then closed her computer.

"All right." She sighed, standing up and stretching her limbs. "Step one of the plan is in motion. What do you say we celebrate with a second glass of wine?"

"I'd say I like where your head's at. Let's do it."

Lena picked up their glasses and headed into her LA loft's sleek white kitchen. Two weeks had passed since they'd planned out their sting operation. She and David had arrived in town early that morning, just before sunrise. He'd offered to stay in a nearby hotel, but Lena insisted she'd feel more comfortable if he stayed with her. David agreed, and she set him up in her guest room.

Lena hadn't cohabitated with a man for an extended amount of time in years. She couldn't deny the fact that having David there felt good.

"So, when is the press release going to go live on the LAPD's website?" he asked.

"According to the PR director, as soon as she gets my approval. My guess is that the minute she sees my email, it'll be posted. Local news stations are going to share the news with the public, as well."

"And then, it'll be showtime. I'm sure our suspect will immediately leave Clemmington and head back to LA. Then when he comes for you, we'll come for him, and that'll be the end of this nightmare."

"From your lips to God's ears," Lena replied. "I can only hope it'll be that easy."

David propped his arms along the back of her gray suede couch and glanced around the living room.

"I love your place," he said. "The aesthetic is really cool. The high ceilings, exposed copper pipes, brick walls, and wide-open floor plan give it a bit of an industrial feel. Then your contemporary furnishings and artwork offer up a really slick, modern look."

Lena leaned back and stared across her marble island. "Listen to you, sounding like you write for *Elle Decor*. Thank you." She refilled their glasses with Pinot Noir rosé, then took a seat next to David. "I have yet to see your house. I bet it looks good."

"Ah, it's okay. Just a simple, rustic, trilevel townhome. Nothing too fancy. But I'd love for you to stop by and check it out when we get back to Clemmington."

"I'd like that," Lena murmured. When she noticed David leaning in and staring at her intently, she took several sips of wine, then changed the subject. "So, I heard from Miles this morning. He confirmed that they'll be arriving in LA this afternoon."

David paused, shifting his body a few inches away from Lena's. "Cool. Who have we got coming from the Clemmington PD again?"

"My dad and brothers, of course. And Officer Underwood. My father asked Russ to stay back and hold down the fort while they're all here."

"Good," David said. "I could use a break from him and his antics."

"You just don't want him flirting with me."

"Yeah, that, too."

Lena's head swiveled as she gazed over at him. "Whoa, okay then. Tell me how you really feel."

David shrugged his shoulders. "Just being honest," he replied before sipping casually from his glass.

"Alrighty then." Lena quickly reopened her laptop and pulled up a Word document. "Listen, why don't we shift gears and run through our plan for catching the killer one more time?"

"Good idea."

"Okay, so, tomorrow night, I'm going to head to the Cucamonga Wilderness hiking trail and revisit the crime scene. Chief Scott has confirmed that he'll have a substantial number of law enforcement officers hidden all along the trail, from the parking lot to the actual crime scene."

"I think I should be posted at the crime scene," David said. "But I'll let you decide where you'd like for me to be positioned."

"Of course I want you posted at the crime scene. That's where the killer will probably try and strike. And when he does, I want you to be there to protect me. Aside from my family, I know that you'll have my back like no one else."

David reached over and took Lena's hand in his.

"Yes, I will," he affirmed.

She leaned back and rested her head on his shoulder.

"Thank you, David."

"Of course." He reached back and slowly wrapped his

arm around her. "I know you're probably tired of being questioned, but are you sure you want to do this?"

"Absolutely," Lena said firmly, sitting straight up and refocusing on her computer screen.

Just as she began scrolling down the page, David leaned over and closed her laptop.

"Hey, why don't we give the whole sting operation talk a rest?" he suggested. "We put the plan together back in Clemmington, perfected it over the past few days, shared it with law enforcement and discussed it the whole way here. Believe me. We're good. Let's just take this time to relax. Maybe order some Thai food and chill out until your family gets here."

Lena sat back and let out a deep sigh.

"That actually sounds good. Really good. I'll pull up Uber Eats and see who can get some food here the fastest. Why don't you scroll through Netflix and find a movie for us to watch?"

"I'd love to."

While David grabbed the remote and turned on the television, Lena curled up on the couch and began searching through restaurants on her phone.

LENA PRESSED HER fingernails into the steering wheel as she sped down Wilson Avenue. She glanced in her rearview mirror for the hundredth time. There, a couple of cars behind her, was the black sedan that Officer Underwood had rented.

She jumped when the shrill sound of her ringing cell phone blasted through the speakers. David's name appeared on the touch screen. She reached out and tapped the accept button.

"Hey," she answered nervously. "What's going on?"

"Just checking in to see how close you are to the hiking trail."

"I'm on Mount Baldy Road now, heading toward Ice House Canyon Road. So I'm about ten minutes away."

"Okay. Your family and I are here at the crime scene, scattered about inconspicuously. And the LAPD is everywhere, posing as joggers, hikers and even a few vagrants."

"Good," Lena breathed, the relief in her voice apparent. "Chief Scott told me he's got several snipers combing the area, too."

"Oh, yeah. We've got this place surrounded. There's no way in hell the killer is going to find his way out of this trap."

Lena felt her tensed back relax farther into the seat. "Hearing that is definitely helping to calm my nerves. But I have to admit, I'm a bit on edge."

"That's to be expected. And that's why I called you. I wanted to make sure you're holding up okay."

"I am. I just hope that after tonight, this will all be over. I'm tired of living in fear—looking over my shoulder and waiting for the next attack. I'm shaken up right now at the thought that the killer might be following me."

"I know you are. Just stay strong. After tonight, you'll be everybody's hero."

"That is if I get through tonight."

She heard David grunt softly.

"Come on, now," he said. "Don't talk like that. Of course you'll get through tonight. Remember, this go-round, you won't be at the crime scene alone. You'll be surrounded by people who love you, who'd never let anything happen to you."

The sound of those words caused Lena's breath to

catch in her throat. She wondered if he was including himself in that group of people who loved her.

"CAN YOU STILL see Officer Underwood in your rear-view?" David asked.

"I can," Lena confirmed after taking a quick look behind her. "I've been keeping an eye out for that obnoxious sports car I think the suspect drives, too. But so far I haven't seen it."

"Well, if he was driving that vehicle all through Clemmington, maybe he was smart enough to switch out cars tonight."

"Maybe…" Lena looked up at the street sign and made a right turn. The sight of vast, rugged mountains came into view. "Okay, I'm heading down Ice House Canyon Road now. So I'll be pulling into the parking lot soon."

"Got it. Once you park your car, just stick to the plan. Let Officer Underwood exit his vehicle first. When he gives you the hand signal that he's got eyes on you, you'll get out of your car and set off toward the trail's entrance."

"Will do. I just need to keep reminding myself that I've got a ton of eyes on me. As vulnerable as I feel right now, I know that I'm safe."

She wasn't quite convinced of her own words. Nevertheless, Lena hoped that saying them out loud would assure her.

"Yes, you are safe," David reiterated. "Now, don't forget to insert your headset before you leave the car. We're all connected through the same network so that we can easily communicate with one another. Anything you see or hear that seems off, let us know. We'll do the same."

"Okay. I'm pulling into the parking lot now. And Officer Underwood is behind me."

"Great. He already has his earpiece in and is keeping us posted on your locations."

Deep breath in, deep breath out... Lena told herself as she parked her car.

The sun had set, and a dark haze covered the canyon. The parking lot had cleared out, and there weren't many vehicles scattered throughout.

Lena turned off her engine and pulled her earpiece out of her purse. She kept her eyes focused on the rearview mirror, waiting for Officer Underwood to make a move.

"Underwood just informed us that he's parked a few spaces away from your car," David said. "He's getting out and heading toward you. Do you see him?"

"I do. He's walking up now. And...he's tapping the screen on his watch. That's my signal. I'm going to disconnect our call, connect my headset and head up the trail to the crime scene."

"Copy that. I'll let the other officers know that you're on the move. Don't forget your forensic kit. We want the suspect to think you're pulling another rogue move and investigating the scene alone."

"I've got it right here on the passenger seat. I'll check back in once I get my headset connected."

"Sounds good. And hey, Lena?"

"Yes?"

"Be careful."

She bit down on the side of her cheek, willing herself to stay calm. Despite being surrounded by law enforcement, she couldn't shake the trembling fear burning inside her stomach.

"I will," Lena said, hoping that David hadn't noticed the crack in her voice.

She ended the call, slipped her Bluetooth headset

inside her ears and tapped the wireless button on her radio adapter.

"Testing, testing, one two," she said. "Can anyone hear me?"

"Coming in clear," Chief Scott replied. "We're all standing by, Lena. I've got officers inconspicuously placed everywhere. You're in good hands."

"Yes, you are," her father added. "I'm positioned at the crime scene with your brothers and David, ready and waiting to move in on the suspect."

"Thanks, everybody. I literally felt my blood pressure easing up with every word you all just spoke."

Lena grabbed her forensic kit and then slowly stepped out of the car. Officer Underwood was several feet ahead, standing along the side of a fence while stretching his calf muscles.

"I'm getting out of the car now," she informed the team.

"We've got eyes on you," Chief Scott replied. "Whenever you're ready, start heading up the trail."

Lena bent down and tightened the laces on her sneakers. She readjusted the waistband on her yellow leggings, then zipped up her white windbreaker.

The colors were much brighter than her normal attire. But Chief Scott had advised her to wear highly visible shades so that she could be easily spotted.

She readjusted the scrunchie holding her ponytail in place and stared up ahead, wondering if the killer was watching her.

"Okay, everyone," Lena said, discreetly moving her lips. "I'm walking through the parking lot and heading toward the trail's entrance."

"Ten-four," Officer Underwood responded. "I'll be right behind you."

Trembling nerves of doubt crept through her limbs. Her eyes darted from right to left in search of the suspect. She couldn't help but feel as though he would appear out of nowhere and tackle her to the ground.

Stay calm, she told herself. *You are not alone. You're being protected...*

Lena sped up. A blustery wind whipped past her, piercing the tips of her ears. The temperature had dropped significantly since she'd left home. She pulled her zipper all the way up to her chin. But as her teeth began to chatter, she realized that it wasn't just the cool air chilling her to the bone. It was fear.

Deep breath in. Deep breath out.

The breathing mantra failed to ease her nerves. Lena turned her head slightly, hoping to get a glimpse of Officer Underwood walking behind her. But when she didn't see him, a sick feeling of dread spread throughout her entire body.

"I'm still with you, Lena," Officer Underwood said.

The sound of his voice speaking through her earpiece immediately put her at ease.

"We're all watching you," he continued. "Just keep moving forward and act natural. We'll handle the rest."

"Thanks for the reassurance," she responded, covering her mouth as she walked. "You must've sensed that I needed it."

"That, plus the fact that I noticed your head swiveling. I figured you were looking for me."

"You figured correctly," Lena said just as she reached the hiking trail's entrance. "Okay, I'm going in. Did anyone notice whether or not I'm being followed?"

"There is no one in our vicinity," Officer Underwood replied.

Several of the other officers chimed in, confirming that they too hadn't seen anybody.

"Good," she told them. "If that changes, please give me a heads-up."

Lena pulled her flashlight from her jacket pocket and shined the beam on the trail ahead. Just as she began maneuvering her way through the rocks and twigs littering the dried dirt, a throbbing pain pulsated over her right eye.

She grabbed her head, praying that a migraine wasn't about to kick in. Flashes of light and blind spots suddenly clouded her vision. She blinked rapidly, wishing she'd taken a couple of aspirin before leaving home.

It's just stress, she told herself. *Shake it off...*

Lena rubbed her eyes and focused on the trail. The crime scene appeared in the far distance. She stopped, contemplating whether she could finish the mission.

Come on. You can do this...

"You okay up there?" Officer Underwood asked her.

"Yes," she said, lying, her shrill tone laced with forced enthusiasm. "Just stopping for a second to catch my breath."

"Keep going, Lena," she heard David say. "I can see you coming up the trail. You're good."

Hearing his voice was all it took for Lena to move forward. Her slow walk turned into a slight jog. She felt ready to hit the crime scene and get this over with.

Yellow tape came into view. It was about twenty feet off the trail where the victim's body had been found.

Lena slowed down. Her courage began to dwindle again. She second-guessed her decision to do this. Their suspect was slick. She didn't trust that he wouldn't somehow manage to attack her, despite being surrounded by law enforcement.

But it was too late to turn back now. So Lena squared her shoulders and continued into the wooded area.

She eyed the bush that the perp had hidden behind before attacking her the first time. Lena shuffled toward it. She flashed her light toward the shrubbery and bent down, eyeing the area closely. Nothing appeared but dirt and fallen leaves.

Why am I expecting to see the two black lumps that turned out to be the killer's boots? she asked herself.

"You're doing great, Lena," Chief Love said. "Just keep walking the perimeter of the scene. If our perp is here, my guess is that he'll be making an appearance shortly."

No sooner had the words left his mouth than a forceful gust of whistling wind blew past Lena. The hood on her windbreaker flew across her face, blocking her vision. The sound of rustling foliage and crackling branches filled the air. It was as if the entire forest had burst into song, playing a haunting melody.

Lena felt herself becoming unnerved. She dropped her forensic kit and pulled her hood away from her face. Flashbacks of the attack flooded her mind. She spun around, searching for the killer. She could sense his presence. Lena knew he was going to attack at any given moment.

The spinning caused her to grow dizzy. The stress wasn't helping. Lena stopped, feeling as though she might pass out.

"Lena!" she heard David say. "Are you okay? Do you need assistance?"

His voice once again calmed her heightened sense of panic. She closed her eyes and took a deep breath in, then out.

"I'm fine," she said. "I just—I've got a headache. It made me feel a little discombobulated. But I'm good."

Lena picked up her forensic kit and kept going. There was no way in hell she could let the entire LAPD down, let alone the Clemmington PD. This case was riding on her, and she was determined to see it through.

The rustling of the tree branches ceased. The eerie wind subsided. A strange sense of peace lingered in the air.

See? Lena said to herself. *Everything's okay. Just stay the course.*

And then…

Boom!

Lena hit the ground. She was pinned against the dirt. What felt like a two-hundred-pound mass was lying on top of her. She tried to scream, but her face was being pressed against the chalky earth.

Suddenly, the weight was lifted off her. She was flipped over onto her back, then pulled to her feet.

A bewildered Lena rubbed the dirt from her eyes and stared straight ahead. She struggled to comprehend what had just happened.

"Freeze!" she heard her father and Chief Scott yelling simultaneously.

A swarm of law enforcement officers were huddled together, hovering over someone.

"Hands above your head! Let me see your hands!" the group roared.

Lena felt someone run up from behind and spin her around. It was David.

"Are you all right?" he asked her. "He didn't hurt you, did he? I'm so sorry we didn't get to you sooner."

Lena embraced him tightly, laying her head against his chest as she tried to catch her breath.

"What—what *happened*?" she stammered.

"The killer just jumped out of a tree and took you down," David replied, wrapping his arms around her protectively. "I'm so glad we were able to get to him before he could harm you. And you did great. Thanks to you, we got him."

"Thank God," Lena whispered, still shaken up but relieved that everything was finally over.

David held on to her as he headed toward the trail.

"Come on," he said. "Let's get you out of here."

Chapter Seventeen

David leaned back in his seat and stared across the table, looking into the eyes of their suspect.

They were sitting inside a small LAPD interrogation room. Bleak gray walls matched the worn carpet. The black plastic chairs were uncomfortable, and the steel metal table was cold. David felt claustrophobic being stuffed between Chief Love and Chief Scott. But he wasn't there for the creature comforts. He was there to get a confession.

David glanced discreetly over at the reflective glass window. He couldn't see through it. But he knew that Lena, her brothers and several other law enforcement officers were standing on the other side, looking on from the observation room.

"How old did you say you were again?" David asked the perp.

"I didn't," he replied defiantly.

"Hmm." David sighed. He ran his hand down his goatee, studying the suspect.

The man appeared to be about five feet eleven inches tall. He had a stocky build and was dressed in tactical camouflage gear. His look fit Lena's description of her attacker to a T.

"Listen," David continued, "I would advise you to

drop the whole tough-guy act. You're currently in police custody, being questioned by two police chiefs and a detective regarding some of the most heinous crimes that the state of California has ever seen. Do you understand that?"

"Um, *no*," the suspect shot back, fiddling with the handcuffs clinging to his wrists. "I'm telling you, you've got the wrong guy. Now can one of you please get me outta these shackles? It's not like I committed a real crime or anything."

"Attacking a woman out on a hiking trail *is* a real crime," David shot back. "Not to mention the rest of the felonies we're questioning you about. So we'll remove the cuffs after we get some answers."

David noticed a sudden change in the suspect's disposition. No longer was his head held high and chest poked out. He was now hunched over, his gaze focused on the table rather than the law enforcement officers.

"Son," Chief Scott began, "why don't you start by telling us your real name."

After several moments of silence, the suspect finally spoke up. "Chris."

"Chris *what*?" Chief Love asked.

"Chris Ware."

"As in Christopher Ware?"

"Yeah."

"And how old are you?" David asked once again while jotting down notes.

"Eighteen."

The detective and police chiefs glanced at one another, their furrowed brows a clear indication that they were all on the same page. None of them expected their perp to be so young.

"Look," Christopher said, "I don't know what type of…

hernias crimes you all think I committed. But whatever they are, I didn't do 'em."

David shook his head in disgust. He didn't know whether to correct or slap him. He decided to do neither and instead continued his line of questioning.

"What were you doing hanging out in the middle of the Cucamonga Wilderness trail? In the middle of a blocked-off crime scene, no less?"

Christopher glared at David, remaining silent. The detective prayed that he wouldn't cut the interview short and ask for an attorney.

"That's what I was instructed to do," Christopher finally blurted out.

"What do you mean, *instructed to do*?" Chief Scott asked.

The suspect shoved his right hand inside his mouth and began biting down on his grubby fingernails. David slid his chair closer to the perp and leaned in, sensing that he was about to break.

"Who instructed you to go out on that trail?" he asked quietly, hoping that the softer tone would encourage him to talk.

Christopher's knees bounced erratically underneath the table. He swiped his hand across his perspiring forehead.

"Come on, Chris," David urged. "You need to tell us what's really going on here. I'd hate to arrest and charge you with multiple counts of first degree murder if you weren't involved in the crimes."

"First degree murder!" Christopher shouted. He shifted in his seat and began rocking back and forth. "Wait, this interrogation isn't a part of the prank?"

"Prank?" Chief Love spat. "What prank?"

"Ugh," Christopher moaned, dropping his head into his hands. "I got set up, man…"

"By whom?" David asked, throwing his arms out from his sides. "Listen. It's been a long, nerve-racking day. We're all exhausted. You need to stop speaking in fragments and tell us what the hell is going on here."

Christopher looked back up at the officers, his red eyes appearing damp. "I'll probably get arrested for what I'm about to tell you. But at least I won't get charged with murder. So, here goes."

When he paused, Chief Scott slid his tape recorder across the table and turned up the volume. "We're listening."

Christopher looked up at the white ceiling tiles and blinked rapidly. "There's this shock site on the dark web called *Gonna Get Got*. The guys who run it post violent videos, extreme prank videos, stuff like that."

He paused once again. David tapped his pen against the table, his skin prickling with irritation as Christopher took several long sips of soda.

Be patient, he told himself. *At least you've got him talking…*

David winced when their perp emitted a loud burp.

"And," Christopher continued, "there's a section on the site that lets members apply for prank master positions. That's what I am. So when *Gonna Get Got* receives requests to have pranks pulled on someone, we're hired to do the job. I've been taking on jobs since last year. This was my eighth assignment. And I have never, *ever* been busted by the cops before. Until now, that is."

"Okay," David replied, staring down at the table while struggling to digest the absurd story. "What exactly did this particular assignment entail?"

"First, I had to send in a photo of myself to prove that I fit the description of the job requirements."

"And what was that description?"

"Male, about five feet eleven inches tall, husky build. Oh, and I had to buy this outfit I'm wearing and send in a photo of it before I got hired."

David paused. He eyed Christopher from head to toe. A cold sweat seeped through his pores once he realized that the real suspect had hired a stunt double to foil their sting operation.

"How exactly do you communicate with these people?" David asked. "Is it strictly through the website?"

"Yeah. *Gonna Get Got* lets its members chat back and forth without revealing their identities."

"So you have no idea who these people are that you're working with?"

"Nope. And as long as I'm getting paid, I honestly don't care."

When David groaned loudly and leaned back in his chair, Chief Scott stepped in.

"Well, you *should* care," he insisted. "Because you're dealing with some really dangerous people here. Now explain to us what you were instructed to do tonight."

"Look, the dude sent me a photo of some woman who he said was an old childhood friend, and a map of the Cucamonga Wilderness hiking trail. I was told to camp out at the taped-off spot last night and wait for the woman in the picture to show up today. When she did, the plan was for me to jump her, knock her to the ground, then yell *gotcha!*"

"Gotcha?" David asked. "Why gotcha?"

"Because that's the site's catchphrase or whatever."

David slid toward the edge of his chair.

"So let me get this straight," he began. "You were

there at the site when law enforcement officers arrived earlier this afternoon?"

"Yep. And when I saw you all coming, I hid in a tree. I didn't know what role you all were playing in the prank. So I got out of Dodge and stuck to the script. I wasn't about to miss out on making five hundred dollars."

"Five hundred dollars," Chief Love repeated, as if shocked at the amount.

Christopher nodded his head arrogantly. "Yes, sirs."

"Wait," David said, holding up his hand. "Do you still have the picture of the woman that was sent to you?"

"I think so. It's on my cell phone. In my jacket pocket."

David glanced over at the chiefs. They both nodded their heads, indicating it was okay to uncuff him.

David stood up and unlocked Christopher's restraints. The suspect pulled out his phone, tapped the screen, then handed it to him.

"Here she is."

David leaned forward. His stomach flipped at the sight of Lena's image splayed across the screen. He immediately recognized where the photo had come from. It was her profile picture on Instagram.

Both of the chiefs moved in closer and eyed the photo. David could feel the anger coming off them as they grunted simultaneously, then looked away.

David turned his attention back to Christopher, anxious to pump him for more information.

"Did the person requesting this job share with you the reason behind wanting to have this woman attacked?" he asked.

"Yep," Christopher said before taking several more sips of soda.

David felt a sudden urge to jump across the table and strangle him.

"*Well*, what was it?" he prompted.

"He said that him and the woman had been pulling pranks on each other for years. A few weeks ago, they were jogging out on that trail, and she faked like she was having a heart attack. The guy thought she was dead. Scared the crap outta him. So he wanted to get back at her. He knew she'd be out there running today and sent me to prank her."

Chief Love slammed his fist against the table and jumped up from his chair.

"Looks like the only ones who got *got* is us!" he barked, before walking out and slamming the door behind him.

David could tell by the distressed frown on Chief Scott's face that he wanted to follow suit. But David wasn't ready to let up.

"So, how do you receive your payments?" he continued.

"Anonymously. Through a mobile payment service."

David closed his eyes and rubbed them rigorously. Chief Love was right. The only ones who'd been had was them.

"So, uh," Christopher began, "am I gonna get arrested? Or can I get sent home for good behavior?"

Chief Scott tapped David's arm and stood up.

"Why don't we take a break?" he suggested.

"I think that's a good idea," David told him. "Christopher, give us a minute. We'll be back soon."

"Yeah, sure. I mean…um—sirs, yes, sirs!" he hollered, jumping up from his chair and saluting them as they left the room.

"Just keep walking," the chief muttered to David.

"Hey!" Christopher called out. "When you corporals come back, can you bring me another soda? And maybe a corned beef sandwich with a bag of chips or something—"

David shut the door behind him before Christopher could finish.

"I cannot believe this…this *foolery*!" Chief Scott roared. "How am I supposed to go inside that observation room and face Lena? We really screwed this up, Detective."

"Chief, we're pulling out all the stops to try and solve this case. Lena knows that. Every plan isn't going to work, unfortunately. But hopefully we're getting closer. And keep in mind we are dealing with a cold, calculated, highly intelligent psychopath here. Organized serial killers like this one are the most difficult to catch."

Chief Scott leaned against the wall. He pulled a handkerchief from his shirt pocket and ran it across his sweaty, balding head. "You're right. But in hindsight, putting out that fake press release was a bad idea. The killer guessed right. He figured out what we were doing and used it against us. Imagine how thrilled he must be right now."

"Yeah, well, it was still a good effort," David insisted, giving the chief's arm a supportive pat. "And if the suspect is in fact gloating, then he'd better enjoy his freedom while it lasts. Because now that he's pissed off your entire force *and* Clemmington's? Trust me. This will be the last time he gets one over on us."

"Let's hope so. We have *got* to get this maniac off the street before he strikes again."

"We will." David glanced over at the observation room door. "Should we go in and check on our girl?"

"Yes. We should. Then we'll regroup and figure out what to do with that goofball *prank master* Christopher."

David stifled a chuckle and followed Chief Scott inside the room. He noticed Lena's father embracing her tightly.

Chief Scott paused. He glanced over at a group of LAPD officers huddled in a corner.

"Could you all please give us a minute?" he asked them. "I'd like to have a word with Lena and the Clemmington PD."

"Yes, sir," the officers said as they walked out.

Once the door was closed, Chief Scott approached Lena.

"I cannot apologize to you enough for what happened tonight," he began. "We put everything we had into this operation. However, I had no idea that our suspect would figure out—"

Lena's father held up his hand.

"I'm sorry to interrupt you, Chief. But that's not why Lena's upset. She just received a very disturbing email."

Miles handed Lena's phone to Chief Scott. David peered over his shoulder, eyeing the message.

My Dearest Lena,
You poor, pitiful soul. Did you and your little comrades really think I would be stupid enough to fall for that amateur trap? Yes? Well LOL, the joke's on you, bitch! The LAPD must really be disappointed in you. Do you think they'll miss you when you're dead? Because for my next act, I won't be pulling a prank. I'll be carving the other half of that heart into your chest, then choking the life out of you. Enjoy your last days while you can...
Yours truly,
Committer of the Heart-Shaped Murders

David's entire body shook with rage. He looked over at Lena, devastated by the sight of her tearstained face.

"Your computer forensics expert is already investigating the origins of the email," Miles told Chief Scott.

"He's assuming that the killer sent the message using a VPN that would hide his identity. But he's going to take a crack at it anyway."

"Good," David said, hoping that no one noticed the tremor in his tone. "The Clemmington PD already looked into another email Lena received from him. It was sent through an encrypted VPN tunnel. And the text messages she's been getting were delivered through a secure app that doesn't store data. So we were unable to trace them back to the sender."

"My God." Chief Scott sighed before handing the phone back to Miles. "Who in the hell are we dealing with here?"

"Have you thought about bringing in the FBI?" Jake asked the chief.

"I have. But I'm hesitant. We've made a lot of headway on this case. I don't want them coming in and trying to take over."

"At this point, maybe we should consider it," Chief Love interjected. "I know we're highly skilled and all, but I think it's safe to say we might be in over our heads with this one."

"What do you think, Lena?" David asked her softly. "Should we continue this investigation on our own? Or is it time to bring in reinforcements?"

She opened her mouth to speak. But instead of a response, Lena shrugged her shoulders.

"David," her father said, "why don't you take Lena home? We'll stay here and wrap things up with Christopher." He glanced down at his daughter. "Are you okay with that, hon?"

She stepped away from him and nodded her head, still unable to speak.

"And you're sure you don't need to go to the hospital and get checked out?"

"No," she said. "I'm fine. I just wanna get out of here."

David walked over and wrapped his arm around her protectively. "Come on. Let's get you home."

Miles gave Lena a quick hug and patted David on the back. "We'll call and check in with you all once we get back to the hotel."

"Sounds good, man," David replied. "Thanks."

"See you soon, sis," Jake said.

Lena threw him a feeble wave, then leaned into David as he held on to her tightly. The pair walked through the station in silence. Just when they reached the exit, she stopped abruptly and turned to him.

"I don't think I can do this anymore," she blurted out. "Maybe we do need to bring in the FBI. And—and I should stop working the case. As a matter of fact, maybe I need to stop working as a forensic investigator altogether. Because at this point, these murders are happening because of me. It's *my* fault these people are being killed."

"Hold on, Lena. Listen to me. You are not the cause of these murders. So don't put that on yourself. Now, you're exhausted and shaken up, which is perfectly understandable. Let's not make any rash decisions. Why don't we go back to your place, order some food and get some rest? Drop all talk of the investigation for now. How does that sound?"

Lena stared up at David. The expression on her face was so soft and vulnerable that he almost bent down and kissed her.

"That sounds good," she whispered before allowing him to lead her out the door.

Chapter Eighteen

"This might sound weird," Lena said, "but I am so happy to be back in Clemmington."

"That does sound weird, coming from you," her mother agreed, reaching across the kitchen table and clutching her daughter's hand. "I'm glad to hear it, though. But once again, I wish your visit was under more pleasant circumstances."

"Yeah. So do I."

It had been three days since Lena left LA. She tried to hang in there and continue assisting with the investigation. But she'd grown frustrated when Christopher was only charged with minor assault and released from the county jail due to overcrowding. He also hadn't provided law enforcement with any information that would help lead them to the killer.

Then when the LAPD failed to make any headway or come up with a new plan to catch the suspect, she decided that she'd had enough. Lena and David packed up and headed back to Clemmington, rejoining her father and brothers, who'd left the city two days after the botched sting operation.

"I just feel more comfortable being here at home, surrounded by my family," Lena said.

"As you should. There's nothing like family, honey.

No matter the situation, you can always depend on us. And I'm including David in that equation, too."

"So am I," Lena responded, giving her mother's hand a slight squeeze.

"Speaking of David, what's going on between you two?"

"What do you mean?"

Betty threw Lena a sly side-eye. "You know what I mean."

"No, actually I don't," Lena insisted, playing coy before jumping up from the table and grabbing their coffee cups. "Time for a couple of refills. Do you want another muffin?"

Her mother chuckled and waved Lena off. "Way to change the conversation, kiddo. You always were good at that."

"Good at what?" she shot back, continuing to deflect from the topic at hand. "Look, all I'm saying is that I'd like to splurge on another chocolate chip muffin. Will you be joining me?"

"Twist my arm, why don't you. Meaning yes, throw a chocolate croissant on a plate for me."

Lena refilled their cups with hazelnut coffee and set them on a tray, added the plate of pastries, and carried it over to the table.

"Can you at least admit that you and David share a special bond?" Betty asked.

Lena sighed as she sat back down. "Yes, I can admit that David and I share a special bond. But as far as us getting back together is concerned, I don't see that happening."

"Why not?"

"Because our past is so rocky. And I can't help but

think that a part of him still resents me for moving away. He believes that's what ultimately ruined our relationship."

"Did he tell you that?" Betty asked.

"In so many words, yes."

Her mother sat quietly, taking several sips of coffee before turning to her daughter.

"A lot's changed since then, Lena. I personally think you and David are good for one another. And with you spending so much time here in town, working down at the station with him and your dad and brothers, it seems to me that everything is falling into place."

"Yeah, except the fact that this serial killer is still on the loose. Honestly, Mom? Until he's been apprehended, I can't even think about anything else."

"I can understand that. I'm sorry, honey. I'll drop it. But I do have something else on my mind. Now that you're back home, please don't run off on your own and investigate any more crime scenes. I don't care what happens. Understood?"

Lena stared down at her muffin and picked at the chocolate chips.

"Understood," she muttered.

The conversation was interrupted when Lena's cell phone buzzed. Her mother stood up and grabbed her coffee and croissant.

"I'll let you get that while I head to my bedroom," Betty said. "My book club's Zoom meeting is starting in a few minutes."

"Okay. Enjoy."

Lena grabbed her cell. The words *No Caller ID* appeared on the screen.

She held her hand to her chest. Her heartbeat stuttered erratically as she debated whether or not to answer the call.

The old you would've picked up on the first ring, she thought to herself.

But things had changed. Ever since the brutal attack, she no longer possessed that fiery sense of fearlessness.

The call went to voice mail. Lena studied the screen, waiting to see if the caller would leave a message.

She jumped back in her seat when the phone buzzed again. The person was calling back.

"Come on, you can do this," Lena said out loud. "Answer the call."

On the fourth ring, she finally got up the nerve to pick up. "Hello?"

"Hel-hello. May I, uh…may I please speak to Lena Love?"

Lena sat back in her seat, confused at the sound of the woman's soft, timid voice.

"Speaking," she said. "May I ask who's calling?"

"Um, I'd rather not say."

"Okay," Lena replied slowly. "How may I help you?"

The caller remained silent.

Lena stood up and walked over to the deck's sliding glass doors. She stared out into the backyard, contemplating whether she should hang up the phone. But something told her to stay on the line.

"Hello?" Lena asked. "Are you still there?"

"I'm here. I just— I'm a little nervous, that's all. Actually, I'm a lot nervous."

"Why is that?"

"Because I've got some information that may help solve your murder investigation."

Lena jumped back so fast that she almost tumbled to the floor. She grabbed hold of the door handle and slid it open, then stepped out onto the deck. Her bare feet pounded against the cedar boards as she began pacing back and forth.

"I'm listening," Lena said, biting her tongue so she wouldn't bombard the woman with a barrage of questions.

"So, the killer. I think you know him."

Lena stopped abruptly. It felt as though a splinter had torn through her heel. But she was too focused on the conversation to acknowledge the pain.

"Really?" she panted. "And what would make you think that?"

"I can't tell you. Just trust me. You do."

Lena looked out at the alleyway in the back of the house, just to make sure that the squad car was still there. It was. Ever since she'd returned to Clemmington, her father had cruisers patrolling both the front and back of the house at all times.

"Well," Lena said, "are you going to tell me who you think the killer is?"

"I want to. But I can't."

"Look, is this some type of prank call? Because I honestly don't have time to—"

"This is *not* a prank call," the woman interrupted. "I'm trying to clue you in on who I think the killer is without saying too much. If I do, I'd never forgive myself."

Lena walked over to the edge of the deck and leaned against the railing.

"Why is that?" she asked.

"Because I know the person. All too well."

"Okay then." Lena sighed. "What *can* you tell me?"

The other end of the line went silent for several seconds.

"Hello?" Lena practically shouted.

"I'm here. Sorry. Like I said, I'm nervous."

Lena closed her eyes and inhaled slowly.

Be patient, she told herself. *Let the woman go at her own pace.*

The sound of heavy panting came swooshing through Lena's eardrum.

"Your suspect runs a website called *Gonna Get Got*," the caller blurted out.

Lena's eyes shot open. She gripped the phone after it almost slipped out of her hand.

This call is legit...

"Wait," Lena said. "How do you know that?"

"Like I said, I don't feel comfortable sharing too much information. For a number of reasons. There's too much at stake. Just take what I'm giving you and go from there. Find the person who runs the site, and you'll find your killer."

"Listen, you have *got* to help me out here. Please. I'm begging you."

The other end of the phone went silent once again.

"Please," Lena insisted as tears filled her eyes. "I'm desperate. And I—"

"I saw the video of you being attacked out on the hiking trail on the *Gonna Get Got* website," the woman interrupted.

"*What?* How? Who recorded it? The LAPD caught the kid who attacked me. He didn't do it. Law enforcement ran an analysis on his phone."

"Your suspect recorded it."

Lena froze. Despite the steamy California heat, she was overcome by a frigid chill. The thought of the killer being at the scene, filming the prank while surrounded by two police forces, almost brought her to her knees.

"Are you still there?" the woman asked.

"Yes. I'm here. I, uh—I'm in shock over what you just told me."

"I can imagine." The caller paused, then inhaled sharply. "Look, I will tell you this. When it comes to *Gonna Get Got*, your suspect usually hires what he calls prank masters to do the jobs. But if a request comes in one thousand dollars or more, he'll perform the prank himself."

"One thousand dollars," Lena blurted out. "What kind of prank is worth that much money?"

"The deadly kind."

"Wait. People are paying this man to commit murder?"

"Not exactly. They're paying him to bring people to the brink of death. Just to mess with their heads."

Lena's mind raced as she began pacing the deck again. A flurry of questions flew through her head. She ran back inside the house and into the dining room.

"And another thing I noticed," the woman continued, "is that your suspect seems to take on jobs that'll give him some sort of personal satisfaction—"

She abruptly stopped speaking. Lena heard the sound of a man's voice booming in the background.

"Jan!" he yelled. "You home?"

"I've gotta go!" the woman hissed.

"Wait! Can you just finish what you were saying? What do you mean by *personal satisfaction*?"

"You're gonna have to figure that out for yourself."

Lena flung open her laptop. "Well, can you at least tell me how to gain access to the website—"

Before she could finish, the line went dead.

"Dammit!" Lena yelled.

Her fingers fumbled as she tried to dial David's cell phone number. On the third attempt, she finally succeeded. But the call went straight to voice mail.

"David! Call me ASAP! I just received some new information about the case."

Lena disconnected the call and frantically typed a text message to him, insisting that he call her immediately.

After sending the message, she thought about her car. She was so tempted to jump inside, rush down to the police station and find David.

Don't do it, a voice inside her head warned. *You made a promise to your family. And to David...*

Lena slammed her laptop shut. A fiery ball of anger exploded inside her chest. She couldn't stand the hold that this killer had on her. It'd left her feeling anxious and powerless.

You have got to think of something. Something that'll catch him at his own game...

Chapter Nineteen

David slid his laptop toward Lena and enlarged the website displayed on the screen.

"My digital forensic investigator was able to download a dark web browser onto my laptop, which enabled access to *Gonna Get Got*," he said. "Our search capabilities are limited, though. We won't be able to view any of the videos or other exclusive content until our membership is approved. Once it is, we can go from there."

Lena leaned forward, focusing on the computer screen while sipping a glass of wine. "Wonderful. I'm just glad we were able to gain access."

She and David were sitting in the middle of his living room, cozied up on his chocolate-brown leather sofa. After receiving Lena's messages earlier that day about the anonymous phone call, David immediately went to work on infiltrating the website.

"It looks pretty sinister, doesn't it?" David asked, pointing at the screen. "That black background against the eerie, bright red font."

"A font that appears to be bleeding, no less."

"Exactly. And the logo, with the GGG lettering and photo of a distorted Japanese oni mask, is quite disturbing. Those three *G*'s actually remind me of the devil's number, 666."

"Well, think about it," Lena said. "An oni is an evil being that haunts the spirit world. Our killer is an evil man who's haunting the entire state of California. Seems fitting to me."

"Yes, it does."

Goose bumps formed underneath the raised hairs on David's forearms as he studied the oni's image. Two large gold horns were growing from its head. Its long, wild hair, cracked red skin, and ogre-like features were chilling.

David tapped the menu button. "We need to figure out how to navigate this site. The administrator certainly doesn't make it easy to access any of the content. Even the stuff that isn't exclusive."

"Seems like that's all a part of the allure. Figuring out how to crack the code just adds to the mystery. If this is how our suspect spends his free time, it gives us even more insight into how twisted he really is."

David could feel Lena's eyes on him as he continued to search the site. When she slid closer toward him, her thigh brushed up against his. A bolt of heat shot straight up his leg and settled in his groin.

Stay focused, he told himself while trying not to squirm in his seat. *Tonight is about business. This is not a social call...*

"Thank you again for having me over for dinner," Lena said. "I really needed this."

"And I need for you to stop thanking me. Like I told you earlier, this was the least I could do. You've been working so hard and taking so many hits with this investigation. So for me to throw a couple of mouthwatering steaks and ears of corn on the grill, sauté a little asparagus, and stop off at your favorite bakery to pick up a silky vanilla key lime pie was nothing."

Lena squeezed David's shoulder playfully, then held her hand to her ear. "What was that I just heard? Could it have been the sound of you tooting your own horn?"

He sat straight up and glanced around the room. "Huh? I didn't hear a thing."

Her hand drifted down toward the small of his back. David was surprised when she kept it there.

"I do have to admit, though," she said, "dinner was delicious. You outdid yourself. It certainly was a big change up from all the noodles, chicken nuggets and tater tots you used to cook back in the day."

"Um, excuse me. Let's not get it twisted. If I can recall correctly, you used to devour everything I made."

"Yeah, I did," Lena quipped. She took a sip of wine, then paused.

When David glanced over at her, she smiled slightly. It appeared as though Lena was lost in thought.

"On a serious note," she continued, "there's something else that I'd like to thank you for."

"Really? What's that?"

"Thank you for always taking care of me. And protecting me. And wanting what's best for me. I do realize that I could've handled things better before I moved to LA. But I was so eager to get my career started that I neglected to deal with our relationship the right way. As well as your feelings. So for that, I apologize."

David parted his lips to speak. But he couldn't find the right words to say. He was too taken aback. Because everything Lena had just said was all he ever wanted to hear.

"And you don't have to respond to any of that," she added. "We can leave it right there. I just wanted you to know how I was feeling."

David cleared his throat. "Well, I appreciate you sharing that with me. It means a lot. More than you'll ever know, actually."

"Now you're making me wish I would've shared it a long time ago."

"You should have. I think it would have avoided a lot of hurt feelings and resentment. At least on my end."

"Mine, too," Lena murmured.

David felt a singeing arousal swirl inside his chest. His eyes searched Lena's remorseful expression and landed on her soft lips. They lingered along the curves of her petite figure, which was well-defined in her fitted white jumpsuit. The sight of her voluptuous cleavage, which was perfectly positioned within the low-cut neckline, caused him to readjust his navy trousers.

"Would you like another glass of wine?" he asked, eager to change the subject in hopes that it would quell his excitement. "Or a second piece of pie?"

Lena placed her hand over her flat stomach. "If I put another morsel of food inside my mouth, I swear my jumper might burst at the seams. So no. I'll pass on the pie. I may have one more glass of wine in a bit, though. But for now, why don't we try and figure out how to find our way around this *Gonna Get Got* site?"

"Good idea. Oh, and didn't you mention earlier that you came up with some sort of plan you think might help us catch the killer?"

Lena twisted her lips and shrugged her shoulders, as if she were having second thoughts. "Eh, I thought I had something, but I don't know if it'll work."

"Look, at this point we need all the ideas we can get. So come on. Let's hear it."

She stared down at her fidgeting fingers. "After we tried to pull off the whole press release ruse and failed, I don't know how you'd feel about this."

"Try me."

"All right. Here goes. Once we receive the confirmation that we're officially members of the *Gonna Get Got* site, we should submit some sort of high-price prank request that we know the killer will take on himself."

"Hmm." David sighed thoughtfully, running his hand down his goatee. "You know what? I actually like that idea. I like it a lot."

"You do?"

"Yeah. I do. But whatever we come up with has got to be foolproof and go off without a hitch. We can't afford another misstep."

"I agree."

"So what type of prank did you have in mind?"

Lena paused once again. As she stared down at her glass, David got the sense that she was holding something back.

"I know that expression," he said. "The rapidly blinking eyes. The tightened lips. I still remember it from back in the day, when you'd want to share something with me but were afraid of how I'd react. As a matter of fact, it's the look you gave me right before you announced your move to LA."

Lena sat back and stared at him intently. "Sometimes I hate that you know me so well. Better than anyone else, honestly."

Maybe it's an indication that we belong together, David almost blurted out. But he quickly caught himself.

"So come on then," he continued. "Let's hear the plan."

"Okay, but before I start, promise me that you'll keep an open mind."

"Uh-oh." David picked up the bottle of Pinot Noir

and refilled their glasses. "Sounds like this is gonna require more wine."

"Trust me, it will." Lena grabbed her glass and took a long sip before continuing. "So, while I don't have an *exact* plan for the prank request that we should submit, I do have a couple of suggestions. First, I think we should set the price high on how much we're willing to pay. That way, we can guarantee that the killer will take on the job himself."

"Good thinking. And I agree."

"I also think that we should use me as the subject. Let our suspect know in advance that the prank is aimed directly at me."

David abruptly pushed his laptop off to the side and jumped up from the couch.

"*Absolutely* not," he insisted.

David noticed Lena flinch as he stormed across the mahogany hardwood floor. He stopped at the picture window, staring up at the bright three-quarter moon in search of the right words to say.

Chill, he told himself. *Don't lose your cool and ruin the evening over a bad idea.*

David turned back around.

"I hope you're joking right now," he said. "Because you cannot seriously be making such a reckless suggestion."

Lena set her glass down on the table and stood up. She walked over to David and took his hands in hers.

Her soft, warm touch caused his anger level to drop several notches. David's heaving chest settled as he stared down at her.

"Just hear me out," she said softly. "You're the one who said we can't afford any missteps this go-round. We've got to do something that will guarantee an arrest. Everything we've tried so far hasn't worked. But finding out that this man runs a website that could give us direct access to him is priceless. We have got to seize this opportunity. And unless we come up with a plan that'll put us in his presence, we'll keep failing, and he'll keep killing."

"But what if your plan gets *you* killed?"

"It won't. I trust that Clemmington's police force, along with the LAPD, will protect me. And honestly, if we don't do something soon, he's going to kill me anyway."

Lena's words chilled David to his core. He remained silent for several moments before giving her hands a gentle squeeze.

"Look," he said, "I can't say that I agree with your idea one hundred percent. But I'm willing to be open-minded while we work on a viable plan."

"That's all I'm asking you to do. Now, why don't we drop the subject for now? Let's sit back down and finish our wine."

David felt the tingling sensation of Lena's thumbs caressing his palms. He stood there for a moment, gazing at her. His mind drifted to the past, back when they were still together and happily in love.

He took a step toward her. She leaned into his chest. Just as he bent down and pressed his lips against hers, his cell phone vibrated inside his pocket.

"Ooh!" Lena gasped, quickly backing away from him.

David couldn't tell which she was more startled by—the kiss or the phone.

"Sorry about that," he muttered, irritated by the interruption.

He reached down and pulled out the phone. A text message from his digital forensic investigator appeared on the screen.

Your membership to the *Gonna Get Got* website has been activated. You'll now be able to create a profile, send and receive messages, and access exclusive content. Let me know if there's anything I can do to assist in the investigation.

"We're in," David said as he wrapped his arm around Lena's waist and led her back over to the couch.

As much as David wanted to cross the line and take their relationship in a more intimate direction, he knew that now was not the time. They needed to stick to the business at hand—catching the killer before he struck again.

Chapter Twenty

Dear *Gonna Get Got* Administrator,

I would like to hire a prank master to pull a stunt on my ex-girlfriend. I want her to think that this is a real-life situation, and I am her hero. My goal is to get her back. Below are the details of the job:

The prank will take place in the city of Berkshire, at a restaurant called The Ocean Grill. I know the owner and will make arrangements for him to rent the place out to me after hours. I'll bring my ex there, giving her the impression that this is a private dinner date and I'm issuing an elaborate apology.

I will drop her off in front of the restaurant while I go and park the car. The prank master will act as the restaurant's maître d' and escort her inside. He'll need to wear a full disguise. Wig, beard, glasses, the whole nine, so that he's unrecognizable. He will take my ex down to the restaurant's lower level. Once the door closes behind them, he'll lock it and pull out a fake gun. He'll then tie her up and hold her hostage, acting as if he's going to rob her.

That's when I'll show up, banging on the door. The prankster will give her the impression that he's going to kill me. I'll kick the door in and rush down the stairs. The fake gun will shoot blanks. I'll act as if I'm dodging the bullets, and the prank master and I will get into a pseudo tussle. I'll overtake him, grab hold of the gun, and keep him at bay until my ex and I can escape. We will flee the scene and I'll act as if I'm calling the police. I won't. I will have someone call me and pretend that the suspect got away before cops arrived.

I have attached a photo of my ex-girlfriend. I am willing to pay $2,000 for this prank. I hope that you agree to these terms, and look forward to hearing back from you. Thank you.

Lena read over the message one last time, then emailed it to David for his approval.

The pair had worked on the plan for three days straight after their dinner at his house. Once they settled on the specifics, Lena agreed to draft the details.

But the plan laid out in the message wasn't the one they intended to follow. An undercover LAPD officer would play the role of Lena's ex-boyfriend and drive her to the restaurant. The Ocean Grill was owned by a friend of Berkshire's police chief, so he'd be in on the stunt.

The Clemmington PD and LAPD would have The Ocean Grill discreetly surrounded. As soon as the undercover cop pulled in front of the restaurant, Lena would step out of the car. When the killer approached the vehicle to escort her inside, law enforcement would jump in and place him under arrest.

That was the plan. Lena prayed that this time, it would actually work.

Her thoughts were interrupted by a ping from her laptop. She rolled over to the other side of her bed and double-clicked the email inbox. A new message from David popped up on the screen.

Your request to *Gonna Get Got* looks great. I'll send it to Chief Love and Chief Scott for their approval. You know that neither of them are fully on board with this idea. They both think it's radical and dangerous. Nevertheless, since you're set on the plan and we've run out of options, they're willing to go with it. We just have to prove that our strategy to keep you safe is bulletproof. I'll keep you posted on their responses.

Lena wrote David back, letting him know that she'd be anxiously waiting to hear back from him. She then closed out her email and pulled up the internet.

Clemmington PD's digital forensic investigator had downloaded the dark web browser onto her laptop so that she could access *Gonna Get Got*. To say that she'd become obsessed with the site was an understatement. Lena had viewed practically every video that'd been posted, from the funnier pranks to the more intense, to those that were downright dark and evil.

For some reason, she hadn't been able to find the video of Christopher attacking her out on the Cucamonga hiking trail. She wondered if the killer had taken it down.

She refreshed the website one last time. Lena suspected that a new video had not been posted within the last few minutes. But she couldn't help but check anyway.

Just as she placed her hand along the top of the laptop to shut it, a huge ball of fire burst onto the screen. The sound of a detonating bomb blasted through the speakers. The words *NEW VIDEO ALERT!!!* flashed rapidly.

Lena shot straight up and pulled her computer in closer.

"What the…"

She leaned forward and double-clicked the play button. The screen faded to black. The word *DISLOYALTY* slowly appeared. Its bold red letters grew larger as they moved to the forefront. The haunting beat of an ominous bass drum boomed in the background.

Lena held her breath. The screen faded to black again. Then a brightly lit kitchen appeared. A woman was standing at a stainless steel sink, staring out the window. Her back was to the camera. She was holding a cell phone up to her ear.

The sound of the bass drum abruptly stopped.

"You're gonna have to figure that out for yourself," the woman whispered into the phone.

She disconnected the call and turned around. The white scrunchie holding her long blond hair in place fell to the floor. Her pale green eyes widened. Her body stiffened at the sight of whoever was holding the camera.

"What are you doing?" Lena heard the man holding the camera ask.

"Nothing," the woman croaked. "I was—I was just, uh, washing up a few dishes."

The cameraman crept toward the woman. She recoiled. Her hands shook as she grabbed a dish towel off the beige granite countertop and rubbed her palms against it.

"Who was that you were talking to?"

"The, um, the gas company. They wanted to know when they could come out and inspect the meter."

"And you told them that they need to figure it out for themselves?" he asked. "How does that work?"

The cameraman zoomed in on the woman's face. A thin film of perspiration covered her flushed, gaunt cheeks.

Lena's heart began to race. She covered her mouth, anxious for what was to come.

"I'm sorry, I didn't hear you," the man continued

after the woman failed to respond. "I said, *how does that work?*" he repeated, his voice rising in anger. "And why would you just hang up on the customer service rep so rudely like that?"

The woman's lower lip began to quiver. Her eyes filled with tears. It was clear that she feared whoever was standing on the other side of the camera.

"I don't know," she whispered.

Lena clenched her hands together tightly. She bit the inside of her cheek as adrenaline-fueled anxiety filled her chest. The video didn't appear to be some sort of prank. Lena felt as though this woman was in real danger, and she had a sinking feeling that things weren't going to end well for her.

"I don't know!" the man mocked her in a whiny tone.

The camera suddenly moved away from the woman. It looked as though the cameraman was walking out of the room.

"Wait, is that it?" Lena muttered aloud. "It's over? What was the point of—"

She stopped midsentence when the cameraman focused on a round wooden table. There was an open laptop sitting in the middle of it.

"Wait, what is going on here?" he asked, zooming in closer.

"No," the woman whimpered. "No, *wait!*"

He aimed the camera back at her as she hurried across the room and lunged across the table. But before she could slam the laptop shut, he pulled it away from her.

"Have you been going through my stuff?" the man yelled. *"Again?"*

"No! I was, I was just looking for some—"

"Don't lie to me!" he roared. "You're still spying on me, and I'm sick of it!"

The man stormed toward her. She ran across the kitchen, screaming out in pain after banging her hip against the edge of the island's granite countertop.

"Oh no," Lena moaned, watching as the woman cowered in the corner against a pantry door.

The cameraman moved toward her, zooming in on her twisted, terrified expression. His sinister chuckle creaked through Lena's speakers. He was clearly enjoying seeing the woman in fear.

"Aw, don't cry!" he insisted, his exaggerated tone dripping with sarcasm. "Now, tell me. Were you snooping through my computer? And did that snooping have anything to do with the call you were on just now?"

"No, no, no," the woman uttered, rapidly shaking her head from side to side. She raised her hands in the air, as if to protect herself.

"You're gonna pay for whatever it is you've done," the man growled.

Lena felt the urge to jump through her computer screen and save this helpless woman.

"*Please*," the woman mumbled, "I didn't do anything wrong."

"Oh, but your little secret phone call and my open laptop tell a different story."

The man's hand slowly inched toward the woman's throat.

"I'm gonna give you one last chance to come clean. Who were you talking to?"

"I told you. The gas co—"

Before she could finish, he wrapped his hand around her throat and squeezed tightly.

Lena screamed at the sight of his fingertips digging into her flesh.

"Stop!" the woman wheezed. "You're hurting me. I can't… I can't breathe. Come on. Stop it, Pe—"

Suddenly, the screen went black. The words *TO BE CONTINUED* appeared, then the video ended.

"Lena!" her mother called out. "You okay in there? Did I just hear you scream?"

"I'm fine! I just got startled by something I saw online."

"Okay. I'm making a pot of chili for lunch. It should be done in about an…"

Lena couldn't focus on what her mother was saying. She was too busy calling David to tell him about the video she'd just watched.

Chapter Twenty-One

David stood inside Walton's Antique Store, which was located next door to The Ocean Grill. Clemmington PD, along with LAPD, was swarming the area. They were waiting for Lena to arrive at the restaurant with undercover LAPD officer Chad Ingram.

David glanced down at his watch. It was a quarter to eight. Lena and Officer Ingram were due to arrive at eight o'clock.

David adjusted the volume on his radio adapter and pushed his Bluetooth headset farther into his ears.

"Ingram, what's your location?" he asked.

"We're heading down Berman Street now. So we should be arriving at the restaurant in about ten minutes."

"Ten-four. Lena, how are you doing? Hanging in there?"

"I am. Feeling good. And confident. I think this is it. This go-round, we're gonna catch that bastard."

"Yes, we are," David agreed, his deep voice filled with conviction.

He'd been worried that Lena would grow fearful as they got closer to the day of the stunt. Hearing her self-assured tone was a relief.

"We're all set on this end," he continued. "The LAPD's undercover officers are tucked away inside The Ocean Grill. We're still waiting for our suspect to arrive. He was supposed to be here at seven, but he sent me a message through the *Gonna Get Got* site claiming he's driving in from LA and got caught up in traffic."

Miles, who was standing next to David, threw him a look of doubt.

"I'm thinking he's going to wait until Lena and Officer Ingram get here before he shows up," Miles said. "Just to make sure that this whole thing is legit."

"Judging by his past behavior, that does sound like something he'd do," Lena said. "Is LAPD's undercover officer Braxton in position at the front of the restaurant?"

"Yes, he is," David confirmed. "And all of the officers have their earpieces in so that we can communicate with one another. Undercover officers are wearing body cams, too, and we're livestreaming the footage. So while Clemmington PD is here at Walton's, we can see everything that's going on next door with the surveillance system we've set up."

"So it sounds like we're fully covered on all ends," Lena said.

"Absolutely. No more slipups."

David and Lena were interrupted by Officer Ingram.

"We're about three minutes away," he said. "Any sign of the suspect's arrival?"

"Not yet," Chief Scott chimed in from the restaurant. "But we're keeping a close eye out. Why don't you all stay in the car until he gets here? When he pulls up, you two can act as if you're getting out of the car. Then when he heads toward the restaurant, we'll take him down."

"Will do," Officer Ingram replied.

David turned around and wiped his damp brow as he eyed the store. The lights were low, and officers were tucked away around the perimeter of the small establishment. They'd promised the owner that they wouldn't disturb any of his precious glass vases, lamps and statues lining the shelves. He made them swear not to go near the glass display cases that stood in the middle of the floor, which housed his fine jewelry, handbags and small heirlooms. So the officers made sure to steer clear of that area.

"We're turning the corner and heading down Roosevelt Boulevard now," Officer Ingram said. "We'll hang back by the end of the block until the suspect arrives."

"Ten-four," Chief Love said. He ducked down behind the antique store's picture window and peered through his binoculars. "I can see you coming this way. When we see the suspect's vehicle approaching, which Lena has confirmed may be a black sports car with large, spiked chrome wheels, we'll direct you to pull up in front of the restaurant."

"Copy that."

David unbuttoned the top button on his crisp white shirt. He ran his hands down the sides of his face as a strong mix of dopamine and adrenaline rushed through his system.

The temperature felt as though it was increasing by the minute. When his heart began to palpitate unsteadily, he closed his eyes and took a deep breath.

Be cool, he told himself. *Lena will be fine. This time, the plan will go off without a hitch...*

Those words ran through his mind over and over again until they were disrupted by the sound of a roaring car engine.

"That's him!" David heard Lena shriek. "That's our suspect's car. I'd recognize the sound of that engine anywhere."

David's eyes shot open. He bent down and hurried toward the window, startled by the unnerved tone in Lena's voice. Gone was the cool confidence she'd exuded just minutes before.

"Stay calm, Lena," David said soothingly, despite the fact that he was struggling to contain his own anxiety. "Everything is under control. We've got the scene completely surrounded, and there's no way that the suspect will even be able to get near you. Okay?"

"Okay," she replied, her tone slightly wavering.

David felt a throbbing pain shoot through his chest. Had he not known better, David would've thought that he was on the verge of having a heart attack. But ever since he'd begun working in law enforcement, he experienced the aching sensation whenever a big arrest was about to go down.

Take your own advice and calm down, he told himself.

David looked out onto the street. He saw a black sports car slowing down, creeping toward the front of The Ocean Grill.

"Looks like our suspect has arrived," Chief Love said. "Chief Scott, Officer Braxton, are you and your team in place and ready to go?"

"Yes, sir," Chief Scott responded. "You have no idea how ready we are."

"Imagine how I feel considering this maniac is coming after my daughter. Before this is all over with, you may have to stop me from choking him to death."

David reached over and gave Chief Love a reassuring pat on the back.

"Don't worry, sir. He's going to pay for what he's done, to Lena as well as all of the other victims."

The piercing sound of screeching tires filled the air. David looked out onto the street. The suspect had stopped his car a few feet in front of the restaurant.

"All right, team," Chief Scott said. "Let's get prepared to move—"

He stopped abruptly when the suspect pulled away from the curb.

"Come on!" the chief yelled. "Where the hell is he going?"

"Do you think we should have Lena and Officer Ingram pull up to the restaurant so that the suspect will see that they're here?" David asked. "Just in case he's having second thoughts?"

"Good idea. Lena, Ingram, head toward The Ocean Grill and park right in front."

"On the way, sir," Officer Ingram responded.

David's eyes remained glued to the street. He watched as Officer Ingram drove up to the restaurant's entrance.

The suspect's vehicle came to a sudden stop, about fifty feet away from the grill. He turned off the engine. The lights went out. But he remained inside the car.

"He's not getting out," Lena said.

David could once again hear the panic in her voice. He clenched his jaws together tightly, feeling uneasy with what he was about to suggest.

"Lena, we're going to need for you to step out of the car. I think that once the perp sees you, he'll get out, and then we'll jump in. Keep in mind he won't get near you. He'll only make visual contact. Okay?"

David waited for her to reply. She remained silent.

"Lena," Chief Love said quietly, "you can do this. We're all here to protect you. We just need for you to take this one extra step, and then it'll all be over."

After several moments passed, she finally responded.

"All right. I'm ready."

David was hit by a mix of emotions. Relief, then angst, then the one that he dreaded most. Fear.

Flashbacks of the prankster pouncing on Lena in the middle of the Cucamonga Wilderness trail filled his head. He was reminded of the sheer terror he felt at the sight of her being pummeled to the ground.

That won't happen again. Heed your own words. Trust that you and your fellow officers have this situation under control.

Despite the words of encouragement, David couldn't seem to stave off the feelings of doubt.

He snapped back to attention when Lena stepped out of the car.

"I'm on the move," she said.

Her sparkling silver pumps caught David's eye. His gaze traveled up her toned calves toward her fitted, shimmering gray wrap dress. The rhinestone hoop earrings she wore complemented her outfit. Even though they were in the middle of his most intense operation to date, he couldn't help but notice how beautiful she looked.

Lena clutched her handbag tightly. David could see her hands trembling from the store window.

"Stay calm, Lena," he said. "You're doing fine. Why don't you hang back by the car. Act like you're looking for something inside your purse while we wait for the suspect to exit his vehicle."

"Got it."

As Lena rummaged around inside her handbag, David turned his attention back to the perp's car. He still hadn't gotten out.

"What is this clown doing?" Chief Love muttered, staring at the suspect's vehicle through his binoculars. "Why hasn't he exited the vehicle yet?"

No sooner had the words left his mouth than the suspect's door opened.

"Hold on," Chief Scott interrupted. "It looks like we've

got movement. Team, the suspect is stepping out of the car. Everyone get in place and follow the plan. Lena, you and Officer Ingram stay put and remain preoccupied for now."

"Copy that," Officer Ingram replied.

David turned toward the perp. His rapid breathing grew shallow as the husky man climbed out of his vehicle.

The suspect was dressed in a black suit, white shirt and black bow tie. It was the exact outfit he was instructed to wear as the restaurant's maître d'. His short, shaggy brunette wig, dark sunglasses and bushy beard completely hid his identity.

"I see our suspect walking toward the restaurant," Officer Braxton said.

"Stick with the plan," Chief Scott told him. "Lena, start heading toward the grill's entrance. As soon as the suspect gets a little closer, the entire team is going to swoop in and take him down. Everybody got that?"

"Got it," Lena and the law enforcement officers replied in unison.

David turned to Chief Love. "This is it. This nightmare is finally going to be over."

"Let's hope so."

David followed the chief as he moved toward the door and hovered in the corner. Jake and Miles lined up beside them. Each of the officers drew their guns.

"The second that the LAPD initiates the takedown," Chief Love said into his earpiece, "Clemmington PD will exit the store and assist you."

David's heart was beating so forcefully that he could feel it in his throat. He leaned forward and peered out of the glass door. The suspect appeared to be taking his sweet time getting to the restaurant.

"Lena, stand down," Officer Braxton said. "I'm in

the grill's doorway now. I'm about to step out and meet the perp."

"And we'll be right behind you," Chief Scott said.

David watched as the suspect finally approached the restaurant. Lena was only a few feet away from him. Before he could approach her, Officer Braxton swung open the door. He reached out, as if to shake the killer's hand. Just when the two men made contact, David sprinted out of the store, followed by the rest of Clemmington PD.

Boom!

An ear-piercing explosion filled the air. David pressed his hands against his ears right before a blinding light impaired his vision.

David fell back against a window front. He closed his eyes, disoriented by the sudden mayhem.

"Hold on!" Chief Love yelled. "I think the perp detonated a stun grenade!"

David choked on the billowing smoke. He stumbled along the sidewalk, ignoring the ringing in his ears and flashes in his eyes.

Despite the explosion, Officer Braxton had managed to detain the suspect.

"Let's move in!" Chief Love commanded.

Clemmington PD ran over just as the LAPD swarmed the street. Organized chaos ensued when every officer approached the perp with their guns drawn.

David swooped in. Officer Braxton forced the suspect to the ground. David held the killer's legs down while Braxton forced his wrists into a pair of handcuffs.

"You have the right to remain silent," Chief Scott began. "Anything you say can and will be used against you in a court of law. You have the right to speak to an attorney…"

Once the perp's ankles had been secured in a pair of

shackles, David jumped to his feet. He stood steadfast with his weapon aimed at the killer. Along with the rush of excitement he was feeling, David was overcome by a calming relief.

We got him, he thought. *We finally got him. Thanks to Lena's brilliant plan...*

David gasped and spun around. In the midst of all the commotion, he had yet to check on Lena. Now that law enforcement had the killer detained, he began searching for her. But she was nowhere in sight.

"Hey, Officer Ingram!" he called out.

"Over here!" the policeman shouted.

David looked to his right and saw him standing against the restaurant's brick wall, coughing profusely.

"Where's Lena?" David asked. "Did she go back to the car?"

Officer Ingram doubled over. "I—I think I saw her run inside the restaurant," he wheezed. "But after that explosion, I'm not sure."

David darted inside The Ocean Grill and looked around frantically.

"Lena!" he called out. "*Lena!* Are you in here?"

There was nothing but silence. He ran toward the back and checked the restrooms. They were empty.

David charged through the restaurant and rushed back outside.

"Has anyone seen Lena?" he yelled, now looking around for her father and brothers.

Miles appeared from the middle of the huddle, just as the officers pulled the killer up on his feet.

"I thought she was with Officer Ingram," he panted.

"Yeah, so did I. She must've gotten disoriented after the grenade went off and tried to get to safety."

"Well, she's gotta be around here somewhere. Did you check Ingram's car?"

"No, good idea."

David darted down the street. On the way to Officer Ingram's vehicle, something caught his eye. He stopped abruptly.

There, on the edge of the cracked beige concrete, was a rhinestone hoop earring.

David gagged as he tried to take in a breath of air. A feeling of dread crept up his back. He turned around and ran back toward the group of law enforcement.

"Hold on!" he called out as Chief Scott and his team escorted the killer to a police cruiser.

The men paused. David approached the suspect. He looked closely at his chubby jawline. Traces of dried white glue lined the edges of his beard. David ripped it off.

"Ouch!" the perp exclaimed.

Without saying a word, David grabbed his black aviator sunglasses and snatched them off his face.

"Hey, what's up, Corporal?" the suspect exclaimed. "So we meet again. I hope I don't get arrested for real this time. It wasn't illegal for me to take on another prank job, was it?"

David felt his lungs constrict. His chest tightened as the air around him seemingly dissipated. He opened his mouth to speak but couldn't utter a word. Because there, standing in front of him, was Christopher Ware. The prankster from the Cucamonga Wilderness trail.

Chapter Twenty-Two

Lena was sprawled out in the back seat of a car. She'd been blindfolded, and her hands were bound behind her back with duct tape.

"I can't believe you people thought I was that damn stupid," she heard her kidnapper mutter. "I mean, seriously, if I was dumb enough to fall for this setup, do you really think I would've gotten away with all of these murders?"

Lena whimpered, her eyes stinging from a mix of tears and perspiration.

"Hey!" the kidnapper yelled. "I'm talking to you!"

"We—I—I don't know!" she stammered.

She shivered at the sound of the killer's sinister chuckle.

"I don't *knooow*!" he repeated, his tone emulating hers. "Well, let me tell you what *I* know. I know that you and your little inadequate cohorts made the biggest mistake of your lives tonight."

Lena bit her bottom lip, struggling to stifle the sobs that were creeping up her throat. She was determined not to show any signs of fear, despite the fact that she was completely terrified.

How the hell did I even get here? she thought to herself.

But once she'd regained her senses after the explosion, Lena remembered.

Back when they were at the restaurant, Officer Ingram was working overtime to protect her. He'd assured Lena that he had her back. Then the grenade detonated. She and the officer were separated. Lena was left standing on the sidewalk, alone.

She'd temporarily lost her sense of sight and sound. Once she came to, an officer dressed in black LAPD tactical gear appeared from a nearby alleyway and jogged over to her.

"Lena!" he said. "We got him! Are you okay?"

"I'm fine," she replied, her eyes squinting as she tried to peer through the tinted visor on his helmet. "I'm sorry, but I can't see very well out here. Could you please tell me who you—"

She was interrupted when one of the arresting officers shouted loudly.

"I said stay down and keep your hands where I can see them!"

The policeman who'd been speaking to Lena gently wrapped his arm around her.

"Oh no," he'd moaned. "The killer seems to be giving law enforcement a hard time. Come on. Let's get you to safety. I'll take you inside the restaurant through the back door so that you won't have to go near him."

"Thank you so much." Lena sighed.

She allowed the man to lead her through the alleyway. Once they'd reached The Ocean Grill, she made a right turn and headed toward the door.

"Wrong way," the man grunted before grabbing Lena's arm and shoving her inside an unmarked black sedan.

He'd moved so fast that she hadn't had a chance to fight back, or even scream. He snatched the earpiece out of her ears and the radio adapter from her hand. Before Lena knew it, she'd been bound and blindfolded. Within seconds, the killer was speeding down the alley.

And now here she was, alone, at the killer's whim, and undoubtedly on her way to being murdered.

"Oh, look!" the killer said. "Your cell phone! Well, let's disable this thing right now just in case your little boyfriend David is trying to track your whereabouts."

Dammit! Lena thought, so out of sorts that she hadn't even realized he'd confiscated her purse.

"You know," he continued, "I'll admit, that was a slick little attempt you made to try and trap me by submitting a prank request through my website. I was actually shocked when I saw your photo. And that price tag? There's no way I was gonna turn down two thousand dollars. But then my sixth sense kicked in. I thought to myself, *self, something is amiss here...*"

Lena forced herself to stop panting. She focused on the man's voice. It sounded eerily familiar.

"I bet you're wondering where we're going," he continued before cackling wickedly, then snorting. "Don't worry. You'll soon find out."

Lena assumed he was taking her to the Cucamonga Wilderness trail. That seemed like something he'd do; finish what he'd started in the same place where it had all begun. In his warped mind, he'd deem it poetic justice. She just hoped that David would somehow figure out a way to find her.

DAVID SHOVED CHRISTOPHER and pushed through the crowd of police officers.

"Get him the hell away from me!" he yelled. "Ingram!"

"He's over here," Chief Scott said.

David saw Officer Ingram standing against the side

of the restaurant, staring down at his black leather cap-toe shoes. His hands were shoved deep inside his pockets, and his distorted expression was riddled with regret. Chief Love, Miles and Jake were surrounding him with their arms crossed.

Ingram appeared remorseful for letting Lena out of his sight. And David knew his mishap wasn't intentional. Nevertheless, he was in no mood to console him.

"Dude!" he hollered, storming over to the group. "What the *fu*—"

"*Detective*," Chief Love interrupted, pressing his hand against David's chest, "please. The man feels bad enough. We're working to retrace his and Lena's steps so that we can track her down. So let's be respectful."

"Yes, *let's*," Officer Ingram interjected, shooting David a death stare.

David pushed past the chief and swung his arm back. Right before his fist connected with the policeman's jaw, Miles grabbed David and pulled him away.

"All right, let's go," Miles insisted, leading him down the street. "Let's walk it off."

"Walk it off? We need to go and find Lena!"

"That's what we're working on. The LAPD has already sent out several squad cars to search for her. Jake and I have been trying to track her cell phone, but it looks like it's been turned off."

"Has anybody tried to contact her cell phone carrier?" David asked.

"Officer Braxton put in a call to the LAPD's digital forensics expert. He's on it."

"Good." David dug his fingertips into his forehead and began pacing the sidewalk. "I cannot believe that idiot let Lena out of his sight. And I never should have let her talk me into this...this *prank*. The killer has been ten steps ahead of us the entire time. I don't know why I thought this time would be any different. And now, he's got my girl. I—I can't…"

David's voice broke. He bent down and pressed his hands against his knees, barely able to take in any air.

"Listen," Miles said, "we're going to find her. Believe me, I'm worried, too. But I'm trying to keep it together for the sake of you and my family."

Just as David felt Miles's hand on his shoulder, he shot straight up.

Miles jumped back, seemingly startled by the sudden move. "*Whoa*. Are you okay?"

David reached inside his back pocket and grabbed his cell phone.

"Did you happen to notice whether or not Lena was wearing her smart watch?" he asked, his eyes peeled to the phone screen.

"No, I didn't. Why?"

"Because she's got a GPS tracking system on it. If the killer has her, I'm assuming he confiscated her phone and turned it off so that we wouldn't be able to track her. But if she's wearing her smart watch, I might still be able to trace her whereabouts."

"Knowing Lena, she's got it on," Miles replied as he peered over David's shoulder. "And if that maniac does have her, hopefully she'll be able to keep it hidden from him."

"Let's hope so."

David pulled up a map on his phone. He tapped on the location services prompt and clicked Lena's name.

David held his breath, waiting to see if the green locator marker would appear.

Come on, Lena. Show me where you are…

"Anything showing up yet?" Miles asked.

"Not yet."

Just as David was hit with a sinking feeling, a green tab popped up on the map. He was so shocked that he almost dropped the phone.

"We've got movement!" he yelled.

"Where?" Miles asked frantically. "Where is she?"

David followed the white arrow guiding the green marker.

"Looks like she's heading toward Clemmington," he replied before taking off running. "I'm going to find her. I'll call you from the car for backup!"

Chapter Twenty-Three

Lena winced in pain as gritty dirt scraped against the bottoms of her bare feet. She stumbled forward, expecting to fall flat on her face until she was abruptly pulled back up.

"Come on!" the killer growled. "You know how to hike these cliffs. You should be a pro by now. Stay on your feet before I throw you over the edge."

Stay strong, Lena told herself, wishing she could peek over the top of her blindfold. *Do not show fear. Do not shed another tear...*

But despite the words of encouragement, feelings of doubt and hopelessness numbed her entire body.

This is really it. I'm going to die this time.

Lena was struggling to figure out where they were. She'd tried her best to move the blindfold by rubbing the side of her face along the back seat of the car. But it'd been tied so tightly that the blindfold had not budged.

The killer hadn't driven long enough for them to be in LA's Cucamonga Wilderness. Lena wondered whether he'd taken her to a new trail, where no one would think to look for her.

"Let's *go!*" her kidnapper insisted. He yanked her arm and pulled her forward. "Someone's waiting on us. And I can't *wait* for you two to meet."

Just as he emitted another one of his sinister laughs, Lena heard a woman scream in the distance.

What the...?

"There she is!" the man exclaimed. "That's her way of greeting you, Lena. Hey! Let's play a game. Good news and bad news. Which do you want first?"

Before Lena could respond, she felt a sharp rock cut into the ball of her right foot.

"Ouch!" she shrieked, once again tumbling forward.

Stinging pain shot up her leg. When the bottom of her foot grew damp, Lena knew she was bleeding. She cried out as grainy bits of earth crept into the fresh wound.

The killer appeared oblivious to her agony.

"I said, good news or bad news!" he repeated, his gruff tone growing more impatient.

Ignore the pain, Lena thought. *Mind over matter. Mind over matter...*

"The good news," she mumbled through clenched teeth.

"All right, cool. So, the good news is, you won't have to die alone."

"Help me!" Lena heard the woman yell. *"Help!"*

Between the sound of her pleas, the killer's threats and her injured foot, Lena felt as though her limbs might give out. But she refused to collapse underneath the weight of the situation.

"Shut up!" the kidnapper hollered into the distance. "Quit being so damn impatient. We're coming!"

The man stopped. Lena felt him lean against her, his hot, stale breath singeing the side of her face. When the tip of his cold nose brushed against her earlobe, she cringed, but kept her composure.

"And now," he murmured, "the bad news. You *are* going to die. Now, let's go!"

Lena gasped as the man grabbed her legs, picked her up and threw her over his shoulder. She lost her breath while he ran full speed ahead. She bounced around wildly, almost falling several times. Lena held on by gripping the back of his jacket so tightly that her fingernails bent against the rough fabric.

The woman's screams grew louder. Which meant they were getting closer to her.

"Jan!" the man yelled. "Shut the hell up!"

When the woman screamed again, Lena heard a loud slap. And then, quiet whimpering.

Please God, Lena thought, *help me…*

"Okay, ladies," the man said. "This is the moment of truth. Are you ready?"

Neither of the women replied.

"I said, are you ready!" he hollered.

"Yes," they responded in distraught unison.

"All right, then. Here we go. Three, two, one. *Ta-da!*"

Lena squealed when she felt the man's grubby fingers grab the blindfold and rip it from around her head. She blinked rapidly, struggling to adjust her vision.

He shined a flashlight in her face. He then aimed it at a woman standing across from her.

Lena was horrified when she realized that the woman was tied to a tree. Her pale green eyes were drenched and swollen. And her long blond hair was stuck to her sweaty face and neck.

Lena froze. She took a closer look at the woman. For some strange reason, she looked familiar. The eyes, the hair…

The name Jan.

And that's when it hit Lena. The woman standing in front of her was the same person in the Disloyalty video on the *Gonna Get Got* website.

"Lena," the man began.

She turned to the killer, hoping to finally get a good look at him. But he was still wearing his tactical helmet.

"Meet Jan," he continued. "Jan, meet Lena. Now, technically, you two have already met. Because when Jan here overstepped her bounds by meddling in my business and finding my website, she had the nerve to call *you*, Lena, and drop a dime on me. Can you believe that? And what's worse, I had to choke the hell out of the bitch just to get her to admit it!"

As his voice grew louder, Jan writhed against the tree. She emitted a guttural howl.

"Didn't I tell you to shut up!" he yelled.

Lena expected him to go after Jan. But instead he lunged at her.

The killer grabbed Lena by the collar and shoved her against the tree. He leaned in and pressed his face against hers.

"You're probably wondering who this snitch is to me," he said, sneering. "Believe it or not, she's my *wife*. But not for long. Because in the next few minutes, she'll be a beautiful corpse, and I'll be a grieving widower. And as you for, Lena Love, you'll soon be nothing but a dead forensic investigator who failed to capture one of California's most prolific serial killers."

The man reached out and tucked several strands of Lena's hair behind her ear. Her chin trembled in disgust. She felt the urge to kick him in the groin.

That urge quickly subsided when he pulled a knife out of his back pocket.

Lena pressed her body farther into the tree. Its bark tore at her dress's thin silk material, scraping against her skin. Her foot throbbed uncontrollably. But she was so focused on the knife's long, sharp blade that she barely felt any pain.

"How are we going to get out of this?" Jan whispered to her. "I don't wanna die!"

Lena glanced over at the man. He slowly pointed the knife at her. She could hear his heavy panting. A slight moan rumbled when he exhaled. Bile crept up her throat as she sensed his excitement.

The blade of the knife grazed Lena's neckline. Jan screamed out.

"Help. *Help!*"

"I thought I told you to shut up!" the man yelled.

He swung the knife in Jan's direction. When she cried out, Lena glanced over at her. She was horrified to see that the man had slashed her cheek. Blood gushed from the gash and streamed down her neck.

"Your *throat* is gonna be next!" he told her.

The killer grabbed Jan's collar and tore at her blouse. Buttons went flying everywhere.

"Why are you *doing* this?" she sputtered. "You're insane!"

Lena tightened her lips, intent on suppressing the scream rumbling in the back of her throat.

The man tapped the tip of the knife against Jan's chin. She closed her eyes as her lower lip quivered. He dragged the blade down her neck, ignoring the blood that was dripping down her chest. When he pressed the knife into her flesh, she screamed out in pain.

"Stop it!" Lena couldn't help but yell.

"Stay out of this!" he demanded, reaching out and grabbing her neck. He squeezed tightly, then pushed her back.

Lena stumbled and fell against the side of the tree. Sharp-edged twigs sliced into her bare soles. She grunted loudly, fighting the pain while somehow managing to stay on her feet.

"You see this, Lena?" the killer barked.

She glanced wearily over at him. He was shining his flashlight directly at Jan. When he pointed the knife above her left breast, Lena saw that a heart had been carved into her chest.

"Aaah!" she shrieked before spinning around and taking off running.

Adrenaline numbed the pain in her feet. She ran as fast as she could, praying that she could somehow get away.

But just as she laid eyes on the hiking trail up ahead, Lena felt the kidnapper's hand on the back of her head. He grabbed a handful of hair, gripping it tightly while pulling her back.

She fell to the ground. But that didn't stop him. Despite her kicking and flailing, he dragged her across the ground like a rag doll. When they reached the tree, he yanked her back up onto her feet and shoved her hard against the trunk.

"Try that again," he growled, "and I'll stab you right in the heart."

Lena's entire body trembled uncontrollably. She was stunned by the sinister evil standing before her. And she knew that if law enforcement didn't arrive soon, both she and Jan would be killed.

Please, David, please come and find us...

Chapter Twenty-Four

"I've got Lena's exact location," David said to Miles, who he'd been talking to from the car. "Her watch is pinging near the Juniper hiking trail. Get here with backup. *Now!*"

"We're on our way!"

David disconnected the call and flew down the street. He pulled over in front of the trail's entrance so fast that his car jumped the curb.

David barely turned the engine off before he hopped out. He grabbed his Glock 22 from its holster and held it close before charging up the trail. When he heard a loud scream in the distance, David quickened his pace.

It didn't take long for him to reach the outskirts of the crime scene. He used the light from his cell phone to guide his footsteps, David ducked down and moved in swiftly, but carefully.

Within minutes, he noticed Lena leaning against a tree, next to a woman he didn't recognize. The killer was standing in front of the woman with what appeared to be his hand wrapped around her throat. He was dressed in all black and barely visible. But the flashlight he was holding shined a beam of brightness in the vicinity.

As he moved in closer, David let out a sigh of relief.

While Lena was far from being out of danger, at least she was still alive.

"Get down on your knees," he heard the killer yell. "Both of you!"

The man untied the rope binding the other woman to the tree. His head dropped down toward the ground as he watched the two women follow his command. David heard him cackle loudly as they knelt in front of him.

When the killer placed his hands underneath their chins and jerked their faces upward, David moved in closer. He cocked his gun and stayed low. The sight of a knife in the man's hands forced him to increase his speed.

Just as he approached the group, the sound of blaring sirens filled the air.

"What the...?" the killer said.

David ran toward him at full speed with his gun aimed at his chest.

"Police! Freeze!" David yelled. "Drop your weapon and get your hands up!"

The man slowly backed away from the women. Lena grabbed the other woman and pulled her to safety.

The killer was still moving away from David with the knife in his hand.

"Stop right where you are!" David ordered. "Drop the weapon and get your hands up. *Now!*"

"Yes, *sir!*" the suspect yelled, right before he jetted off into the woods.

"David!" Lena screamed. "Don't let him get away!"

"I won't!" David assured her as he started to run.

He aimed his gun at the killer, shot and missed.

"Dammit!"

The suspect bobbed and wove in between the trees. David shot again. The bullet ricocheted off a tree trunk and disappeared into the brush.

The killer was getting away. He appeared to know the wooded area well.

David increased his speed, ignoring the rough foliage scraping against his legs. When he heard a loud grunt and thud up ahead, he shined his cell phone's light in the distance.

The suspect had tripped over a thick branch and fallen to the ground.

"Freeze!" David yelled. "Stay down!"

He hurried over to the man, shoving his phone inside his pocket and pulling out his handcuffs, then securing his gun inside its holster.

"Ooow," the killer moaned. "I'm injured. I think I broke my leg…"

David ignored him. He was too busy grabbing his wrists. Just as David went to apply the handcuffs, the suspect quickly rolled over and kicked him in the groin.

"Ahh!" David yelled.

He fell over onto his back. The nauseating sting was excruciating. But when the killer tried to jump up and run off, David kicked out his leg. He hooked his right foot underneath the man's left calf.

The killer tumbled to the ground.

David fought through the pain shooting up his abdomen and sat up. As soon as he did, the suspect reached over and punched him in the jaw. Both men struggled to get to their feet. David made it up first. He hit the man with a swift uppercut to the chin, then unholstered and pointed his gun.

"If you make one more move," David huffed, "I will shoot you. And this time, I won't miss."

The killer slumped his shoulders in defeat.

"Detective Hudson!" David heard Miles call out. "Where are you?"

"Over here!"

The policeman ran up and quickly handcuffed the suspect.

The Clemmington PD and LAPD came rushing over. The women weren't far behind them.

When the law enforcement officers saw that David had finally caught the killer, they gave him a round of applause. Lena walked to the front of the group, clapping the loudest.

"I want you to remove that helmet," she said to David. "I've been waiting for a long time to finally see this man's disgusting face."

"It would be my pleasure," David said.

When he pulled off the helmet, Lena moved in and squinted her eyes, then gasped. She jumped back, covering her mouth in shock.

"Peter?" she uttered. "Peter Ballentine?"

"Wait, you know him?" David asked.

"I—I do. We went to Pacific Western University together. We were both studying to become forensic investigators."

Miles stepped forward, shaking his head from side to side. "Wait, this is Peter Ballentine? *The* Peter Ballentine? The guy who was always competing with you? And losing?"

Peter squared his shoulders and held his head high.

"Yes. That's me. *The* Peter Ballentine. And Lena may have won in the classroom. And gotten the job with the LAPD over me. But look at all the damage I've done to her. How good could she possibly be at her job, considering how long it took for you all to catch me? It took not one, but two police forces to take me down. *Two.* Ha!"

"All right," David said, gripping Peter's arm. "That's enough. We're taking you down to the station."

David noticed Lena's chest heaving up and down, as if she was struggling to catch her breath. Her father and brothers stood around her, offering up words of support.

Just as David stopped to check on her, Chief Scott stepped in.

"Detective Hudson," he said, "why don't you stay here and look after Lena? We can take the suspect into custody. And we'll make sure the other victim gets the medical attention that she needs, too. Lena," he continued, turning toward her, "are you sure you don't want to go to the hospital?"

"No. I'm fine," she said confidently. "I've got a few cuts and bruises, but I can treat them myself. Just get Jan to the hospital."

"We will. And I'll check back in with you and Detective Hudson shortly."

David nodded his head. "Thank you, sir."

Chief Scott and several members of the LAPD took hold of Peter. Before they walked away, Peter glanced back at Lena.

"You obviously aren't as great as everyone thinks you are!" he ranted. "And your investigative skills *suck*. Too bad my killing spree single-handedly ruined your entire career…"

His voice faded off as the officers dragged him toward the trail.

Lena's father and brothers encircled her in a Love family embrace. It appeared as though she hadn't heard a word that the killer had spoken.

"This horrid ordeal is finally over, baby," Chief Love told her. "Now you can move on from it and get back to living your life. Hopefully back here in Clemmington."

"Dad," Miles interjected. "Really? After all that Lena's

been through? At least let her recuperate before you start trying to get her to come back home."

"You're right, son. I'm just glad that my girl is okay."

Chief Love turned to David and shook his hand firmly. "Excellent work, Detective. Without you, we may have had a very different outcome."

"How did you even find me?" Lena asked him.

"Your smart watch. I tracked down your location through it."

Lena reached down and grabbed her wrist. The watch had been covered by her sleeve.

"*Oh my…* I forgot that I was even wearing it. Thank you!" she exclaimed, rushing over and throwing her arms around him.

As he embraced her tightly, Lena's father and brothers gave him a thumbs-up, then walked off.

"I'm so glad you're okay," David said, his voice muffled within her wild curls. "And I am so sorry that tonight didn't go as planned."

"If anybody should be apologizing, it's me. Remember, this whole prank thing was my idea."

David slowly pulled away from Lena, his hands sliding down the sides of her waist before resting on her hips.

"Well," he said, "the bottom line is, it worked. Our suspect is in custody, you're okay and we saved another victim's life tonight. I didn't even get a chance to ask her name, or how she was kidnapped."

"Her name is Jan, and she's Peter's wife. She's also the woman who called me anonymously and told me about the *Gonna Get Got* website. Oh! And that was her in the video I was telling you about, where a woman was being confronted by an unseen man. Peter actually filmed it while she and I were on the phone."

"*Really?* Wow. You and I have got a lot to catch up on."

"Yes, we do. It'll all come out once we get to the station."

David glanced down at her feet, noticing that her shoes had been replaced with a pair of booties. The blue fabric was stained with blood.

"Wait," he said, "what happened to your shoes? And your *feet*?"

"My shoes got lost in the midst of the kidnapping. As a result, my poor feet paid the price."

"Well, we can't have that, now, can we?" David asked before picking her up and carrying her back down the trail.

Lena wrapped her arms around his neck.

"Thank you for coming to my rescue," she whispered.

"You're welcome. Thank you for being one of the strongest people I know," he replied before softly kissing her lips.

Chapter Twenty-Five

Lena and David were sitting out on her parents' deck, enjoying the tranquil sunset.

She leaned back in her lawn chair and took another sip of wine, then turned to him and smiled. When he held out his hand, she reached over and interlaced her fingers within his.

"I still can't believe that this nightmare is over," he said. "But I'm sure no one is happier about it than you."

"*I* still can't believe that Peter Ballentine is the one who committed all of those murders, just to spite me."

"Yeah, what was his beef with you anyway?"

"Well, as you know, I graduated top of my class in college. Year after year, Peter would always try to outdo me. It never worked, and he always came in second. Sometimes third. And he was a smart guy. But he was just… *strange*. And antisocial. Bottom line, he just didn't have *it*. And he resented me, because according to our professors, I did."

"Of course you did," David murmured. "As a matter of fact, you still do."

Lena's eyes lowered as she tucked her hair behind her ears.

"Thank you. So anyway, the competition between Peter and me really came to a head right before graduation. We both applied for forensic science positions with the LAPD. I got hired and he didn't. Peter was livid."

"Oh, I bet he was."

"Then he really lost it when he found out I'd earned a certificate in crime scene investigation, which gave me an edge during the hiring process. He even showed up at my graduation party uninvited, drunk, and dressed in a pair of plaid pajamas. After giving the most bizarre congratulatory speech ever, saying that the streets of LA would probably eat me alive, he stormed out."

"*Wow.* And he ended up being the one to try and take you down. What a coward. You should've seen how smug he was in that interrogation room when he confessed to the crimes. But as hard as he tried to get away with it and turn you into another victim, he failed. And you won. *Again.*"

"Exactly." Lena crossed her legs and shifted in her chair so that she was facing David. "That's what this was all about. And with that being said, thank you for those kind compliments."

"You're welcome. Just speaking the truth." David ran his thumb along the top of her hand. "I'm just glad you're safe now, he's behind bars, and you can live your life again without fear."

"Cheers to that," she replied, reaching over and clinking her glass against his.

"Speaking of living your life again, what are your plans? Do you think you'll be going to LA and getting back to work soon?"

Lena could hear the strain in his voice. She peered over at him. He stared back at her, his eyelids lowered. He raised his head off the back of the chair, seemingly anxious to hear her response.

"We'll see," she replied coyly. "My father did offer

me a pretty lucrative position here with the Clemmington PD."

"Did he really?"

"Yep. He did."

David moved his chair closer to hers.

"And what'd you say?" he asked.

"I told him that I'd need some time to think about it. And that he'd have to meet a few of my demands in order for me to consider it."

"What exactly do those demands entail?"

"Well, for starters, I wouldn't want to be running back and forth between the police station and the crime lab. So he'd have to build some sort of lab for me here in town. And if the cost is a deterrent, I told him I'd be willing to share it with a few of the neighboring towns, as long as they'd contribute to the budget."

David nodded his head. "That sounds reasonable. How did he respond?"

Lena threw her head back and laughed. "Pretty favorably, actually. He said, and I quote, 'I'd build you a lab, a house, a car *and* a boat if that's what it would take to bring my baby girl back to Clemmington.'"

"Oh, wow. How could you say no to that?"

She turned to him and smiled. "I couldn't. So I didn't."

David shot straight up in his chair. "Wait, so does that mean you're moving back home?"

"Yes, it does."

He jumped up, pulled Lena out of her chair, wrapped her in his arms and twirled her around the deck.

"David!" she squealed. "What are you doing?"

"What does it look like I'm doing? I'm celebrating!"

She pressed her lips against his neck while embracing him tightly. When he slowed down, she held his head in her hands.

"Looks like I'm finally gonna get my girl back," he murmured as they gazed at one another.

"Looks to me like you already did."

"So when are we going to LA to pack up your things?"

"How does tomorrow sound?"

"Tomorrow sounds perfect," David replied before leaning in and kissing her passionately.

* * * * *

CAVANAUGH JUSTICE: DEADLY CHASE

MARIE FERRARELLA

To Mama,
Who Gave Me
My First Agatha Christie Book
And Began My
Never-Ending
Love Affair With Murder Mysteries.
I Miss You, Mama,
More Than Words Can Ever Say—
Even Mine

Prologue

It was back.

That itch, that need, that unshakable, overwhelming desire that always began small—sometimes no bigger than a tiny pinprick.

Hardly noticeable at all, he thought with a self-satisfied smile.

But that desire would continue to grow, consuming him until it was all he could think about. Morning, noon and night, it became his constant companion, demanding attention, demanding satisfaction, until that itch, that desire to watch a beautiful face begin to fade as the light slowly went out of that woman's eyes, was all there was.

A light that was extinguished because *he* had been the one to put it out.

Well, technically, he corrected himself, the women were the ones who put that light out, because eventually when they were able to move again, they began to struggle. And when they did, they weren't able to keep their legs up in a position that didn't cause the thin rope he had artfully tied them up with to be pulled.

When that happened, they would wind up strangling themselves, no matter how hard they tried not to.

In some cases, it was a slow, drawn-out process accompanied by tears when the women he had chosen for this demise realized that there was no way out.

Usually, however, the end process was quick, because the woman who thrashed about thought if she moved with enough force, she could break the string.

The string never broke.

The last time around had wound up being so fast, he barely had enough time to make himself comfortable as he began to watch the young woman squirming about.

He felt cheated, like a boxing patron who had paid the high price of a ticket to watch an exclusive match only to have the match over in a matter of moments due to a well-placed knockout punch.

It had barely satisfied his need to exercise dominance over this holier-than-thou woman who enjoyed looking down her nose at him, acting as if he was less than the lint that accumulated on her clothing because of a faulty dryer.

Not one of these women whom he had ended had the brains of a canary, while he was the superior being, the one with not one science degree, but several. He was the one who could not only dispense the medication that some third-rate physician prescribed, but he actually knew how to mix the different ingredients together to create those medications if necessary.

The women who became his victims thought that because they were lucky enough, through no effort of their own, to have been gifted with great faces and fantastic bodies, that made them his superior. That gave them the right to look right past him as if he didn't even exist.

They changed their minds quickly enough in their final hours, he thought with an almost gleeful smile.

After a moment, the smile turned dark.

They deserved what he did to them. Each and every one of them deserved to be on the receiving end of his wrath.

Except for one.

That had been a truly personal act, even though the woman had no idea who he was.

But her husband did.

What he had done was a warning to the man to get him to back off, that he was getting too close, although, now that he thought about it, the cat-and-mouse game between them did invigorate him.

Too bad the messenger had to be sacrificed, but that was the way it went sometimes.

Besides, he hadn't gotten anything out of that particular kill. Killing that woman hadn't satisfied the fire in his belly. If anything, it just made it grow larger.

He needed to feed that hunger.

Because he had a superior intellect, he knew when

things were threatening to close in on him. So he had changed his hunting grounds.

He chuckled to himself. Just when those morons on the police force thought he was in one place, he had moved his location to another part of Southern California. It would take them weeks to make the connection.

Maybe longer.

Those simpletons never communicated with one another, he thought in satisfaction. Even in this high-tech world, so many things didn't register or wound up falling through the cracks, and those morons on the police force just went stumbling off into the dark.

All except for one.

And now, it seemed that Cortland was back in the game.

And he was ready to play, he thought. Oh, so ready.

He felt the hunger in the pit of his stomach growing.

It had nothing to do with food.

It was time to leave the confines of his new quarters and start patrolling the streets, looking for the next woman who needed to be made to pay.

It was time to play the game again.

He couldn't wait.

Chapter One

Shayla Cavanaugh-O'Bannon, the youngest of Maeve Cavanaugh-O'Bannon's five children, was admittedly also the sunniest of that subgroup that comprised the many, *many* members of the Cavanaugh clan, most of whom worked in some capacity for the ever-expanding Aurora police department.

Having recently aced her detective's exam, the sharp, pretty, blue-eyed blonde was still learning her way around now that she was an active member of the homicide division and not just part of the uniformed police force.

From the first moment that she had joined up, Shayla had loved everything about being a law enforcement officer. She saw it as a way of being able to help people. Maeve's youngest always focused on the positive aspects of every situation, no matter how dark that situation might seem at the outset.

Determined to make the best impression she could in her new position—there were those who felt that she had only gotten to where she was because of whom her uncle and the rest of her family were and not because of her own merit—Shayla had come in early, which meant that she had gone for her customary run almost in the dark. Invigorated, she'd gotten ready and was at her desk, completing some paperwork.

Paperwork was regarded as the bane of every living law enforcement agent's existence.

She had just decided to get some coffee to help fully focus her brain when she looked up and saw a dark-haired, exceedingly handsome and moody-looking well-dressed man walk by. She was vaguely aware that a new detective had transferred from Los Angeles, although she hadn't met him yet.

His eyes flickered over her for the briefest of moments, but if her presence had registered—Shayla offered him a bright, wide smile—he gave no indication of it. The newcomer just continued walking.

Coffee mug in hand, the twenty-eight-year-old newly minted detective turned and watched the unsmiling man's progress as he walked out the squad room's door and down the hall and then disappeared.

Shayla had always been a sponge when it came to information, whether it was just harmless office gossip or key information that could very well be crucial when it came to solving a case, Shayla took everything in. Which was why, after a moment's pause, she turned toward her older brother Ronan, who just happen to be standing next to her at the coffee machine, and asked, "Is that him?"

The question, coming out of the blue the way it did, caught Ronan completely off guard. Lost in his own thoughts, he had been busy trying to come up with an anniversary gift for his wife, Sierra. He blinked and looked at his sister, whom everyone in the family still thought of as the baby of the group.

"Him who?" Ronan asked. Looking around, he didn't see anyone out of the ordinary in the room—just the same faces he was accustomed to seeing on a more or less daily basis.

"The new guy," Shayla answered, turning back to face her brother, since the person she was asking about had just left the squad room.

She assumed that the new detective was most likely on his way to see the chief of detectives, Brian Cavanaugh.

"Gabriel Cortland—the detective who just transferred here from LA," she elaborated when her brother just continued to look at her, apparently waiting for more input before answering. "What do you know about him?" Shayla asked.

Ronan absently shrugged his broad shoulders. "Only that Cortland was the one who requested the transfer from his old precinct. Word has it he was a really sharp, first-class detective before he fell into the bottle. Almost drank himself to death, but then one day he just decided to get his act together and sober up. And when he did, he put in for a transfer.

"Oh, yeah, and one more thing," her brother added as an after thought. But then he paused, his voice lingering.

Sometimes, getting information out of her brothers was like attempting to drill for water in a well that gave all the appearances of having gone dry, Shayla thought. But she refused to let Ronan see her get frustrated.

"Oh?" she prodded. "And just what is that one thing?"

"Cortland doesn't talk much. Or, from what I hear, practically at all," Ronan told her, draining the last of the coffee from his large mug.

He had a feeling if he didn't leave right now, his sister would just continue asking him questions.

Shayla looked down the hall, despite the fact that the person she was asking about was long gone at this point.

"In other words," she murmured, "a challenge."

"No," her brother told her, "in other words, I'd suggest leaving the man alone. Detective Cortland doesn't strike me as someone who would be a happy recipient of your endless sunshine. They haven't made the kind of sunglasses that can block what you give off."

That didn't begin to convince her that she should back off, not that Ronan had thought that it would. He viewed his youngest sister the same way everyone else in the family did—Shayla was bright and cheery and the absolute definition of unyielding stubbornness once she set her mind on something.

The next words out of Shayla's mouth proved it. "That just tells me that the poor man needs to be subjected to that sunshine, as you put it, even more."

About to leave, Ronan paused and gave her a weary look. "Don't you *ever* come off that cloud of yours?"

"No. Why should I? I don't view the world as a dark, hopeless place," she said in all sincerity.

Ronan almost laughed at her reply. What stopped him was that he believed she honestly meant what she said, which was incredible, yet in a way, he had to admit, also kind of heartwarming.

"Given what you do for a living—what we *all* do," he amended, "that's rather amazing. You are definitely one of a kind, Shayla."

"I really would like to change that," she told her brother with feeling.

"I'm sure you would," he answered. "I've got to go, Shayla. If I do hear anything more about Cortland, I'll pass it on to you," he promised just before he disappeared down the same hallway that the other detective had taken.

Except that unlike the detective under discussion, Ronan was only on his way to the elevator.

Shayla sat at her newly assigned desk—there hadn't been a place for her when she had initially been placed in Homicide until almost a month had gone by.

She remained at her desk for another half hour. At that point, she had finished filling out the paperwork—which wasn't due until tomorrow, at least not by anyone's standards except for her own. Thanks to the work ethic that her mother had instilled in her when she was a little girl, Shayla didn't believe in being on time. She believed in being early—always. To her way of thinking, being early left her time to tackle other things if they came up unexpectedly.

Right now, she was having trouble focusing her attention on anything other than the incredibly sad look in the newly transferred detective's eyes. Try as she might, Shayla couldn't remember ever seeing sadness to that degree.

Oh, to be sure, she had definitely seen sadness before. There was no way she could have been part of the police force without having come in contact with people who had been touched by the ravages of sadness to a lesser or greater degree.

Shayla could remember that look in her mother's eyes when she had received word that their father, a police officer, had been killed in the line of duty.

Eventually, that sadness had faded to some degree.

But the look in Gabriel Cortland's eyes seemed as if it was deeply embedded and very possibly to remain there indefinitely. It wasn't anything that the detective had said—they hadn't exchanged any words— it was just a feeling she'd had during that briefest of moments when their eyes had met in passing.

Still, she *knew* that man was sad. She would bet anything on it. Somehow, some way, she was going to make it her mission to find out what had caused that look, that sadness, to take root. Because if she didn't know what was behind it, she wouldn't be able to help him get beyond it.

And she was determined to do that. For her, it was like walking by a puppy in pain. There was no way she could ignore that puppy. It was no more in her to do that than it was to ignore a cry for help—even a silent one.

Shayla made up her mind. Detective Gabriel Cortland was going to get her help whether he wanted it or not.

Because, at bottom, she was certain that the former LA detective really wanted that help.

FIFTEEN MINUTES LATER found Shayla summoning her courage and going to her uncle's office.

There was a time when her uncle Andrew had been the chief of police, but then his wife had suddenly gone missing, leaving him with five children to raise. Andrew Cavanaugh never thought twice about his course of action. He retired early from the Aurora police force and devoted himself to raising his children, as well as conducting a search for his wife whenever time permitted.

However his younger brother Brian never had to make that sort of life-altering decision, and eventually his dedication got him placed as Aurora's chief of detectives. A levelheaded man who always kept his priorities straight, Brian Cavanaugh never allowed his position to go to his head.

By everyone's account, Chief Brian Cavanaugh was one of the fairest, as well as the most honest, chiefs of detectives the Aurora police department had ever had. He treated everyone the same, taking their merit, not their last name, into account.

The entire family, Shayla thought as she stood in front of the outer door, was exceptionally proud of the work Brian Cavanaugh had done, proud of the man's

instincts that always had him running the most effi-
cient police department in the entire state.

He had done all this while raising a combined family of eight—four of his own children, as well as the
four offspring that Lila, his former partner, brought
into the union when he married her years after his
first wife passed away.

Shayla stood there staring at the door that led into
her uncle's office, trying to come up with the right
words to say, when suddenly she saw a hand reaching up around her and then knocking on that door.

Startled, she swung around and found herself looking up at her uncle.

"The door usually doesn't open unless you knock
on it," Brian informed her with a cheerful smile.
Opening the door all the way, he glanced down at
Shayla. "Would you like to come in?" he asked, even
though it was a foregone conclusion.

"Yes, sir," she answered quietly.

The chief of detectives gestured into his office.
"Then do that," he coaxed.

Shayla noticed that the desk where her uncle's sec-
retary usually sat, making sure that no one entered
the inner sanctum without her say-so, was empty.

Once the newest member of his family to become
a detective was in his office, Brian gestured for her to
take a chair on the other side of his desk. "And what
can I do for you, Detective Cavanaugh?" he asked,
his mouth curving ever so slightly as he addressed
her formally.

The right words still hadn't come to her. "I'm not sure how to start this, Chief," Shayla admitted nervously.

"The beginning is always a good place to start. That way, you won't lose me," the chief of detectives told her with a wink.

She sincerely doubted that anyone could possibly come remotely close to losing the chief. He was one of the smartest men she knew.

"I might be out of line, sir," Shayla began slowly.

"I'll let you know if you are," he promised in such a friendly tone, they might have been discussing their reaction to one of Andrew Cavanaugh's new dishes, which the family patriarch enjoyed trying out on the family during his far-from-rare get-togethers. It was a well-known fact that the older man used any excuse to throw a party.

Okay. It's now or never, Shayla thought. "Was that the new transfer here to see you earlier? The detective who just transferred from the Los Angeles Police Department," she added in case the chief didn't know whom she was referring to.

"Are you asking about Detective Gabriel Cortland?" her uncle asked.

"Yes, I am," Shayla answered a bit nervously. "Detective Gabriel Cortland," she repeated. "You saw him earlier, right?"

"I did. Shayla." Given the nature of the conversation and her obvious discomfort—an unusual state for her—Brian decided that perhaps it would be better to address the young detective by her first name. "What is this all about?"

"I was wondering, have you assigned him to a partner yet?" she asked, her words pouring out quickly.

"No, I haven't," he replied.

During their meeting, Cortland had specifically
said that he wasn't looking to be partnered with anyone. What he was looking for was to be assigned to
a specific kind of case. He had said he was rather
confident that the serial killer who had been haunting the streets of LA was about to change his hunting grounds.

Brian looked at her with interest. "Why do you
ask?"

"Well, if you haven't already assigned him to a
partner, I would like to respectfully request that I be
the one partnered with Detective Cortland," Shayla
told the chief.

To her credit, she thought, she didn't fidget, and
she made sure to look him directly in the eye.

Brian nodded his head slowly. "Interesting. May
I ask why you're making this request?"

Shayla was confident that the chief of detectives
didn't view her as an airhead, or think she was making this request because Gabriel Cortland was an incredibly handsome man by anyone's standards.

She also knew that Brian Cavanaugh wasn't going
to laugh at her once she explained. Along with the rest
of the family, she and the chief had shared more than
a few meals together. Enough meals, she thought, for
the chief to believe that she was being serious when
she told him why she was making this request.

Still, it took her a moment to try to get her wording just right.

"Because I think he needs me."

Brian looked at her mildly surprised. "Detective Cortland didn't say anything about you," the chief replied, trying to understand just where his niece was going with this.

"That's because he doesn't know who I am," she told him, then realized how she had to sound. "Chief, that man has the saddest eyes I have ever seen. Someone or something hurt Detective Cortland. Hurt him very badly beyond all reason. He needs help in finding his way back among the living." She took a breath. "I know you probably think that I'm crazy—"

"No," he assured her. "I'm intrigued. Continue."

"Those were the eyes of someone who doesn't care if he lives or dies," she told him. "Consequently, he will wind up forging ahead without any hesitation, taking chances the rest of us wouldn't. I would like to be partnered with Cortland so I can watch over him. Possibly convince him that no matter what happened, he needs to go on living. To work his way past whatever put that darkness into his eyes and find something worth living for, no matter how small a thing that might be."

Finished, Shayla looked at the chief of detectives hopefully, waiting for the man's decision.

Chapter Two

When the chief of detectives finally spoke, Brian Cavanaugh did so kindly and chose his words carefully.

"And you believe that you're the one who can help Detective Cortland step back from this abyss that you fear is threatening to swallow him up?" he asked the newest detective in his family.

Shayla never hesitated. It wasn't that she thought so much of herself—she just honestly thought that she could help the man who was so troubled he didn't even realize that he needed help.

"Yes, sir," she answered the chief. "I really believe that I can help Detective Cortland."

She saw the chief smile at her.

It was a known fact, a given, that all the Cavanaughs were good, decent people, but Brian had come to view Shayla as practically goodness personified in the way she went out of her way to try to help people, especially the victims of crimes. If he were to place a bet on the one person who could help the newly transferred detective to step back from the edge of the abyss, it would most definitely be her.

Long ago Brian had made it a point to read the history of anyone who transferred into his police department. Cortland was no different. And while there were glowing things cited about Cortland's abilities to track down murderers, capturing killers who had heretofore managed to elude being caught and bringing them in, there was also a disturbing footnote in his file that would back up Shayla's observation.

Which was why, although she was newly promoted to the position of detective as well as new to the homicide division itself, Brian felt fairly comfortable assigning her to be Cortland's partner.

If things didn't work out, Brian theorized, he could always reassign Shayla to someone else. Heaven knew they didn't lack for personnel when it came to any of the departments.

"Well," Brian replied, "luckily, I think you can, too."

Unconsciously clutching the armrests, Shayla stared at the chief of detectives. "Does that mean you're going to assign me to be Cortland's partner?" she asked, hardly able to believe that she had managed to convince the chief so easily. Family member or not, it usually took her a lot more words than this to get someone to agree with her.

"For now, yes," Brian qualified. It was always a good idea to leave himself a way out if it became necessary.

The careful wording was not lost on Shayla. "And for later?" she couldn't help asking.

"Why don't we just see how this goes first?" he advised.

"Yes, of course," Shayla quickly agreed. She definitely didn't want to seem like she was offending the chief in any way. "Do you want me to find Cortland and tell him about this newest development?" she asked, ready and eager to volunteer for the assignment. The sooner this became a reality, the better.

Brian leaned back in his chair and could only laugh. "Lord, I don't remember any of the others being as eager as you," he told her, the others being the sum total of detectives he had dealt with ever since he had taken over his current position. According to everything he knew, Cortland and Shayla had never actually met. "Why don't you just stay here and leave the introductions to me? I just sent Cortland back down to the homicide division. Lieutenant Hollandale promised that he'd give Cortland a desk where he could set up."

"There aren't any," Shayla felt obligated to point out to the chief. "I got the last one last week."

Listening, the chief nodded, appearing unfazed. "I had another desk sent in just before you came in to request being partnered with Cortland." Anticipating Shayla's next question, he explained why an extra desk had just fortuitously turned up. "Detective Al Chapman retired from Missing Persons the other day. He took a security job position in the private sector," Brian explained and then smiled. "Seems his father-in-law owns the company. You know how it is, working for the family," the chief told her with a knowing wink. His father, Seamus Cavanaugh, onetime chief of police, just like Andrew had been, now ran his own security firm.

"Yes, sir, I am well acquainted with that sort of situation," Shayla answered, not bothering to suppress her smile.

Brian laughed softly to himself. All the Cavanaughs had dealt with snide remarks about privileged behavior because of their last name, but not a one of them had ever been known to actually capitalize on that, a fact that all the senior Cavanaughs were quite proud of.

The chief now nodded his head. "I thought you might be." Turning his chair slightly, he reached over to press a button on the phone on his desk. "Virginia, please call Lieutenant Hollandale for me. Ask him to send Detective Cortland back up to my office."

"What reason shall I give him, sir?" a disembodied, melodious voice asked. "In case he asks," his assistant added.

"Just that I would like to see him again," the chief said. His people didn't usually question why he wanted something to be done, and he was not in the habit of having to explain himself. His people had come to know that there were always good reasons behind anything he asked for.

"Consider it done, Chief," Virginia replied cheerfully.

Brian nodded to himself. He and his assistant had had a good working relationship that spanned over the last decade. "I always do, Virginia," the chief answered.

Releasing the button on his phone, Brian looked over at the other occupant in his office. "When Cortland gets here, Shayla, I'd appreciate it if you let me make the introductions and do the talking to begin with. Cortland needs to know that the decision to team the two of you up came from me. As you might already suspect," he told her, "the new detective isn't overly keen on being partnered up with anyone. As a matter of fact, he specifically told me that he would rather *not* be assigned a partner."

"Did he give you any reason why?" she asked the chief.

"The usual one expressed by every loner I've ever met—he feels he works best alone," the chief replied. "So, if you want to change your mind—" Brian began.

She never gave the man the opportunity to finish. "I don't," Shayla replied emphatically.

Brian was not finished. "However, if for whatever reason, you come to the conclusion that this just isn't working for you—" the chief began again.

"I won't," she promised with feeling. "I'm determined to give this more than a day or two—or thirty," Shayla informed the chief with a wide smile.

Brian nodded. "Ah yes, I forgot how stubborn they told me you could be."

"'They'?" Shayla questioned. The man was exceptionally busy. When would he even have the time to discuss her with anyone?

"I believe that single word would encompass the entire family," he told her.

Just then, Virginia's voice came over the intercom. "He's here, Chief."

The chief briefly glanced in Shayla's direction before he told his assistant, "Send Detective Cortland in, please."

The next moment, there was just the slightest knock on the door. Shayla expected to see the door open and the detective who had been the topic of discussion come walking in.

But the door remained closed. Apparently, Detective Cortland was waiting to be told to come in.

The chief obliged. "Come on in, Detective Cortland."

The door opened, and the newest member of the Aurora detective squad walked into the chief's office.

Shayla couldn't pull her eyes away.

My Lord, she thought, *the man looks even handsomer close up than he did earlier at a distance.*

If nothing else, Cortland's presence was going to create a stir amid a great many of the detectives as well as the regular officers, she couldn't help thinking. Men *and* women—for different reasons.

Cortland looked exceedingly solemn. "Is there something you neglected to tell me, sir?" he asked, obviously at a loss as to why he had been called back.

Gabriel was aware that there was another person in the room, but since he assumed that she was just another member of the force and had nothing to do with him, he didn't spare her a glance or direct even a smattering of his attention toward her.

He was here because the chief had sent for him, no other reason.

Never an overly friendly man, he had completely

withdrawn into himself after his wife, Natalie, had been killed. He had absolutely no interest in playing nice with any of the police personnel at large. He wasn't here to play nice. He was here to resume his pursuit of the Moonlight Killer. The serial killer who had exacted the ultimate payment from his wife.

"I wouldn't exactly say that I neglected to tell you something, Detective," Brian told the young man in response to Cortland's question. "But I have made a decision."

Shayla had been right, he caught himself thinking. Looking at the detective more closely now, it struck Brian that he had never seen such abject sadness in anyone's eyes before. Having Shayla around the detective might really do Cortland some good.

Gabriel waited for the chief to tell him what this decision he had made was all about. The detective had a very uneasy feeling that he knew, but given his pessimistic way of viewing things, he could be wrong, he thought.

He sincerely hoped so.

"I've decided to partner you up with another detective," Brian informed the newly transferred young man.

Surprise, displeasure and disbelief all briefly registered across Gabriel's ruggedly handsome face before fading away again just as quickly.

Gabriel cleared his voice. "I believe we already discussed that, sir," he politely told the chief, adding stiffly, "I don't do well with a partner."

Cortland briefly thought of the last man he had

been partnered with. Jon Wakefield had been a decent enough partner in the beginning, but once Gabriel's world suddenly exploded and he sought relief at the bottom of a bottle, Wakefield had requested a different partner. Rather than realize what he was going through, Wakefield only focused on the way his drinking was interfering with their working relationship.

Angry, hurt, abandoned, Gabriel eventually resolved to drag himself back out of the tailspin that had sent him to a bottle for solace as well as relief from his pain.

Neither solace nor relief happened, but he was determined to stop drinking, so he went cold turkey and never looked back.

No one offered to help him achieve his goal of hunting down the man who had killed his wife—not that he would have listened to anyone had they tried. But it had just taught him that he couldn't count on anyone being there for him. The only one who ever had had been Natalie, and she had been cruelly taken from him.

A year ago, Gabriel had even been on the path to mellowing. Recently married, he was looking forward to becoming a father, becoming part of a real family. Abandoned by a mother who preferred partying to caring for her son, he'd been a loner for most of his life.

And then he had met Natalie, and for a while, he had begun to think that maybe things could change, maybe they could improve for him.

He should have known better.

Things never changed for the better—they only got worse. And he'd wound up paying the ultimate price for believing that happiness actually existed.

"I know what you said, Detective," the chief told him with an amiable smile, "but I decided that perhaps you would do better with a partner after all."

Gabriel made one last attempt to change the man's mind. "Sir, I don't—"

But Brian raised his hand, stopping the protest they both knew was about to come. "Why don't we give this a trial run?" Brian proposed. "Say, a month? A month from now, you can both come in and tell me how it's going."

For the first time since he had walked into chief's office, Gabriel slanted a glance toward the woman sitting in the chair next to his. "Both, sir?" he questioned.

Apparently their partnership had already been taken for granted, he realized, far from happy about the turn of events.

"Yes," Brian replied. "Detective Gabriel Cortland, I would like you to meet your new partner—" he gestured toward Shayla "—Detective Shayla Cavanaugh-O'Bannon."

Gabriel had heard only one word that had caught his attention in that introduction. "Cavanaugh, sir?"

Brian smiled. "Yes, the detective is part of my extended family. After you spend some time here, you'll discover that there are a great many of us here in the precinct. But don't let that get to you. The last name does not entitle any of them to any special treatment not awarded to other members of the force."

Shayla had extended her hand toward the detective the moment the chief had said her name. She was still holding it out toward Cortland, who seemed completely oblivious to the gesture.

It wasn't until the chief nodded in her direction that Gabriel seemed to realize that he had ignored the hand that had been extended to him by way of a greeting.

"Hi," Shayla said, smiling broadly. "Nice to meet you."

Relenting, Gabriel took her hand and shook it, holding it as if were some inanimate object he had been forced to pick up against his will. The connection was broken almost immediately as the detective grunted something in response.

Something that Shayla wasn't able to quite make out. Undoubtedly, she judged, it was not anything friendly. It didn't put her off. If anything, it just convinced her more than ever that the man needed her.

Her smile grew wider. "I am looking forward to working with you."

The look in Cortland's eyes when he briefly shifted them toward her told Shayla that she was alone in that sentiment.

"Well, that's all for now, Detectives," Brian said, his tone, although friendly, telling them that they were being dismissed. "Let me know how things are going in a month or so."

Cortland merely nodded at the chief as he rose and

took his leave. Shayla was quick to follow, thinking that she certainly had her work cut out for her.

Brian was thinking the same thing as he watched the newly formed team leave his office. He really hoped that Shayla knew what she was getting herself into.

Chapter Three

Rather than ask the detective to shorten his stride—
Cortland had to be at least six inches taller than she
was, if not more, she thought—Shayla increased her
stride to the point that she was now almost trotting
in order to keep up with her new partner.

The low heels she was wearing were creating a
staccato beat as they quickly and rhythmically hit the
floor with each quick step she took. When she saw
Cortland about to pass the elevator doors, she realized that the man was headed for the stairs.

"You know, if you're trying to lose me," she called
out to Cortland, glad more than ever that she ran on a
regular basis, "you're going to be doomed to failure. I
know the layout of this building a lot better than you
do, and even if your stride is wider and faster, I will
ultimately wind up in the same place that you do. So
why don't you give up this race so we can walk into
the homicide squad room at the same time like civilized people?"

Even as she made the suggestion, Shayla continued to trot behind Cortland like a stubborn racehorse

in her last race, determined to at least make a good showing since winning the race was out of the question.

Gabriel Cortland stopped moving so suddenly, she almost found herself crashing into him. Shayla managed to catch herself at the very last moment.

Cortland glared down at her as if he couldn't believe she had said that. "You're assuming that I want to appear to be a civilized person."

"Don't you?" she questioned.

Still immobile, Gabriel continued looking down at her. This irritating thorn that had been inflicted on him didn't appear to be breathing hard, and she gave every appearance of being able to keep up this pace for at least a while longer.

Just his luck.

This, Gabriel caught himself thinking, had to be a brand-new high when it came to stubbornness.

"No," he finally bit off, answering her seemingly innocent question. "That would just be inviting interaction with other people here. I have no desire to interact or work with anyone." His vivid green eyes narrowed as he continued to glare at her, thinking that might get her to back off. "Least of all you."

Rather than be intimidated by him, he saw the annoyingly perky blonde actually smiling up at him.

"Sorry, but the chief wants us working together, so that means you're stuck with me, like it or not," she declared cheerfully. "And, between you and me, when you least expect it, you might actually find that you've grown to like it."

"I sincerely doubt that," he informed her coldly, thinking that between his tone and his expression, that should cut this annoying cheerful woman dead in her tracks.

It didn't.

"That's all right," Shayla countered his response. "When it happens, it'll be a surprise."

When the elevator arrived, he gave thought to darting in and boarding the car at the last moment, but that seemed somehow childish in his estimation, and that sort of behavior was reserved for her, not him.

So he walked into the elevator, averting his eyes and completely ignoring her.

At least, that was his plan, but he found it rather difficult to ignore someone who had obviously decided not to stop talking no matter what.

"I think you're going to like it here," Shayla predicted.

"You're entitled to your opinion," he told her in a removed voice that all but said her prediction didn't have a prayer of coming true.

Unfazed, Shayla continued. "Everyone's pretty friendly here."

"Doesn't matter," he informed her in a crisp but cold voice. "I'm not looking to make any friends."

"Sometimes things just happen even if you're not looking for them," she told him innocently.

His eyes swept over her, taking every single inch into account. For a pain in the neck, he had to admit that she was rather attractive—but attractive didn't interest him. Being left alone did.

"Tell me about it," he replied just as the elevator came to a stop.

The moment the doors parted, Gabriel immediately strode out. Shayla braced herself for another race.

To her surprise, this time Cortland did *not* stride ahead of her at a fast clip. The detective maintained a civilized pace that she was more than able to keep up with.

When he didn't suddenly take off, she flashed what he was beginning to think of as her blinding smile and said, "Thank you."

"For what, Cavanaugh?" he asked. To the best of his knowledge, he hadn't done anything for her to thank him about.

"For not making me trot all the way into the homicide squad," she told him. "And you can call me Shayla."

In no way could the look he spared her be classified as a warm one. "And why would I want to do that, Cavanaugh?" Cortland asked, deliberately emphasizing her last name.

Was everything going to be a contentious battle between them, she wondered.

"Because it's less of a mouthful than *Cavanaugh* is—and definitely less of a mouthful than the hyphenated version of my name." When he looked at her blankly, she explained, "Cavanaugh-O'Bannon. But whatever works for you is fine with me," Shayla concluded with a shrug that was meant to appease her new partner.

Gabriel narrowed his eyes practically into slits as he looked at her just before he turned away and walked into the thriving beehive that was the homicide squad.

"What would work for me, Cavanaugh," he informed her, "is working on my own."

She gave him an innocent, contrite look that almost looked believable.

Almost.

"Sorry," she went on to tell him. "We can't all get what we want." The smile she flashed in his direction looked as if it was wired for high voltage.

What Gabriel wanted was to be left alone, to do what he did in peace. But when he came right down to it, the only thing he *really* wanted was to catch the serial killer who had not only killed at least seventeen women and escaped capture but had thumbed his nose at him by killing the only person he had ever loved. A person who had been decent and pure and should have never even come in contact with a creature as demented and depraved as this serial killer was.

"Yes, I know," Gabriel answered in such a quiet, still voice that Shayla immediately knew that he wasn't referring to anything they had been talking about. This went a great deal deeper, was far more painful than anything that had, up until now, been touched upon even briefly.

What was it that tormented Cortland to this point?

For a moment, as she walked into the homicide squad room, Shayla briefly thought of going back to the chief and asking him what he knew about her new partner's background. But she knew that Brian Cavanaugh was very dedicated to the privacy of the men and women who worked for him. He sincerely believed that everyone was entitled to their secrets as long as those secrets did not ultimately hurt anyone else.

No, Shayla thought, if she wanted answers, she would have to look elsewhere. Not to the source, because she sincerely doubted that Cortland would tell her *anything* of that nature. He struck her as the very definition of the term *closemouthed*.

No, if she wanted answers, she had to find another way of delving into her new partner's past.

That was when her thoughts turned toward the computer.

Gabriel Cortland didn't strike her as someone who maintained even the barest minimum of a social media page, but that didn't mean there wasn't some sort of information about him floating around somewhere on the internet.

Almost *everything* was somewhere on the internet if a person just knew where to look or what files to access.

"Valri," she suddenly murmured out loud.

Shayla immediately pressed her lips together, afraid that Cortland had overheard her. But he apparently hadn't, because her unwilling new partner didn't even spare her a glance. Instead, his attention seemed to be focused on the man in the glass office at the extreme end of the squad room.

Lieutenant Dell Hollandale.

Relieved, Shayla went on mentally casting about for a solution. Which was why she had thought of Valri.

Valri Cavanaugh was one of two computer wizards in the family. If a fact could be located *anywhere* on the internet, even on the notorious dark web, Valri was the one who could find it. Shayla immediately made a mental note to talk to her cousin the first chance she got.

Right now, though, she felt that she needed to be at her new partner's side as the detective went through the motions of introducing himself to their lieutenant.

"Lieutenant Hollandale's office is that glass one all the way at the end of the squad room," Shayla pointed out.

Cortland gave her a look akin to the one he would have sent her way if she had just talked to him as if he was the village idiot.

"Yes, I know," Gabriel replied. "His assistant was the one who sent me back to the chief's office so I could be saddled with you."

She forced herself to ignore the obvious insult and focused on attempting to remedy the situation.

"You know," Shayla told the good-looking, brooding detective at her side, "if you think of this as a budding partnership rather than being 'saddled' with me, it might be easier for you to come to terms with this."

The expression on his face told her he didn't see it that way. "What would be easier for me is if you changed your mind and asked for another partner," Cortland told her matter-of-factly.

She was not about to lie to him, not even to attempt to get along with the man. He needed to accept the situation as it existed.

"That's not about to happen," she said with a smile.

"And neither is my thinking of this—" he gestured to the space between them, pointing toward her and then himself "—as a partnership."

Not about to accept defeat, but unwilling to hash this all out right now, Shayla promised, "We'll revisit this later."

Gabriel made no immediate reply. He knew that he needed to remain in this precinct, and it wasn't in his best interest to lose his temper in front of the entire squad on his first day on the job.

He made his way across the floor to the lieutenant's office. Just before he was about to knock on the glass door, he glanced at the woman at his side. "We'll see," he told her.

The next moment, Cortland was knocking on Hollandale's door. There was no more time for any sort of an exchange between him and the incredibly annoying woman at his side.

While he didn't paste a smile on his face, Gabriel did do his best to look unperturbed, at least for his first meeting with his new superior.

"Ah, Detective Cortland and Detective Cavanaugh, I take it you've met one another," Hollandale said, rising from behind his desk to extend a hand to each detective, although he had obviously already met Shayla.

"Just barely, sir," Shayla answered, slanting a look toward her new partner.

"Yes, sir," Cortland answered stoically.

"I've read your file, Cortland," Hollandale said, sitting down again. He nodded for the detectives to do the same, then continued. "Your superiors had some very impressive things to say about you," he observed. "And yet you transferred." He raised his penetrating brown eyes to the detective's face. "Why?"

The answer, in Gabriel's opinion, couldn't have been simpler. "The serial killer I have been pursuing over the last two years suddenly changed his hunting grounds, switching from Los Angeles to Aurora and the surrounding area. I didn't think the Aurora police department would look kindly on an LA police detective pushing his way into their—your—investigation."

It wasn't the entire truth, but Gabriel felt that it would satisfy his new boss. Solved cases far outweighed everything else.

Hollandale continued looking at the new detective. "Is that the only reason?" he asked.

Shayla found herself hanging on every word being exchanged between the two men. She wondered if Cortland would open up or continue repeating the known facts.

Cortland took a breath, then said, "Things in Los Angeles became rather intolerable for me. It was time for a change. Luckily, as it turned out, it came at a good time for the ongoing investigation as well."

"What makes you think that the killer moved

here?" Hollandale asked. "He could have easily taken off for another state."

"He didn't," Cortland replied with conviction.

Hollandale wasn't quite ready to drop the matter. He wanted to be convinced, or at least understand what had made Cortland believe what he did.

"What makes you so sure?"

"Call it a gut feeling," Gabriel replied evasively.

Shayla looked at the detective in surprise. She hadn't expected this sort of an admission from someone who behaved more like a sphinx than a human being.

"You have a gut feeling?" she questioned.

Gabriel felt as if she was talking down to him. One look at the woman's face disproved that, but it was still difficult for him to give her the benefit of the doubt.

However, the lieutenant's office was not the place to allow his dismissive feelings toward this partner he had been saddled with to surface.

So all he allowed himself to say was, "Yes, I have a gut feeling."

Shayla smiled. He noted that it wasn't a mocking smile but a pleased one. The woman was up to something.

"As someone who comes from a family that has made gut feelings into a religion," Shayla told him, "I think that going with a gut feeling is an excellent way to proceed."

Gabriel really thought that this time the bouncy detective was making fun of him. However, a closer look at the woman told him she was serious. He realized that he had stopped talking to his new lieutenant and had shifted his attention to the annoying detective who had somehow managed to latch onto him for reasons that were hers alone.

He had to be crazy, he told himself. And it was her fault. She had burrowed into his life in less than a half an hour, and already he felt as if his life was being turned on its ear.

How the hell had that happened, anyway?

It was the serial killer who needed his undivided attention, not some dippy, privileged little princess who was the unfortunate by-product of what seemed like an otherwise extremely bright, capable family.

Well, with any luck, she would get tired of whatever game she thought she was playing and would request another partner, leaving him alone to do what he had come out to do: rid the world of a serial killer and live up to the promise he had made at Natalie's grave.

To kill the man who had killed her.

Chapter Four

"Well, for the city's sake, I hope this guy doesn't turn up anywhere near here," the lieutenant said to the two people in his office. "But, on the other hand, we're never going to catch that sick SOB by sticking our heads in the sand while keeping our fingers crossed that he stays away." Hollandale's normally easygoing expression turned momentarily dark. "That scum has to be brought down—and as soon as possible."

Shayla glanced toward Cortland and decided to answer for both of them, since the latter wasn't being very vocal. "You're preaching to the choir, sir."

"I realize that," the lieutenant answered. Looking at the newest detective on his squad, Hollandale said, "I assume that when you were working the serial killer cases, you kept records."

"I did, yes," Gabriel answered.

Hollandale eyed him a little closer. "Detailed records?" he emphasized.

"I'd like to think so," Gabriel replied honestly, without any fanfare.

"And would you have kept any copies of those

detailed records when you moved out here?" Hollandale asked.

Gabriel paused, wondering if this was a legitimate question or if his new lieutenant was attempting to trip him up for some reason. Ordinarily, when a detective left a precinct, the files he had worked on remained behind, because they were the property of that precinct. Technically, he had no business bringing those files with him, but everyone knew that copies of notes had a habit of turning up in places where they normally didn't belong.

"I don't believe that I still have any of those files, sir." That would have been the standard, expected denial. But because he was honest to a fault, Gabriel threw in a proviso. "However, I would have to look through my papers to make sure."

Hollandale nodded his head at the nonadmission. "Do that as soon as you get a chance," he encouraged. "In the meantime, settle in and get to know the people you'll be working with. You'll both be complaining that you don't have time to even breathe soon enough," the lieutenant assured them with conviction. "Detectives Joan Mateo and Greg Jordan are just wrapping up a murder-suicide case. You might want to look over their shoulder and see how we handle things here," Hollandale suggested, looking directly at Cortland as he said it.

Shayla took that to be their cue to leave and rose to her feet.

"Yes, sir," she responded, then looked at Cortland

to see if he was getting up as well. The latter seemed to stand almost reluctantly.

"Sir," he began, searching for a way to state what had occurred to him without sounding pushy or being thought of as offensive.

One of the by-products of having taken over this job, the lieutenant had learned, was developing the patience of a saint. "Yes?" Hollandale asked.

"If a killing does come up that matches the LA Moonlight Killer's pattern—" Gabriel began.

Cortland didn't have to finish his request. The lieutenant knew where this was going, and he nodded at the detective. Cortland's knowledge of the serial killer's pattern was one of the reasons the man had been welcomed to the homicide division of the Aurora police department.

"I will be sure to call the two of you in," he assured Cortland.

"The two of us?" Gabriel questioned. For the briefest of moments, he had forgotten all about the albatross hung around his neck.

"Yes. Detective Cavanaugh is, after all, your partner," Hollandale reminded the new man. "Or did you forget that?" he asked, amusement curving his mouth.

Gabriel felt like a man who had been placed on a medieval torture rack and had somehow managed to pass out, temporarily forgetting where he was.

"It slipped my mind for a minute, sir," Cortland admitted.

Hollandale actually chuckled as he looked at Shayla.

"I am sure Cavanaugh will be happy to keep reminding you, Detective."

"I'm sure she will," Cortland agreed darkly. The humor in the situation, as seen by his lieutenant, escaped him.

"Well, that's all for now," Hollandale said with a note of finality in his voice. He spared the new detective another smile. "Welcome to the unit, Detective Cortland."

"Thank you, sir," Gabriel murmured politely, feeling as if he had just officially walked through the gates of hell.

"Well, that went well," Shayla cheerfully commented as they came out of the lieutenant's office.

Gabriel merely grunted something completely unintelligible in response.

"I'm going to need a handbook on how to interpret those grunts of yours," she told her partner honestly. "Was that a good grunt or an indifferent grunt?"

"You're the detective, you tell me," Cortland said.

She sidestepped what she viewed as a trap. "I'm going to need more input before I can form an intelligent opinion," Shayla answered. "What I can tell you right off the bat is that I'm your friend, Cortland. At times, when we're out in the field, I might be your only friend. And I will have your back each and every time. But you are going to have to stop viewing me as the enemy, because that is the one thing I am not.

"Now, that's your desk over there." She pointed toward the newly placed piece of furniture that, as it happened, was right in front of hers, although she didn't tell him that yet.

Cortland was going to love this, she couldn't help thinking. The next moment, the look on his face told her she was right.

Out loud, Shayla suggested, "Why don't you settle in, and once you finish doing that, I can introduce you around."

"Why would you do that?" Gabriel asked suspiciously.

It looked as if this partner of hers was going to fight her every step of the way. Well, she had asked for this, so she couldn't really complain about it, she reminded herself.

"Because," she explained patiently, "these are the people you're going find yourself working with at one point or another."

"I've got a better idea," Gabriel countered. "Why don't we wait until that time comes up before you start playing the hostess with the mostest?"

Okay, she thought. She needed Cortland to back off a little before she found herself losing the temper she was striving so hard to hold on to.

"I want to make one thing very clear," she told Cortland. "I grew up with three bossy, overbearing older brothers and a whole bunch of obnoxious male cousins. More than you could possibly shake a stick at. If I didn't kill any of them then and am on good terms with all of them now, you don't have a prayer of driving me off with your less-than-amiable behavior," she informed him point-blank.

"So you might as well give it up, because, barring an earthquake where the ground opens up right under my feet and swallows me whole, I am *not* going anywhere."

Her eyes met his, and for the first time since he had met the woman, Gabriel noticed that her eyes were a vivid shade of light blue.

"Have I made myself clear?" Shayla asked.

"Yes," Cortland replied, his lips barely moving.

Her smile was as wide as his frown was pronounced. "Great!" she declared. Gesturing toward the empty desk again, she told him, "There's your desk."

He retreated to it as if it was his last bastion of refuge. The next moment, that notion was totally sacrificed when he saw her sit down at the desk that was right beside the one he had just been directed to.

The scowl on his face resurfaced and looked even more intense than it had just a little earlier. Shayla pretended not to notice. The detective was going to need time to adjust, she thought.

Probably more than the usual amount.

But she had absolutely no doubt that Cortland *would* adjust, because she had no intentions of giving up, and, as her mother had once noted—rather proudly when she thought that she hadn't been overheard by her daughter—her youngest child could be stubborn as hell when she wanted to be.

And however briefly she'd been in Cortland's company, Shayla most definitely intended to be *very* stubborn and wait out this deeply hurting detective.

Shayla gave her new partner an hour to settle in,

and then, because they hadn't been placed on an actual case yet, she began to slowly bring some of the older detectives by Cortland's desk.

Granted, she was a newly promoted homicide detective, but she knew almost all the people there thanks to having interacted with them both on the force and at any one of her uncle Andrew's numerous gatherings and parties.

Among other things, it bred a sense of camaraderie within the police force. Practically everyone chipped in to defray what could have been a prohibitive cost if the former chief of police had to bear the expense on his own.

Consequently, relatives and friends were more than happy to contribute. The real draw to these parties, other than the company, was the way Andrew cooked. Cooking had been a passion of his when he was putting himself through school. It only grew more so as the years went by.

To Cortland's credit, he didn't actually say anything to show that he had no interest in broadening his circle of acquaintances. But his body language did seem to reinforce that particular message.

"Your new partner isn't exactly sunshine in a bottle, is he?" Brianna commented at one point after her sister introduced Cortland to her. A few seconds later, the detective had excused himself and retreated.

Feeling somewhat protective toward the man, Shayla said, "It takes him time to warm up to people."

"Are you sure he's capable of warming up?" her

sister asked skeptically. "Hell, I've seen icebergs melt faster than your new partner."

"He's dealing with some things," Shayla replied. She only wished she knew what, she added silently.

"We're *all* dealing with some things, Shay. There's no reason to give anyone frostbite when they make the mistake of walking by," Brianna told her. And then her tone softened as she looked at Shayla. "I don't want to see you put yourself out there and get hurt, kid."

"Hurt?" Shayla repeated with a scoff. "Haven't you heard, Bri? I'm invulnerable."

"Yeah, yeah." Brianna waved her hand, humoring Shayla because she knew there was no way to talk her sister out of doing something once she had set her mind to it. "Look, in honor of you being the last of us to pass the detectives' exam," Brianna said, doing her best not to grin, "why don't you come down to Malone's and join us all for a celebratory drink?"

It was just after hours now, and none of the inner group were out working a case at the moment. To Brianna it seemed like the perfect time to get all of them together.

"Sure. Just let me go and ask Cortland if he wants to join us," Shayla said.

She turned toward where she had last seen her new partner.

Brianna scanned the immediate area. "Doesn't look as if he is, kid," she told her younger sister. "I think your new partner just ducked out when you weren't looking and went home."

Shayla began to protest, but she saw that Cortland's desk was empty.

And he was nowhere to be seen.

Brianna was right.

DOING NOTHING WAS a great deal more tiring than actually working a case, Gabriel thought angrily. He had forgotten that.

He let out a long breath as he walked into his sparsely furnished ground-floor garden apartment. It wasn't home, but it was a refuge, he thought. And that was all he was interested in.

Because of that incessantly chipper partner he had been saddled with, he had begun to feel as if today was just never going to end. It was just going to go on and on like a merry-go-round whose mechanism had gotten stuck and somehow was doomed to continue, having him go around and around in an endless circle until he eventually expired.

It was days like today that made him really regret giving up drinking. Having a tall, cold Black Russian would have really gone down well right about now.

He took down an all but empty box of crackers and extracted the last of them. Bringing the box over to the sofa, he began to dispose of the last of the crackers. They were stale.

He thought longingly again of a Black Russian. It would have been an easy enough matter just to go to a local bar or restaurant and order one. But he knew he couldn't give in, not even for a single drink, because it was *never* a single drink. One drink would lead to another and another until he was right back to where he had been nine months ago.

After he had found Natalie's body, he had tried so desperately to find a way to cope with the pain, to mute it, drown it, do something, *anything* to make it stop haunting his every waking moment. So he had a choice between being haunted or being a hopeless drunk who couldn't cope with life.

Hell of a choice, he thought as he ate another stale cracker.

The bottle had come incredibly close to winning him over to its side but giving in to that sort of an existence was an insult to his late wife on several levels. Natalie wouldn't have wanted him to devolve to this state.

More importantly, if he gave in to his pain and drowned his sorrows to the point that he was incapable of even thinking, how could he ever make that disgusting subhuman who had done this to Natalie pay for what he had done? Pay for stealing not just the rest of her life, but their baby's life as well?

Not to mention their life as a family?

But to do that, to capture the serial killer, he had to remain sober. Not just occasionally, but at all times.

And once he had tracked this ruthless creature down and made him pay the ultimate price for what he had done—not just to his beloved Natalie and their unborn child, but to all the women he had killed and the families he had robbed of their presence—once he had done that, Gabriel didn't care what happened to him. He would have done what he needed to do.

The rest of his life after that didn't matter to him. Because without Natalie, there was no life for him.

Gabriel pressed his lips together, wishing he could have just one single drink. But that wasn't possible, which was why he didn't bring any alcohol into the apartment he had rented. Not even to help him sleep.

Sleepless nights had become the norm for him, but he has gotten used to them. All he needed was just enough time to recharge and he could keep going.

The knock on his door had him stiffening. He'd lived here for almost a month and knew absolutely no one.

So who the hell was that?

Chapter Five

Because the person at his front door wasn't showing any signs of going away despite his inclination to ignore them—whoever was there had already knocked a total of three times—Gabriel decided he needed to make them leave.

Muttering under his breath, he stormed over to the front door.

At first, when he looked through the peephole, Gabriel thought his imagination had gotten the better of him. Cavanaugh had relentlessly been dogging his tracks ever since the chief had given him the bad news that he was teaming the two of them up.

Seeing Cavanaugh standing on the other side of his door now was just a continuation of the nightmare he felt he was having.

Except, apparently, it wasn't a nightmare, because, no matter how much he blinked and willed her gone, she was still standing there.

"Cortland," Shayla said, "I know you can see me. I can hear you breathing."

"I'm off duty, Cavanaugh. We're done for the day," he informed her curtly.

But Shayla stood her ground. The dinner she had brought with her from Malone's was beginning to cool. She needed to give it to him now.

"Open your door, please, Cortland."

The door remained closed with its lock in place. "Why should I?" he asked. Didn't this woman ever give up and stop making a pest of herself? What the hell had he done to be plagued like this?

"Because I'll make it worth your while, Cortland," she promised.

He sighed, debating what to do. He could ignore her. It wasn't easy, but it could be done. However, if he didn't let her in, this nutcase was liable to stand out there all night, making noise and talking endlessly. Eventually, one of the neighbors was going to get irritated enough to call 911 and complain.

Gabriel swore under his breath. That was all he needed.

Flipping the lock, he yanked open the door, but he didn't hold it open all the way. His arm was up, barring her access. "What are you doing here?" he demanded angrily.

Ignoring the fact that he hadn't exactly invited her in, Shayla ducked under his arm and wiggled her way into his apartment.

A warm, tempting smell accompanied her.

"You haven't eaten, have you?" she asked, turning around to face him. It wasn't really a question on her part but more of an assumption.

"Now you're answering a question with a question?" Gabriel asked. Frowning, he closed the door, but he didn't flip the lock into place. He wanted to be able to pull it open quickly.

"It's not really a question," she confessed. "It's more like intuition." She looked pointedly at the almost empty container of stale crackers in his hand. "And the fact that I didn't see you eat anything all day."

"I wasn't hungry." His eyes narrowed as he all but pinned her in place. "Something kept killing my appetite."

"Well, sorry to hear that," she responded with an innocent expression, "but I figured that your appetite might have made a reappearance by now, so I brought you a thick steak sandwich from Malone's as well as a bag of their fries."

"Malone's?" Gabriel was unfamiliar with the name. Actually, he was unfamiliar with most of the different places in Aurora. He had even chosen the apartment where he was currently living solely because of its proximity to the police precinct. To Gabriel, being able to roll out of bed and go directly to work was a major plus. He was not interested in the scenery.

Shayla had taken the wrapped sandwich and fries out of the bag and placed them on the small table in his equally small kitchen.

Flattening the bag, she held it up for him to see the Malone's logo.

"It's a local bar and grill run by a retired detective. Actually, everyone who works there used to be with the police force," she added. "You should come down sometime." Her face lit up at the thought. "I can take you there."

If he told her not to come, Gabriel sensed that wouldn't be enough to put the woman off, so he told her shortly, "I'm not planning to have any time for that."

"You can't work all the time," she told him, thinking about the old saying that all work and no play made for a dull person. Shayla pressed her lips together, deciding that saying so out loud could probably just lead to an argument that she didn't want to have right now.

He focused on what she had just said about his not being able to work all the time. His eyes narrowed, taking it as a challenge. "Try me," Cortland told her.

"Right now, I think you should try the steak sandwich," Shayla urged, deliberately changing the topic. "It tastes good cold, but it's even better warm."

It did smell good, Gabriel thought almost against his will. The tempting aroma just reminded him that stale crackers for dinner didn't quite cut it. But he wasn't about to have this bossy little fresh-out-of-the-box detective telling him when and what to eat.

And he *really* wanted to get her out of his apartment.

"Maybe later," he told her as he took a step back toward the front door.

But Shayla didn't move. She remained exactly

where she was and nodded toward the food she had placed on the table.

"Let's just say that you're not getting rid of me until I see you eating." She deliberately didn't phrase her statement to say, "Start eating." She wanted the process to include finishing the meal, otherwise, she wouldn't put it past him to stubbornly throw the food out.

She could see by the look on Cortland's face that he was definitely considering that unspoken option.

"You really do know how to make a pest of yourself, don't you?" Cortland said, stunned by her behavior and, at the same time, rather surprised by her single-mindedness. It occurred to him that she would be a driven detective if she applied that same stubbornness to a case she was on.

Rather than be insulted that Cortland had called her a pest, Shayla smiled complacently at him and said, "I have a PhD in it."

Gabriel came close to laughing. "I just bet you do," he answered. Turning on his heel, Gabriel spared his annoying partner a glance and said, "Well, c'mon," and then walked into the small kitchen.

Buoyed and hopeful, Shayla followed.

Against the wall there was the small table where she'd placed the sandwich and fries. Three chairs surrounded the table. Cortland took a seat directly opposite the one that Shayla slipped into.

"Good?" she asked after Cortland had had a chance to take a couple of bites of his sandwich.

The sandwich was still warm, but Gabriel just shrugged. "It's okay," he said in between more bites.

"I'll pass that heady praise of yours to Reese, who currently does all the cooking at Malone's. I'll just make sure all the knives and meat cleavers are out of reach before I say anything," she confided, a smile playing on her lips.

Sharp green eyes narrowed ever so slightly as Gabriel looked at her. "Is sarcasm your first language or your second?" he asked.

"Second," she answered without hesitation. "Being around certain types of people just seems to bring it out of me," she said innocently. And then, still looking up at him, Shayla promised, "I'll try to keep a lid on it."

Gabriel shrugged again, trying not to allow his irritation to surface. Ever since Natalie had been killed, he'd had trouble holding on to his temper. It was better now than when he was drinking, but it still wasn't the way it used to be.

"Suit yourself," he told her.

"I usually do," she answered honestly. "But I also like taking the people around me into account."

He found himself wondering again if she was on the level. "Must get tiring," he noted.

"At times," she agreed. She was still looking at him pointedly. "But at other times it can be extremely satisfying." She sat back and continued to watch him eat.

Gabriel realized he was waiting for her to stop. To grow tired of being this cheerful Pollyanna and allow her true colors to finally surface. This woman had been perpetuating this act all day, and even people pretending to be Santa Claus had to give it a rest eventually, right?

But this eager beaver seemed to enjoy this act she had been playing all day, and she gave no sign of stopping or even of backing off the tiniest bit.

"You seem really invested in having me finish every last bite," Gabriel noted. "Is that when the cyanide kicks in?" he asked sarcastically.

"No, not until a day or two later," she answered with such a straight face, for a second Gabriel actually thought that she was being serious.

And then she started to laugh, giving herself away and, coincidentally, annoying the hell out of him.

"That wasn't funny," he informed her icily.

"Neither is treating me like the enemy or some invading force," Shayla countered. Pausing, she told herself to regroup. "Look, why don't we both return to our corners and start over?"

For the sake of getting along, she had placed herself in with him, but in her honest opinion, her grumpy partner was the only one who needed to return to his corner and start over.

But she wasn't here to judge him, Shayla reminded herself. She was here to try to win him over and make him realize that she wasn't just his partner. She could be his friend if he only let his guard down a little and let her in.

When Cortland made no response, she leaned in a little, reached up to take hold of an imaginary bell and said, "Ding, ding, ding."

He frowned at her. Maybe it was her imagination, but the frown didn't seem quite as intense as it had been initially. *Progress?* she thought hopefully.

"You missed your calling," Cortland told her. "Maybe you should be doing voice-overs in cartoons."

"Maybe," Shayla replied, nodding as if she was giving the idea some thought.

He watched her for a long moment, unable to understand her motives any more now than he had when she had first arrived. "I take it this is what people mean when they refer to bending over backward," Cortland guessed.

"I wouldn't know," she replied innocently. "I'm not bending."

The expression on his face was the last word in skepticism. She was kidding, right? Still, he asked, "So this is normal behavior for you?"

Her smile was almost blinding. "Now you're learning," she told him.

He realized that he had almost eaten the whole sandwich—and it had been exceptionally thick, as well as good. But what really bothered him was that the food—and his no longer empty stomach—had managed to distract him.

He never should have opened the door.

"Look," he started, "I don't know what your game is, but—"

"I already told you this morning when we were first introduced. There is no game. All I care about is working with you and, just possibly, if we do it right, making this small part of the world a better, safer place for the people who are in it." Shayla's eyes met his. "Nothing else really matters."

She was some actress, he thought. Another man might have believed her. But another man hadn't been through what he had.

"And you expect me to believe that?" he challenged.

Shayla's eyes never wavered from his. "Yes," she replied, "I do. Maybe not today or tomorrow or even the next day, but eventually. Because it's true."

Cortland grunted just the way he had done earlier in the office. *Nobody* was this sunny, he thought. *Nobody.*

"And if you happen to cut your finger, is sugar going to come pouring out?" he asked.

He was goading her. It was hard to keep the smile on her face, but she managed even as she rose to her feet.

"I really wouldn't recommend doing that to see if you're right," she told him.

It took him a second to realize that she was heading toward the door. He had wanted her to do that since she had arrived, yet now that it looked as if it was really happening, he almost couldn't believe it.

Belatedly, he came to and followed her, walking his so-called partner to the door a step behind her.

"Well, thanks for the steak sandwich—and the fries." His own voice sounded almost awkward to him.

"My pleasure," she answered, her tone bright again. "I figured there was no advantage in having a partner whose stomach was rumbling at inopportune times."

Gabriel took offense at the offhanded comment. "My stomach wasn't rumbling," he informed her.

"It was only a matter of time," she promised. "Don't forget, I did grow up with all those brothers and cousins. I am well acquainted with the sounds of hunger, and to the best of my recollection, you hadn't eaten."

"I could have gotten something to eat after I left the precinct," he pointed out.

"Then I wouldn't have found you with a container of stale crackers in your hand," she told him.

Now she was just reaching. "How would you even know they were stale?" he asked.

"The noise they made when you bit into one," she answered cheerfully. "Fresh crackers sound different from stale ones."

"And you've investigated crackers?" Cortland asked cynically.

She didn't answer him directly. "It's all just part of conducting intense investigations," she informed him. "You never know when one small piece of information can suddenly fit in and make everything else just click into place." She glanced at her watch. "Now, it's getting late, and I should go so you can get some sleep."

He stared at her. Just how old did she think he was? "It's not even eight o'clock."

"I know, but it probably takes you a long time to finally fall asleep. I had better leave so that you can get started."

His sleeping patterns had been off for the last nine months. He couldn't fall asleep for hours, and when

he finally did, nightmares would quickly materialize
and haunt him. He would wake up feeling even more
tired than when he had finally fallen asleep.

But he had never told anyone that. He wasn't the
kind to share. This partner of his was getting to be
downright creepy.

"How would you know that?" Gabriel asked.

"You have bags under your eyes. The kind that
come from lack of sleep. Since you're currently not
working a case, there's only one thing that could keep
you up—your own thoughts. And those are hard to
bury," she told him knowingly. The next moment, she
opened his door. "See you tomorrow, partner," she
said cheerfully as she slipped out the door.

Cavanaugh was an annoying, pushy woman who
had managed, in the matter of just hours, to get under
his skin like some sort of infectious rash, Gabriel
thought as he watched her go.

And, he supposed, judging by her conclusions, she
also seemed like she had the makings of a half-de-
cent detective.

Biting off an oath, Gabriel flipped the lock on his
door, closing it.

Unless the woman had learned how to slip under
the door like some sort of witch, that should keep her
out, he decided.

Chapter Six

Gabriel arrived at the precinct the next morning at seven thirty. It wasn't so much that he was eager to get started. Oddly enough, the quiet in his apartment after his chatty pseudopartner had left began to get to him. Every sound seemed to be amplified.

He could hear his ears ringing.

Gabriel had thought of putting on the television in order to have some background noise, but there was nothing on except for either inane programs that insulted his intelligence or sickeningly "clever" newscasters who thought they were entertaining because they were bantering back and forth while making little sense.

At that point, Gabriel had given up and just gone to bed.

Going to bed turned out to be another futile endeavor for him. Not for lack of trying, Gabriel had managed to get in about five hours of sleep. Not straight through, but in broken snatches.

The last time he woke up, he figured he was done

for the night. Because he was, he decided to go in earlier than he was actually scheduled to come in.

Aurora was known as one of the more peaceful, law-abiding cities in the country. Still, he reasoned, there had to be *something* happening now that he could sink his teeth into.

And, if he hadn't missed his guess, this city was exactly the type of setting that the Moonlight Killer, as he had been dubbed by some journalist, was looking for in order to leave his new mark.

The heartless ghoul enjoyed nothing better than bringing fear into the hearts of heretofore peaceful people.

Because of the proximity of his apartment to the precinct as well as the lack of traffic, Gabriel managed to make it from his apartment to the precinct in no time flat.

The homicide squad room was practically empty when he walked in.

Or so it looked at first glance.

And then Gabriel stopped dead.

Apparently nightmares continue even when you're awake, Gabriel thought, seeing his partner already at her desk.

Approaching Shayla, he asked, "What are you doing here?"

Shayla had barely made it in a few minutes earlier, managing to get an abbreviated run in before taking a quick shower. Pleased with herself, she looked up at her partner, a hint of an amused smile curving her mouth.

"I work here, remember?"

Oh, he remembered all right, Gabriel thought. He had thought—hoped, really—that by coming in so early, he would be able to avoid her for at least an hour, possibly longer. Obviously, he had thought wrong.

"I know," he answered formally. "But you don't work this early."

"Actually," she told him, "I like getting an early start." Shayla nodded toward her computer screen. "I decided to read everything I could find about that serial killer in LA and the surrounding area. By the way, that coffee is for you," she said, tilting her head at the large, covered container standing in the middle of his desk.

He hadn't even noticed it. She had been what had caught his attention, front and center. "Where did it come from?" Cortland asked.

"Well, if I said the coffee fairy, you probably wouldn't believe me," Shayla laughed, "so why don't we just say that it came from the coffee shop at the end of the block?"

He made no move to pick up the container. Instead, he continued just looking at it with suspicion. "What's it doing here?"

"Standing?" she supplied, amused.

"Damn it, Cavanaugh—" The woman had just managed to make him lose his temper in record time, he thought, frustrated.

"Ask a stupid question, you force me to give you a stupid answer," Shayla said, then decided to tell him the truth. "I stopped to get my morning coffee at the shop and decided that you might want something a little stronger than the discolored dishwater that passes for coffee around here." She looked into his eyes. "I am trying to make this as hospitable a workplace as possible for you, but you're going to have to work with me a little here."

"I didn't ask you to do that." Gabriel stopped.

He had to get hold of himself or he would wind up being fired before he had a chance to even start working at this precinct. There was no getting away from the gut feeling that the fiend who had stolen Natalie from him was going to bring his killing spree here next—if he hadn't already.

He couldn't explain why—he just *knew*.

So Cortland forced himself to reel in his temper and did his best to sound civilized. "Sorry. Thank you. What do I owe you?" he asked, reaching for his wallet.

"I'll take a smile," Shayla told him cheerfully.

His eyes met hers. "You don't give up, do you?"

She grinned in response. "Ah, you're learning." Cortland's expression appeared almost frozen, and then, slowly, there was just the slightest movement at the corners of his mouth. "I guess that's good for a first effort," Shayla told him, nodding her approval. "After all, you can only go up from there."

With that, she lowered her eyes and looked back at her computer screen.

Working diligently, she had managed to find a

number of stories about the serial killer, each one more bone-chilling than the last.

The killings, she discovered, all appeared to have been committed in the evening, and oddly enough, none of the victims had been sexually assaulted.

Then there was the fact that all the bodies had been tied up in that same painful, hog-tied fashion.

After reading the tenth story, sickened, Shayla had had to stop for a second.

She blew out a breath, shaking her head.

"What?" Cortland asked, curious as to what seemed to have gotten to her.

She realized that her partner was sitting at his desk, drinking his coffee and watching her. Was he trying to get a handle on her reaction, she wondered, or was there something else going on? She didn't have a clue. Cortland wasn't the easiest man to read.

"By definition," she said, answering his vaguely worded question, "serial killers are all sick people, but this one, it's like he goes out of his way to be particularly sick."

Gabriel certainly wasn't about to argue with that. "Yeah."

Cortland's voice sounded painfully flat to her, as if he didn't just agree with her assessment, he felt it all the way down to his bones.

Shayla glanced at the date of the last article she had read, which apparently was about the serial killer's last victim.

"Am I reading this right? This ghoul hasn't surfaced for the last nine months?" she asked her partner.

"Yeah, you're right," he answered curtly.

It had been nine months, he thought. Nine months ago when his life came to a painful, skidding halt and the walls of his life came crashing in on him. It was also the last time that anyone had supposedly heard from the Moonlight Killer.

Shayla was studying the screen. "There're a lot of reasons why the killer would just disappear from the scene," she said, thinking out loud. "Someone could have killed him and his body hasn't been discovered yet. Or he moved on to another city or state to continue his killing spree.

"Or," she speculated further, "he could have been arrested for some unrelated crime and is currently serving time in prison right now." These were just some of the things that had been known to happen to other killers, causing them to disappear from the scene and keep them from conducting what they felt driven to do.

Cortland waited for her to pause, then said, "Maybe."

"But you don't think so," Shayla guessed, observing his expression.

He was not about to say he had a gut feeling again. In his opinion, saying so the first time had been a mistake on his part. Even though she said he shared that instinct with some of her family, he felt it made him appear foolish.

So he flippantly said, "Fortune-telling is not in my realm."

"Not mine, either," she answered. "Just making a

calculated guess based on past events. Enjoy your coffee," she told him, ending what she felt had become a stilted conversation at best.

Shayla went back to reading through the various serial killer stories, because, unfortunately, there were more.

But she couldn't keep her mind on what she was reading. The stories were upsetting, to say the least, and she had to admit that she was being distracted by her new partner. Not because of anything he had said specifically so much as the unsettling vibes she was picking up.

The man had been through hell, and he didn't give her the impression he was back yet. She needed to find out what had happened to him. How could she have his back if she didn't know what was going on?

Shayla had already decided that asking Cortland about it wasn't going to get her anywhere except insanely frustrated, and going to the chief of detectives would bring her to the same dead end.

What she needed was input from a friendly source.

She had thought of Valri yesterday and hadn't had a chance to touch base with her cousin yet. Maybe it was time to do that.

Rising, she stopped by Cortland's desk. "I'll be right back," she promised.

Leafing through a report that had been on his desk when he came in this morning, Gabriel shrugged.

"Take all the time you want," he told her.

Shayla couldn't resist telling him, "Try not to miss me," before she headed for the squad room doorway.

The expression in his eyes when he raised them told her that he definitely wouldn't.

Shayla walked faster. If she discovered that there was nothing responsible for those sad eyes of his and he just had a nasty disposition, she promised herself that Cortland was going to be a very, very sorry human being.

Shayla took the elevator down to the basement, where both the morgue and the computer research department were located—fortunately not next to one another.

The door to the computer research department was open. There appeared to be several people in the room, but she didn't hear any voices. What she did hear was the rhythmic clicking of computer keys.

Stepping just inside the large, square room, Shayla knocked on the side of the door.

Valri was located on the far side of the room, completely involved in what she was doing. She usually was.

Even so, alert to any different sound, the computer expert raised her eyes in response to the knock.

"Hi!" Shayla greeted the woman everyone who availed themselves of her services referred to as "the computer wizard."

"Are you busy right now, Valri?"

She knew the woman obviously was, but it was a way for her to initiate the conversation she needed to have.

Humor played across Valri's lips. "Compared to me, Santa Claus is sitting still, twiddling his thumbs.

Why? What is it that you want me to do that I can't possibly do without growing a second pair of hands?"

Shayla began slowly. "You might have heard that Detective Gabriel Cortland has recently joined the homicide division."

"I have minions who tell me things, yes," Valri responded. Even as she talked, she seemed to be going full speed ahead at her keyboard, her fingers flying. "What about him?"

"Well, he's very closemouthed," Shayla continued, trying to find the right way to word her request.

"Heard that, too," Valri confirmed. Making a notation for herself, she moved her chair slightly and switched to another screen. That was when Shayla realized that the woman was working two monitors at the same time. She began to talk faster.

"Well, the chief of d's partnered us up," Shayla told Valri.

The latter flashed a smile at her.

"At your request, wasn't it?" It wasn't really a question, but Valri was curious to see what the family's newest detective would have to say about that.

"Yes." Shayla quickly launched into an explanation. "Detective Gabriel Cortland has the saddest eyes I've ever seen. I thought that maybe, if I was partnered with him, I could find a way to bring him around, help him rise above that sadness."

"Very noble. And how do I fit into this, since you're obviously here because you need something from me?" Valri concluded.

"I need to know *why* Cortland is so sad. It's nothing that he said—heaven knows the man doesn't talk," she told her cousin. "It's just the look in his eyes that gets to me." She lowered her voice so that it wouldn't carry to the other computer techs who worked under Valri. "I thought that maybe there's something in his personal records that would give me a clue, point me in the right direction." Shayla looked hopefully at her extremely proficient cousin.

Valri's expression didn't change. "In other words, you're hoping I would breach his privacy to satisfy your curiosity?" she guessed.

"It's not curiosity," Shayla told her. "I can't help him if I don't know why he's the way he is."

"Why don't you try asking him?" Valri suggested.

Shayla gave the computer expert a look. "If it was that simple, I would have already done it. The man is more closemouthed than a clam whose top and bottom were sealed together with crazy glue. I can barely pry 'hello' out of him. Predominantly, he speaks in grunts. I need help here. Specifically—" she looked at Valri pointedly "—I need *your* help."

Valri frowned slightly, looking at the various piles of folders on her extra-wide desk, all of which corresponded to different requests she had received. Gesturing at the stacks of folders, she said, "I have all these requests ahead of you. I haven't seen the bottom of my desk in months. Maybe even years," she added wistfully.

"I just need a hint, Valri. Something, *anything*, to get me moving in the right direction. I have this really uneasy feeling that the man is going to implode if I don't find a way to help him," she confided, leaning over Valri's desk again. "The man hardly eats, doesn't sleep much. I practically had to force-feed him a steak sandwich from Malone's."

"He is bad off, isn't he?" Valri commented. "The steak sandwiches from Malone's are my idea of heaven.

"I won't ask how you know he doesn't sleep much," Valri continued. "Okay, take a seat over there and give me a few minutes. I won't be able to give you much, but I can gather the basic headlines, and then you can take it from there. How's that?"

"That's terrific! I'm really grateful to you, Valri," Shayla told her cousin with feeling.

"Yeah, yeah. Go. Sit," she ordered, pointing toward a chair that was some distance away from hers.

Shayla did as she was told, crossing her fingers as she walked away. If anyone could help shed light on the situation, it was Valri.

Chapter Seven

Shayla was prepared to settle in and wait for a while in order to get some sort of an answer. She realized that she was interrupting Valri, and whatever the computer expert came up with, she would gladly run with it, because, right now, she had nothing.

To her surprise, she didn't have to wait all that long. She barely had time to sit back in the chair before she saw Valri's body language become rigid as her eyes scanned the screen before her.

A moment later, the computer wizard looked up and was beckoning to her to come over.

Extremely hopeful, Shayla didn't even remember crossing the floor back to her cousin's desk. However, her eagerness was tempered with a note of caution. *That* was coupled with an underlying feeling of dread. If anyone had asked her why she felt that way, she wouldn't have been able to explain the origin of the sensation in the pit of her stomach—she just knew that it was there.

"What did you find?" Shayla asked, still attempting to interrupt the expression on the computer expert's face.

Valri glanced toward her cousin, then back at the screen she had just pulled up. "You do know that Cortland had been tracking the LA Moonlight Killer, right?" she asked. When Shayla nodded, the computer expert continued, "Cortland transferred here when it looked as if the killer was taking his spree away from LA."

"Yes, I know," Shayla said.

Valri measured her next words carefully. "Did you also know that, when Cortland was getting too close, the Moonlight Killer killed Cortland's wife?"

Shayla didn't remember sitting down in the chair next to Valri's desk, but she must have, because she found herself there when her knees suddenly gave way.

"No," she whispered in a horrified voice, "I didn't know that."

But Valri wasn't finished giving her all the heart-wrenching details yet. "His *pregnant* wife," the computer expert emphasized.

Shayla's hands flew to her mouth to keep the cry of horror back. She could almost feel her scream ricocheting in her throat. The information made her sick to her stomach.

Her eyes filled with tears, but she managed to keep them from spilling out.

"Oh, how awful for him," Shayla cried. It all made sense to her now. She could totally understand why Cortland was so obsessed with catching this particular killer. And why there was so much sadness about the man.

Valri looked up from the screen she had been scrolling. "It looks like this killer is obsessed with your Detective Cortland," she commented to her cousin.

Shayla was about to correct her cousin that Cortland wasn't *her* detective, but since she was partnered with the man, it might sound like she was just splitting hairs, she thought. What really mattered here was that Cortland had lost his wife to this maniac. He was going to need help in tracking down this serial killer and bringing him in.

Shayla swallowed, trying to keep her breakfast down. The details Valri had just given her made that a challenge.

"Anything else?" she asked, doing her best to come around.

"Isn't that enough?" Valri asked her in surprise.

"Yes, it is," Shayla acknowledged sadly. "I just wanted to know if the report contained any other bombshells I should know about."

Valri looked back at the report on her monitor. "Only that when his wife was killed—he discovered the body, by the way," she added as a potent footnote, "Cortland went on an extensive bender that all but killed him. Because he had been such an exemplary detective and this crime was such an unspeakably horrific blow to him, his superiors tried to look the other way," she told her cousin as she quickly scanned the information. "Luckily, Cortland eventually cleaned up his act and asked to be transferred. I gather that his sole purpose in life became finding the killer and, I'm assuming, bringing him to justice."

Finished with her update, Valri sighed as she looked at Shayla. "I certainly don't envy you, Shay," she said, thinking about her cousin leaving here and trying to deal with her partner armed with this information.

"That makes two of us," Shayla murmured.

Valri's curiosity got the better of her. "So what are you going to do?" she asked. "Ask for another partner?"

Shayla's eyes met her cousin's. Valri knew better than that, she thought. "No way on earth," she told her cousin firmly.

Valri laughed softly. "I didn't think so," she replied. "Let me know if there's anything else I can do to help."

Shayla barely heard her. Nodding, she murmured, "Will do," as she quickly left the computer lab.

That poor man, Shayla couldn't help thinking as she hurried to the elevator. What Valri had told her kept replaying in her head. Fighting back tears again, Shayla tried to picture herself in his place, coming home and discovering the murdered body of his wife. It was just too awful to contemplate.

No wonder he had trouble sleeping. She wouldn't have been able to close her eyes in his place, not without being haunted by visions of what he had seen.

Impatience overwhelmed her. She had no idea how she was going to handle the situation once she was in the same room with Cortland. The main thing she had to remember was to curb her desire to throw her arms around the man and just hug him in an attempt to comfort her partner.

That was the way things were done in her family, but Shayla knew Cortland wouldn't appreciate that. The detective would most likely view it as a display of pity on her part rather than having her really feeling for him.

Well, she would find some way of comforting the man, she promised herself. To assist him with his mission—because that's what it was—and help him eventually come back to the living.

She knew now what she was up against. Armed with this information, she needed to get on with what needed to be done and, along the way, help Cortland take possession of his soul again.

He couldn't be allowed to let despair overwhelm him.

Determined, Shayla got off on her floor. It took her a second to hear the sobbing.

Heart-wrenching sobbing.

The sound was coming from a young woman one of the uniformed officers was attempting to talk to. He was also trying to quiet her down.

The officer was failing.

Shayla quickened her pace and walked up to the unusual pair. When she drew closer, she realized that the officer was trying to bring the young woman into the homicide squad room. The distraught young woman didn't even seem to hear him. Or, if she did, she wasn't processing what he was saying to her.

The moment that Shayla walked up, the officer's eyes darted in her direction, and he looked incredibly relieved.

For her part, Shayla looked from the police officer to the distraught young woman he was unsuccessfully trying to calm down.

"Can I help you?" Shayla asked the officer.

The story instantly came pouring out. "I found her like this downstairs, Detective. Every time I asked her what was wrong, she choked up and couldn't answer me. She just kept crying." The look on the young officer's face said that he realized his narrative was disjointed. He tried to explain his reasoning. "I saw a trace of blood on her shirt and thought maybe I should bring her up to Homicide."

The shell-shocked brunette's eyes widened a little at the mention of the word *homicide*, but she still didn't say anything. She just kept on sobbing.

The officer mutely appealed to Shayla for help. "I'm already late for my shift," he told her.

She knew what was probably coming. He was going to ask her for help. Given the situation, she felt she couldn't refuse. "I'll take it from here, Officer—"

She looked at the policeman, waiting for a name.

The man finally came to. "Yates," he said, raising his voice to be heard above the sobbing woman. "Ron Yates."

Shayla made a mental note of the officer's name in case she had more questions for him later.

"I'll get in contact if there's anything to tell you," she promised, then turned her attention toward the woman. "Why don't you come in with me so you can sit down?" she suggested kindly. "And then you can tell me just what happened."

"I don't know," the woman gasped, her voice cracking.

They were the first words the woman had offered, and Shayla seized them immediately. "Maybe if we start at the beginning," she coaxed, taking the sobbing woman by the hand and slowly leading her into the squad room.

Everyone in the front of the squad room turned to look at them, especially when the young woman finally managed to choke out an attention-getting phrase. "She's dead!"

And just like that, the room was alive with detectives and police personnel, all converging around Shayla and the sobbing woman with her.

Doing her best to focus on the distraught brunette, Shayla led her to her desk and had the woman sit down in the chair that faced hers.

Shayla noted that Cortland had drawn closer as well.

"What happened?" Cortland asked his partner before anyone else had a chance to voice the question.

"I haven't been able to get that out of her yet," Shayla told him honestly. "Maybe you'll have better luck."

The commotion had succeeded in drawing Hollandale out of his office as well. He immediately made his way over to Shayla's desk. The other detectives drew back, giving the lieutenant space.

"What's going on here?" he asked, his eyes sweeping over the scene.

"Officer Yates brought her up here," Shayla explained. "He said he found her like this. He couldn't get her to talk, but he saw the blood on her clothes, so he thought that she might have either witnessed a homicide or been part of one," she guess, filling in the details into Yates's anemic narrative for the lieutenant's benefit as well as Cortland's.

Hollandale nodded. He had learned to roll with the punches a long time ago.

"Why don't you come into my office, ma'am?" he politely requested, making it seem that the choice was hers to make instead of his.

The woman rubbed the heel of her hand against her tearstained face, trying to dry it.

"Cavanaugh, since you brought her in, why don't you come along, too?" Hollandale suggested. He began to turn, then paused. His eyes swept over her partner. "Cortland?"

It was all he said and all that he really needed to say.

The dark-haired detective followed in their wake.

Like a deflated balloon, the sobbing woman collapsed into a chair the moment the lieutenant directed her toward it.

"Would you like something to drink?" Hollandale asked the woman. "Water? Coffee? Soda?"

She shook her head in response to each suggestion.

Instead, she pressed her hands against her lips as if attempting to pull herself together so that she could finally say some intelligible words.

Shayla moved closer to the woman. Ever so gently, she took the woman's hands into her own. "Take your time," she told her. "I'm Detective Shayla Cavanaugh. This is Detective Cortland, and this is our commander, Lieutenant Hollandale." She looked at the woman, who was marginally beginning to settle down. "When you're ready, you can tell us your name."

"Maureen," the brunette finally said. "Maureen O'Hara." A knowing half smile quirked her mouth. "My mother loved old movies," she explained. Her voice broke just then, and she struggled to continue.

"Take your time, Ms. O'Hara," the lieutenant advised gently.

Maureen raised her head, still struggling to contain her emotions. After a moment, she began talking again, although it was obvious difficult for her to keep her voice steady.

"I came in early to get my check. The door wasn't locked, but—" Her voice broke again, and she pressed her lips together.

"But what?" Hollandale asked kindly.

Shayla noticed that Cortland hadn't said a word since he came in with them. Instead, he was watching the young woman intently, like he was waiting for something to rise to the forefront.

"But it didn't look like there was anyone there," she said helplessly. "At first," she added belatedly. Fresh tears rose to her eyes.

"Where do you work, Maureen?" Shayla asked the young woman.

"It's a twenty-four-hour convenience store on Alton and Yale," the woman said, studying her fingertips as if the answer was somehow found there. "It wasn't my shift, but I wanted to get my check, so... so I stopped by and...and...that's when I saw her," she sobbed, her voice breaking.

"Saw who?" The deep voice startled them. All three people in the room turned to look at Cortland, who had finally spoken up.

"Shirley." There was almost a look of agony in the young woman's eyes as she answered the question.

"Shirley?" Cortland repeated.

"I don't know her last name," Maureen lamented. "I should, but I don't. Didn't," she corrected herself, as if that information existed in the past but no longer in the present.

"Where was Shirley?" Shayla asked. She was aware that the lieutenant was observing both her and Cortland, undoubtedly wanting to see how they performed under strained circumstances, she thought.

"On the floor," Maureen answered, her voice cracking. "She was all tied up in this awful, bizarre way. There was a thin rope around one of her ankles, and it led up to her throat. It looked as if she had choked herself, but that doesn't make any sense." Maureen looked at Hollandale. "Does it?"

There were details that had been left out of news reports on the serial killer's murders. The detectives who had been involved in trying to catch the killer were aware of them, but the public had been kept in the dark about the killer's very strange way of tying up his victims that brought about their demise.

"Anything else?" Hollandale gently coaxed.

The young woman looked down at the blood on her sleeve.

"Yeah," she answered, her voice hollow, as if she was trying to separate herself from the image that hovered in her mind's eye. "There was blood on her left cheek, and it looked like someone had—had—" She covered her face with her hands, as if that could somehow wipe away the image she saw—but it couldn't.

"Had carved initials into her face," Cortland filled in.

The woman looked at him, stricken. "Yes!" she cried then began sobbing again.

Chapter Eight

It wasn't easy, not to mention somewhat time-consuming, but by speaking slowly and calmly to the distraught young woman, Shayla and Lieutenant Hollandale eventually managed to piece together the choppy information Maureen gave them.

They found out that the traumatized clerk had practically tripped over the other woman's body. Horrified, rather than calling the police, Maureen had run out of the store and away from the crime scene.

The details were all jumbled up as they emerged from her mouth. She didn't even seem to know how long it had taken her to get from the convenience store to the precinct, but somehow, she had eventually managed to stumble into the police station.

That was where, Shayla told the other two men, Officer Yates had found her. Listening, Hollandale nodded. He looked far from pleased. "Looks like that LA serial killer did resurface here after all." The lieutenant looked at the two detectives in his office. "Cortland, Cavanaugh, take a couple of uniforms with you, call in a CSI team and head over to the crime scene."

Maureen looked horrified at this turn of events. Her eyes darted from the detectives to the lieutenant. "Please don't make me go back there!" she begged as she began to shake.

"Don't worry about that," the lieutenant told her in a comforting tone. "Right now, all we need from you is the address of the convenience store. We would like you to stay here and give your statement to Detective Lorenzo."

Maureen nodded numbly. A small woman, she looked as if she wanted to fold up into herself if she possibly could.

"The store is on the corner of Alton and Yale," she said, her voice cracking.

The lieutenant called in two uniformed officers. He gave the two policemen the address.

Meanwhile, Shayla was calling the CSI division, requesting that a team, along with an accompanying coroner, be sent to the scene of the crime.

It was all attended to in record time.

"SHOULDN'T YOU WAIT until you're sure that there *is* a crime scene?" Gabriel asked her as they took the stairs out of the building and headed to the parking lot.

"Did she sound as if she was making all this up to you?" Shayla asked in surprise.

Gabriel shrugged. He'd had time to think, and he realized that hoping the serial killer would materialize might have colored the way he viewed everything. Maybe it made him believe the young woman's story when he should have held it somewhat suspect.

"People lie about all sorts of things for all sorts of reasons," Gabriel told her.

"Maybe," Shayla allowed. "But Maureen looked too sick to her stomach to be making all this up. And if we wait to verify the information before calling in CSI, that's that much more time that we've managed to lose. We've already lost more time than we should have."

Reaching the bottom of the stairs, she looked at Cortland. She was determined to have him think of her as his partner, not a cross he had to bear. Which was why she asked him, "You want to take your car or mine to the crime scene?"

Cortland didn't hesitate for a second. "Mine."

Shayla smiled to herself. She thought so. Cortland struck her as someone who needed to be in control at all times. Given what Valri had told her, she saw no reason for her to point out the obvious to her partner—that she was far more familiar with the area than he was. If he wanted to drive, then so be it.

Turning on her heel, Shayla made her way over toward where his vehicle was parked. Standing next to it, she surprised Cortland.

He scowled at her, confused. "How did you know which one was mine?"

"I like being prepared," she told him cheerfully. "That car was parked in the space that corresponded to your apartment number when I came by last night to bring you the sandwich and fries."

That gave him pause for a moment. "All right," he

said, hitting the button on his key fob that opened all the locks on his vehicle.

Getting in, he looked at the GPS on his dashboard. He didn't want to admit that he needed help, but he knew he had to. It was either that or waste time driving around in circles. "What did you say the address of this convenience store was?" he asked.

Rather than tell him, Shayla leaned over and typed in the address on his GPS. Finished, she smiled at him. "There."

"Thanks," Gabriel bit off. Putting the car in gear, he took off.

The two uniform policemen had gotten to the destination a couple of beats ahead of them. Drawing closer, Gabriel saw that telltale yellow crime scene tape stretched across the store's doorway. A very small crowd had begun to gather outside, speculating on what had happened.

Shayla wove her way through the small crowd, ignoring their questions for the time being. Cortland walked ahead of her, forging a path for both of them.

Walking into the convenience store, Shayla saw the victim lying on the floor behind the counter. The woman was tied up the way Maureen had described.

Shayla instantly looked up at Cortland for his reaction. In her opinion, her partner looked numb and pale.

"Are you all right?" she whispered to Cortland.

"Yeah," he snapped, then looked at her accusingly. "Why shouldn't I be?"

"No reason," she answered, attempting to brush the whole thing off.

But it wasn't in her to lie. Being part of a police-oriented family had its consequences. One of which was to always tell the truth, no matter what.

So she did.

"I just thought it might bring up some bad memories," she admitted.

Was she implying something, he couldn't help wondering, growing defensive. "There are no good memories when it comes to homicide," he informed her coldly.

"No, there aren't," Shayla readily agreed. Taking out her cell phone, she bent close to the victim and snapped a few photographs.

"I thought CSI did that sort of thing," Gabriel said, surprised to see that this woman he had to put up with was taking pictures of the grim scene.

"Oh, they do," she assured him. "I just like to have my own set. Maybe I can see something in the ones I take that aren't visible in the other photos," she explained.

Crouching next to the victim, Shayla could feel her heart aching. "Poor thing never had a chance," she murmured. She looked the dead woman over carefully. "I think the killer took her completely by surprise. There aren't even any defensive wounds on her. She didn't have a chance to fight back." Shayla could feel a chill slithering down her spine. "This guy's a sick monster."

"Well, we agree on that," Cortland told her.

He slowly surveyed the entirety of the small, crowded crime scene. Unlike some convenience stores that had several aisles customers could wander down, this store was relatively small, crowded with displays that took up almost all the available space.

"We're not dealing with a big guy," Shayla concluded.

"What makes you say that?" Cortland asked, curious as to the thought process that led her to this conclusion.

"Nothing's knocked over," she pointed out. "If the killer was a big man, in a place like this, all sorts of things would have been toppled over."

She looked at the woman on the floor again. She wished the coroner would arrive so those awful ropes could be taken off the victim. They were dehumanizing.

"The second he put his hands on her," Shayla continued, "she would have tried to run away."

"Not necessarily," Cortland told her, circling the woman's body like a bloodhound that had caught the scent of something and was now zeroing in on it.

"Are you saying he charmed her?" Shayla asked, trying to follow Cortland's thinking.

"No," he answered, still circling the inert body, "I'm saying that he gave her a shot of something that immobilized her, knocked her out so that he could tie her up like some lassoed rodeo calf. Probably walked up behind her like he was going to ask her a question, then injected her." He had his guess as to what the killer might have used.

She looked at Cortland, horror stricken. "I hadn't thought of that."

"I did," Gabriel answered grimly.

Moved, thinking of what he had to have gone through, finding his wife this way, before she could stop herself, Shayla said, "I'm sorry."

Gabriel thought she was referring to what the victim had gone through before she died and allowed himself a moment to feel sorry for the murdered woman.

"Yeah," he replied, looking at the dead woman. "Me, too."

Shayla read what the detective was thinking in his face. She was about to correct him, then decided that it was better this way. He wouldn't suddenly turn defensive on her, and she wouldn't have to admit that she knew about what had happened to his wife. She thought it would be better if she was more prepared to voice the right sentiments in the right way. She didn't want to give the detective cause to snarl at her.

The next moment, she heard her uncle's deep voice.

"I'm not sure we're all going to be able to fit in here," Sean Cavanaugh said as he arrived at the convenience store with his team in tow. He paused just inside the doorway with its yellow tape. "I'm not even sure there's enough room for our equipment." Sean nodded at the new detective he didn't recognize and then smiled at his niece. "What do you have for me?"

"Apparently the Moonlight Killer's latest victim, I think," she told her uncle when Cortland made no response to her question.

"The Moonlight Killer?" the CSI leader repeated, somewhat taken aback. "It's been over nine months since anyone's heard from that creep. I was hoping that, if nothing else, maybe he had retired. Or died."

"Not hardly," Gabriel replied, rocking back on his heels.

Shayla had noticed that her partner had been combing through the various debris on the floor, obviously searching for something.

From the look on Cortland's face, Shayla judged, he had just found it.

"What do you have?" she asked, nodding at his hand. His glove-covered fingers were curled around something.

"A broken syringe." The item was lying in the center of his blue-gloved hand.

"You were right," Shayla cried excitedly, standing on her toes and peering over Cortland's broad shoulder.

"Of course I was right," he answered.

"Would either of you want to let me in on what you're talking about?" Sean asked.

Rather than speak up the way Gabriel assumed that his partner would, Shayla took a step back and gestured toward him, giving him the floor.

"Go ahead," she said. "You're a lot more familiar with the way this sick SOB operates than I am."

Cortland's face was grim as he slowly described how the Moonlight Killer managed to get the drop on the women he singled out to be his victims. "It looks like he manages to come up behind them and

injects them with some sort of a neuromuscular blocking agent."

Sean looked surprised, then nodded. "I'm familiar
with that substance. It's fast acting and immobilizes
the victim so that they can't move, can't speak, but
they're not unconscious. They're aware of everything
that's going on around them. I once heard of couples
supposedly using it to enhance the whole sexual experience, but that's just a line of bull," Sean concluded.
"It's an awful way to victimize someone."

"That's not available to just anyone, is it?" Shayla
asked her uncle.

"No, a person would have to be a doctor to get
their hands on it. It's meant as a fallback during sur-
gery," Sean told her.

"A doctor or some kind of other medical professional," Shayla expanded, thinking out loud. "Like
a nurse practitioner. Or maybe a pharmacist," she
guessed.

"All possibilities," Sean agreed. He snapped out
of his thoughts. "Well, I've got a crime scene to process," he told the duo, excusing himself.

Shayla moved out of her uncle's way and looked at
her partner. He was looking particularly grim at the
moment. "Are you all right?" she asked.

Irritated, he almost snapped at her. If they had
been alone, he would have. "Why do you keep asking me that?" he demanded.

"You look pale," she explained. "I would have
thought that by now, you would have reached a satu-
ration point with these murders."

He shrugged. "No more than anyone else dealing with homicides," he said. And then he looked at her more closely. "There's something else, isn't there?"

There was, but she didn't think now was a good time to broach it. Maybe when he had gotten to know her better—and trusted her more—she could tell him what she had found out. "Why don't we question some of the people in the area, find out if they might have seen something last night, instead of quizzing each other?" she suggested brightly.

He gestured for her to lead the way, but he wasn't convinced that there wasn't something she wasn't telling him—something she was holding back.

THEY COMBED THE AREA, but after canvassing the nearby stores, all of which had been closed at the time the murder had taken place, they weren't able to find anyone who could tell them anything had might shed any light on the circumstances.

As they made their way back toward the convenience store, Shayla noticed a restaurant across the way. She pointed it out.

"It has a surveillance camera outside the window that might have picked up something," she suggested to her partner, "but I wouldn't get my hopes up."

"I'm not," he told her.

As it turned out, she was right. The camera was broken and had been left up to hopefully deter robberies until it was fixed, the embarrassed restaurant owner explained.

After several hours of canvassing the local stores

in the area, they had nothing to show for their trouble. None of the surveillance cameras—the working ones—had captured anything worthwhile.

The Moonlight Killer, Shayla thought, remained as big a mystery now as he had been before the convenience store worker had lost her life.

It felt like forever before they finally returned to Cortland's vehicle and got in.

He glanced in Shayla's direction as he buckled up. "You look drained," Cortland commented.

"I am," she said, sighing. "This is my first serial killer. How do you do it?"

Cortland started up the Crown Victoria. He had no idea what she was talking about. "How do I do what?"

"How do you manage to keep going?" she asked Cortland.

He didn't answer immediately. Instead, he waited until he could stop at a light, and then he looked at her. He understood where she was going with this now.

"Because throwing up my hands is not going to capture this SOB and get those women the justice that they all deserve," he told her. He tossed her another pointed glance before continuing to drive back to the precinct. "Anything else?" he asked.

"No," she answered quietly. "Not right now."

Chapter Nine

When they walked into the homicide squad room, Shayla and her partner went to see their lieutenant. She assumed Cortland would be the one to describe the crime scene to their superior. But he sat down in front of Hollandale's desk, remaining silent, so she was forced to start talking, giving Hollandale a summary of what they had seen and dealt with.

Finished, Shayla slid forward to the edge of her seat and asked the lieutenant, "Do you think that there is any way you could put pressure on whatever coroner is on duty today to do the autopsy on the convenience store victim first? Or at least complete that autopsy before the end of day?"

The lieutenant looked at both of the detectives. "Is there some question about the way the woman was killed?" Hollandale asked. From the input he had already received, the cause of death seemed pretty cut-and-dried.

It was on the tip of Shayla's tongue to tell the lieutenant about Cortland's theory regarding the drug that may have been used to render the poor woman immobile. But that information belonged to her partner.

She forced herself to look at the detective sitting next to her. "Cortland found something," she told the lieutenant.

Hollandale turned his chair slightly to face the silent detective. "I'm listening, Cortland," he said, waiting for the man to start talking.

Gabriel preferred *doing* to *talking*, but it was obvious to him that he had no choice, so he told his superior, "I think the killer uses a neuromuscular blocking agent to render his victims immobile before he ties them up." Each word cost him, and he tried not to think about Natalie suffering at this maniac's hands.

"You think?" the lieutenant asked, clearly asking for some sort of proof to back up this theory.

Gabriel frowned. He wasn't keen on performing like some sort of trained seal, but he also knew he couldn't go on operating on his own. Everyone in this precinct supported teamwork. If this serial killer was going to be caught, he needed to accept that fact and be part of that team.

"I know," Gabriel corrected himself, enunciating the two words in a clear, firm voice for the lieutenant's benefit.

Seeing her partner's discomfort, Shayla immediately jumped in. "That's why we need that autopsy done as soon as possible," she explained. "So we can get a clearer picture of what we're dealing with."

Hollandale nodded agreeably. "If the coroner on duty is swamped for some reason, I'll see if I can get another set of hands down there to handle the clerk's autopsy," he promised, then asked, "Did any of the locals see anything that might prove useful?"

Shayla shook her head. "No one was even out walking their dog when this happened," she answered. "Cortland and I went around the neighborhood, but it was mostly stores and restaurants, all of which were closed for the night at that time."

She knew what the lieutenant's next question was going to be and beat him to it. "There weren't very many surveillance cameras in the area, either, and the ones that were there either weren't working, or, according to the store owner, hadn't recorded anything."

The lieutenant turned toward the newest detective to join the squad. "Anything to add, Cortland?"

"No, Cavanaugh covered everything, sir," Gabriel told his superior respectfully.

"From what I'm told," Hollandale said with a smile, glancing toward Shayla, "she usually does." The lieutenant moved forward in his chair. "All right, write up your reports and see if you can come up with any connections to the other victims who were killed by this psychopath. We still don't know what makes him single out the women he kills."

Shayla rose to her feet, as did Cortland. "Yes, sir," she said, answering for both of them. "You will be the first to know if we find a pattern."

Gabriel expected her to say something about the meeting, but she didn't. Instead, she hurried back to her desk. The moment she got there, Shayla sat down and picked up the telephone receiver.

Normally, curiosity was something Gabriel could easily contain and ignore unless it was directly related to a case he was working on, at which point he would explore—on his own—whatever it was that had aroused his curiosity in the first place.

But this woman he had been forced to work with had somehow managed to affect his usual way of thinking and had spurred his curiosity.

Gabriel heard himself asking her, "Who are you calling?"

About to answer him, Shayla was forced to hold up her hand like a traffic cop, telling him to hold on to that thought as she heard the receiver on the other end being picked up.

"Kristin, hi, it's Shayla. Christian's sister," she added since there were so many family members floating around, sometimes it was hard putting a face to a name. Now that she had the lieutenant's blessing, she wanted to get this autopsy moving along as quickly as possible. "I need a favor—it's sanctioned by my lieutenant, in case you're wondering. Lieutenant Hollandale," she supplied, adding, "He's the new man in charge of the homicide division."

Shayla heard the medical examiner pause for a moment, as if she was thinking, then say, "I'm familiar with him. What do you—and he—need?" Kristin asked.

"We need an autopsy done on this convenience store clerk who was found dead this morning, and we need the report as soon as possible." In case the medical examiner had misgivings, Shayla added, "Apparently, the Moonlight Killer has moved his base of operation from LA to our fair little city."

"Oh Lord, we didn't need this." Kristin sighed. "Is there anything in particular that you are looking for or hoping to find in this report?"

Shayla give her a quick summation. "My partner found a syringe near the victim's body. He believes that the killer injected his victim with a neuromuscular blocking agent in order to paralyze her. If you can find any indication of that in her system, it might help us narrow our list of people to look at and consider."

"Because not everyone can get their hands on this drug," Kristin guessed.

"Exactly. So, do you think you'll be able to get down to the morgue?" she asked hopefully.

"I need to make a phone call first," the medical examiner told the young woman she had inherited the day that she had married Malloy Cavanaugh, "but yes, I can get down to the morgue. Nothing I like doing better on my day off than an autopsy," she told Shayla with a laugh.

Shayla breathed a sigh of relief. "Thank you, Kris. I owe you."

"Yes," Kristin agreed. "You do. And I plan to collect on that promise when I find myself needing a babysitter."

Shayla nearly dropped the receiver. "You don't mean for Malloy, do you?" she asked.

"Nope," Kristin answered.

Shayla could practically hear the grin in her cousin-in-law's voice. Malloy had to be pleased as anything, she thought, herself immensely delighted. "When?"

"Seven months from now. You have time," Kristin told her.

"I think that's wonderful! Keep me posted," she said.

Kristin laughed. "I plan to keep everyone posted. As for your other request, I'll be at the morgue as soon as possible."

"Are you sure you can handle it?" she asked, concerned now that this newest piece of information had come up.

"Hey, I'm a Cavanaugh," Kristin reminded her. "Even if it is by marriage. We Cavanaughs can handle everything—or so it said on my wedding certificate. See you," she said just before she hung up.

Shayla could almost feel Cortland's eyes on her the entire time she had been on the phone. The moment she put down the receiver, he asked, "What was that all about?"

"We have a medical examiner in the family," she told her partner. "I just got her to agree to come in on her day off to do our victim's autopsy. Otherwise, we might have to wait until sometime tomorrow or even the day after that to find out if that immobilizing drug you mentioned was in her system. From what I gather," she went on, "there are a number of autopsies at the morgue waiting to be done ahead of our victim's."

But that wasn't what he was asking about. "Do you always squeal gleefully when arranging for an autopsy?"

She had forgotten about that, Shayla thought. She hadn't meant to let that sound slip. Gabriel was obviously waiting for an answer.

"No, that was personal," she said, hoping that was enough to satisfy him. It wasn't. She sighed, continuing. "The medical examiner, Kristin Alberghetti Cavanaugh, is married to my cousin Malloy Cavanaugh."

It still wasn't making any sense to him. "Is that why you squealed?"

To be honest, Gabriel didn't even know why he was asking. But since he had gotten stuck in this work relationship, he felt that he might as well try to make it work. Or at least understand it—and her.

Who knew, her answer might even turn out to be useful to him down the line, although he did have his doubts. So far, working with this woman who had relatives hiding in every nook and cranny at the precinct was one great big chaotic mystery—not to mention a pain.

"No," she answered, searching madly for a reason to give him to explain why she had suddenly sounded so joyous. Normally, she would have had no problem telling him—or anyone—the real reason. This pregnancy was just wonderful news.

But in this case, it would just unearth some terrible memories and subject Cortland to a great deal of pain. Pain she didn't want him experiencing.

"So why did you squeal?" Gabriel asked.

Shayla pressed her lips together. If Cortland did stay in the homicide division for a while, he was bound to see Kristin's condition for himself. He might as well hear it from her now.

"I just found out that my cousin's wife is pregnant," she told Gabriel. Shayla never took her eyes off her partner's face.

A whole barrage of emotions passed through him before Gabriel was able to completely shut down his expression and get hold of his thoughts.

Shayla could see the man's pain, and for the second time since she had found out about his wife, she felt that overwhelming desire to comfort him, to somehow attempt to take away at least some of the pain that Cortland had to be feeling.

"I'm sorry," Shayla said as she put her hand on his shoulder.

Gabriel shrugged it off. Not trusting himself to speak, he strode toward the doorway and crossed the threshold, going out into the hall.

For half a second, Shayla thought of just letting him go. But she had never been one to step away and hope that things would just take care of themselves. She knew that wasn't the way things were done.

So instead of watching her partner go, she was on her feet, moving fast and hoping to catch up with Gabriel before he disappeared.

She managed to reach him just as he was about to open the door to the stairway. Well, at least he hadn't disappeared into the elevator.

"Wait," she implored, making a grab for his shoulder.

Unlike in the office, this was not a hand on his

shoulder that was meant to offer comfort. What she was trying to do was to hold her partner in place until she could get the man to listen to her.

Gabe knew he could very easily shake her off and keep going until he could get hold of himself. But instead, he just looked at her, waiting for some sort of an explanation and trying his damnedest to get hold of his rampaging emotions.

"What?" he demanded.

There was no way around this. She had to tell him and fervently hope that instead of shutting off communication between them altogether, it would somehow magically open it up.

"I know," she told him, lowering her voice at the last second as someone walked by. Shayla didn't want the woman in the hall to hear what she was about to say.

He waited until the person passed. "Know what?" he all but growled.

She never took her eyes off his. "I know about your wife."

His first instinct was to pull away and storm off. But instead, Gabriel forced himself to say, between clenched teeth, "Know what?"

"That she was a victim of the LA Moonlight Killer," Shayla answered. They were not the easiest words to for her to utter, especially since she was still looking her partner in the eye. But she felt that looking away would have somehow been insulting to the memory of the woman he had lost. "I am so sorry," she told him again, unable to find another way to offer him her condolences or to comfort her partner.

She had learned a long time ago that everyone who had ever lost a loved one had to find their own way back. The only thing she could do was offer her presence to him whenever he felt like talking about what he was going through—if he ever even got to that point.

"Yeah," Gabriel bit off dismissively. And then he suddenly looked up at her. He had a feeling that wasn't all. "What else do you know?" he asked, pinning her in place.

This was even more difficult to say than the first part had been, she thought. She debated pretending that there wasn't anything else, but she had a feeling that Cortland wouldn't be so easily led astray. With all her heart, she wished she had made her call to Kristin in private so that none of this would be coming to light anywhere around her partner right now.

Shayla forced the words out. "I know that your wife was pregnant at the time the serial killer snuffed out her life."

"She wasn't a candle," Gabriel shouted at her before he could get hold of himself.

None of this was coming out the way she wanted it to. "I didn't mean to imply that she was. I'm trying to apologize here, Gabriel," she explained, then added, "I don't usually walk into something that I need to apologize for. I'm usually the one who says the right thing at the right time, even when everyone else is at a loss for words." She blew out a breath, wondering if there was anything else she could possibly say to somehow make up for the fact that she had walked right into this.

He knew she meant well and that she was trying her best to say the right thing. But he just felt so angry about everything, including having his privacy invaded, that he couldn't immediately forgive Shayla.

Waving a dismissive hand at her, Gabriel told her, "Forget about it," in a detached, distant voice.

"I can't," Shayla told him honestly. "But now that it's out and you're aware of the fact that I know, I want *you* to know that if you ever need someone to talk to about what happened—or about anything at all, for that matter—I'm here for you. You can always talk to me if you need to."

He looked at her as if she had just told him that she intended to keep poking at the wound he'd suffered. All he wanted was for her to back off.

"I don't need or want to talk to anyone," he informed her pointedly. "Have I made myself clear?"

She wanted to argue with him about it, to tell him that no man was an island or could consider himself to be one.

Not even him.

But for now, she knew that the best thing she could do for her partner was back off and give him some time to heal—or at least go through the motions of attempting to heal.

"Perfectly." Regrouping, Shayla said, "All right, let's

find a way to bring this killer in." With that, she turned on her heel and walked back to the squad room, hoping that he would decide to follow her.

After a couple of minutes, Cortland finally did.

Chapter Ten

They were back the following day, working with the meager input they had gathered on the serial killer. As it turned out, Kristin had been unable to come in late yesterday, but she was in this morning and had called to tell them so.

Shayla noticed that Cortland kept checking his watch every so often. She knew he was waiting for Kristin to call back with information.

After observing his behavior several times, Shayla felt obligated to tell her partner, "Most autopsies take between two and four hours. Sometimes longer."

She was going to add that time didn't go by any faster if he kept looking at his watch, but she decided to keep that remark to herself.

Gabriel arched an eyebrow and gave her a look. "Your point?" he asked.

"No point," she answered innocently. "Just a fact that I wanted to throw out there." Because she felt her partner needed something concrete to hang on to, she went on to tell him, "Since we gave the medical examiner something specific to look for, she'll probably call us once the results of that test are in. Until then," she continued, looking down at her desk, "we've got all this paperwork to keep us busy." Leaning back in her chair, she blew out a breath. "And I don't know about you, but I feel like we're going around in circles."

Gabriel merely grunted. She took that as his way of agreeing.

They continued writing the reports and studying what they had managed to collect, which didn't amount to all that much. But in her opinion, "something" was always better than nothing.

After another hour had gone by, Shayla felt like everything was aching. She moved her neck back and forth, trying to get rid of the kink that seemed to have gathered at the very base and was now throbbing.

Closing her eyes, she took a minuscule break. A number of thoughts had been crowding in her brain. Opening her eyes again, she glanced at her partner. "You know, there's also the possibility that this wasn't the work of the Moonlight Killer at all."

Cortland eyed her sharply. "What do you mean?"

"Maybe she was killed by someone she knew, like an old boyfriend she had cheated on who was looking to get even with her and that's why there were no defensive wounds found on her. He caught her by surprise before she realized what he was up to and could fight back."

"You're forgetting about the syringe," Gabriel pointed out.

She *had* forgotten about that, Shayla realized. The

way the clerk had been bound was also identical to the other victims, but the detail about the syringe had been left out of the other accounts, so only the killer and the LA police would know about that.

She hadn't known about that detail until Cortland had mentioned it.

"And you came across a syringe at one of the Moonlight Killer's murder scenes before?" she asked, just to be sure.

"Yes, I did," he answered flatly. His expression was dark.

She didn't have to ask her partner for further details. Instinctively, she knew that he'd probably found a syringe at the site of his wife's murder.

Shayla was about to go back to reviewing the files stacked on her desk for the umpteenth time when the phone next to her rang.

"Hopefully, that's the cavalry," she murmured, reaching for the receiver. "Cavanaugh."

"Shayla, can you and your partner get down here?" Kristin asked.

Up until the phone rang, she had felt as if she was in danger of having her eyes shutting on her. The moment she heard Kristin's voice on the other end of the line, Shayla felt as if she had suddenly come to life.

"Did you find something?" she asked, cradling the phone against her neck and shoulder as she pulled her files together into one neat, orderly pile.

"I think so," Kristin answered, trying to keep the excitement out of her voice. "Since you gave me something specific to look for, I had the test identifying a neuromuscular blocking agent in her system fast-tracked. The results just came back a minute ago."

This could just lead them to the break that they were looking for, Shayla thought hopefully. At the very least, it was a start.

Pushing her chair away from her with the backs of her legs as she rose, Shayla told her cousin's wife, "We'll be right there."

Gabriel was on his feet immediately. "Your friend found something?" he asked. There was actually what passed for a hopeful note in his voice.

Shayla caught herself mentally crossing her fingers. "It sounds like it," she answered, already on her way into the hall.

Gabriel caught up to her in fewer than three strides and was ahead of her by the time he reached the elevator. Punching the down button, he looked over to the opposite wall at the door to the stairway when the elevator didn't immediately materialize.

It seemed as if he was planning on taking the stairs, Shayla thought.

"Why don't we just wait for the elevator?" she suggested. She wasn't in the mood to go dashing down the stairs unless it was absolutely unavoidable. "After all, you already know what the medical examiner is going to tell us." All the evidence pointed to the fact that Cortland was right about the drug in the victim's system.

"Maybe I like being validated," he answered in an

offhanded manner. When his partner started laughing at his response, Cortland looked at her sharply. "What?"

"You are the very last person I would *ever* say actually needed to be validated," she told him. Just then, the elevator arrived and opened its doors.

She noticed that Gabriel looked relieved that there was no one else on it.

They got on quickly. Cortland jabbed the button for the basement as well as the one that closed the doors quickly. The elevator rumbled in response, then proceeded down to their destination.

"I'm not about to argue with you," Gabriel told her, referring to her comment about his not needing validation.

"Wait, let me mark that down," Shayla cried, pretending to make a notation of the date in the air. And then, thinking maybe she had gone a bit too far, she flashed an apologetic smile. "Sorry, most of the people I work with know when I'm kidding. And I kid a lot," she added. She looked at him to see his reaction. He still appeared rather solemn. "Kidding helps to relieve the tension. You should think about trying it sometime."

"Maybe later," he replied.

"Something to look forward to," Shayla said just as the elevator doors opened again.

Getting off, Cortland took a step toward the right.

"The morgue is in the other direction," Shayla told him as she began to walk toward the left. "It used to be located in another building that was off the premises, but they found that having the morgue in the same area where the CSI team did its research wound up saving time and effort," she explained.

Gabriel merely nodded and fell into step beside her. He discovered that he had to concentrate in order to keep from moving ahead of his partner.

As if reading his mind, Shayla told him, "In case you're wondering, I *am* walking fast." She punctuated her statement with a grin.

For a moment, she thought she caught a glimmer of a smile flicker in response to hers.

"Yeah," Gabriel answered. "I can tell."

Humor, wow, she thought. There was hope for the man after all.

"As long as you know," she said with as straight a face as she could manage. And then she grinned.

The hallway at this end of the basement broke into two different areas. The far larger area housed the crime scene investigators that her uncle Sean oversaw, while the much smaller area was reserved for the morgue, with its autopsy tables as well as the very deep drawers that housed bodies that were waiting either to be autopsied or to be moved to their final resting place. There was also the computer lab area which in essence was part of the Crime Scene Investigation department.

Walking into the morgue, the first person they encountered was Greg Allen, the medical examiner who was on duty for the day.

The person they were looking to speak to was all the way in the back of the room, dressed in her scrubs.

Much to her mother's everlasting disappointment, Dr. Kristin Cavanaugh had decided to give up her medical practice and become a medical examiner. She felt that she could do the most good in that capacity, speaking for the dead who were no longer able to speak for themselves.

"Kristin," Shayla called out as she and Gabriel walked in, "we got here as soon as we could." Reaching the medical examiner, Shayla paused. "You two haven't met yet, have you?" she realized. "This is my new partner, Detective Gabriel Cortland. Detective Cortland, this is Dr. Kristin Alberghetti Cavanaugh, the wonderful medical examiner who agreed to come in on one of her days off and fast-track this autopsy for us."

"Nice to meet you," Kristin said, nodding at Gabriel. "I'd shake hands, but…" Her voice trailed off as she held up her gloved hands.

Aware of the necessity to keep everything clean in the autopsy area, Gabriel returned the nod. "Same here. Thanks for coming in," he felt obligated to add.

"Shayla explained that you believed the victim was killed by the Moonlight Killer. I thought he only stalked his victims in LA," she commented as she led them back to the table where the latest victim had been autopsied and was now neatly sewn back together.

Gabriel tore his eyes away from the young woman's face. Despite the fact that she was partially draped with a sheet, seeing the convenience store victim like this just brought back too many vivid, painful memories of his wife.

Memories that had taken him a great many months to come to terms with.

Turning away from the victim, Gabriel looked at the medical examiner. "Did you find the neuromuscular blocking agent in her system?" he asked.

Kristin nodded. "She tested positive for the substance. How did you know?" she asked, looking from Gabriel to Shayla.

"The credit all belongs to Cortland," Shayla told her. "He was the one who saw the small puncture mark right behind her ear and found that near-empty syringe on the floor next to the victim." Because she thought that Kristin might need some further clarification, she added, "Cortland was also one of the detectives who had been working on the serial killer case back in LA."

Kristin nodded, thinking about what she had read about the case at the time. "I heard that there was a nine-month break in between LA's last case and now this one."

"There was," Gabriel answered grimly.

When he didn't say anything further, Kristin asked innocently, "Do we have any idea why that was?"

Shayla decided to step in, trying to save her partner from having to put up with any more questions at the moment.

"Just unproven speculation," she answered quickly. She saw the pile of pages lying on the side table. "Is that the autopsy report?" she asked the medical examiner hopefully.

"The unofficial one," Kristin answered. "It's not the formal version. That hasn't been finalized yet."

"Can we hang on to this until you've had a chance to write one up formally?" Gabriel asked, already reaching for the pages.

Kristin looked a little surprised at the request. "Sure, I guess," she answered.

"Right now," Shayla said to her cousin's wife, "since from all indications, the killer moved his base of operations from LA to Orange County—more specifically, to Aurora—it's like we've been moved back to square one. So far there are no eyewitnesses and no leads." She pointed to the pages that her partner was now holding in his hands. "This could very well wind up pointing us in the right direction to start our search."

Kristin smiled. "Well, after that sort of a buildup, how can I possibly say no?" she asked. "Sure. Take the preliminary report. I've got a copy of it. I can use it to extrapolate and further embellish on my findings. Do you want me to send that to you when I'm done?"

Shayla smiled warmly at the other woman. "I'd consider it an early Christmas present," she told Kristin.

The medical examiner pretended to roll her eyes. "If only the rest of the family was that easy to please."

"All you have to do is tell them your news and you can sit back and consider your holiday shopping done. Everyone will be thrilled."

Nodding, Kristin glanced over toward the other detective. He had become almost eerily quiet since she had turned over the preliminary copy of the autopsy report to him.

From the looks of it, he appeared to be absorbing every word that had been written down. "It's still rather sketchy," Kristin told Shayla's partner, apologizing for the lack of depth in the report.

After a beat, Gabriel realized that the medical examiner was addressing him and not his partner.

"That's okay," he assured her, looking up. "I can work with this. But call once you have the final copy."

Kristin nodded. "Will do."

Rather than remain behind as they walked out of the autopsy area, Kristin went out with them. Once outside the area, she deliberately drew her husband's cousin aside.

"How long have you been partnered up with this guy?" she asked, interested.

"Just since two days ago," Shayla answered. Gabriel had moved aside and was back to reading the report. "Why?"

"He's cute." Kristin kept her voice low, but there was definitely enthusiasm in it.

Shayla knew what was going on in the woman's head. Matchmaking seemed to be second nature to the Cavanaugh women once they had a ring on their own finger.

"Kristin, you're a married lady who's going to have her first baby," Shayla reminded her.

"All true, but I can still see—and appreciate. As

I remember, your last partner was a patrolman who was on the verge of retirement—and looked a lot like Rip van Winkle," she added.

"And your point is?"

"Just that this guy is a huge improvement," she declared with approval. Leaning in, she whispered, "Don't let the grass start growing under your feet, that's all."

"You just take care of you and that little peanut growing inside, Kristin. I'll take care of me."

With that, Shayla moved over toward where her partner was leaning against the wall, still reading through the report. He had already gone through the report once and now appeared to be reviewing it for a second time.

"Let's go back to the squad room," she said to Cortland, using her regular speaking voice. "And go through that autopsy report." She saw that he was about to say something—most likely that he had already gone through the report—and she told him, "Some of us haven't had a chance to read it yet. We were too busy thanking the medical examiner for coming in and doing the autopsy for us."

Gabriel inclined his head, acknowledging her point.

"Sorry, I got caught up in the report," he confessed. Looking over his shoulder, he smiled at Kristin and said, "Thanks!"

"Don't mention it. As Shayla will tell you, that's what I'm here for," Kristin replied, returning to the autopsy room to collect her things.

Kristin was right, Shayla caught herself thinking as she looked at her partner just before they went back to the elevator. Cortland was really good looking.

Chapter Eleven

It was getting late, and Shayla felt that they weren't making all that much headway. Ordinarily, she would be inclined to call it a night, but she had a feeling that Cortland wasn't about to retreat. She had the impression that he would keep on working until he dropped.

Glancing to her right, she looked at him. He was still combing through his notes, as if he was hoping to find something that he had overlooked the first ten times.

Something occurred to her. "I take it that you've read the other autopsy reports on the Moonlight Killer's victims."

He hardly looked up. "I have," he answered dourly.

"Just how many victims were there?" she asked. She remembered reading a number, twelve, but somehow that didn't seem right.

"Too many," he replied, continuing to read his notes.

"I agree," Shayla said since in her opinion, even one murder qualified as too many.

"But in this case, what's the actual number?"

He put down the pages he was rereading. "Seventeen," he told his partner. "He killed one woman every few months—until his spree suddenly increased. And then he stopped." Gabriel tried to distance himself from the memory but found he still couldn't. "Looking back now, it seemed almost as if he was waiting to see if I was ever going to come back and play his sick game again."

She heard the pain in his voice. She wished she could back away from the topic altogether, but there were questions that needed to be answered if they were ever going to get this killer.

"You mean after he killed your wife and you went on that prolonged bender," Shayla guessed quietly.

For a moment, his eyes flashed, and then he said grimly, "Yeah."

"When you were in LA, were there other detectives working on the case as well?" she asked.

"Of course there were," he answered. "But once the Moonlight Killer's spree abruptly stopped and no more bodies turned up, there were other homicides that required more immediate attention. Some of the homicide squad even thought that maybe something had happened to him."

Shayla had stopped pretending to look at her notes. Her attention was completely riveted on her partner and what he was saying.

"But you didn't think that." It was more of a gut feeling than a guess.

He wasn't looking at her. Instead, he was staring into the air just above her head. He was in an entirely different place right now. "At the time, the only thing I could think of was that I had failed my wife, that she was dead because I wasn't there to protect her. I just wanted to drown that awful feeling of guilt any way I could. Suicide by bottle, I guess," he said cryptically with a shrug.

Shayla was utterly amazed that he was sharing this with her after having been so closemouthed and defensive up to this point. She had thought it would take her a lot longer and infinite patience to get him to open up. She hadn't counted on what an effect reading the autopsy report would have on him.

Shayla wanted to tell Cortland that she was touched to have him tell her all this, but that would be placing too much emphasis on the fact that he was verbalizing his pain. She decided it was better to make no comment on his revelation.

"Do you think the Moonlight Killer followed you out here?" she asked. "So that this sick game of his could continue?"

Cortland shrugged. He really didn't know for sure, but— "I guess it certainly looks that way," he told her. And then he shook his head disparagingly. "Not exactly the way I pictured my life going, being a serial killer's main adversary." He looked at Shayla. "But right now, there's no other way I *can* look at it. I need to end this man. Or at least his killing spree."

She had already assumed that Cortland had read all the other reports. "Did you get copies of the other autopsy reports and save them so you could look for possible overlapping similarities?" she asked. He struck her as someone who would do that. She knew she would in his place.

Gabriel laughed dryly in response. "One of the other detectives, a Guy Fergusson, accused me of having one hell of an odd hobby."

An odd hobby that could come in very handy, Shayla thought. Out loud she asked, "Did any of those reports make mention of that paralyzing drug that was administered to the convenience store clerk?" She couldn't help wondering if that was a new development or if the killer had used it all along and Cortland had only recently noticed it.

"Not to my knowledge," he admitted. "I only noticed that puncture mark behind the ear at the last scene in LA," he confessed, his face drawn and haunted-looking. "That's when I found that syringe on the floor. But at the time, I wasn't able to piece two sentences together, much less think clearly."

All he could think of at the time was that his wife was gone and his life was over.

Shayla had been exhausted a few moments ago thanks to all the work they had put in. Now her mind was racing.

"Is there any way the coroner who worked those cases could go back to run that test, looking for some sort of paralytic agent?"

He shook his head. "The only way the coroner could do that was if he could get some of those bodies exhumed."

"Is that even possible?" she asked. Physically, she assumed that at least some of the victims had been buried rather than had their bodies cremated. But of the ones that had been buried, there would undoubtedly be all sorts of awful feelings attached to exhuming them, she couldn't help thinking.

"The next of kin for those victims would have to be approached and authorize the exhumation, but in the name of catching that bloodthirsty maniac, I'm sure some of them would agree." He could feel his own stomach tightening, but he knew that in his wife's case, he would have to agree to the exhumation. "It's not like they would have to witness it being done," he added.

"No," she agreed, "they wouldn't." The more she thought about it, the more it seemed like the way to go. Shayla nodded her head. "I think it might be a good idea to see if any of those people would be willing to have an exhumation done. We just need a few to say yes."

Gabriel had another idea. "Before we ask the department to go to the expense, both monetary and emotional, of digging up those bodies, why don't we go through the victims' autopsy reports to see if there was any mention made of defensive wounds found on those victims?"

"If there weren't any," Shayla concluded, "it might be a pretty good argument that the killer had rendered them immobile. Conversely, if the victims did have defensive wounds, that meant that the victim tried to fight him off. They wouldn't have been able to do that if they had been injected with that paralytic agent."

"Good point," he said. "I don't have those other autopsy reports here," he told her. "They're at my apartment."

That made sense, Shayla thought. "Well, it's well past quitting time," she pointed out. "Time for all good little detectives to call it a night and go home." She looked at her partner. "We could get started reading those reports first thing in the morning."

"We could," he agreed.

That did *not* sound convincing to her. "Why do I think you plan to be up all night, reading?" she asked.

He didn't bother confirming or denying her supposition. Instead, he said, "Because you're probably the most opinionated woman I've ever crossed paths with."

Rather than take offense, Shayla pretended he had meant it as a joke. "Flatterer."

Gabriel opened his mouth to say something, then closed it again, shaking his head. "It wasn't meant to be flattering."

Shayla's mouth curved. "I always try to make the best of a situation. Are you really determined to read through those reports you have tonight?"

He knew he could just dismiss her assumption, but he also knew that she wouldn't believe him. Those blue eyes of hers just seemed to have a way of looking straight into a man's soul.

The idea both intrigued him and made him uncomfortable.

Rather than answer her directly, he replied with

a question of his own to see how she would react. "And if I am?"

"You could invite me over so I could help you with all that reading. Autopsy reports make for unsettling reading, especially late at night."

What was she telling him? "You afraid of the dark?" he asked her.

"I was as a kid," she admitted.

"I never was," he told her, then explained his reasoning. "There's nothing there in the dark that wasn't there in the light."

She thought that over for a second, then asked, "Does that mean you were perpetually fearless, or that the idea of ghosts got under your skin just as much in the daylight as it did in the dark?"

How did the conversation turn into something so personal, he couldn't help wondering. He certainly hadn't tried to direct the subject toward a personal nature. As a matter of fact, he had done his best to keep things from veering into that territory.

But how could that have even been possible, he thought the next moment, given the fact that this whole thing was incredibly personal to him?

"Why don't we focus on what needs to be done and not on me?" he suggested.

"Okay," she agreed brightly. "Does that mean you're inviting me over? To help read those reports," she added when he made no effort to answer her question.

Gabriel looked as if he was actually considering her suggestion for a total of about five seconds before disregarding the entire idea. Although he had to admit—to himself and no one else—that she hadn't been as annoyingly overwhelming as he had expected her to be. Some of the things she had proposed had even made sense. Gabriel felt as if he should quit while he was ahead in this game, at least for now.

The autopsy that had been done today had taken more out of him than he had thought it would. While it did give credence to his theory, it also depressed him to no end, because it made him think about what Natalie had had to endure at the hands of this psycho, not to mention what their unborn baby had to have endured by proxy.

From the moment Natalie had told him she was pregnant, he had thought of the baby as a person in the making, with all the features, all the attributes of a child of his. He had been alone for most of his life, passed from one person to another while his mother searched for a way to enjoy her life and have someone take care of her.

The life he had been determined to forge with Natalie was going to be different, he had promised himself. All the pieces for that happiness had been put in place—and then this maniac had stolen it all from him. From Natalie.

It had been almost more than he could bear—until he had forced himself to focus on his renewed purpose—to avenge Natalie and all the victims who had died at this depraved man's hand.

"Why don't we get an early start tomorrow?" he

suggested, thinking that he had put the topic to bed for now.

He saw her looking at him as if she could see answers there that he was trying to keep to himself.

"No offense, Cortland, but I still don't believe you," she told him. He was going to go through those reports, and she didn't want him doing that alone.

"What?" Cortland questioned, hoping she wasn't talking about what he thought she was talking about.

"You're not planning on getting an early start tomorrow. You are going to go home and start reading those reports the minute you close the door behind you," she told him. "I just figured two sets of eyes are better than one."

She gave him the impression of someone who was not about to back off. "I said I was going to get started tomorrow. Why won't you believe that?"

"Well, there is one way you could convince me," she told him.

Suspicion washed over him, but he was committed to playing this out. "Go ahead, I'm listening."

"Invite me over."

He scowled. "We've already gone through this," he informed her.

"Yes," she allowed. "But not to my satisfaction. And, if you're actually not planning on staying up to read those reports, I'll follow you home and you can just hand them to me. And I'll get started on them tonight."

He stared at her. The woman had to be kidding, he thought. "You want me to hand them over to you so you can take them over to your place?" he questioned, stunned that she could even suggest such a thing.

She could see the problem had multiple layers. She tried to strip it down to the basics.

"No, I can curl up on your couch and read the reports there. That way, they never actually leave your apartment, you can get some much-needed rest and the work can still get started. Did I manage to check all the right boxes?" she asked him cheerfully.

"All except for the one that you should be locked up in," he answered.

"We can talk about doing that later," she promised. "Right now, from what you mentioned earlier, there are a number of autopsy reports that need to be gone through, and I'm eagerly volunteering to do the reading."

His eyebrows drew together. "Eagerly?" he repeated incredulously.

"Well, maybe not eagerly, but my heart's definitely in the right place," she told him.

Gabriel snorted. "I'll take your word for it. Well, since I'd rather not have you breaking into my place in the middle of the night, you might as well come along."

"I really won you over?" she cried in surprise, pleased at having managed to turn him around to her way of seeing things.

They left the squad room and went down to the first floor, then proceeded to leave the building. He noticed that she had waved goodbye to the person manning the front desk. Was there no one this woman didn't know?

"No, it's more like you wore me out so I'll go along with this wild idea of yours—for now," he stipulated. He led the way down the stairs and to the parking area.

She deliberately ignored his last phrase. "Hey, I'm not greedy. A win is a win," she told him happily.

Gabriel sighed. "Whatever you say," he muttered dismissively.

"In the interest of that—" she began, only to have him cut her short.

"No," Gabriel declared, opening his vehicle door.

"But you don't know what I was going to say," she pointed out when he had so quickly shot her down. She got in the passenger side and buckled up.

"I don't care. Whatever it is, the answer's no," he told her.

She looked at him, innocence personified. "I was just going to suggest that we stop at a takeout place to pick up something to eat on the way to your place."

"Oh." He scowled at her for a moment as he drove away from the precinct. Leave it to her to have effectively taken the wind out of his sails, Gabriel thought. Refusing to agree didn't do either one of them any good. "I suppose we can do that," he said.

He saw the grin blooming on her face, and although he wanted to maintain his silence, he found that he couldn't. He needed to know what had prompted her to smile like that.

"What?"

"Nothing," Shayla said. She could feel herself smiling so hard, she was fairly sure that her cheeks were going to crack at any moment. "It's just that, considering how you feel about being partnered with someone, you seem to be coming along rather nicely," she told him.

Gabriel's hands tightened on the steering wheel.

Shayla's unwilling partner blew out a breath. For the time being, he felt it best just to keep his silence.

Chapter Twelve

Gabriel slowly raised his head as he opened his eyes.

He didn't remember falling asleep, but he obviously must have. Why else had his head wound up on the kitchen table, nestled between pages of the autopsy reports and the paper wrapper that initially had held a chicken salad sandwich?

His neck cracked a little, playing a symphony and reminding him that he wasn't ten years old anymore and that was why pillows had been invented—so that sane people wouldn't wake up feeling as if they had spent the night on a hard, unforgiving surface.

Gabriel rubbed his neck, trying to massage out the kink.

The first thought that hit him when his mind started to focus was that he wasn't alone. He remembered that that annoying Cavanaugh woman had been here with him, reading reports as well.

Blinking, he scanned the room. He didn't see her at first, but he doubted that he could have been lucky enough for her to have gone back to her own lair.

Could he?

Just as a glimmer of hope began to rise in his chest, he saw her. She had made herself comfortable on his sofa, taking along her share of autopsy reports.

The glimmer of hope disappeared.

Although he tried to recall details, Gabe couldn't remember the woman curling up on the sofa.

Actually, he could barely remember anything after they had settled in and eaten the takeout food she had insisted that they pick up. He did remember announcing that he was going to read through the reports he had, and she had insisted that she take half of them.

But after that, the rest of the evening was all a blur. He must have been more tired than he'd thought, Gabriel decided.

Taking in another long breath, he got up and crossed over to stand next to the woman who seemed so bent on driving him crazy. Lying on the sofa like that, fast asleep and holding a report in her hand, she looked almost harmless.

Gabriel smiled to himself. He imagined that her coworkers probably thought the same thing about Typhoid Mary as she moved among them in the hospital kitchen where she had worked—spreading the disease.

Gabriel thought about waking his partner up, then decided to enjoy the peace and quiet for a little while longer.

With that in mind, he moved soundlessly over to the coffee maker on the counter. Coffee would definitely help him wake up.

Gabriel measured out the necessary coffee grounds

and was about to pour in a cup's worth of water when he stopped. Cavanaugh would probably want coffee, too. Muttering under his breath, he measured out more coffee before finally pouring in enough water to brew two cups rather than just one.

Within moments, the coffee maker began to make brewing noises.

"Smells good."

He turned around to see that his partner was sitting up on the sofa. So much for peace and quiet.

"It's nothing special," Gabriel told her.

She swung her legs off the sofa, and the papers she had been holding when she had fallen asleep went raining down onto the floor.

"Oh damn," she murmured, looking at the resulting chaos.

Gabriel crossed over to the pile of papers to pick them up at the exact same time that his partner bent over to do the same. The end result was that their heads collided rather unceremoniously.

Shayla could have sworn that she saw stars, and for a second, she lost her bearings and nearly her balance. Gabriel moved quickly and caught her by the shoulders in an attempt to steady her.

"Are you all right?" he asked, afraid that the collision might make her pass out.

Gabriel had surprised her by displaying the first concern she had heard from him. It managed to momentarily catch her up short.

"Oh yeah, I'm fine," she assured him, although she winced as she passed her hand over her forehead.

Nevertheless, she denied any bad effects. "I've got a pretty hard head. Just ask any of my brothers—or my mom, for that matter," she added with a self-deprecating grin. "My mother runs an ambulance company, so she should know about things like that," she added, her eyes dancing in amusement.

Looking at her uncertainly, Cortland went to the freezer and took out an ice pack. The worn ice pack was a holdover from his drinking days. Holding on to it served as a reminder that he could never allow himself to go down that rabbit hole again—at least not until after he caught the Moonlight Killer and put the man away.

Filling it, Gabriel brought the ice pack back with him and held it out to his partner. "Here, apply that to your forehead before you have a bump on it the size of a small planet."

"I thought you were bringing the coffee," she said with a note of longing.

"This will do that bump on your forehead more good than the coffee," he said. Returning to the kitchen, he set out two cups and filled them. "I'm sorry about your head," he finally apologized.

"That's okay. It's not like you did it on purpose," she told him. The next moment, applying the cold pack, she shivered. "This is really cold," she said. After several seconds had gone by, she held the ice pack away from her.

"Keep it on for at least five minutes," he instructed.

"I'm afraid it I do, it'll freeze my brain." Shayla was only half kidding.

"You never know, that might be a good thing," Gabriel commented, bringing the two cups of coffee over and placing them on the coffee table in front of the sofa.

"Is that humor?" she asked him in surprise. Shayla smiled. "I didn't know you had it in you."

Gabriel nodded toward the cup in front of her. "Drink your coffee," he said, sitting down on the far edge of the sofa.

When he saw Shayla getting up, he automatically put his hand on her wrist to stop her. The last thing he wanted was her falling down. "Where are you going?" he asked.

"I know you drink your coffee black, but I need milk in mine. I actually like cream better," she admitted, "but I figure that would be too much to hope for, so I was going to look for a container of milk."

She pulled a little, attempting to free her hand, but he continued holding it. A warm feeling began to inch its way up her arm, spreading out as it went.

"Sit," he ordered, rising to his feet to get her the milk. "What would be too much to hope for is for you to be quiet for at least a few minutes."

"More humor," Shayla commented, looking over toward her partner. "Granted, not enough for you to pack up and take your show on the road, but it is definitely a step in the right direction."

Gabriel shook his head at her droll assessment. "I guess you didn't get hit as hard as I thought," he said, setting a half pint of milk next to her coffee cup. "You're back to your usual babbling."

"Please," Shayla said, leaning forward a little so she could put some milk into her coffee, "you're making me blush." She pored over the pages that had caused them to collide in the first place. Gabriel had set them on the side of the coffee table. "I didn't find anything in my share of the autopsies, and by anything I mean mention of defensive wounds. Did you?"

"No," he answered flatly.

They both knew what that meant. Shayla put it into words first. "We've got a bunch of people to approach about exhuming their loved ones."

As an afterthought, she looked at the cup in her hands she had just sampled and said, "This is good."

"Just store-bought coffee," he told her, shrugging off her compliment. He had nothing to do with it other than opening the can.

"Must be the loving way it was prepared," she told him.

Heaven help him, he was practically getting used to her flippant remarks. Maybe that collision had affected him as well.

Draining his cup, he set it down and said, "Why don't I drop you off at the precinct so you can drive to your place, take a shower and then drive yourself over to the precinct?"

Shayla deliberately blinked her eyelashes at him. "Are you giving me the bum's rush, Detective?" she asked.

"No," he bit off. "What I'm being is practical."

"And what else are you going to be doing while I'm gone besides being practical?" she asked.

Shayla couldn't shake the feeling that he would use any excuse he could to ditch her and go off on his own in this investigation.

"I'm planning on taking my own shower before going back to the precinct," he told her. "Why, isn't that allowed? Or would you want to supervise my shower to make sure I do it right?"

For just the tiniest second, her mouth went dry. Where had that come from? And why was it creating these images in her head?

After a moment, she managed to form words. "I just wanted to make sure I went on working with you on this case. I have visions of you taking off," she admitted honestly.

His eyes met hers. He caught himself conjuring up a different sort of vision of his partner, just for a moment. The kind of vision that reminded him, if only for the smallest moment, that he was a man and not just a crime-fighting robot.

"I have no intentions of taking off," he informed her dryly. "Now, are you ready to go?"

"Just as soon as I rinse out my coffee cup," she told her partner, getting up with the empty cup.

"Leave the coffee cup," he ordered, sounding like a drill sergeant. "I know how to clean up."

And then he looked her over one final time as she rose to her feet. "Are you sure you're okay?"

His own head hurt a little and, in his opinion, she had sustained a much harder blow than he had. The last thing he needed or wanted was for the chief of detectives' niece to get hurt while in his care.

"I have a partner who knows how to clean up after himself as well as after me. I'm great," Shayla declared cheerfully.

Gabriel closed his eyes and shook his head, then looked at her. "You're crazy, you know that, right?"

Shayla grinned in response as she looked at him, then crossed toward the door and picked up her purse. "Let's go, Gabriel. We're burning daylight."

"Daylight," he pointed out, nodding toward the front window, "just got here."

"Still, we're burning it nonetheless," she answered with authority. "You can't argue with that."

"Apparently," he told her wearily, "you can—and do—argue with absolutely anything, and everything."

"Not true," she told him as she followed him out the door.

"See, you're even arguing about this," Gabriel pointed out.

Shayla decided that, for the time being, the best way for her to proceed was just not to say anything.

Because he was concend about the bump on the head she had received, once she picked up her car at the precinct, he decided to follow her to her house—just in case.

Gabriel pulled up in front of Shayla's house. The recently painted building was located in one of the older residential developments in Aurora, one of the first five that had been built at the time the city had been incorporated.

He noted that her house was a single-story model,

and, in a state where land was quickly going at a premium, he was surprised to see just how large a plot her house was sitting on.

Gabriel had planned to just stop his vehicle and look around, then quickly take off back to his own place, but his curiosity aroused, he just had to ask her.

"Does this land all belong to the house?" He knew that in some residential areas, they had something referred to as a zero property line, where the land on one side of the house or the other actually belonged to the house that was located right next door. Supposedly it was to make the yards the houses were on just appear bigger, although he thought of the whole thing as being some sort of a visual trick.

Gabriel's question caught her off guard for a moment, but then she realized what he was asking her.

"It doesn't belong to the house," she corrected him. "The lot the house is standing on belongs to me."

Gabriel had just assumed his partner was renting the house, especially since she was so young. "You own this house?" he asked her incredulously.

"Well, the bank and I do," Shayla told him. "But eventually, it'll be all mine when I pay it off."

In his estimation, she seemed too young to be a homeowner. The only people he knew who weren't renters were older family men with kids—kids they were attempting to convince to go to college. These Cavanaughs, Gabriel decided, were a whole different breed than what he was normally accustomed to.

As if reading her partner's mind, Shayla told him, "My mother thought it was a good idea for all her kids to buy a house as soon as they were financially able to make a down payment. When my father was killed in the line of duty and she had to go back to work, my mother decided that each of us needed to have something stable to hang on to—other than each other and the rest of the family, of course," she added with a smile. "My mother is a really great believer in earning your own way. She always has been."

Gabriel nodded, barely listening. His mind was already back on the case. He needed to make a list of people to get in contact with, as well as putting together the professions that would allow someone to get their hands on the drug that was used without attracting attention.

"I'm going to get going," he announced, his body language saying that for all intents and purposes, he was already gone.

"I'll hurry," Shayla promised needlessly. "I'll see you back in the squad room."

Gabriel barely nodded. "Yeah."

Starting up his car, he was just about to drive off when his cell phone suddenly began ringing. He turned off the engine and took out his phone.

Just as hers started to ring as well.

She looked at Gabriel through his window. They were being summoned into the precinct, she thought. Any other explanation just seemed like too much of a coincidence.

"I think our showers just got put on hold," Shayla said, taking out her phone.

Gabriel was already talking on his.

"Cavanaugh," she declared, swiping her phone on.

"There's been another killing," the deep voice on the other end of her phone said. "The victim was tied up just like the convenience store clerk."

Chapter Thirteen

Shayla put her cell phone away in her small shoulder bag. Cortland had already slipped his into his pocket. There was silence for a moment as their eyes met.

"This isn't normal, is it?" she asked through his opened window, fairly sure that she knew the answer before her partner said anything.

"The guy's a homicidal maniac," Gabriel answered. The disgust was meant for the serial killer, not for the woman who had just gotten out of his car. "There's not a damn thing normal about him."

Shayla shook her head. "I meant timing wise. He doesn't usually kill his victims so close together, does he?" Something was up, and she hated thinking about what that might mean.

"No," Gabriel answered her grimly. "He doesn't."

She looked over toward her vehicle, parked in her driveway. "Should we just drive back to the precinct in yours?" she asked.

Leaning all the way over to his right, Gabriel strained to reach toward the passenger side and threw open the passenger door for her.

"Get in," he instructed.

"Well, since you asked so nicely," she began, trying to inject a little humor into what was a completely humorless moment. She stopped short when she saw the impatient look creasing his brow. "I'm getting in, I'm getting in," Shayla told him, sliding into the passenger seat and pulling the door closed behind her.

Shayla was still securing her seat belt when her partner took off. Instead of sitting in her seat, she found herself sliding first to the right and then the left as Gabriel tore out of the development. Even when she finally did secure her seat belt, the ride she was on couldn't exactly be described as a very stable one.

To finally stop moving so erratically, Shayla firmly braced her hands against the dashboard. She was just grateful that she hadn't had breakfast yet, although the coffee she'd had at his apartment wasn't exactly sitting all too well in her stomach. She understood why he might be in a hurry, but he really needed to slow down a little.

"Do you charge extra for this?" she asked, doing her best to hold on as Gabriel made another fast turn.

"No," Gabriel bit off, making it clear that this was no time for any of her so-called witty humor.

Her eyes widened as he took another really fast turn.

"I think you took the wrong turn," she told him, reading the street signs as they whizzed by. "This isn't the way to the precinct."

"I know," he answered. "It's the way to the crime scene." With that, Cortland made a rather unnerving turn at the end of the block.

"You know where the crime scene is?" she asked, surprised. No mention of that had been made in the call she had gotten.

"Garza told me," Gabriel said, referring to one of the detectives he had been introduced to in the last couple of days. All their faces had merged together, but their voices had set them apart. "He was the one who took the initial call."

"So?" Was he going to keep her guessing? "Where is the crime scene?"

"The victim's body was found in the stacks in the university library," he told her, then gave her the details that Garza had passed on to him. "One of the librarians found her when she came in early to open up," he said. Gabriel spared her a glance just before he took another left turn, this time making his way directly onto the university campus. "Now you know as much as I do."

When Shayla made no response, he looked at her again, reminding himself that she had received a rather substantial bump on her head when their heads had unceremoniously collided. Maybe it was interfering with her ability to process information. "Are you up to this, or should I have dropped you off at the precinct first?"

She saw that he was more than ready to turn back. "I'm fine," she quickly assured him. "And I'm a great deal better off than that poor woman the librarian found in the stacks." This whole thing had her wondering again about the killer they were dealing with.

"Why do you think the Moonlight Killer has upped his game?"

Her partner frowned. He wished she'd stop asking questions. "My guess is that he's trying to make up for lost time," he told her.

"You mean for those nine months you dropped out?" she asked bluntly. She knew the question made him uncomfortable, but these were questions that needed to be answered so they knew if they were ultimately going in the right direction. "Why do you think he singled you out this way?" There had to be a reason why the killer was so fixated on Cortland.

Gabriel shrugged. "Who knows? Maybe I got closer to finding him than the other detectives did." Reaching his destination, he pulled up in a parking spot near the library.

Getting out of the car, Gabriel took out his badge and detective ID, preparing to show them to the police officer who was approaching them. It was obvious that the latter was about to tell them that they had to move their vehicle and couldn't enter the crime scene.

Looking at Cortland's badge and identification, the officer gave Shayla a confused look. She quickly followed suit.

Satisfied, the uniformed officer waved them on their way, saying, "Everyone and his brother wants to see what's going on," by way of an explanation for why he'd been about to bar them a moment ago.

"At least they're still alive to do that," Gabriel commented.

The officer nodded. "Yeah, I guess that's one way

to look at it." He followed the two Aurora detectives as they headed toward the library entrance. "You want me to get one of the officers to show you to the stacks?" he asked, explaining, "I've got to stay out here."

"That won't be necessary," Shayla answered. "I know where the stacks are. I graduated from this university."

Gabriel turned to look at her. "You went to school here?"

She didn't know if he was impressed or about to say something disparaging. Most likely the later, she decided. "I did."

Gabriel stepped to the side and gestured for her to go through the entrance first. "Then, by all means, lead the way, Cavanaugh," he told her.

She took the steps leading to the front doors quickly. She couldn't remember how many times she had been here, studying or writing papers. Never once had she ever thought this would be the site of a murder.

"I always figured I'd come back here someday, but not because I had to investigate a crime scene," she confessed sadly. Shayla looked around as she was about to enter, memories flooding her mind. "This always seemed like a safe space to me."

"Just shows that you can never take anything for granted," Gabriel told her.

There was another police officer posted at the library's entrance. Seeing their badges, she quickly stepped aside.

"You'll find the victim all the way downstairs," the police officer told them, then warned, "Brace yourselves."

Gabriel stopped and looked at the young woman. "Why?"

The police officer shrugged, somewhat embarrassed by her reaction. But she answered the solemn-looking detective.

"It's the stuff nightmares are made of," she told him. "At least mine will be from here on in," she lamented. The woman's voice dropped as she confided to Shayla, "I think I picked the wrong line of work."

"Well, I hate to tell you, but it doesn't get any easier," Shayla told her. "But after a while, you develop a tougher skin and find that you can put up with things a lot better."

Pointing toward where they needed to go, the officer remained at her post. "The poor librarian found the victim tied up and at the bottom of the stacks. She screamed so loudly, several people called 911."

"Is the librarian still downstairs?" Shayla asked. "We'll need to ask her some questions after we view the victim." Shayla couldn't get herself to say, "dead body." Somehow, calling the poor young woman that just felt too disrespectful. The victim had been a human being, most likely a student, with a life. A life that had been cut far too short, Shayla thought.

"I think her name is Josephine," the officer interjected. "After Josephine finally stopped screaming, she was shaking so badly, one of the other officers called for an ambulance and had her taken to the ER. She's probably still there now."

Shayla could see that Gabriel was anxious to go downstairs into the stacks to see the victim for himself. Thanking the officer for the information, Shayla told her, "We'll go there when we're done here."

The young woman nodded. "The crime scene investigators are already down in the stacks," the officer said, adding, "They just got here a few minutes before you two did."

Shayla didn't remember seeing the CSI vehicle, but she knew that there was parking available on three sides of the library, so she could have easily missed it. She had been focused on getting here as quickly as she could and viewing the crime scene while it was still relatively fresh.

"Thank you," she said to the officer. "You've been a great help."

The young woman beamed at the compliment. It was obvious to the Shayla that the officer's ego could use a little bolstering.

Gabriel looked as if he was straining at the bit and walked into the building ahead of her.

The area was wide-open and airy, perhaps just slightly smaller than she recalled. Shayla could remember getting lost here a number of times in her first year at the university. Now it all seemed so familiar—and it had been violated by the Moonlight Killer, she thought angrily. He had taken what had once been such a safe space to her and turned it into a place of unimaginable horror.

She had to struggle to keep herself from being overwhelmed with waves of anger. Striding toward the stairs leading into the stacks, Shayla glanced over her shoulder to make sure she hadn't lost Gabriel.

He was still looking around, methodically taking everything in. She could tell by his expression that Gabriel was viewing it all through the victim's eyes. Shayla could only guess what was going through her partner's mind, but she felt for him.

"This way," she told her partner, leading the way to a stairwell off to the side.

Gabriel's pace quickened until he had caught up with her. Shayla was moving down the stairs quickly, her heels clicking almost rhythmically against the metal.

Gabriel was right behind her.

There wasn't really enough room for two people to go down together. The stairway, he noted, had a rather dated appearance, like it had been initially put in when the university had been built, some forty-odd years ago.

Despite the fluorescent lights illuminating the stairs and beyond, there was a somber darkness to the area that only grew more so the farther down they went.

By the time they reached the bottom of the second stairway, she could make out the sound of voices, talking.

"I guess we're the last to get here," Shayla commented to her partner. Gabriel merely grunted in response.

Shayla saw that her uncle had come out to review

the scene with his team again. Usually, he varied his involvement, sending someone else to head the team if he had come out the day before. But here he was, leading his team again. Apparently, her uncle had made catching the serial killer a personal priority, just the way Gabriel and she had.

Sean Cavanaugh raised his eyes when he saw the two detectives approaching him. "We've got to stop meeting this way," he commented sadly.

"Tell me about it," Shayla said.

Rather than answer her, Sean looked toward his niece's partner. "You're the expert here, Cortland. Is this the Moonlight Killer's usual mode of operation, to practically follow up one killing with another, or is this something new for him?"

Gabriel had walked by the CSI team, who were cataloging the various data that had been found at the crime scene, even though that data proved to be scarce.

Gabriel seemed intent on absorbing everything. Finally, he turned toward Sean.

"This is something new," he admitted. He had really hoped that the Moonlight Killer would have reduced his pace and that he would be caught before he killed again.

No such luck, Gabriel decided.

"Well, maybe since the Moonlight Killer has stepped up his game, he'll get sloppy and that'll give us more of a fighting chance," Sean theorized.

Gabriel allowed himself to savor that thought, although he had some grave doubts.

"Maybe," Shayla's partner said without any real conviction.

So far, Shayla thought, turning back to the victim, who had been roped and tied up in the same unnerving fashion as her predecessors, there seemed to be no connection between the young women, other than the fact that they were all in a certain age range.

Beyond that, there was no similarity in looks, nationality or what they did for a living. And, from what she had managed to learn, the women had nothing in common. The victims had been employed in a wide range of work.

Gabriel's wife, she recalled reading, had taken a leave of absence three months into her pregnancy because she had felt too tired to be able to do a good job. She had been fighting a constant battle against fatigue.

Maybe if the woman had remained working, she wouldn't have been in the wrong place at the wrong time and caught the killer's eye.

Gabriel bent down, getting as close to the victim as he could. As he shone the small, powerful flashlight he always had in his possession along her body, he didn't detect any defensive wounds on her hands.

"What are you looking for?" Sean asked as he turned around to see Gabriel conducting what appeared to be a methodical search of the victim's body.

Shayla began to answer for her partner, then pressed her lips together. This was Cortland's show. It was up to him to answer her uncle.

"Whether or not the woman has any defensive

wounds on her," Gabriel answered, "and if there's
any evidence of a drug being administered."

As Shayla and her uncle watched, her partner
slowly went over every square inch of the victim's
upper body—until he finally found what he was
looking for.

Chapter Fourteen

"There it is," Gabriel declared, moving to the extreme right so that the head of the crime scene investigative team could see what he had managed to locate.

Gabriel pointed to the area where the needle had gone in to inject the paralyzing agent into the victim.

The injection had created a minuscule pinprick at the very back of her neck. The injection had turned that small area into a rather angry shade of pink.

Obviously, Gabriel concluded, the victim had been allergic to the paralytic agent that had been used on her.

"I thought that was an insect bite. I was going to ask the coroner if I was right or if that was caused by something other than a bug," Sean said to the two detectives. He looked at his niece's partner. "Nice catch."

Gabriel shrugged off the compliment. To him a "nice catch" would have been applicable if he had managed to capture the serial killer.

"It helps if you know what you're looking for," he told the head of the investigative team.

Gabriel looked around on the floor, but found no syringe.

"What are you looking for?" Sean asked, pausing to look on the library floor as well.

"The last couple of times, the Moonlight Killer discarded the syringe with the paralyzing agent he used. This time it looks like he took the syringe with him—or threw it out someplace," Gabriel theorized.

Shayla had trouble looking away from the victim. The woman looked so young. She'd obviously had her whole life before her—until it had been brutally stolen from her.

She turned toward her uncle. "Do we have a name for the victim yet?" Shayla asked.

"Amanda Quinn. She was working on her master's thesis in English literature. It was on the evolution of comedy," Destiny Cavanaugh, Sean's right-hand assistant as well as his daughter-in-law, volunteered the information. "I looked through her backpack, trying to find her name."

Gabriel gazed down at the victim's face. "There are no defensive wounds," he noted. Just like the last victim. This woman had apparently been dead a number of hours. "She never even saw this coming. Most likely, the killer has to wear soft-soled sneakers." Rising, he turned toward Shayla. "We need to talk to that librarian who found the victim—and to anyone who might have been on duty late last night."

His eyes swept over the scene, taking it all in.

This time, the Moonlight Killer had tied up the victim and hung her from one of the massive library shelves. "Maybe we'll get lucky and find someone who saw something." Although he had to admit, he had his doubts. He turned to look at his partner again. "Students don't have to sign in to use the library anymore, do they?"

Shayla had heard that was once a thing, but not for a very long time. "Not for years and years," she told him, then she looked at her cousin's wife. "Are there any surveillance cameras around?"

Destiny looked as disappointed as Shayla felt. She shook her head. "I already asked. The students said they felt as if the people in charge were spying on them, so the cameras were all taken down or disconnected."

Shayla's eyes met her partner's. It was hard to say which of them was more disappointed. "Too bad. A little bit of spying might have come in handy right about now," she said. "It could have helped us get this guy instead of having him out there, hunting for more victims."

Sean Cavanaugh was taking photographs of the victim from several different angles. Gabriel waited until the man paused. "We're going to need to see the autopsy report as soon as it's available," he told the CSI head, stressing, "I need the coroner to have the lab test Amanda's blood for any and all neuromuscular blocking agents."

Sean looked very interested. "Is that what you think was used on the victim?"

"Victims," Gabriel corrected, stressing the plural. "To my knowledge, at least two of the last two victims before this one were injected with a paralytic agent, instantly rendering them unable to fight back. In all likelihood, there were more victims that were injected," he added. "If that turns out to be the case, the information could help us narrow down the list of people to look into and investigate. A neuromuscular blocking agent isn't something just anyone can get their hands on."

Sean turned toward his niece, smiling. "Looks like you got partnered up with a good one right out of the gate," he told her, nodding his head with approval.

"WHAT WAS YOUR uncle talking about?" Gabriel asked as, armed with the name of the hospital the librarian had been taken to, he and Shayla made their way out of the library stacks.

She realized that Cortland had probably forgotten this fact. She was fairly certain that she had told him this on their first day. "He was referring to the fact that you are my first partner since I passed my exam and got my detective's shield," she explained. She saw doubt enter his eyes and quickly said, "Don't let the fact that I'm a newbie bother you. I grew up surrounded by detectives and absorbed an awful lot facts and procedures just through osmosis."

The grin she flashed at him was all but disarming. It took him a moment to tear his eyes away.

"Yeah, right," he muttered dismissively.

"No, really," Shayla insisted. "Every family gathering we ever had—and there have been an awful lot of them—the older generation always talked shop. That went on until we suddenly *became* the older generation."

He shrugged, trying to appear as if he was indifferent, even though he really wasn't—and that did bother him. "Whatever. I guess I'm stuck with you for the time being."

She wondered if that meant that he was going to attempt to get another partner. She really doubted that he would—at least, not until they could bring down the Moonlight Killer. Cortland had too much of himself invested in this, and she was fairly certain that he knew she could be an asset, not a liability, in this pursuit.

Once upstairs in the main library area, Shayla and Cortland went in search of the person in charge, a Mary Ann Elder, according to one of the officers. Miss Elder looked as if she could very well remember the days when students had to sign in before availing themselves of any of the books in the stacks. After showing the woman their shields and IDs, Shayla told the head librarian, "We need to find out who was working here on the late shift last night and if any of those people saw anything out of the ordinary at that time," Shayla asked.

The woman looked as if she would rather talk to Gabriel instead of his partner, but she forced herself to address Shayla's question. "Josephine Juarez had the late shift last night," she told the detectives.

"Josephine," Gabriel repeated. "Isn't she the young

woman who had the first shift here this morning?" he questioned.

"Yes," Mary Ann answered. "She was pulling a double shift. Josephine is getting married next year and asked me for extra work so she could save up as much money as she could." The woman dropped her voice, as if she was about to impart some great secret. "If you ask me, the gown she's buying is far too expensive, but then, nobody asked me." The woman sighed, as if this had all happened just to annoy her. "Now I have no idea if she's up to working at all, and I'll need to find someone who can come in and sub for her."

"In other words, this Josephine person is the only one we can talk to about what went on here last night?" Gabriel asked.

Mary Ann beamed at him. "You catch on quickly, Detective."

Shayla took out her card and placed it on the desk in front of the librarian. "If you or any of the other people who work here remember anything at all, please give me a call and let me know." Turning away, she looked at Gabriel. "Let's see if we can go talk to Josephine at the hospital," she proposed.

She felt that spending the extra minutes here had turned out to be a waste of time. Hopefully, the young woman in the ER could tell them something more helpful.

As they began to walk out of the library, Shayla looked at her partner. "Do you know how to get to the hospital from here?"

He hated to admit it, but he had no choice since he was the one who was driving. "No, not offhand."

"It's not that far from here," she told him. "I'll give you directions."

He laughed shortly. "I figured you would," he answered, hurrying down the stairs, away from the library.

Gabriel lost no time in getting to the parking lot. When he didn't hesitate but went directly to where he had parked his vehicle, Shayla had to admit that she was impressed. With three sides to the library parking lot, she had gotten lost finding her car the first few times when she had used the library.

Gabriel, on the other hand, seemed to have unerring instincts when it came to finding the vehicle. Opening the doors, he got into his car and waited for her to do the same.

As she settled in, he told her, "Okay, start giving me those directions."

She pretended to pout. "You're taking all the fun out of it. Isn't your manhood supposed to make you grumble about having to ask for directions?"

"My manhood is very secure," Gabriel informed her.

"Good to hear," she told him with a wide smile. Glancing at her, he got the impression that she actually meant it.

Shayla watched as her partner put his key in the ignition. "You know, we could just trade places and I could drive us there."

"My manhood might be secure," he told her, "but

I haven't taken leave of my senses. I'll drive. Now, left or right?"

"Neither," she told him. "Just go straight until I tell you where to turn."

He slanted a look in Shayla's direction. "You're enjoying this, aren't you?"

Her eyes were twinkling. "Maybe just a little."

She had to give her partner a few more directions, which incorporated several more turns, before they were finally able to pull up in the hospital parking lot.

"You know, the streets here are a lot less busy than they are in Los Angeles," he couldn't help commenting. "In LA it feels like I'm practically driving around in circles. The streets in Aurora seem like they're a lot more straightforward," he said in quiet appreciation.

In the parking lot, Gabriel found a parking space some distance away from the actual ER entrance.

The moment he parked his car, he and Shayla immediately got out and hurried directly toward the emergency room entrance. The dark gray electronic doors sprang open the moment they came close to them.

There was a middle-aged woman sitting behind the admissions desk. She seemed rather harried, and it wasn't even nine in the morning yet. Shayla wondered if it had been very busy in the ER or if this was just the way the clerk normally looked—like a wilting flower.

To save time, both Shayla and Gabriel had their IDs and shields out as they approached the woman behind the desk.

"Did a Josephine Juarez come into the ER this morning? She would have been brought in by ambulance from the UC Aurora library," Shayla explained, adding, "According to the police officers on the scene, she had been rather badly traumatized."

The description immediately struck a nerve. "Oh yes, she came in and she's still here." The woman looked at her monitor to confirm something before she disclosed the information. "It took Dr. Benjamin a long time to finally calm her down. She just wouldn't stop wailing and crying."

"Where is she?" Shayla asked, immediately following that up with another question. "Can we see her?"

The receptionist turned from her desk and called over to one of the nurses who was leaving with a tablet. The latter kept glancing at the screen, reading something on it even as she was walking away.

"Donna," the reception called to her, "can you take these two officers—"

"Detectives," Shayla corrected the receptionist before her partner could speak up. She was afraid that he might see the "demotion" as an insult for some reason.

"—these two detectives," the receptionist corrected, "to see that woman who was brought in from the UC Aurora library? Josephine Juarez," the receptionist clarified. "I think they put her in bed number twelve in the ER."

The heavyset older woman nodded her head, her short-cropped dark hair bobbing around her face. Tucking the tablet under her arm, Donna told the pair that had been entrusted to her, "If you just come this way," and then turned on her rubber-soled heel.

"Do you know if Josephine said anything to anyone about what happened?" Shayla asked the older woman.

Donna shook her head. "Far as I know, the poor thing was too busy screaming to say anything actually coherent," Donna replied. "We don't even know what happened to her." She glanced over her shoulder at the two detectives. "The doctor couldn't get her to stop screaming and crying long enough to tell anyone why she was having this breakdown. Would you know?"

Shayla glanced at her partner. She felt that it was really more his story to tell than hers if he wanted to.

"Josephine Juarez came across the Moonlight Killer's latest victim. The victim was down in the library stacks at the time," Gabriel finally said when he realized that Shayla was waiting for him to take the lead. "It's a pretty unsettling sight," he said, deliberately leaving out the more unnerving details. "I can see why the poor woman would freak out the way she did."

"In your medical opinion, do you think that she will be able to talk to us?" Shayla asked the nurse.

She didn't want to make things worse for the traumatized young woman, but she was anxious to talk to possibly the only witness that they had—if the woman had actually even seen anything.

"It certainly is worth a try," Donna said, bringing them over to a curtained cubicle. All the beds in this part of the ER were equally divided. There were more empty beds than Shayla had thought there would be.

"Slow day?" Shayla asked, looking toward the nurse.

"It's the middle of the week. It'll pick up in a few hours," Donna predicted.

The nurse brought the two detectives over to the young woman who had had the misfortune of discovering the body hanging from the bookcase. "These detectives are here to see you, Josephine," Donna told the woman in the hospital bed, smiling at her.

Josephine Juarez slowly turned her head in their direction.

The disoriented look on her face quickly turned to one of abject terror.

Chapter Fifteen

Josephine Juarez appeared as if she desperately wanted to disappear into the bedding. Her breathing became much more labored, and her eyes darted back and forth between the two strangers at her bedside.

"Go away. I didn't see anything. Please go away," she begged frantically. It seemed as if she was saying those words to Cortland.

Watching the librarian's reaction, Shayla made a quick judgment call. "Cortland, could you step away for a few minutes and meet me out in the hallway? I'd like to have a word alone with Ms. Juarez."

To be honest, she half expected her new partner to fight her on this. But to her surprise, Gabriel nodded his head, walked away and disappeared down the hall without a word.

The moment Cortland left, Shayla immediately turned her attention back to the distraught librarian. The woman had acted far too agitated around her partner. Something just didn't add up here.

"Josephine," she said in a soft, kind voice, "are you

sure you didn't see anyone in the stacks before you went down there this morning?"

"No, not this morning," she denied, shaking her head.

"But…?" Shayla let her voice trail off as she waited for the librarian to offer more information.

Josephine swallowed hard, forcing herself to speak. "But he…bumped into me…as I was leaving the library last night." Her voice was trembling again, as if she felt she had said something she was going to wind up paying for.

"He?" Shayla cocked her head and looked at the young woman quizzically.

The librarian's voice dropped down to barely a whisper, not wanting to be overheard as she said, "Your partner."

"Detective Cortland?" Shayla questioned. "*He* was the man who bumped into you?"

She nervously pressed her lips together and finally answered, "Yes. Last night. It was around nine o'clock. I was in a hurry to leave, and I walked right into him. He looked surprised to see there was someone there—surprised to see me," she explained, "but he didn't say anything."

Shayla didn't protest or say that it couldn't have happened that way because at that time Cortland was with her in his apartment. That was when they were reviewing the pile of autopsy reports.

Instead, she calmly asked Josephine, "You're sure it was him?"

"Yes," the woman answered, although she did

shrug her shoulders somewhat helplessly. But then she went on to describe the man she had bumped into. "Tall, muscular, dark hair." And then she shrugged again as if to explain why her description wasn't more detailed. "It happened really fast."

"Go on," Shayla urged gently, trying not to sound too eager as she continued to entertain the idea that had presented itself to her. "Tell me everything."

The devastated young librarian looked somewhat at a loss. "That's all there is to tell." Josephine pressed her lips together to keep from crying again. "Until I came in this morning and saw…and saw…" The young woman couldn't bring herself to finish her sentence.

Shayla patted the distressed librarian's hand, trying to comfort the other woman as best she could.

"Ms. Juarez, would you mind if I sent in a sketch artist to see you so you could give her a description of the person you saw in the library last night?" Shayla paused, then added, "It would be a really great help to us."

The librarian seemed confused by the request, but she nodded even as she said, "He looked like the detective who was in here with you."

"Still, it would help to have a sketch," Shayla said. And then she looked back at the nurse. "Is Ms. Juarez going to stay here for the day?"

Donna responded, "The doctor wants to run the patient through a battery of tests to check her out. If everything turns out to be negative, then the hospital will be able to release her and send her home. Most likely by tomorrow morning."

Taking all this in, Shayla nodded, then looked back at the woman in the hospital bed. "We'll send in that sketch artist to see you later on today, Ms. Juarez," she promised. Giving Josephine's hand another squeeze, she told the young woman who had, mercifully, stopped trembling, "I'll see you later today."

With that, Shayla walked out of the ER treatment area. Making her way down the hallway, she looked around to see if she could spot her partner somewhere.

He was nowhere to be found.

This was what she got for not being specific, Shayla upbraided herself. She should have told Cortland that she would meet him at the vending machine or some other more precise location.

"So," a deep voice from behind her said out of the blue, "what did the librarian wind up telling you?"

Startled, Shayla swung around, her flying blond hair all but whipping her partner in the face. She managed to comb it back with her fingers.

"You really need to make more noise when you're sneaking up on a person," she told him.

"Then it wouldn't be sneaking up, would it?" he challenged. There was just the barest touch of amusement in his voice.

Shayla spread her hand out on her chest. "Just let my heartbeat go back down to normal."

Taking a deep breath, she waited for a second until

her heartbeat *did* settle down. She took another deep breath before she felt ready to answer his question.

This, she knew, wasn't going to be easy.

"I've got some good news and some bad news," she told her partner. "Oddly enough," she went on as she saw his eyebrows draw together quizzically, "it's the same news."

Gabriel frowned slightly. "You certainly know how to keep someone on pins and needles," he commented dryly. "Since it's the same news, out with it."

"I think we might have a clue as to what this guy looks like," Shayla began, choosing her words carefully. She also felt as if his eyes were drilling right into her.

"Go on," he told her.

Shayla pressed her lips together as she raised her eyes to his face.

"According to the librarian, the reason for her freaked-out reaction when we walked into the room together is that Josephine Juarez swears she bumped into the Moonlight Killer at the library last night."

Her partner paused. It was like waiting for a shoe to drop in slow motion.

"And?" he asked, never taking his eyes from her face.

"*And* she said that the man she bumped into was you," Shayla said, continuing to look at him for his reaction to this piece of news.

"Was *me*?" he questioned in complete and total disbelief.

"That's what she said."

"That's not possible," Gabriel denied. "I wasn't anywhere near that library last night—or ever before this morning, for that matter."

"I *know* that. I'm your alibi, remember?" Shayla pointed out—which was a good thing, she thought. Because if they hadn't been together last night all the way up to and including to when they had received the call to come in today, she might have been tempted to entertain some doubts about her partner's innocence.

But any possible doubts had been entirely wiped out before they could even form, because she and Cortland had spent all that time together.

That fact brought her to only one possible conclusion. She shared her suspicions with her partner before this whole thing could get more out of hand.

"Everyone out there supposedly has a doppelgänger," she told him. "That's when—"

"I know what a doppelgänger is, Cavanaugh. Are you saying that our witness actually thinks that she saw me at the library last night?"

"I'm saying that Josephine admitted to being in a hurry and that as she was dashing out, she bumped into a tall, handsome, broad-shouldered man she could have very easily mistaken for you in her haste to leave the library."

Listening to this, his expression grew very solemn. "That explains things," he said more to himself than to his partner.

It had always bothered him that it appeared Natalie had let her killer into the house. If the Moonlight Killer resembled him, that would have given him just enough advantage and time to get the drop on Natalie and kill her.

The thought made him incredibly sick to his stomach.

Shayla was looking at Cortland's face. She could tell by his expression that he had gone to a very dark place and, if he was going to be of any use to himself and to her, she needed to get him out of there.

"Wherever you are, come back," Shayla ordered him. "We've finally been given a lead to work, and we need to use it to our benefit."

Gabriel assessed his partner. She was right. He couldn't allow himself to sink back into that quicksand bog that had threatened to swallow him up whole.

Taking a breath, as if that would help him clear his mind, Gabriel looked at her and asked, "Handsome, huh?"

She had been trying to figure out what was going on in his mind. His question managed to throw her.

"What?"

"You just used the word *handsome* to describe me," Gabriel pointed out.

"Josephine used the word, I didn't," she told him. "Just think of the word as a placeholder. I told our witness that I would send in a sketch artist to draw the man she passed in the library. Once she does, we can get started showing that sketch around to the library staff." Her eyes widened as she thought of something else. "And to any of the people who might have used the convenience store where our last victim was found.

"Who knows, maybe our killer stakes out his victims? He strikes me as being too methodical to just walk in cold and kill his victims without planning ahead. He doesn't seem like the type to do that," she told her partner.

Gabriel was inclined to agree with her. If the Moonlight Killer hadn't been so careful and had just been consumed with this overwhelming desire to kill, Gabriel was certain that the man would have been caught a lot sooner.

Maybe even before he had killed Natalie.

Gabriel dismissed the paralyzing thought. He wouldn't be able to get anywhere if that event remained front and center in his mind.

WHEN THEY GOT back to the precinct, their first order of business was to report to their lieutenant.

Hollandale looked pleased to see them and impressed at the headway they seemed to have made. And it also surprised the lieutenant to hear that the witness currently in the ER had almost gone into shock when she saw Cortland come walking into the room.

When he finished listening to everything Shayla had to say, Hollandale remarked, "Lucky thing you had Cavanaugh to vouch for your whereabouts, Cortland." The librarian's accusation could have raised quite a few questions and gotten pretty messy before it was cleared up, the lieutenant thought. "Bet you're glad now that I didn't listen to you when you said you didn't want to be partnered up with Cavanaugh."

Gabriel had no choice but to agree. He nodded. "I guess it would have made things really complicated otherwise."

Shayla grinned as they walked away from the lieutenant's office. "I didn't know you had a gift for understatement."

Gabriel decided it was safest just to ignore her.

"Want to grab some lunch?" Shayla asked after a moment.

He blew out a long breath, searching for patience. The emotion continued being among the missing. "What I want to do," he finally said, "is get to work."

Now that they had something to work with, Gabriel found he was more anxious than ever to continue following up leads on the murders. Eventually, they would have to take him somewhere.

"Okay," Shayla responded cheerfully, "we'll compromise and pick up some takeout."

That hadn't been a choice he was entertaining, but he knew she was probably right. Even a train needed fuel to keep going, he conceded.

"You pick the place," he told her.

Her grin grew wider. "Isn't it nice when we cooperate?" she told her partner with enthusiasm.

He slanted a look in her direction. "Don't push it, Cavanaugh," he warned, but Shayla could have sworn she detected a hint of a smile curving the corners of his lips.

He seemed to be coming around a great deal faster

than she had anticipated he would, she thought. But then, she had never been around anyone who had so much room for growth and progress in his makeup.

Most people she had worked with only had to go from a D to an A. This man had a huge area for growth, going from the absolute last letter of the alphabet to the very first one.

"What are you grinning about?" Gabriel asked.

"Just glad we're working together and that things appear to be going so well."

Gabriel shook his head. "Maybe I shouldn't ask."

"Oh, but then you'd miss out on so much," she pointed out.

His eyes met hers. "My thoughts exactly."

"Admit it, I'm getting to you," she replied, smiling.

"Oh, I admit it all right," Gabriel answered, barely containing his temper. "I just have no idea what to take in order to combat the feelings that are being stirred up."

"Feelings?" she questioned. Was he saying what she thought he was saying?

"Like nausea," he supplied.

Gabriel expected his partner to take offense. Instead, she smiled at him, and then told him, "The detective doth protest too much."

"Uh-huh." The single annoyed word was meant to dismiss her, but no such luck. Instead, it just made her think of something else she needed to tell him.

"By the way, remember those parties I told you about? The ones my uncle Andrew likes to throw frequently and for no apparent reason?"

He remembered. "What about them?"

"He's throwing one in a couple of weeks."

He shrugged as he got back into his vehicle. "Good for him."

She continued watching his face as she got in on the passenger side. "And you're invited."

About to put his key into the ignition, Gabriel stopped dead. "Why?"

"Because you're my partner," she said simply.

That didn't seem like a good enough reason for anything, he thought, annoyed. What was it about this family that got under his skin like some sort of bad itching powder? All he wanted to do was be left alone and do his job.

"You know, I think it's time to dissolve this partnership," he told her.

"Too late," she said cheerfully. "I'm afraid you're stuck with me. At least for the time being." She pointed out the window. "The way's clear now. You can go at any time."

If only that were true, Cortland thought, turning on the car's ignition.

Chapter Sixteen

"I have an idea," Shayla announced.

She and Gabriel had been working on the last two murders committed by the Moonlight Killer for the past two days, talking to as many people—hoping to find possible witnesses—as they could.

Sadly, they were getting absolutely nowhere.

They were back at the precinct now. Shayla had been going through the current mug shots on file, looking for a criminal who even vaguely resembled Cortland and the likeness that the precinct's sketch artist had drawn based on Josephine Juarez's description.

So far, Shayla hadn't been able to find anyone.

Caught up in the files he was going through, Gabriel took a few moments before he raised his eyes and looked at his partner. "Can't wait to hear this one," he murmured.

"You know, you could sound a little more supportive," Shayla told him, although she knew it was useless pointing this out.

"This *is* me being supportive," Gabriel replied.

"When I'm not being supportive, trust me, you'll know it."

Considering his sarcastic responses at times, that might prove rather difficult. "I'm not so sure about that," Shayla told him.

This back-and-forth was getting them nowhere, Gabriel thought. "All right, what's this big idea of yours?"

"Well, I've gone through all the current perpetrators we have in the pages of these books," she told him, indicating the numerous volumes on her desk. "I was thinking that maybe our guy was never arrested in Orange County. Consequently," she extrapolated, "there might not *be* a current mug shot of him in our books. *But* there might be a current poster that we can find in the mug shots of the criminals in Los Angeles."

Gabriel thought her words over and decided that she might actually have a point. "I suppose it's worth a shot."

Shayla smiled. "I'll take that as high praise," she quipped, then turned serious. "Do you know anyone back in your old squad room who we could call to get our hands on those mug shot books?"

Cortland shook his head. "Not really. Anyone I knew has either retired, transferred or, in one case, died."

They had hit another wall, she thought. Apparently the people he worked with didn't exactly have an overly long work expectancy.

"That doesn't sound very helpful. Maybe, since

you're my partner, I should make sure that my insurance is all up-to-date."

It occurred to him that although he knew she was part of the Cavanaugh family, he really didn't know any personal information about her.

"Why?" he asked, deciding this was as good a place as any to start. "Are you married?"

She looked at him in surprise. "No," she answered, thinking he'd already known that.

"But you have kids?" Again, it was a question, not an assumption.

"No." Shayla watched her partner, amused. "Is that your way of finding out if you can ask me out?"

"No," he responded defensively. There was a small part of him that felt she had hit a little too close to home. The moment that occurred to him, he immediately stripped the thought from his consciousness. "It's my way of finding out why you would want to carry life insurance if you're not married and don't have any kids."

She decided that his world had to be exceptionally narrow. "Maybe I want to leave something to my mother," she informed him, "not to mention that I'd also want to make sure that no one would have to put out money for my funeral expenses."

Gabriel shrugged. He saw no reason for elaborate funerals of any sort. "To my way of thinking, once you're dead, you're dead. What happens after that doesn't really matter," he concluded.

His wife's death—or, more accurately, her murder—

must have really done a terrible number on him, she thought, aching for her partner. She could only imagine what he had gone through and was probably still going through to some degree. If she was going to find a way to bring this man around, Shayla thought, she really had her work cut out for her.

"Oh, it matters," she assured him with enthusiasm. "You might not think so, but it does."

He looked at her incredulously. "You're trying to tell me that my death matters," he asked, amazed.

"Absolutely," she responded with feeling.

"To whom?" he questioned, stunned, even though he knew he should just drop the whole matter and not get embroiled in a discussion. He had learned rather quickly that engaging in a verbal battle with this woman would not lead to a victory for him.

"I don't have a family," Gabriel told her. "To whom could my death possibly matter?"

Shayla never hesitated for a moment. "To me," she answered, then went on, "and to the people you work with."

Gabriel closed his eyes, searching for his fragmented patience. It didn't help any that it was growing late and they had been at this for hours.

"Give me a break." He wasn't prepared for what she said in response.

"I think *you* should give yourself a break," Shayla told him. "Stop pushing people away so hard. Just drop those defenses of yours and let things happen."

She was going to go on like this until he could find

a way to get her to stop, Gabriel thought. Taking out his cell phone, he put it on the desk in front of him.

"Let me see if I can get hold of someone and have them forward those mug shots," he said.

"Then you *do* know someone at your old precinct," she said.

"No, but I'll find someone," he answered, adding, "Anything to get you to stop talking endlessly."

She beamed at him, happy that she had managed to get him to come up with a possibility, even if it was strictly intended to get her to stop talking.

"Whatever it takes," Shayla told him cheerfully.

Gabriel made the call to his old precinct. He had to put up with being transferred a number of times— and disconnected once—but in the end, he managed to find someone who promised to get the photo books sent over to his office.

It struck Gabriel, as he hung up the phone, that he actually thought of this squad room as *his* office. He had never even thought of the LA office in those terms, he realized.

"The mug shots are being sent over," he informed Shayla.

"Are they being sent or couriered?" she questioned.

Gabriel knew what she was saying. That "sent" referred to a haphazard directive, while "couriered" implied a process that was safeguarded.

Rather than answer her question, Gabriel sighed inwardly and picked up the receiver, dialing the number again so he could speak to the person in LA again, appealing to that person to take care of the job for him.

Twenty minutes later, talked out, Gabriel hung up again.

It was done.

"Anything else you want, Princess?" Cortland asked. "Need a dragon slain or maybe a mountain climbed?"

"No, I'm fine," she told him brightly. And then she thought of something. "Did that person you talked to tell you when he was bringing the albums with the mug shots?"

"Tomorrow. Why?" he asked suspiciously, eyeing her. Was she going to have him drive into LA to pick them up himself in the interest of efficiency, not to mention making sure that the albums with the mug shot posters actually arrived safely?

But she surprised him.

"Well, if we don't have to wait for the mug shots to be brought over today, then, seeing what time it is, we're free to leave." She began to gather her things and lock up her desk. "Can I buy you a cup of coffee or a soft drink?"

He scrubbed his hand over his face as if to wipe away the sleepiness that had been descending over him. He needed to wake up.

"I'd rather have a drink," he commented.

She looked at him. Was the man slipping up? "I thought you weren't supposed to have those," she said.

"I'm not," he confirmed. "Doesn't mean I still can't want one."

"No," she agreed, "It doesn't. Tell you what, why don't you come to Malone's with me?"

"To the bar?" Gabriel questioned.

"Malone's also serves food," she reminded him. "Pretty good food at that. I brought you that steak sandwich from there." She watched his expression for some indication that he knew what she was referring to. With Cortland, it was really hard to tell.

Gabriel shrugged. "No, thanks, I'll pass."

"I don't think you should." She saw her partner staring at her as if she had just suggested that he needed to run around buck naked for his own good. "You need to get out, to do something besides eat and sleep serial killer," she pointed out.

His eyes washed over her dismissively. "I have you," he said darkly.

"Yes, you do, but you're getting fairly good at ignoring me. You need more input and more people," she told him. She saw him about to protest and quickly added, "Trust me, the more you interact with people, the more your brain cells get stimulated.

"Cases get solved because of the oddest things," she went on. "For instance, the Son of Sam, that serial killer who swore that this dog told him to kill people, was caught because of an outstanding traffic ticket."

"Now you want me to look into unpaid traffic tickets?" he asked, not certain exactly what she was driving at.

"No, wise guy," she told him with a sigh. "What I'm saying is that you never know when you might come across something that gets you thinking and might actually point you in the right direction."

"So you're saying that talking to the people at Malone's will wind up pointing me in the right direction?" he asked.

"No," she corrected, "going to Malone's will keep me from beating on you And maybe, just maybe, something that's said there might just get you thinking about other possibilities. Bottom line, Cortland, is that you need to get out, to socialize a little more. It'll get those rusting wheels in your head greased up and moving in the right direction."

"I'm not going to get you to stop until I agree to go to this Malone's, am I?" Cortland asked.

"Not agree," she corrected, not about to be placated by a few meaningless words. *"Go,"* Shayla emphasized.

She had lost him. Again. This was becoming an annoying habit of hers. "You want to run that by me again?"

"In simple terms, I am not backing off until you and I walk into Malone's together." She gave him the highlights of the evening: "You get something to eat, you say a few words, listen to a few more words and then I'll untie you."

"Untie?" Gabriel echoed, his brow furrowing.

"That was a joke, Cortland. If you can't tell the difference between that and a straight statement, you're worse off than I thought and you *really* need to get out more and mingle with people." She could see that her partner was really resisting her suggestion. "Give me forty-five minutes. Forty-five minutes there and then you can go home. I'll leave you alone."

"Does that mean you'll stop nagging me about your family's party or get-together or whatever you call it?" he asked.

She sighed. She should have known that would be his bargaining chip. "One thing at a time, Cortland."

"In other words, no," he guessed.

"No, in other words, one thing at a time," she repeated. "Right now, let's go to Malone's. And next Saturday, we'll see about my dragging you over to Uncle Andrew's house."

He thought that was rather an apt description for what she was threatening to do. "Dragging me might be the only way you'll succeed in getting me over to that event," he said.

Shayla gave it one more shot. "I know that you haven't had time to figure out all the family connections here, but I think you should take note of the fact that as well as being the former chief of police before he had to retire to take care for his family, Uncle Andrew is also Uncle Brian's big brother. And, in case you forgot, Uncle Brian is—"

"The chief of detectives, yes, I remember," Gabriel said impatiently.

She nodded, then continued, "And while Uncle Brian does not believe in throwing his weight around in any manner, shape or form, you might think twice before disrespecting his older brother by not coming to one of Uncle Andrew's gatherings that you've been invited to attend."

"Point taken," Gabriel answered, none too happily. Switching off his computer, he got up from his chair. Maybe if he faced the first battle, he'd be lucky and the second one would fade away. "You want to lead the way to Malone's?"

Her eyes were shining as she told him, "I would love to."

Chapter Seventeen

Malone's was located a little more than a mile and a half away from the precinct. The reason Gabriel hadn't even noticed the friendly little establishment until now was because Malone's was a small, single-story building, only slightly larger than a yarn shop. Moreover, it was recessed from the middle of the block and, from a certain angle, appeared to be hidden.

At first glance, it was hard to say just where the front of Malone's actually was. Customer parking surrounded the rectangular building on three of its four sides, and most nights, the parking was far from adequate. Patrons had to leave their vehicles parked out on the street, either close by or somewhere in the immediate vicinity.

Shayla and her partner had arrived early enough to avail themselves of parking within the lot that surrounded Malone's rather than somewhere down the block—or farther.

"Looks like they're not all that busy," Gabriel commented, getting out of his car just as his partner walked up to him. He was looking around the parking lot just before he walked into Malone's.

There were a number of people inside, but it wasn't exactly crowded.

"It comes in waves," Shayla told him. "People on the force drop by for a little company, to exchange a few words, have a drink or two, maybe even get something to eat, and then they're gone."

It sounded like an experience that would be over before it even began. He couldn't see why it had been so important to her for him to come to the establishment.

"And why again am I here?" Gabriel asked. As far as he could see, this place looked singularly unimpressive.

That was simple enough for her to answer. "To get your feet wet socializing with your fellow police officers and detectives."

Gabriel looked at her as if she had lapsed into some sort of foreign tongue. Shayla tried again to explain what she was saying in as simple a language as she could.

"I think you need to get used to it. What you see here is nothing compared to Uncle Andrew's parties," she told him. "It's like comparing a World Series game to the first game being played at the beginning of a kindergartner's Little League season.

"At one of Uncle Andrew's gatherings, people don't come in shifts the way they do at Malone's. They stay for as long as they can. Not only that," she continued, "but they bring their wives, their husbands, their significant others and their children." She smiled, thinking about those gatherings. "And Uncle Andrew feeds all of them," she told her partner as she found two empty seats at the counter for them.

"And he feeds all of them," Gabriel repeated, stunned despite himself. "Isn't that a little pricey?" he asked, unable to imagine anyone wanting to voluntarily go to all that trouble and expense.

Shayla hadn't expected him to remember. "Like I mentioned before, the guests all contribute to the cost."

He frowned slightly. Whether or not he intended to turn up—and right now, he was leaning heavily toward "not"—Gabriel felt obligated to put in some money. Just because he wasn't going to attend didn't mean that the food intended for him didn't have to be paid for.

Taking out his wallet, Gabriel asked his partner, "How much?"

But she shook her head, stopping him before he could take out any money. "This is your first time. There's no need to pay until you turn up to at least a few of Uncle Andrew's gatherings."

"So, some people don't turn up after their first time?" Gabriel asked, pleased to be proven right.

She shot her partner down very quickly. "Hasn't been known to happen yet," she told him. "Don't worry, Uncle Andrew's gathering isn't happening for more than a week yet. There's plenty of time for you to get used to the idea."

Gabriel frowned. "Why does my showing up at

your uncle's house mean so much to you?" he asked. None of it made any sense to him, not turning up at the so-called family gathering or even here, at Malone's.

"Because I figure on some level, it'll actually mean something to you," Shayla told him. She smiled at her partner. "Think of it as a free lunch around your fellow police personnel. Free is always good, isn't it?" she asked, peering into his eyes.

"Not if I have to pay for it with my time," he answered.

Shayla blew out a breath, shaking her head. "You are a very stubborn man, Detective Gabriel Cortland. You are aware of that, aren't you?"

For the first time, she saw a small grin appear and slowly move over his face.

"Vaguely," he admitted.

The man behind the counter made his way over toward Shayla. He smiled at her. Sharp, blue-gray eyes took the measure of her companion.

"This your new partner, Shayla?" the gray-haired man asked.

"Yes, he is," she told the man. "Casey, let me introduce Detective Gabriel Cortland. Cortland, this is Sergeant Casey Buchanan, one of the sharpest men to ever retire from the Aurora police force."

Casey wiped his hand on his apron before offering it to Gabriel. "Hear you two are tracking down the former LA Moonlight Killer," Malone's newest owner said. "How's that going for you?" He looked from Shayla to Cortland.

Gabriel raised his brow as he glanced at Shayla. "Does everyone know?" he asked.

"First of all," his partner explained, "Everyone who walks through those doors talks to Casey. It's an occupational hazard. Casey knows *everything*. Second, like any police department, the Aurora Police Department is its own small, self-contained community. That's why I thought that coming here might just stimulate your thinking process. Get it moving in a different direction than it had been going previously."

Casey had always been able to read a situation and had become quite good at defusing possible explosions practically from day one. With a genial expression, the slightly heavyset man suggested, "Since this is your first time here, how about a drink on the house, Cortland? Your choice."

"Better yet, how about a hamburger on the house?" Shayla countered. "We've both put in a really long day, and Cortland's hungrier than he is thirsty," she told Casey.

The former sergeant nodded. "One hamburger coming up. You, too, Shayla?" he asked, looking at the young woman he had known since before the day she was christened.

Shayla smiled her answer. "You talked me into it, Casey."

"Knew I could." His gaze swept over the duo. "Be right back," he promised.

The moment he left, Gabriel regarded his partner. "And this—" he waved a hand around in general "—is supposed to stimulate my brain cells?" he questioned.

"Give it a chance, Cortland," Shayla counseled. "It's a process."

"If you say so," Gabriel muttered under his breath with a dismissive shrug.

"Hey, newly minted detective," a male voice called out by way of a greeting. Her oldest brother, Christian, came up to where Shayla and her partner were sitting. "I hear the lieutenant put you to work on the Moonlight Killer case." Christian nodded his dark head. "Impressive for your first time out, kid."

The detective turned to look at the man sitting next to his baby sister. "Hi, you must be her partner." Christian put his hand out toward Gabriel. He made a mental note to find out all he could about this new detective.

"I must be," Gabriel answered. After a beat, he shook the hand that was being offered to him.

"You have to forgive him," Shayla felt obligated to tell her brother. "People aren't all that friendly where he comes from."

Tickled, Christian laughed. "He'll learn. Being partnered with you, he'll have no choice." He glanced at his watch. "I've got to get going. I promised Suzie Q I'd be home in time to help put the kids to bed. If I hear anything about that serial killer, I'll be sure to pass it on."

Turning from Shayla, he glanced in Gabriel's direction and said, "Nice meeting you. And I'd remember to take my vitamins if I were you, Cortland. Your new partner is a tough woman to keep up with."

"Exactly what did your brother mean by that?" Gabriel asked after Christian had left.

Shayla raised and lowered her shoulders. "I haven't the slightest idea," she answered—a little too innocently for Gabriel's liking.

Casey had just walked out of the kitchen carrying a tray with two hamburgers, each nestled in separate baskets and resting on top of a bed of French fries.

He had just set the tray down on the counter between them when each of their cell phones began to ring.

They all knew what that meant, including Casey.

"Take the baskets with you," he instructed. "You can bring them back the next time you come by."

"Cavanaugh," Shayla declared the second she brought the phone close to her face.

"Cortland," Gabriel said into his phone.

Both fell silent as the persons on the other end began rattling off information that made their blood run cold.

Gabriel listened closely to the directions he was being given. Both calls were over with in less than a minute.

Standing nearby, Casey read their faces and shook his head. "This guy can't stop himself, can he?" he asked as Shayla and her partner rose from the counter.

"That's why we have to, as quickly as humanly possible," Shayla told her late father's friend. She nodded at the basket that she was taking with her. "Put this on my tab, Casey," she said. "I'll catch you next time."

"Don't worry about it," the former sergeant told her, waving her words away. "Just get this SOB," he called after the two departing detectives.

"He's not taking a break," Shayla said in disgusted amazement as they walked out of the bar. "He used to let months go by, but now it hasn't even been twenty-four hours."

"Actually," Gabriel said just before he got into his car and took off, "I think this one was done before the other two."

Shayla found herself standing there, staring after the departing vehicle. What Cortland had just said left her totally in a daze. The person from the precinct who had gotten in contact with her hadn't given her any of those details. All she had been told was that another one of the Moonlight Killer's victims had been discovered in a freshly painted gas station bathroom.

It was supposed to be opened up tomorrow, but the attendant had decided to check the bathroom out first and to air it out as well. The gas station attendant had just peeped in to make sure that everything was as it should be in the single-stall bathroom before leaving for home.

Obviously, she thought, chewing her lower lip, it hadn't been.

Shayla got into her car and quickly drove to the gas station that was the scene of the latest gruesome discovery. Ironically, it was located less than a block away from another, almost identical gas station.

Given the close proximity between the two, what had made the killer choose one gas station above the other? Was it the victim he was stalking or the location that had drawn him in?

And why had Gabriel said that he thought this murder had been committed before the murders of the convenience store clerk and the master's degree candidate in the library stacks?

And, even more importantly than that, why had the killer upped his killing spree? she couldn't help wondering.

Was there a reason for it, or had the bloodlust just completely overwhelmed the killer, pushing him to kill even more victims faster than before?

There were so many questions involved here and so few answers, she thought.

The next moment she promised herself that she would find the answers as well as find the killer.

She had to believe that.

She was aware that some crimes were never solved, but those were usually single crimes with single victims, not crimes perpetrated by serial killers, because the more times the man—and sometimes the woman—ventured out to kill a victim, there was that much more of a chance that he would make a fatal mistake, one that would trip him up and lead to his capture.

Turning in to the gas station in question, she noted that there was a convenience store located almost right next to the gas station bathroom.

She wondered if there was some significance in that or if it was just a simple coincidence. From what she had read in the autopsy reports, which included where the murders had been committed, this was apparently only the second convenience store that was involved in the serial killer's spree. In the first convenience store, the victim had been hung from one of the sturdy shelves, then cut down by the killer.

In this one, according to the woman who had given her the information, the victim had been suspended from the bathroom stall.

As she drew closer to where the crime had been committed, she saw that once again, the crime scene investigative unit had arrived on the scene ahead of her. Given that they were driving a larger vehicle, one that they had to load up with all the items that were necessary to carefully document everything that happened at the crime scene, she was surprised to see the CSI vehicle there.

She was even more surprised, Shayla realized, to see that her partner had beaten her to the site as well.

The man didn't even know his way around Aurora yet—how the hell had he managed to get here first?

She had to give the detective his due, Shayla thought as she pulled her vehicle up next to his and parked it. He was obviously boning up on the city.

Chapter Eighteen

Cortland was standing just inside the gas station bathroom, solemnly studying the victim. Dressed in pants and a soft, frilly blouse, the dark blonde had been hog-tied exactly like the other victims. This time the victim was suspended from a rope that was thrown over the top of the bathroom stall.

Shayla drew closer to her partner. He looked so deep in thought that, for a moment, she debated whether or not to say anything that might intrude.

Eventually, he snapped out of it, which was when she asked, "What did you mean by saying you thought that this victim wasn't the latest one?"

He rose to his feet. "Something the person who called me from the precinct said about the crime scene," he told Shayla. "That the bathroom had been remodeled and painted and then locked up for a couple of days to keep the public out while the paint dried.

"And then there's this," Gabriel said, pointing to the mirror just above the newly installed sink. Painted across the mirror in what appeared to be leftover beige paint were the words *Missed you, Det. Cort-land* in large, bold letters.

Shayla's mouth dropped open. She had no idea how she could have missed that. She supposed that it was because her attention had been entirely drawn to the victim—and to Gabriel's reaction to the woman.

"He's made this purely personal," Shayla said, stunned.

"He made it personal when he went after my wife and killed her," Cortland corrected, doing his best to keep the hurtful words at bay.

She had noticed how carefully he had gone over the body. "Did you find another injection site on her?" Shayla asked.

He shook his head. "Not yet, but all that means is that he might have injected her through her clothes. Most likely, he snuck up on her, but I'm guessing she turned around and he had to make do with what-ever area he could get to in order to inject her with the neuromuscular paralyzing agent," Gabriel said.

That made sense, she thought. Shayla looked around, trying to find someone on the CSI team. She wasn't necessarily looking for her uncle, but that was whom she spotted. Sean Cavanaugh was talking to another member of his team. She quickly made her way over to her uncle. She noticed that Gabriel fol-lowed in her wake.

For once, her uncle was not smiling. Nodding at the duo, Sean said grimly, "Looks like the serial killer upped his game. I'm not sure how much longer we can keep this out of the papers. The second this gets out, we're going to have a full-scale panic on our hands. This looks like it's personal," he said, echoing Shayla's words.

Because this sort of attention made her partner uncomfortable, Shayla answered for him. "Cortland was closing in on the killer back in Los Angeles," she explained, lowering her voice. "And then the Moonlight Killer did away with his wife."

She still wasn't sure how her partner managed to function. This sort of thing would have devastated so many other people.

Glancing toward Gabriel, who had stepped away for a moment, Sean nodded. "I am aware of the background details on the case," he told his niece. It was his way of telling her that there was no need to go any further with her explanation. "Obviously the serial killer found out that Gabriel had transferred to Aurora, and he had decided to bring his game out here to punish him.

"What amazes me," Sean continued, "is that the killer actually waited for your partner to dry out and get his act together before he resumed his gruesome spree."

"Maybe that's why he upped his count so quickly, to make up for the long break and lost time," Shayla said grimly. She watched her partner as he moved around just outside the bathroom. She didn't want him overhearing her ask her uncle, "Why do you think the killer feels so connected to Cortland?"

"That is anybody's guess," Sean told her seriously. "Because he's a sick SOB and doesn't really need a reason for anything he does," Gabriel said as he rejoined the two inside the crime scene. Obviously, Gabriel had overheard despite his partner's precautions. "Personally, I don't care why he does what he does. I'm just interested in making him stop as soon as possible. I want to get this homicidal maniac off the streets, one way or another."

"Amen to that," Shayla agreed with feeling. "Do we have an approximate time of death for this woman yet?" she asked, turning toward her uncle.

"Not yet, I'm afraid. But we do have a name," Sean told her. "Her name is Gayle Parker, according to her driver's license."

Something struck her as being a little odd. "You notice that the serial killer never tries to hide his victims' identities?" Shayla asked her partner.

He had already thought about that. "My guess is that he's proud of his kills and wants everyone to know about them," Gabriel told her. "The faster his victim can be identified, the more people can be affected by her death. And the more people who are affected, the more gratified the Moonlight Killer feels."

Shayla frowned at the very idea. "Just what the county needs, a serial killer who's an overachiever." She looked at her uncle. "Has anyone been sent to notify her family or next of kin yet?"

"Not that I know of," Sean told her. "Her wallet was just turned up. Are you volunteering?"

"Not willingly," she admitted. "But someone has to do it." As she said the words, she glanced in her partner's direction.

Gabriel knew what she was asking him, even if her lips weren't moving. He nodded. "I'll go with you."

She knew he didn't have to. It only took one person to do the notification. "I appreciate that," Shayla told him.

"We'll go in the same car," Gabriel told her, then surprised her by saying, "You drive."

She hadn't expected him to surrender the cherished male position of being the one behind the wheel. It had her wondering what was behind this. "Are you sure?" she questioned.

"No," Gabriel answered. "So let's go before I change my mind."

The site of the latest murder to be discovered, if not the actual latest murder to be committed, was in a parking lot that was adjacent to a much larger lot. That lot provided parking for a grocery store, a pharmacy and several stores that specialized in high-end clothing at low-end prices.

Leaving Gabriel's vehicle parked there posed no problem. What they were about to do, however, did.

The address on the driver's license was for a ground-floor apartment in a development of close to a hundred garden apartments.

Shayla pulled her vehicle up in guest parking closest to the apartment number she had. Considering the number of apartments in the immediate area, the available guest parking was sparse.

After getting out of her car, she waited for Gabriel to do the same. "Apartment eighty-one is right over there," she said, pointing it out.

As they approached, she saw that there were lights on, "Let's get this over with," Gabriel said, leading the way to the apartment's front door.

It took three rings before anyone responded.

The front door flew open and an exasperated man of about thirty-five or so cried, "Where the hell have you been?" before he realized that he wasn't talking to the victim.

Alex Reynolds looked at the two people standing on his front step, holding official-looking shields.

"Sorry, I thought you were my girlfriend," he apologized. "She's been missing for three days and I've been worried sick. This just isn't like her."

Shayla took an inward breath and held up the victim's license for him to look at. "Is this her?"

"Yes!" he cried. And then he turned pale as he stared at the driver's license. "Where did you get that?" he asked fearfully, his eyes darting from Shayla to the man standing next to her.

"Mr. Reynolds, I'm afraid we have some bad news for you," Shayla began very quietly and respectfully.

The man's knees buckled. Had Gabriel not been standing right there to catch him, Reynolds would have wound up passing out on the floor in his doorway.

As it was, Gabriel caught the man and half carried him into the apartment he now lived in alone.

THEY WOUND UP staying with the dead woman's boyfriend for close to an hour. Gabriel remained silent for the most part, with Shayla doing all the talking as well as doing what she could to comfort the bereaved man.

She discovered that Reynolds and the woman he had reported missing as soon as the missing persons department was able to take the information had planned to get married at the beginning of next year.

Shayla filed that bit of information away for later.

What she and Gabriel managed to do, once they got Reynolds to calm down a little, was question him about if there was anyone in Gayle's life that she was afraid of, or who might have followed her, wanting to harm her.

But Alex shook his head. The grief-stricken man couldn't think of anyone who would have wanted to harm his fiancée.

"Our life together was close to perfect," he told the two detectives, his voice breaking. "That's why, when she went missing, it just didn't seem like her. One of my friends said that maybe she just got cold feet, but she wouldn't have taken off like that. She would have come to me and talked things out. She certainly wouldn't have taken off and left her clothes behind," he insisted. "She just wouldn't have," Reynolds lamented as fresh tears came to his eyes.

In the end, Shayla called around to the distraught fiancé's friends and got several of them to come over and stay with Alex. She and Gabriel waited until the friends arrived.

"Sorry to make you wait," she told Gabriel as they walked out of the ground-floor apartment and to her car. "I should have had you take your own vehicle," she conceded.

Within moments, they were in her car and finally on their way back to where they had left his car.

"No reason to apologize," Gabriel told her. And then, after a beat, he looked at Shayla. He wasn't the kind to give compliments, but this had struck him at the time. "You were pretty good with that guy, breaking the news to him," Gabriel told her. "You seem to know just what to say, even though the poor guy must have felt like his very heart was being ripped right out of his chest."

It occurred to Shayla that that was a very concise description of what Reynolds had to have been going through.

But then, of course her partner would know all about that feeling.

"Was that how you felt?" Shayla asked him in a low, compassionate voice.

The moment the words were out of her mouth, she could feel her partner stiffening. She knew she had hit a nerve. Hit it hard.

But rather than make a denial or say something flippant or dismissive and change the subject, her partner actually answered her question.

"Yes. I felt like someone had stabbed me right in my heart. I kept hoping that it was all some sort of a nightmare, or that if I bargained hard enough, I would be the one who was dead and not Natalie." He sighed, vividly remembering the whole awful ordeal. "The pain grew so intolerable, I tried really hard to drown it, but I couldn't. For some reason, no matter how much I drank, I couldn't drown me, either. I'd always wind up passing out before I could drink myself to death," he said with a dark laugh.

"What made you decide to sober up and live?" she asked him, hoping that if she got him talking about his ordeal, he could finally begin to put it past him.

Gabriel stared at her for a long moment. No one had ever asked him that before, not even his old captain at the LA precinct. Captain Kelvin was just happy to sign the release documents, getting rid of someone who had once "been a really good detective," the man had said to him as his final parting words.

"Because I realized that I couldn't die before I avenged my wife and unborn baby, bringing that scum to justice." He knew that had to sound hokey, but he didn't care. That was how he felt. "And I realized that I couldn't do that if I was drinking, no matter how much I wanted to drown the pain I was feeling. So I stopped."

They had reached the parking lot where they had left Gabriel's vehicle earlier, and he looked at her.

For a second, the silence in her car was almost deafening. And then Gabriel finally spoke. "Any other questions?"

"Only how can I help?" Shayla asked.

"You're already doing it," he told her. She hadn't backed away from him, hadn't thrown her hands up and just walked away from the investigation. If anything, she kept at it just as intently as he had. Though he had initially complained that she was annoying, he realized now that her support meant a lot.

Shayla nodded. "Well, I intend to keep on doing it until we finally have a resolution," she told him. "My advice to you is to go home and get some rest, but I have a feeling that you have no intentions of listening to that, so I have an alternate suggestion."

"Which is?" he asked, curious despite the fact that he felt he should just tell her he'd see her later, get whatever sleep he could and return in a few hours.

"We've got cots set up at the precinct for people who pull all-nighters," she told him.

He had no idea where this was going, so he urged her to continue. "Go on."

"We go to the precinct with this new information and put down everything we know on one of those boards we use in the squad room. You know, the ones to try to find some sort of common denominator that threads through the cases."

"Other than the fact that so far, all the victims we found were under forty, what else is there?" he asked Shayla.

"There's that paralytic drug used on them and the fact that two of the victims were getting married in the coming year."

"So?"

"That's what we need to find out," she said. "So is that just a stray fact, or does it mean something? And if it does, what does it have to do with the other victims?"

His hand was on the door, opening it. It was obvious that she had gotten him thinking.

And then, just as he slipped out of the passenger side, Gabriel said, "I'll meet you in the precinct parking lot."

Victory! Shayla thought, doing her best not to smile too hard.

Chapter Nineteen

Gabriel walked into the squad room. There were only a few people in there at this time of night, as opposed to the regular number of detectives and officers during the daytime.

"You looking for Shayla?" a redheaded detective near the back of the room asked. Gabriel vaguely recognized the man as someone his partner had introduced him on the first day. The woman had insisted on introducing him to a lot of people, he thought.

He seemed to recall that the man's name was Jeff Anderson or something along those lines.

"Anderson?" Gabriel asked, not altogether sure that he remembered the name correctly.

"That's me," the detective confirmed. "Shayla's in the conference room. Said to send you in there once you got here."

"Conference room?" he repeated. What was she doing there? That was where suspects were usually brought in for interrogation. Had she found someone to question in the time it had taken him to get here?

He had already sensed that she was an overachiever, but at the moment, he didn't know what to expect.

Gabriel walked into the large, windowless room with its single long table. Right now, there was not just one but two bulletin boards set up side by side against the back wall. Shayla was there, her back to him, busy taping up photographs of all the Moonlight Killer's victims, both in Los Angeles and Aurora.

Surveying the photographs, Gabriel stopped dead when he saw the picture of his wife just before the photographs of the latest three victims from Aurora.

"What are you doing?" he asked, his voice dark and demanding.

She had heard him come into the room and was ready for the confrontation.

Shayla gave him a simple answer: "Looking for any and all similarities between the victims."

He forced himself to turn away from Natalie's picture. Looking at it hurt too much. "What are you looking to find?"

"Hopefully, a reason why they were killed," she told him. "The one thing that put them in someone's path to be murdered."

"Something they had in common," he said. "You mean like the two women who were going to be getting married sometime next year?"

They had already discussed this. Maybe Cortland was just looking for reaffirmation. "Yes, like that," she told him.

Gabriel walked over toward his wife's photograph.

Other than her name and date of death, there was nothing posted beneath her name except for his.

"Natalie was already married," he pointed out.

Shayla could hear the pain in her partner's voice despite the fact that he was all but spitting the words out.

"Granted, Natalie is the exception," she agreed. "You already said that you felt the serial killer killed her to teach you a lesson. We need to find out what the other sixteen LA victims had in common—if anything." Shayla nodded at the stack of files on the table, the ones she had just brought in. "I had all the files on the previous victims sent over from Los Angeles. *Something* has to tie them together."

He looked at the stack of files. It wouldn't hurt to go through them a second or third time, he thought. There could be something in the files he had missed.

"Where do you want me to start?" Gabriel asked.

She was surprised that he was so easy to instruct. She had expected Cortland to fight her on this the way he had fought her on almost everything.

"Just pick a file, match it to the photograph on top of the bulletin board and start reading," she told him. "Make a note of *anything* that strikes you. Oh, and when you get tired and want to sack out, the cots are set up in the back room." She could see by his expression that he didn't know where that was. "When you walk out of here, turn left, not right. The room's right there in the middle of the hall."

He nodded, taking in the information. "You are a

handy woman to have around," he murmured under his breath.

Picking up on his barely audible comment, Shayla's mouth curved. "I try," she answered, getting back to the file directly in front of her.

THEY SPENT ANOTHER couple of hours going through about half the files between them. They wrote down everything and anything that appeared as if it might have possibilities on Post-it notes, which, in turn, they put up under the photographs of the corresponding victims.

As it turned out, only a few of the victims had been planning to get married the following year. And, reviewing the information about the brides-to-be, none of them were using the same wedding planners. Different wedding planners working out of different organizations had been recruited. The same went for the places where the receptions were to be held.

"Well, it *was* a decent idea," Gabriel told her when another victim's file proved not to contain anything about the victim getting married any time in the year after her death. He tossed the file back onto the stack on the table.

"Just because they don't have a future wedding in common doesn't mean that there isn't something else going on in their lives that brought them to the killer's attention."

Shayla set aside the file she had been looking through and sighed. "But right now, I'm just too tired to think. I'm going to go get some shut-eye."

He was surprised by that. "You're not going home?" After all, she didn't live that far from here.

"Not in this sleepy state I'm not," she told him. "I'm liable to fall asleep at the wheel and hit someone. And drinking coffee to wake up is out. It would be counterproductive at this point, and I'd wind up much too wired for this time of night."

Shayla rose, leaving the files behind and making her way to the door. "I'll just grab a catnap and be ready to go in about an hour or so," she told him.

With that, she left the room.

He stood there, staring up at the photographs spread out across the two bulletin boards.

Crossing back to the desk, Gabriel picked up another file and opened it. He thumbed through several of the pages. Then, dropping the file, he sighed.

He hated to admit it, even to himself, but the words on the page were beginning to get blurry. He was as tired as his partner had told him she was. Maybe even more.

Gabriel supposed that grabbing those forty winks or so wasn't such a bad idea.

Dimming the lights, Gabriel walked out of the conference room. It took him a minute to remember where Shayla had said that the back room with the cots was located. That was his first clue that he was *really* tired. He usually had no trouble remembering things.

Making his way to the back room, Gabriel tried the doorknob on a whim. He had assumed that since she was in there, she would have locked the door for her own protection, making him have to knock to gain access.

But the door turned out to be unlocked. Turning the doorknob very slowly, he opened the door and saw that Shayla was lying on one of the cots up against the wall on the far side of the room.

His partner appeared to be asleep. He did his best to enter and make his way very quietly into the room. He chose a cot was closest to the door. Gabriel didn't like to be caught napping if someone entered the room, even if that person was most likely another police officer. The sound of the door opening would be enough to wake him.

Lying down on the cot, he stretched out very slowly and then sighed.

Who would have ever believed that he would wind up here like this, he thought. After his wife's murder, he had just assumed that he would have been resting—permanently—on a slab at the morgue by now, not on a cot behind a police conference room.

Well, he was here now, at least for the time being. He might as well make the best of it.

Gabriel promised himself that all he wanted to do was to catch a few minutes of sleep and then he'd be back at it again, going through the victims' files and searching for that one common thread that Cavanaugh insisted was what had brought the Moonlight Killer into those poor women's lives.

Just a few minutes, Gabriel told himself. That was all that he needed.

And then he'd be back at it full force.

He didn't remember closing his eyes.

If anyone had asked him about what happened, he would have easily sworn on a stack of Bibles that he had just intended to get a few minutes' rest.

That was all, just a few minutes.

"WAKE UP, SLEEPYHEAD."

Gabriel started, all but jumping up when he felt the hand on his shoulder, gently attempting to shake him into consciousness.

He found that he had to rise to the surface, pulling himself out of the deep disorientation that only seized a mind during those times when it had fallen into an all-absorbing, penetrating sleep.

Gabriel jackknifed up, bumping his head against the wall next to his cot.

"I wasn't asleep," Gabriel informed her curtly.

The smile on her face was skeptical. "Do you usually snore when you're awake?"

"I don't snore, either," he told her.

"All right," Shayla said gamely. "Just what would you call it?"

"Resting," he answered, swinging his legs off the bed and preparing to stand up.

She nodded as if taking in the information. "You were resting very soundly," she told him, amused. Apparently, admitting to something as human as needing to get some sleep was beneath some people, she thought.

Her eyes slid over her partner. He still looked a little tired, but she knew he would protest the assessment.

"Ready to get back to it?" she asked. "By the way, I ordered some breakfast."

"Breakfast?" he repeated, still feeling a wee bit disoriented.

She nodded. "You know, the most important meal of the day, etc., etc. I figured if I had it delivered, neither of us would have to take any time out to go pick it up." On her feet, she waited for him to get up and join her. "How do you feel about French toast?"

He thought over her question as he got to his feet. "I don't think I'm ready for any kind of a steady relationship with it, but it's not bad once in a while."

She rolled her eyes. He had a penchant of making some minor things sound almost bigger than life.

"Well, you have some waiting for you in the conference room," she told him, leading the way back.

"I didn't ask you to get me breakfast," he called after her.

"No, you didn't. I just figured you might be hungry. Pursuing a serial killer is hungry work," she told him, adding, "You know, you don't have to treat everything as if it was a challenge to your authority because most of the time, it's not." She smiled at him as they sat down at the conference table. "It could just be thoughtfulness."

"Sorry," he apologized, thinking how different the work atmosphere was here than it had been back in his old precinct. There everyone was too busy with their own cases to spare a few words of cheerful camaraderie and send them in anyone's direction. That was obviously not the case here.

"I'm not used to anyone caring if I ate or not," he told her.

"I see," she observed. "Well, here in Aurora, we don't just have a partner's back, we have his front, his insides and all the parts in between," she told him with a smile. A smile that, like it or not, was beginning to get to him. "Now eat," she told him, indicating the Styrofoam carton on the table in front of him.

He sighed as if what she had just told him to do was a hardship for him, but she noticed that Gabriel quickly disposed of the contents of the carton.

"Where's your breakfast?" Gabriel asked.

She nodded toward the wastebasket. A white container was peeking out of the top. "I already ate it."

They continued with what Shayla had come to think of as "the elimination game." They would take something that she had found in one of the folders and see if either one of them could find something similar in one or more of the other files.

Having nothing better to work with, Gabriel made a list of both similarities and differences between what Shayla had found in the victims' files.

Three hours later, Shayla sighed. "This is getting us nowhere," she complained.

"Yes, it is," Gabriel contradicted, surprising her. She looked at him quizzically, wondering if he was actually being positive.

"Come again?" she asked.

"I think that idea that the victims had to have something in common in order to attract the killer's attention is a good one. The trouble is that we haven't been able to find what that one thing is yet," Gabriel said. "Doesn't mean we won't."

She sat back in her chair and looked at him from top to bottom. "Who are you and what have you done with my partner?" she asked Cortland.

"Apparently, I think better on a full stomach," he said with a short laugh. "I also think we need to talk to some of the victims' next of kin. They might be able to enlighten us about some of their relatives' habits that didn't find their way into the files," he suggested, nodding at the files on his side of the table.

"That," Shayla said, impressed with his suggestion, "is an excellent idea." She looked at the folders, each, she thought sadly, representing a victim. "We've got a lot of people to choose from. Most of the victims had someone in their lives who might be able to tell us something that wasn't in these files," she said, her enthusiasm growing right before his eyes. "All we need is a hint to point us in the right direction.

"Tell you what," she continued, her mind racing, "before we throw ourselves into the heart of LA traffic, why don't I come up with a list of questions we can ask the victims' next of kin, see if we can get an idea of what interested the victim. You know, if they went to ball games, did volunteer work, belonged to unusual clubs, things like that," she told Gabriel, excited about this new avenue of possibilities. "Somewhere in that mixture is the answer we're looking for. But," she guessed, "we're not going to know it until we come face-to-face with it."

"Sounds like it's worth a try," he agreed. "Because so far nothing else is panning out."

"At least he appears to be taking a break from killing women," she said, thinking about the fact that there had been no reports of the killer striking in the last few hours.

"Either that," Gabriel said, "or he's getting ready to strike again."

She wrinkled her nose as she pulled over a legal pad, preparing to write the list of questions she had mentioned. "I could have done without that."

The unbidden thought that his partner looked cute wrinkling her nose like that flashed through Gabriel's mind before he could block it.

Where the hell had that come from? he silently demanded.

The idea of getting out and questioning people began to look better and better to him.

Chapter Twenty

"How do you not let it get to you?"

The question had come out of the blue. They had been at this for several hours now, questioning a number of victims' next of kin for information. Consequently, they had also been forced to witness the sadness that these questions stirred up within the family members they spoke to.

What the purpose of these questions were, Shayla had told her partner, was to get some sort of feeling for the kind of women these victims had been and how they, as opposed to other women, might have attracted the serial killer's attention.

There had to be some kind of common denominator amid these women that they could find.

Cortland had lapsed into silence since they had finished questioning the last person on their list. She wasn't altogether sure that she had actually heard him saying anything at all. Her thoughts had been busy ricocheting in her head, so that might have gotten in the way.

Taking a chance, she turned toward him and asked, "What?"

Gabriel blew out a breath and approached the subject from a different angle, because he was really curious what made this woman tick.

"Dealing with all the chaos and havoc that this sick individual has caused to the victims, to their families and friends, why would you even *want* to have a career that deals with something as revolting as that? And how are you even able to smile like that?" he asked, mystified how she could possibly keep going after seeing what had been done to the victims.

"Well, for one thing, I think of my job as preventing killers from getting away with what they'd done and, even more importantly, from killing more people.

"If it weren't for people like us, Gabriel, people like the Moonlight Killer would be free to continuing destroying lives and growing more and more bloodthirsty," she told him. "And I'm doing this to avenge Gayle and Shirley and Natalie and Amanda and all the other victims whose lives that hateful creature has snuffed out."

He understood all of that, but he was having trouble wrapping his mind around the fact that she seemed so upbeat.

"But the things you've seen," he said, "don't they ever haunt you?"

She compartmentalized, but she didn't think she could explain that properly to Gabriel, so instead, Shayla told him, "They would if I wasn't completely focused on doing something about it. And," she added—and to her, this was the important part— "luckily, I have a great family, all of whom know exactly what I'm dealing with and who somehow, miraculously, know just the right thing to say when I do hit a stumbling block and feel like I'm not able to go on."

She smiled at him. The smile was so bright, he caught himself thinking he could see it in the moonlight. "That's the good thing about having so many of my relatives working in the police department."

"Yeah, well I guess that does make you lucky in a way. I don't have that," he said grimly, staring out through the windshield at the road in front of him.

"You can," she told him softly.

He looked at her. His partner was babbling. She knew he had no family. "What are you talking about?"

She worded her answer very carefully and deliberately. "You can start by coming to Uncle Andrew's gathering."

"And they'll do what, adopt me?" he asked sarcastically.

"Not right away," Shayla told him in all seriousness. "But you can talk to them, tell them about the case we're working on. They can offer advice, and more than that, they can commiserate. I guarantee there'll be a number of them who have dealt with the same kind of thing, or at least something close to it. Sharing like experiences can help lighten the way you're feeling."

He spared her a stunned look. "You're serious," he realized.

Shayla smiled even though she knew he couldn't see her face. "Completely. It's been known to happen. More often than you'd think," she told him. She could feel him growing impatient with the conversation, so for now, she changed topic.

"It's getting late. Why don't we stop somewhere for dinner?" she suggested, then instantly changed her mind. "Better yet, why don't we go to my place and I'll make you dinner?"

"I don't feel like having eggs again," he said, remembering what she had offered to make for him the last time. He just assumed that was her entire menu.

"I make other things than breakfast," she told him, amused.

"Like what?" he challenged, thinking she probably couldn't come up with anything right away. She didn't strike him as being domestic, which was all right, given her choice of careers.

Shayla thought for a moment, not because she had no immediate answer but because she was trying to remember what she had in her refrigerator.

"How do you feel about chicken parmesan or pork chops?" she asked. "Either one is fast, simple and you don't have to worry about getting a food taster," she told him, her lips curving at the end of her sentence.

He frowned. "Sounds like a lot of trouble for you to go through."

Why would she even want to put herself out this way, he wondered. The day she had put in was just as long as his had been, and she had to be tired, he reasoned.

"No, it's not," she contradicted. "You obviously don't cook much," she went on. Before her partner could demur further, she quickly said, "All right. That settles it, you're coming with me. No more arguing."

"I wasn't arguing," he protested.

"Certainly felt that way to me," Shayla told him. "But now that's all over with."

Gabriel was about to protest that they didn't have time for this, that he still had work to get to. But glancing at the clock on his dashboard, he realized that more time had gone by than he had initially thought. Somehow, amid all the questioning and driving they had done since they left the station earlier, the day had gotten away from him. It was actually past normal quitting time—and then some.

"Look," Gabriel began in an authoritative voice he assumed would put an end to all this, "you don't have to do this."

What he wanted to do was take her back to the station, where she could get her vehicle and go home, not take him to her place and feed him.

At least that was his plan.

It died a quick death.

"I don't *have* to do anything," Shayla informed him, then insisted, "I *want* to do this."

The woman was going to argue him to death. "Why?"

Shayla rolled her eyes and sighed. "Stop asking questions and just drive like a good little partner."

Offended, Gabriel was about to protest again, then decided that winning an argument with her just wasn't in the cards, at least not tonight.

Besides, now that he thought about it, he had to admit that he really was hungry. As far as he recalled, there was nothing in his refrigerator either to defrost or for him to make a weak stab at cooking. All he had was a quarter of a loaf of bread, and he wasn't inclined to stop to pick up something.

His partner, he thought grudgingly, had won the argument by default.

"Okay," he said, turning his car in the direction of her house.

Shayla was really tempted to say, "That's more like it," but she knew he wouldn't welcome her cavalier assessment. So she just kept quiet and smiled to herself.

It was slow going, but the man was definitely coming around.

"WHAT CAN I DO?" Gabriel asked once they walked in through her door.

A thought occurred to her, but it had nothing to do with being helpful, and she knew that in his present state of mind, he definitely wouldn't welcome it.

But for all his scowling, she really found the man to be attractive, she couldn't help thinking.

She pushed the thought onto the back burner. The really far back burner. If this partnership was going to work, she couldn't allow herself to think that way.

"Well, you can lock the door behind you and then sit down," she told him cheerfully.

"You don't want me to help out in some way?" he asked. He wasn't all that handy in the kitchen, but there had to be something he could do.

"Well, if it's not too taxing for you, you can talk," she told him.

They had talked off and on all day. Mostly about the case, but that was still talking, he reasoned.

"About what?" he asked.

Shayla shrugged. "About anything you want. The case, a program you watched recently that you liked—or hated—and why." She paused for a moment as she took the pork chops out of the refrigerator. "Or you can tell me about your wife."

She saw him look up sharply at her. "I think we've had our fill talking about the case today. And I don't watch TV," Gabriel told her. "And as for—"

He didn't get to finish, because what he had said just prior to that had caught her attention.

"You don't watch TV?" she questioned, surprised. She wasn't glued to her set, but she did turn it on for background noise when she was home alone. Everyone she knew watched TV programs at some point or other.

"No," he told her with finality. "I don't."

"Ever?" Shayla questioned. He sounded so definite about it, it surprised her.

The next moment, she found out why. "I don't own a TV."

"Oh. Well, that would explain why you don't watch it," she commented. "Can I ask why?"

He hovered over her as she began to prepare the

pork chops, suddenly feeling too antsy to sit. "Because I deal with tragedy every day. I don't want to spend my night welcoming it into my home as well."

"There are other things to watch," she told him as the pork chops sizzled on the frying pan. "A whole wealth of things, actually. Comedies, old musicals, classic movies."

He shrugged his shoulders, dismissing all the choices she had come up with in one gesture. "Not interested."

She had the flame on high. Flipping the pork chops over, she was nearly done with them. She had two pork chops for each of them. While the food cooked, she tossed a bag of frozen vegetables into the microwave in an attempt to round out the meal.

"Did Natalie feel the same way?" she asked.

"She watched old movies. Made me watch them with her." He had gotten rid of the set after her death. He couldn't bear to turn it on. Watching it stirred up too many memories, as did everything else in his house. He'd walked away from all of it.

Gabriel looked at his partner accusingly. "Why do you keep bringing her up?"

The answer was simple. "Because that's how we keep people alive who we loved but are now gone. By talking about them. And because every time you or I mention her, you look like your gut had just been vivisected. Why is that?" she asked gently.

"Because I failed her. Because she's dead because of me." The words came tumbling out before he could stop them. "We went to school together, high school *and* college, and she could have had anyone she wanted. Anyone. But for some reason, she wanted me." Gabriel shook his head. "If she had married anyone else, she'd still be alive today," he insisted, feeling his throat closing up.

"You can't know that," Shayla insisted. "Life has a way of arranging itself when we're not looking and there's not much we can do about that. Tell me," she said, removing the frying pan from the cooktop and placing the pork chops on two plates, "was she happy with you?"

Cutting open the bag of mixed vegetables, she poured out the contents, dividing them between the two plates.

"Yeah, I guess. For the most part," he qualified as an afterthought, not sure of anything right now. All he was sure of was that she was gone and he wasn't.

Shayla sat down opposite her partner at her dining room table.

"Well, that's all anyone can ask for," she told him. To keep the somber mood from taking over, she asked Gabriel, "What would you like to drink?"

"A Black Russian," he answered without hesitating. Before she could say anything, he said, "But I'll settle for a soft drink."

Relieved, Shayla inclined her head. "One soft drink coming up."

"I can get it," Gabriel protested as she bounced up.

"I'm already up," she told him, going to the refrigerator and taking out a can. Rather than pour the contents into a glass, she placed the can next to his plate. "Tell you what, you can rough it and drink it straight out of the can."

"Wow," he said, pulling the tab, "makes me feel like a rebel."

Her eyes crinkled as she smiled at him. "Whatever works." She sat down opposite Gabriel again and began eating her dinner. "I hope the pork chops are to your liking. I made them to suit my taste," she confessed.

"They're fine," he told her. "Actually," Gabriel reconsidered his words, "better than fine."

She nodded, smiling at his assessment—and the fact that he had corrected himself. "Glad you like them."

Shayla watched as he made short work of the two pork chops on his plate. She hadn't seen him enjoy something to this extent and decided that he wasn't just paying her lip service.

She slowly consumed one of her pork chops and then waited until he was finished.

"Would you like another one?" she asked.

"That's your dinner," he protested.

"It's dinner," she corrected, leaving out the possessive pronoun. "To be shared any way I see fit. And I want you to have it." Her eyes crinkled again as her lips curved. "It's nice seeing you enjoy something."

Why her words suddenly made him think that what he really wanted to enjoy was her, not food, he really couldn't fathom. It wasn't that he didn't find her at-

tractive. Heaven help him, he did. But just because
a woman was attractive had never left an impression
on him, not since he had first began going out with
Natalie—and certainly not since she had been taken
from him.

In his case, his relationship with Natalie had truly
brought new meaning to the phrase "One-woman
man."

And yet, all these stray thoughts kept popping up
in his head, being brought to life by something Shayla
said, or the way she looked at him—or the strange
longing he had been experiencing of late.

Working with Shayla made him extremely conscious of the loneliness that had been his companion for the last nine months. Conscious of how very
empty his life had become since he had held his wife's
lifeless body in his arms.

But, by the same token, working with Shayla had
managed to fill up all those empty spaces inside him
as well as helping to give his life a new purpose.

As much as he hated to admit it, Shayla was sharp
and kept him on his toes. In addition, she kept his
mind going, and most of all, she kept alive his hope
that despite the odds, he would be able to capture
Natalie's killer and bring that fiend in so that the serial killer could face justice.

"Yeah," he finally said, nodding toward his plate
and responding to her comment about seeing him
finally enjoying something. "This wasn't half-bad."

Shayla widened her eyes and suddenly clutched at
her heart. "Please, be still my poor little heart." And

then she looked at Gabriel, amused. "I don't know if I can handle such a heady compliment."

Gabriel responded by throwing a balled-up napkin at her.

Chapter Twenty-One

Quite honestly, Gabriel didn't really know just what had possessed him to throw that napkin at Shayla. It was truly the first lighthearted moment he had experienced in over nine months and without thinking, he had just gone with it.

Caught by surprise, Shayla laughed, batting away the balled-up napkin.

She managed to hit him square in the face. But since it was simply a napkin, there was no impact, just laughter. The kind of laughter that represented a release of stored-up inner tension.

Gabriel caught Shayla by her waist as she pretended to wipe his face with the napkin. He went on to pull her onto his lap.

Still laughing, their eyes met, causing them to share what was definitely a very atypical moment.

Quite honestly, Gabriel hadn't thought his actions out any further than that. His next move hadn't even occurred to him until it materialized, seizing him.

Encompassing her.

The kiss surprised him no less than it surprised her.

The moment their lips touched, this overpowering aura of disbelief came over each of them.

Each, for reasons of their own, began to draw back. And then, for those same reasons, they just continued to lose themselves in what they had started.

Guilt instantly sprang up within him—momentarily threatening to undo him—but it was no match for the throbbing joy that flooded through all of him.

Lord, but he had missed this. Missed feeling this alive, he realized. Missed feeling as if he was being completely drenched in rays of sunshine.

Still holding Shayla on his lap, Gabriel put his hand to the back of her head, drawing her just a fraction closer to him.

Drawing in that exquisite sensation he felt being created inside him as well.

Shayla hadn't planned for this to happen. It just seemed like one thing followed another and suddenly, here she was, kissing Gabriel and feeling incredibly stimulated and aroused by the simple act.

And then, just like that, he was drawing back, just as she feared he would.

"I'm sorry," Gabriel told her, feeling he had allowed himself to get carried away. Somehow he had taken advantage of the situation—and of her—when he hadn't intended to.

Shayla's eyes met his. On some level, even though she hadn't known him for that long, she sensed—or thought she sensed—what Gabriel was feeling. She did her best to help him push his feelings of guilt aside.

Guilt of this nature was, in her opinion, counter-productive, if not actually destructive.

"I'm not," she told him, her voice sincere and hardly above a whisper.

And then she kissed him to show him that it was all right. That there were no hard feelings and that anything that happened between the two of them to-night had her stamp of approval.

The kiss seemed to go on for a very long time.

It grew more and more heated by the moment until the very sensation of desire seemed to surround them. It succeeded in pushing back the rest of the world and caused it to remain outside the very small, intense circle that was being created by just the two of them.

Gabriel rose then, his lips still sealed to hers.

Some part of him had every intention of taking his leave and going back to his apartment. But in order to do that, he needed to stop kissing her, and right now, the thought of doing that left him feeling bereft.

So instead, he picked Shayla up in his arms, ready to carry her to the ends of the earth—or at least into her bedroom.

He drew his mouth away from hers and said only a single word.

"Where…?"

Shayla pointed toward his left.

Brushing his lips against hers, Gabriel carried the woman who had created a fire in his veins to her bedroom.

Once inside the small, cozy room, he elbowed the

door farther open so he could walk in without any bumping into any obstacles.

Still carrying Shayla, Gabriel brought her over to the queen-size bed and gingerly placed her down, handling her as gently, as if she was a snowflake, easily destroyed by the slightest wrong move.

Almost dazed, Gabriel drew his head back, looking at her, all sorts of half thoughts vying for space in his head.

"This isn't supposed to be happening," he told her, his voice thick with emotions.

"No doubts, no misgivings," Shayla warned him, gently gliding her hands along his face as if she was committing it to memory by virtue of touch alone. "If this wasn't supposed to be happening, it wouldn't be," she assured him. "But it is. So just go with it," Shayla counseled, planting an array of light kisses all along his face and his neck.

Gabriel discovered that he was unable to resist her. Unable to just get up on his own power and walk away from her. It was as if he had been placed in some horrid state of suspended animation, desperately trying to get back to the life that had been so savagely ripped away from him.

Except that this wasn't his wife.

And yet, he couldn't just walk away from Shayla. Couldn't force himself to stop the wild, erratic and almost celebratory feelings that were racing through his system, rejoicing right now.

It was insane, he knew, but he just wanted this to continue.

Heaven help him, he had been so very empty inside for so long, it felt wondrous to feel alive again, even just a little while. Overwhelming to experience all these wonderful sensations that were shooting up and down his body, reminding him that he was a man capable of feeling a wealth of fantastic things.

It was wrong, he knew, but heaven forgive him, he wanted this woman. Not *any* woman, but *this* woman.

It had been an eternity since he had felt this way, Gabriel thought.

He had been convinced that he would never feel anything even close to this ever again. Convinced that, in all likelihood, he would never feel anything at all.

And yet, here he was, wanting to be with this woman.

Wanting this woman.

Desire was heating his body, bringing it up to temperatures Gabriel could only vaguely remember having ever experienced before.

But this wasn't right, he suddenly insisted in the next moment.

It just wasn't.

As if his thoughts had suddenly transferred themselves into her mind, Shayla took his face in her hands and intensely delved into his green eyes.

"It's all right, Gabriel," she assured him in a whisper. "Natalie wouldn't want you suffering like this. She loved you and would want you to be happy, or at least to *try* to be happy."

And then she concluded her argument by pressing her lips against his.

At that very moment, it was as if something had been ripped open within him. Even if he had wanted to, he couldn't resist Shayla a second longer.

Unbuttoning his shirt, Gabriel never drew his lips away from hers. It was as if they were hermetically sealed to one another—and only growing more so.

Tossing his shirt aside, Gabriel went on to divest Shayla of her blouse.

Their clothing managed to disappear at lightning speed until they were both nude, both eager to run their hands over one another's bodies.

Both eager to create a network of warmly pressed kisses along their quivering, hot skin.

Shayla found herself enthusiastically responding to Gabriel. More than anything, she wanted to experience that wonderful, hot, ultimate sensation—and yet she was trying to force herself to slow down a little rather than go racing to the end goal and all that meant.

But it was hard to slow down when she felt her body vibrating and humming the way it was. Hard to slow down when she could feel the sensation building inside her and growing to almost overwhelming heights.

And then suddenly, there he was, looming over her. Gabriel stroked her body, creating more fires inside her as he parted her legs. And then, smiling into her eyes and moving with almost incredible gentleness, Gabriel entered her.

Shayla caught her breath, doing what she could to steady herself even as her heart began pounding wildly.

The pounding increased at the same time that his movement within her grew to ever greater, more intense heights.

Shayla dug her fingertips into his shoulders, holding on to him tightly as her anticipation of the final explosion within her grew to huge, overwhelming proportions.

And then it happened.

That final moment came, seizing them and rumbling through both of them.

And then it was over.

Shayla felt Gabriel sink against her as the moment slowly slipped away.

She could feel her smile filtering all through her, but the next moment, she wasn't thinking about that. She was concerned about how Gabriel would react when he finally found himself floating back down to earth.

Would he feel guilty about betraying the memory of his wife? Disappointed in himself for weakening and giving in this way?

Angry at her for having "led him astray"?

She wanted to be prepared to talk him out of any negative feelings he might be experiencing. She wasn't sure how to go about that, or even, possibly for the first time ever, how to read his expression.

Since she had been raised to always be as direct as possible by a mother who valued the truth above all else, Shayla turned toward Gabriel after he had moved off her, and she searched his face.

"Are you okay?" she asked.

She had caught him off guard. "I thought I was supposed to be the one who asked that."

"These are extenuating circumstances," she told him philosophically. "Besides, you're the one with the heavy weight on your shoulders, not me. So, are we okay? Is everything all right?" she pressed, her eyes holding his.

A half smile curved his mouth. Instead of answering her question, he said, "She would have liked you."

"Natalie?" Shayla guessed, her heart quickening. This had to be the ultimate compliment, she thought.

"Yeah," he affirmed. Without thinking, Gabriel slipped his arm around her shoulders and drew Shayla against him.

"Not that I'm not flattered," she quickly made clear, "but why?"

That was easy enough to answer. "Because you're trying to get me to move among the living instead of just curling up and dying by inches every day."

She thought over his explanation for a moment. "I can accept that," she told him with a smile. Turning in to Gabriel, she leaned her chin against his chest and searched his face. "So we're okay?" she asked him.

He kissed the top of her head. "We're okay," he told her.

And then he pressed another kiss against her hair. And another. He could feel the same stirrings begin to unfold within him that he had felt earlier, yearnings that were flowering and taking possession of him even more intensely than they had in the first place.

His arm tightening around her, Gabriel brought his mouth down to Shayla's, kissing her and unleashing the feelings he had thought had been completely spent just minutes ago.

Apparently not.

Her eyes were smiling at him when brought his mouth to hers. "What's so funny?" he heard himself asking.

"Not funny," she corrected. "Nice. Very, very nice."

"I'm not sure I understand," Gabriel replied.

She placed her fingertip against his lips. "You don't have to," she told him. "Just keep kissing me." Her eyes were shining. "It'll come to you," she promised.

He shook his head, stifling what felt like the beginning of laugh.

He didn't feel like thinking right now. Feeling had so much more going for it. Gabriel opted for that.

GABRIEL EXPECTED TO wake up and find her still in bed next to him. He wasn't quite sure how to deal with that, waking up beside a woman. He hadn't done that since Natalie had been taken from him.

But as it turned out, he didn't have to deal with that. When he woke up, the place beside him was empty.

His mind racing, Gabriel grabbed his pants and pulled them on. He was about to hurry out into the hall when Shayla walked in, dressed and smelling of shampoo and some sort of enticing body soap.

"Hi," she said. "You can shower here and then go get a change of clothes at your place. I've already showered."

"I can tell." What she had used smelled enticing, but it was definitely not meant for a man. "That the only soap you have?" he asked.

She paused to think. "Well, I have dishwashing liquid and also detergent."

"So in other words, no," he translated. "I'll shower at my own place, thanks."

"Okay, have it your way," she told him. "But before you do that, drop me off at the precinct."

He didn't quite follow her. "Why?"

"Because my car's in the precinct parking lot," she reminded him.

He thought for a moment, reconstructing his agenda. "Okay, change of plans. I'll shower here, then go to my place, and then we can go to the precinct so we can get back to work."

She saw no reason to argue with that and had just agreed when both of their phones began to ring.

Shayla felt her stomach sink.

Another murder?

She tried to think positive thoughts even as she said, "I think your shower might have just been put on hold."

With that, Shayla went to answer her phone. Out of the corner of her eye, she saw Gabriel trying to track down his cell phone, following the sound of ringing.

His expression looked far from happy.

Chapter Twenty-Two

"I'm sorry, is this too early to call you?" the woman's voice on the other end of Shayla's cell phone asked apologetically. The next moment, the caller seemed to realize that she hadn't even identified herself yet. "Oh, this is Rose D'Angelo. You and that other detective came to my house yesterday and asked me questions about my sister, Cynthia Wells. You told me that if I thought of anything else about Cyndie, I should give you a call."

Shayla breathed a quiet sigh of relief. At least this wasn't about another serial killer victim.

"And you thought of something else," Shayla guessed.

She heard the woman on the other end of the call hesitate. "Well, I don't know if this means anything," she qualified slowly.

Shayla sat down on the edge of her bed. She could see Gabriel, on his own cell phone, watching her.

"Trust me, Rose, the smallest thing could lead to solving a crime. What did you remember?" she asked.

"It's something that Cyndie said to me about a week before she was killed."

"Go on. I'm listening, Rose," she coaxed. She saw that Gabriel was still looking at her, his body language asking if this was going anywhere. All she could so was raise her shoulders in a noncommittal shrug.

"Well, like I said, this is probably nothing," the woman repeated before telling Shayla, "Cyndie complained to me about her pharmacist. She said he was kind of creepy, to the point that she was thinking of changing pharmacies. I'm probably just reading things into that."

Maybe, maybe not, Shayla thought. "Would you happen to know this pharmacist's name, or the name of the pharmacy where your sister went to fill her prescriptions?" She crossed her fingers as she asked the question.

"I think she said his name was Stewart. The thing that struck my sister as kind of funny is that he told her he used to work in LA, but he liked the homey feel of Aurora better. He claimed it suited him, but it just made her feel really uncomfortable.

"And she left one of her prescriptions at my house, so I can give you the name of the pharmacy," Rose told her, then quickly added, "Don't get the wrong idea. Cyndie wasn't a pill popper or anything. She just gets—got," Rose corrected herself, her voice cracking for a moment. Shayla quietly waited for the woman to continue. "She *used* to get these awful migraine headaches that would all but stop her in her tracks."

This had all the signs of going on for a while, Shayla thought.

"Rose, why don't my partner and I come over to your place so we can continue this in person?" Shayla suggested.

"If you don't mind, I'd rather come down to the police station." The woman paused for a moment, then explained, "It's a matter of closure, I suppose."

"Of course," Shayla told her. "Whatever works for you. My partner and I can be at the precinct in about twenty minutes," she promised, giving the woman the exact address. "Will that be enough time for you to get there?"

"Yes, I think so," Rose D'Angelo answered. "I'll meet you there." The woman sounded excited and hopeful as she terminated the phone call.

Shayla put her phone away. Gabriel had already put his own phone in his pocket.

"Anything?" Gabriel asked, trying to read her expression.

"Hard to say. Maybe," Shayla qualified. "That was a victim's sister calling. What she told me would explain how the killer got his hands on the drugs he injected into his victims."

She had definitely aroused his interested. "Go ahead," Gabriel told her.

"Rose D'Angelo said that her sister told her that her pharmacist made her feel really uncomfortable. She said the victim was actually thinking about changing pharmacies so she wouldn't have to interact with him."

"This could be promising," Gabriel said.

Shayla nodded. "The woman is coming in with the guy's name and the name of the pharmacy he works for. Oh, and one other thing she said," she remembered.

Whatever it was, it obviously had to have left an impression on his partner, or she wouldn't have felt it was important enough to mention, he thought.

"And that was?" he asked.

"According to Rose D'Angelo, her sister said that the pharmacist told her that he used to work in Los Angeles, but he liked the 'homey feel' of Aurora better." Shayla raised her eyes to his. "I'm trying not to let myself get too excited."

A half smile curved his mouth. "We can save that for later," he told her, thinking of last night and how surprised he had been by what had happened and his own reaction to it. "But this definitely looks promising."

"That it does," she agreed wholeheartedly. "What was your phone call about?" she asked as she quickly retrieved her shoes from under her bed and slipped them on.

Gabriel smiled. "It was from someone I used to work with a couple of years ago."

"I thought you said you no longer knew anyone there," she reminded him. Obviously he had stretched the truth.

"Yeah, well, I forgot. Anyway," he continued, "Diego heard I was looking to find out if one of the wanted posters in the LA precinct was of someone who resembled me. Diego got it into his head to look through them late yesterday." It was the kind of thing that would have tickled the detective, Gabriel recalled.

"Diego got the biggest kick when he found one. The guy's getting on in years," Gabriel confided, "and not exactly tech savvy, but he's going to get one of the other guys who works there to scan the wanted poster and send it to me. The poster isn't about a current case—it's about eight or nine years old—but Diego swears the person he found could have been my twin."

"And where is this twin now?" Shayla asked.

Gabriel shook his head. "No clue," he answered. "According to what Diego said, the guy was never located."

This was getting more interesting, Shayla thought. "Sounds like it might be another piece of the puzzle."

"Or it could be just a coincidence—or nothing," Gabriel pointed out.

"Your optimism is really overwhelming."

"I've learned to be cautious," he reminded her.

Shayla's mouth curved. "Me, I thrive on optimism," she told him needlessly. "It gives me the energy I need to keep going."

"To each his own," Gabriel said philosophically.

"My sentiments exactly," she said, her smile widening. "Okay." She rose to her feet. "Let's go, Gabriel—unless you want to take that shower first," she told him, giving him a choice. "I can call Rose back and tell her that we'll be a little late getting to the squad room."

"I can grab a quick shower at the precinct once we get our hands on the information she's bringing. Besides, Diego is going to have someone email me that wanted poster," he reminded Shayla. "I'm curious to see if this guy really does look like me."

"He might resemble you," Shayla allowed, "but I'm sure that you're far better-looking."

"A compliment?" Gabriel questioned, looking at her.

"Don't looked so surprised, partner. You must have a mirror somewhere in your apartment, right? You know what you look like."

"Yeah," he answered dismissively. "I know exactly what I look like—like that serial killer's worst enemy."

She nodded, going with the change in subject as they left her house. "We'll get him. We're getting close. I can feel it, Gabe."

Shayla was surprised to see his expression suddenly change. Was that pain she saw in his eyes?

"What's the matter?" she asked.

"Natalie used to call me that. Gabe," he told her.

The last thing she wanted to do was stir up any painful memories for him, especially after last night. Last night had given her hope that he was actually moving on.

"Would you rather I didn't?" she asked.

He thought for a moment, then reminded himself what Shayla had said—that Natalie would have wanted him to move on. And she was right. "No, that's okay. It just caught me by surprise, that's all," he admitted.

Still, Shayla thought, she would refrain from using

the nickname, at least for now. They had already taken a huge step forward, and she didn't want to mess that up by insisting on using the shortened form of his name. It really wasn't worth it.

She could save that for a later date.

Provided, she qualified, there *was* a later date.

THEY MANAGED TO get to the precinct approximately ten minutes before Rose D'Angelo arrived. Gabriel parked his vehicle several spaces away from where Shayla had left her car the day before. It was early, but judging from the number of cars in the lot, it looked like it was going to be a busy day.

"Think she's here yet?" Gabriel asked, getting out and looking at Shayla over the roof of his vehicle.

"Rose D'Angelo is coming in from Mission Viejo, so I don't think so—not unless she wanted to get a speeding ticket."

"Mission Viejo," Gabriel repeated, trying to remember how far away that was from the precinct. They had interviewed a number of people yesterday, and he was still trying to get the lay of the land. "I've really got to start memorizing the names of the different cities and just where they're located around here."

"It'll all fall into place for you eventually," she promised him. "For now, let's just go in. I'm dying to see if that friend of yours found someone to help him send you that wanted poster. It would be interesting to find out if Josephine was just hallucinating or if she was actually right about bumping into someone she thought looked like you."

They got into the elevator. Gabriel frowned slightly. "Maybe I should start wearing a disclaimer on my jacket that says, 'Sorry, I'm not the serial killer you're looking for.'"

Shayla didn't find his comment the least bit amusing. "You know, that just gives us more reason to find this Moonlight Killer, because if you actually *do* resemble him, someone might just get it into their head to bring you in—or even worse, shoot you."

"Now who's letting their imagination run away with them?" he asked pointedly, glancing at her as they got off the elevator and headed toward the squad room.

She supposed he was right, but that didn't stop her from worrying. Out loud, she agreed, "One step at a time."

ROSE D'ANGELO ARRIVED shortly after they did. Shayla was immediately on her feet, escorting the woman into the office along with Gabriel. She watched the woman's reaction as she came into the squad room, but Rose didn't appear to be unduly nervous. As a matter of fact, the victim's sister looked rather hopeful.

Shayla brought the woman to her desk. "Take a seat," she encouraged, indicating the chair next to her desk. Gabriel brought his own chair over.

Before sitting down, Rose took out and placed a half-filled prescription bottle on Shayla's desk.

"Oh, and Cynthia told me the guy's name was Stewart," Rose told her.

Rose had already told her that when she called, Shayla thought. Before she could say anything, though, Gabriel asked the woman, "Did she happen to know or hear his last name?"

Rose shook her head. "If she knew it, she never mentioned it. Like I told Detective Cavanaugh when I called this morning, Cyndie said she intended to change pharmacies, or at least go to another branch so she wouldn't have to run into him. She sounded pretty adamant about it, and my sister wasn't the kind who scared easily, so there had to be something to this, don't you think?" she asked, looking from one detective to the other.

"How long before she was killed did she tell you she was going to change pharmacies?" Gabriel asked.

Rose thought for a moment. "A couple of weeks, I think," she finally answered. The woman's breathing became a little more pronounced. Her expression was a combination of anger and fear. "Do you think he was the one who killed my sister and all those other women?"

"That would be jumping to conclusions," Gabriel answered, his voice almost deadly calm. "We're going to have to check some things out first."

"But you will tell me once you know, won't you?" Rose pressed. "You have to tell me," she insisted.

Gabriel nodded. "You have our word on it," he promised.

ROSE D'ANGELO REMAINED in the squad room, answering a few more question dealing with her late sister, and then she left.

"So what do you think?" Shayla asked her partner

the moment the woman walked out of the squad room. "Do you think this Stewart person is just a weird guy— or the Moonlight Killer?"

"Being a pharmacist would explain his being able to get his hands on the drug that he used to inject into his victims. At the very least, we have to track him down, This is possibly the first real lead we've gotten. The first order of business is to find out his last name and then get as much information on him as we can," Gabriel said.

"He could just be a creep," Shayla reminded her partner. "*Or* he could turn out to be *our* creep. By the way," she said as she grabbed her shoulder bag and rose from her desk, "did you get a chance to look at that wanted poster from your friend?"

He had forgotten all about that when Mrs. D'Angelo had walked in. Moving over to his desk, he tuned his computer on and scrolled through one message after another.

"This thing takes forever to warm up," he complained.

"Ah, but the anticipation makes the end product all worth it," she joked.

Gabriel leveled a look at her. "You know, Cavanaugh, if this job doesn't work out for you, you could always get one doing voiceovers for corny movies."

So, they were back to "Cavanaugh" again, she thought. Was that because the effects of last night were already beginning to fade away, or because they were at work and he felt more comfortable maintaining a distance between them here?

She decided that whatever worked for him was fine with her.

Shayla looked over at his screen, waiting for the details of the wanted poster to materialize. "You know, once we get a free moment, I'm going to request a new computer for you. You can get old waiting for this to warm up and give you a clear picture."

"Tell me about it," he muttered.

And then the screen began to grow clearer as an image finally formed.

The second it did, Shayla looked at it more closely, and then her mouth dropped open. "My Lord, it *does* look like you," she cried as she stared at the screen.

The more she looked at it, the more similar it seemed. It was, Shayla decided, positively eerie.

Chapter Twenty-Three

Shayla looked away from the computer screen and at the man standing next to her. Granted, it looked like an old shot from his late teen years, but the resemblance was rather unnerving.

"You don't have any brothers or male cousins?" she asked Gabriel.

"I don't have *any* family," he told her. "The second I graduated high school, my mother took off with her then boyfriend. That woman changed boyfriends like most women changed clothes," he added. "I haven't seen or heard from her since. I figured she found someone to pay her bills. As for any siblings or cousins, male *or* female, that's a no."

Shayla turned so that her back was to the others in the squad room and no one would overhear them.

"How do you *know* there was no family?" she questioned. To her way of thinking, he only had his mother's word that there were no other relatives floating around.

"Trust me, if there was any family at all, my mother would have been on their doorstep with her hand out. She would have had me dressed in my oldest clothes and holding me in front of her to generate empathy as well as sympathy for her." Gabriel looked closer at the wanted poster on his monitor. "It says here that the guy's name is Howard Stewart. He was wanted for assaulting a woman nine years ago." He looked at his partner. "According to this, they're still looking for him."

"Send a copy of that to your phone—in case we need it," she told him. Picking up the prescription bottle Rose had brought to them, Shayla glanced at the address on it, then tucked it into her shoulder bag. "Let's see if we can get any information on that creepy pharmacist," she said as she walked out of the squad room.

"Information," Gabriel repeated. "You mean like his name?"

Shayla nodded. "That would be a good place to start."

THE BRANCH OF Good Health Pharmacy that Cynthia Wells had frequented before her untimely death was a large, modern-looking pharmacy that, unlike some of its other branches, was open twenty-four hours a day.

When Shayla and Gabriel walked in and approached the rear counter, they found that there were two pharmacists currently on duty, both women in their forties. There was also a clerk to ring up the sales, as well as a young man who looked like he was still in college.

They began by showing their shields and IDs to

the first pharmacist they saw, and Shayla requested to speak to the person in charge.

"That would be me," the woman told them. She was somewhat tired-looking, with short, dark blond hair. The name tag she wore proclaimed her name to be Christine Madison. "What can I do for you, Detectives?"

Without thinking, Shayla took the lead. "Do you have a pharmacist who works here by the name of Stewart?" she asked.

"You mean Stewart Howard?" Christine asked. "He's not here right now. He's working the night shift this week." Her curiosity stirred, the woman looked from Shayla to her partner. "What's this about?"

"We'd just like to ask him a few questions," Shayla replied, deliberately not being specific.

Listening in, the other woman behind the counter laughed shortly. "Careful what you wish for," she told Shayla.

Gabriel's attention was instantly piqued. "What do you mean by that?"

The other pharmacist—Kim Jordan, according to her name tag—came over to join them at the counter. "Well, nothing, if you're the one who's asking the questions," she told Gabriel. "But if your partner's the one doing the asking, and if he takes a shine to her, that man can go on and on. And *on*," Kim emphasized.

"Kim," Christine said sharply, looking far from pleased by Kim's comment.

Unperturbed, the other woman merely shrugged.

"Just letting them know what they're in for, Christine," she said.

"This Stewart person talks a lot?" Shayla asked Kim.

"Depends if you're a male or a female," Kim answered. When her boss gave her a censoring look, Kim withdrew. "Excuse me, I've got a lot of prescriptions to fill," she told the detectives.

"Don't mind her," Christine told them. "She and Stewart got into it the other day and Kim is the type to carry a grudge, but they're both good workers. Especially Stewart. I can always count on him to take the night shift without any complaints, which is more than I can say for some of the others here," she added without bothering to lower her voice.

"Do you have an address on file for this dependable pharmacist?" Gabriel asked.

The head pharmacist appeared rather taken with Gabriel, but not so much that she was about to rush off and give up the employee's address without asking any questions.

She glanced from one detective to the other, clearly debating the situation. "What did you say you wanted with him?"

Gabriel was ready with an acceptable excuse. "He was an eyewitness to a car accident earlier today. We just needed to ask him a few more questions, get the sequence of events straightened out," he explained.

Christine nodded and then pulled up the necessary information on her computer. "I guess that makes it all right," she said more to herself than to the sexy detective standing before her. She wrote the information that came up on the monitor down on a pad, tore off the sheet and then offered it to the tall, handsome man on the other side of the counter. "There you go."

Gabriel smiled his thanks and tucked the single sheet into his jacket pocket. "You've been very helpful."

The woman all but preened in response. "My pleasure, Detective. Please don't hesitate to come back if I can be of help to you in any other way," the woman called after Gabriel as he and Shayla walked away and headed out of the store.

"I had no idea you would turn out to be such a secret weapon," Shayla told him.

"What are you talking about?" he asked as he led the way to his vehicle parked at the curb.

Getting in on the passenger side, Shayla pretended to bat her eyelashes at him. "Oh, I think you can figure it out. Hey, I'm not complaining," she laughed as she saw Gabriel frown. "Christine was putty in your hands and gave up the guy's address without making us jump through hoops or get a court order—and she could have," she reminded her partner. "On top of that, you were so charming, we won't have to worry about her calling Stewart to warn him that he might be getting some unexpected visitors."

Pleased at how things had gone, Shayla shifted in her seat and smiled at him. "We make a pretty good team."

He didn't bother arguing. "Okay, partner," Gabriel said. "Now what? You want to see if this Stewart guy is home? If he's not, we could wait outside his place for him to come back."

"Now that we have the guy's current last name, we can track down his license plate number through the DMV and find out the make and model of his vehicle. With any luck, we can get hold of his cell phone number as well so we can see if he's mobile right now."

Starting his car, Gabriel decided it would be prudent to drive over to the pharmacist's residence while they focused on tracking down the rest of the information they needed.

He did have one question for Shayla. "What do you mean by his *current* last name?" he asked.

"Didn't you notice that the order of the names were reversed?" she asked him. She could see by the look on his face he had no idea what she was talking about. "That guy on the wanted poster your friend sent over, his name was Howard Stewart..." She let her voice trail off as she waited for her words to sink in.

Gabriel felt like an idiot. He had been so caught up with the rest of it that this one glaring detail had managed to escape him. "The guy we're trying to find now is Stewart Howard."

"Could be a coincidence," she said. The last thing she wanted was to cause him to beat himself up over this.

The look on Gabriel's face told her he saw right through her attempt. "You know as well as I do that that would be one hell of a coincidence," he told her. Gabriel looked totally disgusted by his oversight as well as by the man they were looking to speak to. "That guy is just too full of himself."

"I guess that getting away with twenty murders, possibly more, just filled him with much too much confidence," she said. "Okay, let's drive over to our egomaniac's residence and I'll see if I can get those missing pieces of information we need to catch this guy," Shayla told her partner.

It TURNED OUT that their suspect lived in a small house, which he was currently renting from a retired couple who had recently moved to Florida.

Shayla called Valri to get the rest of the information they needed.

"I can't talk right now, Shayla. I'm really busy," Valri said when she finally answered her phone. "More so than usual."

Shayla interrupted her cousin. "I wouldn't ask you if this wasn't an emergency, Valri."

"With you they're *all* emergencies, Shayla," Valri said wearily.

"This is an *emergency* emergency," Shayla emphasized, talking quickly. "I think Gabriel and I might have found the Moonlight Killer."

There was momentary silence on the other end of the call, and then Valri urged, "Go on."

Shayla gave her a very quick summary about the pharmacist they were looking for, concluding with, "I need to know what kind of car he's driving and his license plate number. And if you have any cell phone listing for him I can track, that would really be the icing on the cake."

Valri sighed. "No promises, but I'll see what I can come up with."

"Cortland and I are sitting outside the guy's house right now," Shayla said by way of an added detail. "If you can come up with that information, I'll owe you my firstborn."

"By my calculations, you owe me your first twelve born," Valri told her cousin. "But I'll consider your tab closed for another steak sandwich from Malone's."

"You got it," Shayla promised excitedly, happy to comply. She closed her phone.

"So?" Gabriel asked, looking at her.

"She's looking into it and will call us back when she comes up with something," she told her partner. "Meanwhile, I suggest we call the lieutenant, tell him what we've found out so far and then get comfortable. I've got a feeling we might be here for a while."

He sighed. "My favorite part of the job," he muttered. "A stakeout." Gabriel shook his head. "Fastest way known to man to develop stiff joints," he complained.

"Well, there's no rule that says we both have to stay here," Shayla pointed out. "You can call for a cab and go back to the station."

"I could," he agreed. "The only trouble is, this is my car."

"I won't steal it," she promised innocently. Shifting in her seat, Shayla dug into her pocket and pulled out a set of car keys. "I'll even give you the keys to my car, and you can use them to drive yourself home once you get to the station and quitting time comes."

"Yeah, right," he said, dismissing her suggestion.

"Well, you can," she told him.

"Shut up, Cavanaugh. You'll make this a whole lot easier on both of us if you don't talk for a while."

— Shayla stared at him, not sure whether or not to believe him. "Are you serious?" she asked Gabriel.

"No," he answered with a sigh. "I'm not. At this point, I'd probably find the silence deafening. But I do think you should call the lieutenant to let him know what we've decided to do at this point."

"It might sound better coming from you," she told him.

He shrugged. "Okay." Taking out his phone, Gabriel stepped out of the vehicle.

Gabriel had no sooner concluded his call to their commander and opened the driver's side door to get back in than Shayla's phone rang. Her body language when she answered the phone told him that the call was the one she had been waiting for, undoubtedly supplying the missing—or at least some of the missing—information that they needed.

Deciding the hell with privacy at this point, since Shayla would tell him about the call soon enough, he got back into the car.

Shayla's cousin slowly enunciated the license number before saying, "He owns a 2021 silver BMW sedan."

"That's not exactly an inconspicuous car," Shayla commented. Nor was it inexpensive. Where was he getting the money?

"A BMW does stand out," Valri agreed. "But silver blends in. That's the color of over a third of the cars out on the road, so it's a tossup," the computer expert said. "But the good news is that it's the latest model, so while I don't have a cell phone number for you to track, you *can* track his vehicle—and the better news is he's parked in his garage right now, so you can go and question him."

"Thanks, Valri. I owe you," Shayla said.

"Yes," Valri answered, "you certainly do. Good luck."

"Thanks," Shayla said as she terminated the call.

"Well?" Gabriel asked the second she lowered the cell phone.

Her eyes met his. "You'd better get some supplies," she told him, nodding toward the convenience store on the corner that they had passed on the way to the residential complex. "We both know that bringing in Stewart Howard—or Howard Stewart, or whatever he chooses to call himself—for questioning without any real evidence isn't going to get us anywhere. In order to get this sleazy serial killer off the street and into a prison cell, we're going to need to catch him in the act."

As much as he wanted to grab the man and haul him in for some close-quarter interrogation, Gabriel knew Shayla was right. He opened the door on the driver's side and got out, ready to head toward the convenience store.

"I guess it looks like we're going to have a long night ahead of us," he said just before he began walking toward the end of the block.

Chapter Twenty-Four

Gabriel could feel an ache setting into his shoulders and his back. He rotated his shoulders, attempting to stretch a little in the limited space in the front seat. He glanced toward Shayla.

"Why don't you get into the back and stretch out there for a couple of hours?" Gabriel suggested.

They had been sitting out here, parked down the block from where their suspect lived, for hours. There had been no activity of any sort for a while now. An hour earlier, they had heard the unnerving sound of an approaching ambulance, but the emergency vehicle had continued on its way, and the distinct sounds eventually faded into the background.

Since then, there had been nothing except for the occasional vehicle passing by.

"That's okay," Shayla replied. "I'm fine right here."

Gabriel had different take on the situation. "Your eyelids are drooping," he pointed out.

"They're not drooping, I'm just blinking hard," Shayla countered stubbornly.

"Whatever," he said dismissively. "The point is

that there's no need for both of us to lose sleep over this character. I'll stand watch and wake you up if I think there's anything going on."

"I can stand watch and wake you up just as easily," she replied.

It was dark inside the vehicle, but she just knew he was rolling his eyes. "Why is everything an argument with you?" Gabriel asked wearily.

"I am not arguing," she contradicted. "I'm just stating a counterpoint."

Gabriel sighed as he shook his head. This was futile and he knew it, so he just dropped the subject.

"For all we know," he told her, "the most likely suspect might not even go out tonight."

A movement down the block caught her eye, and she immediately sat up straight in the passenger seat. When she looked in his direction, Gabriel looked as if he was about to doze off himself. She reached for his forearm and shook it.

"What?" he asked Shayla.

"I think that's his car." Her eyes were glued to the silver BMW pulling out of the underground parking garage. "What time did Christine say Howard's night shift started?"

"Two a.m.," he answered, watching the same vehicle.

Shayla glanced at her watch. "It's eleven thirty," she said. "Kind of early for our pharmacist to be leaving for his shift, wouldn't you say?"

Gabriel was in total agreement. "It is. Let's see where this guy is going," he said. He started up his car but continued to keep it in Park. Watching the other vehicle intently, he mentally gave it to the count of fifteen before he finally started to follow the suspect.

Shayla could feel her entire body growing tense as she never took her eyes off the silver BMW. She knew that they couldn't follow it too closely or they might tip their hand. But on the other hand, they couldn't allow the vehicle to get too far ahead of them or they could lose track of it.

All things considered, this could all be a wild goose chase and she knew it, but somehow, Shayla didn't think so. There were just too many things pointing to the fact that this was their guy, however he might deign to arrange the order of his name.

Gabriel began to consider the possible places that the killer might choose to go, hunting for his next victim.

"What's open this time of night around here?" he asked Shayla.

She thought for a moment. "Not much. Some all-night pharmacies, a few bars, a couple of convenience stores. The restaurants in the area are either already closed or are closing down."

The We're Open sign in front of a Tex-Mex restaurant went out just as she said that.

Shayla suddenly leaned forward, squinting a little as she tried to focus. She almost grabbed Gabriel's arm again. "Wait, I think our guy just circled back around the Tex-Mex restaurant and went down the back alley behind it." Shayla bit her lower lip, examining possibilities. "He could have a girlfriend working here and he's picking her up after she closes the place down."

Gabriel appeared rather dubious, even though he nodded. "I suppose he could."

"Or," she amended, her eyes sweeping over the almost-empty parking lot—there was only one vehicle there, an old, two-door car that had seen better days—"this could be his next victim."

She looked at Gabriel. He hadn't answered her. Instead, as he drove up slowly, he was intently staring at the area behind the restaurant. A silver vehicle was parked some distance away to the far side.

"That's his car," Gabriel said, his voice barely audible. There was no sign of the pharmacist. "My guess is that he must have slipped in the back."

This was it, Shayla thought. This was the crime scene they needed to make their arrest. She could *feel* it.

"Let's go," she urged Gabriel.

"It takes him a while to tie up his victims," her partner reminded her.

"All we need to do it catch him in the act of tying the woman up. And if Howard has that syringe in his possession…" Shayla's voice trailed off.

He knew what she was getting at, and it was all the urging he needed. Gabriel was out of the car like a shot. Reaching the back door, he pulled at it to open it, but it wouldn't budge.

Stunned, he looked at Shayla. "He must have locked it."

One of the things her mother had taught her was

to always be prepared for unexpected eventualities. This was one of them.

"Move over," she told Gabriel as she fished something out of her back pocket.

Gabriel stared at the long, thin metal object in her hand.

"What is that?" he asked. At first glance it looked to him like some sort of unorthodox skeleton key— but not quite.

She moved slightly so that her body blocked his view. "Something you never saw," she told Gabriel.

Inserting the thin, rodlike item into the lock, she angled it into position until it finally made a clicking sound.

Triumphant, she looked at her partner. "Push it."

He did, and at first the door stubbornly remained where it was. But on the second attempt, the door finally opened and moved.

Weapons drawn, Gabriel and Shayla made their way into the rear of the restaurant. They carefully walked through the darkened kitchen until they reached the edge of the actual serving area.

Howard was there, elaborately tying up his latest victim. Sensing their presence, he looked up and then bolted. He left his paralyzed victim half tied up and partially suspended from a low-hanging beam.

"Get her down!" Shayla cried to Gabriel as she ran after the serial killer. "If I try to do it, I might accidentally wind up strangling her." She knew that Gabriel was strong enough to hold the woman up as he cut away all the ties that surrounded her.

Caught in the act, Howard was running through the restaurant toward the exit, his one goal to get into his silver BMW and get away. Shayla kept pace, increasing her stride until she was almost able to catch up to him, silently blessing all those times she had gone running for exercise.

Suddenly, just as he reached the exit, the man she was chasing spun around to face her. At that moment, she realized that he was still holding the syringe in his hand.

Had he emptied the contents into his victim, or was there something left in the syringe?

The next moment, Howard was lunging toward her, the hand holding the syringe raised up high, ready to drive into her. The man was apparently banking on the idea that there was still something left in the syringe to inject.

Holding her weapon with both hands in order to steady her aim, Shayla cried out, "Stop where you are. I can't miss at this range."

"You're bluffing. You're not going to shoot me," Howard jeered, ready to drive the syringe into her.

"But I am!" Gabriel cried, materializing almost out of nowhere.

Pushing Shayla behind him, her partner got off two shots. Each shot hit the Moonlight Killer in one of his knees.

Shrieking, the man went down, his body hitting the floor like a dropped bowling ball. The syringe he was all set to drive into Shayla fell from his hand.

Relieved, Shayla all but sagged against Gabriel. His arms quickly went around his partner to steady her.

Her heart was pounding so hard, she had trouble pulling herself together for a moment. Her first thoughts immediately focused on the intended victim's condition.

"Is the woman he was tying up alive?" she asked.

"I cut her out of that lethal spider's web he had spun around her," Gabriel told her, contemptuously looking down at the shrieking serial killer writhing on the floor. "This maniac injected her with that same drug he used on the other women. Fortunately, it's not a lethal dosage, so she should be able to come around within a few hours. They'll be able to give her something at the hospital to help counteract the effects more quickly."

Shayla couldn't begin to describe the relief she felt flooding through her. "Thank heavens for that," she said. It would have been absolutely awful if the woman had become the Moonlight Killer's latest victim.

"You tried to kill me!" Howard accused, rage emanating out of his every pore as he lay there, still bleeding.

Gabriel looked down at the Moonlight Killer. There was pure hatred in his eyes. "If I had wanted to kill you, you worthless piece of scum, you would have been dead by now," he said. "But you're not worth my going to prison for." He looked at Shayla, his tone changing as concern slipped in. "Are you sure you're all right?"

"I am terrific," she assured him with enthusiasm, her smile wide. Taking out her cell phone, she pressed a series of numbers on the keypad.

The moment she heard the other end being picked up, she stated her name and badge number, told the dispatch agent the nature of the crime that had been foiled, then requested that an ambulance be sent out.

Hanging up, she looked at Gabriel. "It's over," she said, hardly believing the words she was uttering. This had been such a nightmare. "It's actually over." Shayla looked back at the shrieking man on the floor with nothing but sheer contempt. "This slimeball's reign of terror is finally over."

"But not before he killed all those women," Gabriel said, his voice hollow.

She knew that Gabriel had to be thinking of his wife. Her heart ached for him. There was nothing she could do to change what had happened and she knew it, but she could try to get him to refocus his thoughts and look at the events that had happened now in a positive light.

"Think of it this way, Gabriel—you stopped this maniac from killing a lot more women. Because of what you and I just did, there is an entire legion of women who owe their lives to you, even if they don't realize it," she told her partner.

He wanted to see it her way, but it wasn't easy. "You do have a way of exaggerating."

She shook her head. "Not this time."

"Hey," Howard called out angrily. He tried to get

up, but his knees just couldn't support him and he fell. "I'm bleeding here!"

In the background came the familiar sound of approaching sirens.

Shayla regarded Howard with sheer contempt. "Looks like help is on the way." Turning toward Gabriel, she said, "I'm going to go see how our almost victim is doing. Would you mind staying here with him?" She wouldn't put it past the killer to try to crawl away.

"I mind staying in the same universe as this piece of garbage, but go, see how she's doing. I tried to make her as comfortable as possible under the circumstances, although how comfortable could she be with all her systems paralyzed? However, all things considered, I have to admit that my mind was on you, not on Howard's victim."

She smiled at Gabriel. "To be continued," she told him. "For now, I'll be right back," she promised as the sirens grew louder.

Gabriel had laid the Moonlight killer's potential victim down, cutting away the ropes and ties that Howard had used in order to get her to bring about her own demise.

She was conscious but still unable to move. Her eyes were alert and followed Shayla as she moved closer to her.

"I know you probably don't think so right now," she told the young woman, "but you are a very lucky lady. All the other victims who caught this maniac's attention are dead, but we managed to get to you in time to save you."

Crouching down, thinking that the woman was struggling to try to talk, Shayla leaned in closely to the woman's face.

The woman's lips did not move, but a single tear did trickle from her left eye and slid down her cheek.

"It'll be all right," Shayla promised the young woman, moved by her plight and what she had gone through. "You're a survivor. You need to hold on to that. No matter what else is going on, you *are* a survivor."

The sirens had finally stopped blaring. That meant that the ambulance and, hopefully, the crime scene investigative team had arrived and could begin working the scene.

Shayla squeezed the young woman's hand and then rose to her feet. "I'm going to let the CSI unit in so they can get started," she told the young woman. "The EMTs will take you to the hospital. All this—" she swept her hand in a circle over the victim, indicating the paralytic agent that had been used "—will all wear off soon."

Returning to the area where she had left Gabriel, Shayla saw that her partner was exactly where she had left him. He hadn't taken a single step toward the serial killer he had shot.

Shayla had to admit that she was relieved. There had been a small part of her that had been worried he might have allowed his fury to come to the surface.

Rejoining Gabriel, she only had enough time to

tell him, "I think she's going to be all right," before the first responders began arriving.

Gabriel nodded. "She's in a lot better shape than she would have been if we had gotten here ten minutes later," he agreed.

The next moment, the darkened restaurant came alive with police personnel: ambulance attendants and the CSI team, as well as several uniformed police officers, a couple of homicide detectives who had recently been assigned to the task force and Lieutenant Hollandale, who was keen to learn all the pertinent details how two of his detectives had managed to catch a serial killer had terrorized Southern California.

Chapter Twenty-Five

By the time they finished giving their statements to
the lieutenant and were finally free to go home, it was
approaching dawn.

With Hollandale's congratulations ringing in his
ears, Gabriel drove Shayla to her house, then followed
her in and promptly fell into bed beside her, too exhausted to do anything but hold her.

They did wake up a few hours later and, fueled by
the excitement of bringing down the notorious Moonlight Killer, they made love with an extreme intensity, not once but twice before they were finally spent
again as they lay in each other's arms, silent except
for the sound of their breathing.

Finally, Shayla turned toward her partner and,
grasping at a sense of normalcy, she asked, "So,
you're coming, right?"

Oddly enough, though the question came out of the
blue, Gabriel knew exactly what she was referring to.

"Your uncle is still having that gathering?" he
questioned.

She pulled up the sheet a little closer as she curled

her body into his. "Oh, now more than ever," she told him. "Uncle Andrew doesn't need an actual reason to throw a party. This gives him one, and to his mind celebrating the successful capture of a cold-blooded serial killer is just about the best excuse for a party ever."

She could tell by the look on Gabriel's face that he was hoping to be able to wiggle out of going. "I have to tell you that once Uncle Andrew makes up his mind to have a party, nothing deters him. He once had a party right after an earthquake hit because, according to him, he had planned his first and the earthquake had only caused damage out in Death Valley, where no one lived." She smiled at Gabriel as she ran her hand along his cheek. "He's a very stubborn man."

"So, I have to come?" Gabriel asked, resigned that there didn't seem to be a way out without causing a great many problems.

"You have to come," she confirmed. "Besides, Uncle Andrew wants to celebrate the fact that you're a hero." She knew how the patriarch's mind worked. "You brought down the Moonlight Killer."

With the aura of lovemaking still tightly wrapped around him, Gabriel drew her closer to him and pressed a kiss to her forehead.

"It was a joint effort, Shayla," he reminded her.

"At the end, yes," she allowed. "But you were hunting him long before I ever joined forces with you." Her partner's determination was admirable. And then she laughed as she ruffled his hair, grateful that he wasn't giving her a hard time about going to the family gathering. "I promise you'll have a good time."

Gabriel smiled into her eyes. "I thought I just had a good time," he said, caressing her gently. He was utterly amazed at how much she had come to mean to him in such an incredibly short amount of time. If it wasn't physically impossible, he felt he could go on making love with her until he just expired.

"A *different* kind of good time," she said with a laugh.

In her heart, Shayla felt that Gabriel needed to be exposed to her family outside the parameters of work. He needed to discover firsthand what being around a family like hers meant. There was camaraderie, laughter and warmth involved, not to mention the bonding effect of being part of the family of law enforcement agents.

Turning her body farther into him, Shayla made her appeal. "Please? Do it for me."

The words took him by surprise, and he looked at her. "Are we at that point?" he asked her. "At a point when you can ask me to do something I wouldn't normally do because it's for you?"

The fact that they had gotten here without his even realizing it completely stunned him.

Shayla turned her face up to his, giving him no indication that her heart was pounding even harder now than it had been when she had faced down the serial killer.

"Aren't we?" she asked.

The ten seconds of silence that followed were possibly the longest ten seconds she could ever recall enduring.

And then he smiled at her. "I guess we are."

With a relieved laugh, Shayla sealed her mouth to his.

The next hour melted away as he made love with her all over again—for the first time.

AT THE LAST MINUTE, as they stopped in front of Andrew Cavanaugh's large, welcoming two-story home, Gabriel drew Shayla aside and asked her seriously, "Do I genuflect before or after I enter?"

She hit his shoulder with the heel of her hand. "Neither. You smile and shake hands. Uncle Andrew will take care of the rest," she promised, then suggested, "Think of this as the first day of the rest of your life—if you so choose." She looked deeply into his eyes as she made the pronouncement.

Gabriel sighed. "You make it hard to say no," he told her as he rang the doorbell.

She winked at him. "I make it impossible to say no," she corrected playfully.

Whatever he might have said in response never materialized, because just then the front door swung open and Gabriel found himself looking up at a slightly older version of the chief of detectives, Andrew Cavanaugh, who had once been Aurora's chief of police.

At the moment, the still-handsome retired chief was wearing a large navy blue apron, which, Gabriel caught himself thinking, that, strangely seemed to suit him…

The broad-shouldered family patriarch flashed a welcoming smile at the man standing beside Shayla. Clasping Gabriel's hand, Andrew shook it heartily.

"Andrew Cavanaugh," he said by way of a very unnecessary introduction. "Welcome to my home. It's not every day that I get to meet a hero for the first time."

The greeting left Gabriel momentarily speechless.

Andrew never missed a beat. Putting his arm around the younger man's shoulders, he drew Gabriel into his home, which was teeming with warm smells and even warmer conversation.

"Come in, come in," Andrew urged. "Meet the rest of the family." He glanced toward his niece. "Shayla can act as your tour guide. I'd do it myself, but I'm afraid that the quiche Lorraine is being temperamental at the moment and requires my attention," he explained. Gesturing around the interior of his house, he instructed, "Make yourself at home. Please." Then, turning toward his niece, the onetime chief of police said, "Shayla?"

It was enough.

She threaded her arm through Gabriel's and took over. "It'll be painless," she whispered into Gabriel's ear. Her eyes sparkled as she added, "There won't even be a quiz at the end of the evening."

The expression on Gabriel's face as she led him off to the next room said he had his doubts about how painless this experience was going to be.

But it turned out that he was wrong.

Shayla made the initial introductions, but then the other members of her very extended family took over, wanting to learn firsthand the details regarding the capture of the cold-blooded serial killer who had trolled two counties and brought fear and death to what had turned out to be, at last count, a total of twenty young women.

Gabriel found himself sharing details he had forgotten he knew. In the process of doing that, he found that the dark aura that had haunted him for so long—intensified by Natalie's murder—began lessening until it reached the point that it no longer threatened to steal the very air he breathed.

"He looks like he's enjoying himself," Valri told her cousin as the computer tech joined Shayla.

Shayla smiled. The same thought had occurred to her as she watched her partner. She was thrilled to see Gabriel like this. The radiating anger and pain that had been the first things to strike her about the detective were no longer there, she thought.

Gabriel appeared younger somehow. And happier. It was an incredible improvement.

"Yes, he does," Shayla agreed. She turned toward her cousin. "Listen, I wanted to thank you again for everything that you did to get us moving in the right direction. We wouldn't have been able to do it without you."

Valri waved away her cousin's words. "No need to thank me. We're all part of one big team. That being said, I wouldn't say no to a steak sandwich from Malone's if it happened to appear on my desk," Valri said with a wink. And then she moved on to join another cluster of people.

Shayla smiled as she walked over toward her partner, who was, at the moment, talking to her brothers Ronan and Luke and her cousins Dugan and Bryce.

They were, of all things, comparing notes on serial killers.

This had all the signs of going on all night. Trying to prevent that, Shayla sneaked into the middle of the group.

"Sorry, guys, but I'm going to have to steal him away from you so he can get a breath of fresh air on the patio," she told the foursome gathered around her partner as she wove her arm through Gabriel's.

Ronan shook his head. "Trust our little sister to interrupt just when it was getting really interesting," he pretended to lament.

"Don't worry, I'll bring him back after we all get something to eat," she promised.

Gabriel didn't bother hiding his smile as soon as he had gotten a few feet away from the other men. "Were you coming to my rescue?" he asked, amused.

"Not your rescue, exactly," she answered, then admitted, "Much as I love them, my brothers and cousins have been known to be a little overwhelming at times."

"I didn't notice," Gabriel told her honestly. "This was the first time I was ever talking to a group of detectives when one or more wasn't trying to top me or each other. Your brothers and cousins seem like nice guys. I like them."

"You have no idea how happy I am to hear you say that. Not that I thought you could honestly say anything else," she told him in all sincerity. "They care about you, I can tell. As a matter of fact, my family is strongly invested in caring—about each other, about the community, about protecting those who can't protect themselves. However," she qualified, her eyes shining, "sometimes, it's nice to call a time-out and get a little space from them."

The afternoon air was cool and inviting as they stepped outside. Turning toward Gabriel, she smiled at him broadly. "I'm really glad you're here. In case you don't realize it, you have a standing invitation to come over any time you want."

"You mean for the next gathering?" he said, wanting to make sure that he understood.

"No, any time," she told him, then grinned. "It's like Uncle Andrew has this magic box in the kitchen. Any time anyone one comes over to the house, day or night, there's always something in the refrigerator to eat. Somehow, the man never seems to run out of food."

Amused as well as intrigued, Gabriel nodded. "I'll have to put that to the test sometime," he said.

Happily, Shayla immediately jumped on the obvious. "Does that mean you intend to keep coming over?"

He rolled that over in his head. "It might. As long as I keep getting invited."

"Consider this an open invitation," she told him.

Rather than dispute it or argue about the invitation, he surprised her by saying, in all seriousness, "I think I'd really like that."

Shayla found that her pulse was doing some really erratic things, especially when he slowly ran his hand along her back.

ALTHOUGH GABRIEL COULDN'T wait to get her alone tonight, they wound up being two of the last people to leave. It was as if now that he had actually managed to stumble across a situation he had only believed existed in storybooks meant for the very young, part of him was almost reluctant to leave. He was afraid that this was just a dream, or, like in the classic old musical *Brigadoon*, a place that only existed once every hundred years.

But finally, it was time to go.

He expressed his thanks to his host and hostess, not once but several times, and then with Shayla beside him, he left and drove his vehicle to her home.

"You were right," he told Shayla as he walked her to her door.

"I usually am," she answered, doing her best to keep a straight face. "But about what this time?"

"About your family. I really thought going there would be uncomfortable at best."

"And?" she coaxed.

"It wasn't," he said.

Shayla put her wrist to her forehead like an old-fashioned heroine. "Such effusion. I'm not sure I'm up to dealing with it."

"All right, wise guy," Gabriel conceded. "It was great."

"So the next time you're invited…?" She looked at him, letting her voice trail off.

He surrendered. "I'll come."

"Good," she declared. "Because you're invited for next week. I'll go into the details later."

He didn't understand. "Why aren't you going into them now?"

"Because now," she said, slowly unbuttoning her blouse, which, in his opinion, had many too many tiny buttons running up the front of it, "I have something better to do."

He began to watch her intently. "You have my full attention."

"Not tired of me yet?" she teased.

"Maybe—in a hundred years or so. But definitely not yet," he said just before he drew her into his arms and kissed her, long and hard, stealing her very breath away.

Kissed the woman who had miraculously remained with him despite his surly countenance and turned out to be his salvation, now and forever.

* * * * *

COMING SOON!

We really hope you enjoyed reading this book.
If you're looking for more romance, be sure to
head to the shops when new books are
available on

Thursday 9th June

LET'S TALK

Romance

For exclusive extracts, competitions
and special offers, find us online:

MILLS & BOON
A ROMANCE FOR EVERY READER

- **FREE** delivery direct to your door
- **EXCLUSIVE** offers every month
- **SAVE** up to 25% on pre-paid subscriptions

SUBSCRIBE AND SAVE

millsandboon.co.uk/Subscribe

MILLS & BOON

Desire

Indulge in secrets and scandal, intense drama and plenty of sizzling hot action with powerful and passionate heroes who have it all: wealth, status, good looks…everything but the right woman.

MILLS & BOON

MODERN

Power and Passion

Prepare to be swept off your feet by
sophisticated, sexy and seductive heroes, in
some of the world's most glamourous and
romantic locations, where power and
passion collide.